PART FOUR

DRAKE THOMAS
IDOLS & TRINKETS

TYLER SVEC
JORDAN SVEC

DRAKE THOMAS
IDOLS & TRINKETS

This novel is a work of fiction. Names, descriptions, entities, and incidents
included in the story are products of the author's imagination. Any
resemblance to actual persons, events and entities is entirely coincidental.

Cover Image © by Tyler Svec
Cover Design © by Tyler Svec
Interior Design by Tyler Svec

ISBN: 9798863323145

Other works by Tyler Svec

Super Hero Stories
Crunch

Boom

Bang! Pow! Splat!

The Kingdom
I. Alliance

II. Rebellion

III. Redemption

DRAKE THOMAS
Rise of Grimdor

Deception of Merderick

The Dead Mountains

More at svecbooks.com

PART FOUR

DRAKE THOMAS
IDOLS & TRINKETS

TYLER SVEC
JORDAN SVEC

DRAKE THOMAS
IDOLS & TRINKETS

Chapters

INTRODUCTION

SYNOPSIS

1. A PILLAR OF SALT	1
2. ILLUSIONS	14
3. FELLOWSHIP	26
4. AN UNINVITED GUEST	46
5. MANY PARTINGS	64
6. THE TOWER OF IMRAHUNE	75
7. HOPE AND DESPAIR	92
8. LUMAFLOR	102
9. NAIN	116
10. HALLS OF JERMIN	132
11. HEALING OF HADASSAR	144
12. GOVERNOR OF NAIN	154
13. THE LIFTING OF CURSES	170
14. TO THE HIGHEST BIDDER	184
15. BATTLE FOR NAIN	192
16. THE BURNAKS HEIGHTS	213
17. LAST STAND	223
18. TRIALS AND FIRE	244
19. THE GRIM ISLANDS	269
20. PROPHETS OF NAROTH	282
21. MELCHIZEDEK	296
22. JIKE	309
23. THE ROAD HOME	331
24. DURIO HELMAR	348
25. HOMECOMING	360
26. A MATTER OF CONSCIENCE	375
27. GAMES OF DECEPTION	390

28. QUESTIONABLE MOTIVES   411

29. CONTENTION   422

30. ESCAPE FROM HARBRIGGE   437

31. THE WAGES OF WAR   456

32. KING OF THE ELVES   467

MAPS

Stories & References

Introduction

Welcome to *Idols & Trinkets*, the long-awaited fourth book in the Drake Thomas series! If you've never done it before, a lot goes into writing a book and in the case of this book, it took nearly two years to complete.

This book proved to be one of the hardest in the series to write, but maybe not in the way that you would expect.

To start with, the third book was supposed to be the end of the series. But as we got to the end of the third book I thought to myself, for a series about Drake Thomas, you never actually learned that much about Drake Thomas.

It was with this in mind that we decided to put our minds to work and wondered just what else we could do with the series. Whereas most stories would end as the third book ended, I always find myself wondering what happens to the characters after the adventure.

With that in mind, we got to work planning and let's just say that this series is going to be far larger than we originally thought.

One of the challenges that came with continuing this series was picking up where the characters left off. In some ways, it worked out almost perfectly because in the story, 11 years have passed between the *Rise of Grimdor* and this book, and in real life *Rise of Grimdor* was started 11 years ago.

Probably the biggest challenge of writing *Idols & Trinkets* was that some of the characters go in different directions and never see each other again for the rest of the book. It made it very difficult to figure out how the timelines of the different adventures matched up with each other. We had the chapters rearranged several different times before finally arranging them the way we did, which we felt was best for suspense.

The next challenge was that we decided that the series of Drake Thomas was going to span his whole life. That might sound a little crazy (and it might be) but we wanted to show not only Drake Thomas's good moments but bad ones too. Life is full of ups and downs and sometimes we make stupid decisions, so the book series should reflect that.

So going forward the series will be sorted out into trilogy's. But in the sense that each set of three books will tell of a milestone. I wouldn't expect every three books to be its own separate story with perfect endings. Books 1-3 are kind of about Drake's memory, and of course, in the end of the 3rd book, *The Dead Mountains*, he gets his memory back but it still sets up this book.

Without further delay, we certainly hope you enjoy *Idols & Trinkets*!

Tyler Svec & Jordan Svec

SYNOPSIS

This is the fourth part of Drake Thomas

Eleven years ago Drake Thomas woke by the side of the river. After a few moments, it became clear that he had no memory of his life before that moment.

After being pursued by the Sorcerer to the borders of Ariamore, the threat of war was inevitable. The battle ragged and the Sorcerer was overthrown. The land was restored and Drake and Gwen were chosen to lead the new nation of Rhallenin. However, Drake and Gwen appointed Ellizar and Lily as the intern King and Queen. During the night they left, heading north.

Aiden returned to them five years later, to find that they now lived in the northern city of Avdatt. He and Gwen were asked to come on an adventure, which led them through peril which ultimately claimed Gwen's life.

Five years later, the Sorcerer began to gather back his strength, and Drake and his friends prepared to stand against the forces of the Sorcerer Merderick once again.

Before the battle, Isabel came and took Drake to a house that was his own. Among other things, she revealed that her real daughter was Rachal and that the Sorcerer had her as a prisoner.

In an instant, his memories began returning to him. The Sorcerer was defeated and Rachal and him began rebuilding their relationship.

Then in the dead of night, Aiden arrived unexpectedly and asked the both of them to go east.

Chapter 1

A PILLAR OF SALT

Fire and rock were spewed from the cavern as Ellizar and the others dove toward the ground. The mountain shook and trembled. For a moment they lost all sight of each other, surrounded by smoke and debris. A stiff hot muggy breeze soon came over the mountains, lazily removing the smoke until they could see.

Ellizar stood, resting against the rocks. He coughed and shook the dust off of him. After a moment he searched the devastated landscape for any signs of the others.

"Yeh, guys alright?" Ellizar asked into the fog. The sounds came from his lips but fell dead in the air as though some force worked against them. He called out again, finally hearing something to his left. He remained where he was, remembering what he was told.

"We're here and alive, but not completely unscathed!" Morgrin called out. Ellizar, strained his eyes in the fog, finally seeing Morgrin limping through the fog. His wife, Isabel in his arms. Ellizar rushed towards them.

Together they set Isabel down on the hard rocky ground. Blood came from her temple and several of her fingers appeared to be broken.

"She's alive, unconscious, but alive," Morgrin stated. Ellizar breathed a sigh of relief as they both sat down next to her. Morgrin turned his attention to his leg, which had also taken a hit from a piece of debris.

"How is it that I'm the only one out ov the three ov us who came out unscathed?" Ellizar asked. Morgrin chuckled.

"I'll say it's the Dwarvish in you and leave it at that."

They both laughed.

"All I'm goin' teh say is I hope that I was brought along fer more than just causin' an explosion!" A small white owl came and set on the rock next to him, cocking his head.

"I'm sure there is another reason," Morgrin answered, turning his attention to Isabel. "I don't know what it is, but I'm sure there is one."

"That's comfortin'," Ellizar replied. "What's the next move?"

"I'm not sure," Morgrin stated, trying to wake Isabel. "I've learned to not ask what my wife is planning."

"Why not?"

"Because if I don't know, then I can't get freaked out by the prospect of whatever she had been planning for us to do."

"Doesn't the thought ov that freak yeh out?"

"Sometimes, but after all these years I've gotten used to it," Morgrin answered. "I always wanted a life of adventure and Lathon knows I got what I asked for. How about you?"

"My childhood? Not as adventurous as I would've liked and far harder than I would have chosen. I did not have a pleasant childhood."

"Sorry to hear that."

"It is what it is. Got a lot better once Lily came into my life."

"I imagine so," Morgrin answered. Isabel began to stir. Morgrin helped her sit up and rest against a tree.

"Ow," Isabel said plainly. The other chuckled. "That was a much more forceful explosion than the one in my shop years ago."

"I was wonderin' about that myself," Ellizar replied. "I guess the difference is the shop was built out ov wood and the cave out ov rock!"

"Good analysis," Isabel said, wincing as she leaned forward. "We just thought of it two minutes too late."

"I hope no one heard the explosion," Morgrin said, peering at their surroundings.

"We'll be fine. Sounds rarely travels far in the Dead Mountains, plus Aspen did a sweep before we got here and said the area was clear of inhabitants." She motioned to Morgrin who frantically began searching through their pack.

Finally, he produced a small wooden box with a lid. Inside the box was a purple and black powder. Isabel and Morgrin both rubbed it into their various injuries, wincing as they did.

"Dare I ask what that is?"

"Quym," Isabel answered. "Rare plant that grows down south. It smells horrible but has healing qualities. Won't fix the injuries, but does stop the bleeding amazingly fast." She held up her hand, which was now free of cuts and pain even though some of her fingers were still broken. They bandaged her hand and Morgrin's leg. A few moments later they stood to their feet. "Onward."

They followed her up the embankment to the cave opening, which was now significantly larger, thanks to the explosion. They lit a torch, from some of the dying embers and walked into the cave. Their footsteps echoed through the dark chasm. The walls were dark green and filled with crystals that glowed various shades and hues of red and orange. Ellizar's foot splashed in water, making him pause for a moment.

"There was just an explosion in this tunnel, how is there water in it?"

"Mysteries of the Dead Mountains! Who can explain them?"

"Naturally we thought you could," Morgrin said. "You've spent far more time in these mountains than anyone else."

"And still, in this case, I have no explanation," Isabel replied. They turned a sharp corner and came to the place where the explosion had been set off. The white owl flew over their heads and landed by the wall. Isabel shot a look at Ellizar. "Don't touch that thing!"

"Don't worry. Twice is more than enough for me!" Ellizar cried. They walked to the fractured wall at the end of the tunnel. Isabel began feeling over the cracks, searching for any loose pieces. Finally, she pushed on one and it fell from its place, clanging noisily. "Might have been a crazy idea, but it seems to have worked. Uninjured friend of ours, would you like to do the honors?"

"I'd be most honored," Ellizar said, grabbing a large hammer from his belt. He swung at the rock wall, which shuddered. A couple of minutes later a hole had been made, big enough for Ellizar to crawl through. He helped Morgrin with the packs and lastly, Isabel came through the hole. He reached into their bag and pulled out torches that Morgrin quickly lit with a tinderbox. The light from their torches illuminated a vast and intricate arrangement of ruined walls and crumbling em-battlements.

"Welcome my good friend and husband, to the ruined city of...I actually don't know what the city was called, but this is exactly what I expected to find!"

"What happened here?" Ellizar asked. The roof of the mountains went up and up and up until it reached the top, where three large wholes led to the outside world. They had only walked a few feet, but it became clear that what was once a great city, was now a tomb littered with bones and skeletal remains.

"The price of that which separates us from Lathon on so many levels," Isabel said. "I remember clearly that day. Long has it lingered in my mind."

"In all my years living on this earth, I can't recall feeling despair and hatred in one place, quite as much as this one. Despite that the inhabitants of this city have been dead for some time, I still feel afraid that someone is watching us," Morgrin stated.

"Speak nothing until we leave the city gates. It appears empty, but I discern that it is anything but," Isabel warned. "Stay close to each other and soon we will be free of this place."

They fell silent and began finding their way through the mass grave. The bones were picked clean and many of them were scattered or piled in large mounds. Every step felt like a mile in the darkness beneath the mountain.

Ellizar resisted the urge to speak, feeling dread and misery come over him. Whispers were heard in the darkness. Ellizar tried to listen to what the voices were saying, but it was soon discovered to be useless as the language was one that Ellizar couldn't understand.

Each second felt like an hour, and each step became harder to take. Their legs filled with lead and their weariness began to conquer their will. In the darkness, strange and horrible thoughts began to creep into the corners of their minds.

The darkness became thicker and a dense fog filled the air, making it nearly impossible to see. For an hour they wandered in the darkness, making sure to keep hold of each other. Finally, a far distant roar echoed. How far away it was none of them could say. Ellizar heard it again and again and he knew the others were hearing it as well. The sound relaxed them.

A gentle wind moved through the city, freshening up the air that they were breathing. Soon after, it felt as though a great burden had been lifted from them and they were able to travel with great speed until at last they reached the city gate.

They stepped through the crumbling arch, and immediately their weariness left them, and their spirits were revived from the dark thoughts that had taken hold. They continued to walk away from the city, stopping when they reached a great pillar of white.

"What is this?" Ellizar asked. Morgrin and Isabel didn't answer for a moment, a wave of sorrow coming over their faces.

"Gwen was told not to look back as we fled this city nearly six years ago. She didn't listen."

"So this is where she lies?" Ellizar asked. "In the heart ov a mountain? With no livin' souls ov any kind teh care one way or another that she's here?"

"It's not fair, but death rarely is," Morgrin answered. Ellizar looked at the pillar of salt, her name etched into one side. They were silent for a while, forcing themselves to continue, though their thoughts and minds were focused on Gwen for the remainder of the journey that day. When they could walk no further they threw down their packs and collapsed on the ground. After a time, they decided to start a small fire.

The fire revived their spirits and not long after, they pulled out a few of the food items they had brought with them and shared them with each other. They lay in the firelight, imagining they could see the dark stone ceiling.

"What was in your mind?" Morgrin asked. "When we were in the city, my mind was filled with dark thoughts. What was yours? If you don't mind me asking?"

"I had visions of a strange, distant land," Isabel answered. "My father was there. I showed up and he tried to kill me. I could spend all night telling you about the great mysteries that have surrounded him my entire life, but I am certain that what I saw was a half-truth. I know in my heart that my father loved me dearly, even if he died too soon."

"I dreamt that I returned to my ancestor's town and was not allowed to enter for the shame that I brought upon my family for leaving in the first place," Morgrin explained. "I've never even been there, but I know I wouldn't be welcome."

"Why'd yer family leave?" Ellizar asked. "Where'd yeh grow up?"

"I was born and raised in Cos, but my father came from Nlufe; a small island nation a couple hundred miles from the coast of Epirus. There was a heavy influence of the Sorcerer in those parts, though I didn't know it in those terms at the time I heard the stories. For those that were coming of age, there were rituals and ceremonies and a test before you would be considered a full adult. It was different for men and women. For men, who were required to serve in the army for at least a year, they brought out an innocent person, sometimes someone from your own family, and with everyone watching you would have to kill them and *appease* the gods.

"My father didn't know Lathon at the time, but a deep place in his heart wouldn't let him do it. People called it weakness, authorities called it shame and disgrace. He left immediately afterward and never went back. But though I am haunted by what was brought to my mind, my heart is at peace." Morgrin's thoughts trailed off and then finally their eyes shifted to Ellizar.

"I too had a vision ov myself much younger. But it was as if I was watchin' it from someone else's view. In my vision, Lily bought me teh torture me. I know this is not true. She has the purest heart ov anyone I've met. Hence, why I married her right?" Ellizar laughed.

"What do you mean she bought you?" Morgrin asked.

"I was a slave up fer auction at a town even I can't remember," Ellizar explained. "Teh this day neither ov us can tell yeh why she was so far north. But I now know that it was Lathon who made everythin' work out the way it did. I was just a young lad in those days, not quite eleven. She bought me fer a few silver coins. She never said why, or what moved her teh do so. But things have turned out quite well I would say."

"I'm sorry she couldn't come with us," Isabel said. "Is she getting any better?"

"Not really," Ellizar said. "She still has complications with her lungs. At times she is as good as new and can live life with no problems, and other times she is in too great a pain teh do more than get out ov bed in the mornin'. I hope when it comes time fer Drake's weddin' she's on one ov her good days."

"I'm sorry," Morgrin said. Ellizar shrugged.

"In sickness and in health," Ellizar replied. "That's what we vowed and that's what we'll do. I only hope she's doin' alright while I'm here with yeh."

"Don't worry, I'm sure your children are doing their best," Isabel encouraged. They sat in silence for a while.

"Where are we headed tomorrow?" Ellizar asked when finally he felt the urge to talk again.

"If I'm right, we're about a day's walk away from the tunnel we're looking for. Let's hope our presence goes unnoticed."

"What are we lookin' fer?" Ellizar asked. "I came on this small adventure because yeh said yeh needed the kind ov help only a Dwarf can provide. What do we have in store?"

"We're looking for a tunnel that should take us into the deepest and darkest lair of my former friend Enya."

"The Enya that I've heard so much about?" Ellizar asked. Isabel nodded. "I thought she was dead."

"She is, but her house still stands. She is much darker and more dangerous than I was aware of at the time and there's something of hers that I need."

"What is it?" Morgrin asked. Isabel shrugged her shoulders.

"I'm not exactly sure," Isabel answered. "Aiden gave me this quest and he said I would need Ellizar's help to achieve it, but he didn't tell me anything else. I can only assume once we get into her house we'll know what it is."

"Why are we goin' teh such efforts teh sneak in the back? Is there somethin' wrong with goin' through the front door?"

"Aiden said we couldn't use the front door and I don't doubt that he's right. With as many people as Enya knew, they are likely having a small civil war to see who gets to plunder her belongings."

"Interestin' place these Dead Mountains," Ellizar commented. "Quite a place teh visit."

"Try living in them."

"I'll pass, but nonetheless I am glad teh help yeh and assist in whatever way a Dwarf can! After all that's what friends are fer."

"Well said!" Morgrin exclaimed as quietly could be done.

"We'd best get some sleep," Isabel said after a while. "Put out the fire. There are things in the dark places that would love to come see it and then have us as a snack."

"Guess we better sleep with our swords handy," Morgrin said, laying his next to his spot. Ellizar grabbed his axe and laid it next to him. The fire was put out and they were left to the darkness of the mountains.

Ellizar was awoken by Morgrin who was shaking him vigorously. Ellizar stared at the top of the mountain far above them, aware of torchlight flicking to his right. He sat up, immediately seeing several light brown horses in the distance. Their riders sat tall upon their mounts, looking expressionless yet full of thought and depth.

"What's goin' on?" Ellizar asked, unable to move his eyes from the riders. The rider at the head of the company, as if knowing that he was being watched looked into Ellizar's eyes. Ellizar winced feeling an unknown power that might take over him. He shrunk in fear and then pulled his gaze back to Morgrin.

"Aiden came, not ten minutes ago. Said we needed to move now, or never," Morgrin answered.

"What about them?" Ellizar whispered, referring to the horsemen.

"I'm too afraid to ask," Morgrin said. "But be ready soon." Ellizar was packed and ready within a couple of minutes. Morgrin was also ready, both kept an eye on the strange horsemen who still stood unmoving.

Large two-handed swords were clasped to their sides and their armor bore a strange marking that Ellizar had never seen before. A couple more minutes passed before Aiden and Isabel came into view.

"I'm glad teh see yeh!" Ellizar exclaimed.

"Indeed! I'm glad to see you too," Aiden greeted. They embraced. "It has been far too long, and I'm glad to see you still have your axe. We may need our weapons before the day is over."

"What's so urgent?" Morgrin asked. Isabel didn't speak and instead busied herself with packing her few other things.

"Among other things, I am unfortunately here to inform you that rumors of Enya's death have reached the dark corners of the world. They are currently arriving to take everything and plunder her many belongings. I was hoping they would be slower," Aiden explained. "We have a small window of time to get to the tunnel and get what we need before we could be walking into the middle of a war zone. We move now!"

They mounted horses which were provided for them, and despite Ellizar's grumbling, they pulled him onto Morgrin's horse.

Throughout the ride, which lasted for what was probably three hours, each of them kept looking behind to see if the strange horsemen were following. At times they thought they could hear the echo of horse hooves or the sound of armor. Sometimes they thought they could see distant dark shadowy shapes to either side or in front of them. Still, as time went on, they became less and less certain.

They rode at a gallop nearly the entire time and Ellizar was amazed at the horses' stamina as they didn't appear to falter or show any sign of fatigue. They passed over bridges and small streams, and even in one place a series of bridges that were no more than three feet wide. Yet their horses easily and confidently picked a smooth path for them.

As they rode, the air was slowly becoming fresher and a light breeze began to blow. They took comfort, knowing that there must be other shafts that ran out of the mountains.

Finally, they came to a sheer wall of dark red rock. Aiden pulled his horse to a stop and dismounted. The others got off and they entered a small tunnel to the left. It started tall and wide, but soon grew narrow and short. In some places, Ellizar was the only one who could walk through it comfortably. An hour later they came to a large hall with numerous shafts running in all directions.

"Where are we exactly?" Ellizar asked.

"We are nearing the back entrance to Enya's caves," Isabel answered. "This is starting to look familiar to me, though I can't say I remember this hall."

"The hall was added some time ago," Aiden said. "It was not likely built when you would've been spending any great amount of time with Enya. It is legend though that she and a king under these mountains had quite an interlude. This was built for their own private use."

"I never met this Enya, but I'm not sure she sounds like the greatest character teh walk the earth."

"Indeed not," Isabel replied. "She was much different when I first met her, but somewhere along the way she sold herself to the Sorcerer."

"At least you could see the truth," Morgrin encouraged.

"I would advise silence until further notice," Aiden urged. "There are many dark things buried in the heart of these mountains and I do not wish to meet them face to face if it can be helped."

They heeded the advice and walked in silence. Only then did they begin to hear the sound of footsteps walking with them and occasionally they would hear swords clanging together somewhere far in front of them. They stopped in the middle of the great hall as a large horse emerged from the shadow. The rider quickly dismounted. Ellizar recognized the rider as one who had been with Aiden when he had first appeared.

"Any luck?" Aiden asked.

"Luck no, but I have good news," the rider replied. His voice was smooth and deep, but even so, it filled them with terror. "We have located the shaft you'll need to get into. It was right where you said it might be."

"Very good," Aiden replied. "What news from the outside world?"

"More people keep coming and more people keep fighting. If something doesn't change soon, you'll have the entire population of the Dead Mountains fighting each other for the horrors of Enya's halls. We have formed a plan for-"

"We'll get to that later," Aiden said. The rider bowed and then effortlessly mounted his great horse and vanished into the shadows. Aiden and Isabel led the way, seeming to know where they were headed with Morgrin and Ellizar following close behind.

They entered a series of tunnels until Ellizar was quite certain that he had no idea which direction they were headed. At last, a large spiral staircase carved out of stone loomed in front of them. A large red crystal sat atop a pole in the middle of the space. They began climbing the staircase, rising higher and higher until they reached a landing with a balcony and an old wooden door.

Aiden and Isabel removed the bolt and together all of them were able to pull the door open. Immediately after they stepped through, the door swung itself shut leaving them surrounded by darkness.

A torch was lit, bringing to light a smoothly carved tunnel. Moisture dripped overhead and far in the distance, the sound of a small war. Several more men appeared out of the shadows, but they bowed to Aiden as they approached. Ellizar watched them carefully, unsure if they were Elvish or Human.

"Don't worry we are plenty distant from them," one of Aiden's men said. "Besides, they're too busy with their fighting to hear anything we might be doing."

"Are we in Enya's house yet?" Ellizar asked, his nerves starting to get the best of him.

"These are her lower halls," Isabel answered. "I'm sure she had more of them though, even these I only saw once in all my years."

The men who had come with Aiden went ahead to set up a guard as the rest of them came to an old wooden door. The door was five feet wide and just as tall. Aiden grabbed the handle and threw the door open. Inside the tunnel was much smaller; dashing any hopes of them entering.

"That's small," Isabel said.

"Even smaller than I was expecting," Aiden replied. Silence lingered for a moment until all eyes shifted to Ellizar.

"I suppose *this* is why I was brought along?"

"Aiden's idea," Isabel said. They all laughed. "You willing to try it?"

"Sure I'll try it, just be prepared teh give my wife and kids a long explanation as teh how I died if I get stuck in there."

"I talked with her," Isabel said. "She actually knew this is why we wanted you to come. She said not to tell you or else you wouldn't have gone."

"Blasted elf kind!" Ellizar cried.

"I'm not an elf," Isabel replied.

"I am," Aiden said.

"So is my wife," Ellizar stated. They laughed and Ellizar began taking off his weapons. He stepped up to the tunnel entrance, which offered nothing but darkness. "What am I looking fer and how am I going teh see?"

"This should give you light," Aiden said, pulling a small spherical shape from his pocket. It was dark and hot to the touch. "It won't work until you get into complete darkness. You're looking for a map."

"What kind of map?"

"A map of the northern regions, beyond these mountains, so you may not recognize much of it. There are two of these maps in existence. I believe Enya had one of them."

"Why only two? Granted, I was aware at least a little bit ov the world north ov here, but yeh speak as if it's much larger than I think."

"You'll know the map when you see it, trust me," Aiden said. Ellizar nodded and then climbed into the small shaft in front of him. The sphere Aiden had given him lit up bright. He pulled himself along with his hands and struggled to move at certain parts as his clothes would snag on pieces of rock that lay in his path.

"Ov course! Always got teh send the small one into an impossible tunnel that seems teh have no end," he grumbled.

Ellizar crawled a little further hitting the light ahead of him a few inches at a time. Suddenly the sphere tumbled and rolled down a steep incline. Panic filled Ellizar for a moment until the sphere rolled into view, illuminating the area, which housed shelves of books and scrolls. Ellizar crawled forward and tumbled down the steep incline coming to a thud at the bottom.

"You alright?" Aiden's voice rang out.

"Yeah, I'm fine," Ellizar answered. "Looks like a big library, it might take longer than we want."

"Take as long as you need, just be careful not to take anything other than the map!" Isabel said. "If the map is as rare as we think, Enya would have it protected somehow."

"Thanks," Ellizar said. "If yeh need me yeh know where I'll be!"

Chapter 2

ILLUSIONS

$\mathbf{T}$hree hours passed and still the distant the sounds of fighting managed to make their way down the tunnel. From deep in the library Ellizar felt himself growing restless and though everyone else was making an effort to not complain about the amount of time that had passed, Ellizar knew they were getting anxious.

A large pile of books, parchments, and texts were piled in a corner, having already been looked at. Aiden had seemed sure that Ellizar would recognize whatever he was supposed to retrieve. In the vastness of the library, Ellizar's hope began to wane. With as many shelves and rooms that made up this large library, a person could easily spend a lifetime searching for anything.

Ellizar stood from his spot, eager to stretch his legs and explore the library for a moment. He grabbed the glowing sphere, which was now cool to the touch, and started walking among the shelves and halls that branched off. Ellizar paused as he passed by a small wooden door not much bigger than he was.

He walked up to the door, running his fingers over a worn and faded set of runes that were carved into the door. He grabbed the large handle and easily pulled the door open. Darkness lay in front of him. Strangely the light in his hand seemed to be dimmed.

He took a deep breath and stepped into the darkness. For a moment all light was gone. Dread and regret filled him in that moment and though Ellizar tried to turn and run away he found he couldn't. He was trapped in the darkness with no hope of ever getting out.

He took another step, having to shield his eyes as the darkness vanished and instead was replaced with dazzling light. His eyes adjusted and he looked at his new surroundings.

He stood in a large room, at least twenty feet high and a hundred yards in either direction. The entire room was filled with shelves like he had just walked through.

Strange lights floated in the air just above his head. He studied them as he walked, noting they were the same kind of object that he held in his hand, except they were not spherical, but instead strange and deformed shapes, as though they had been broken and sloppily repaired.

He strode into the room, hearing pages being turned. A moment later he saw an old Dwarf sitting at a table with numerous books piled up all around him. The Dwarf had a grey beard which was unkempt and looked like a bush on his face. The Dwarf was short and fat and smiled when he glanced up and saw Ellizar.

"Good to finally see another person," the Dwarf said. His voice was familiar to Ellizar, though he couldn't place it. "Sorry, I'm not trying to frighten you, I'm just trying to help you make sense of everything that's happening."

"Who are you?" Ellizar asked with much effort. Every second that passed fear and uncertainty grew stronger. The Dwarf got up from his pile of books and walked closer.

"Someone just like you," the Dwarf replied. "Like you, I recognized the name on the door. *Belshazar.* I came across this room a long time ago. I went in and much to my surprise I couldn't get out again. I assume you must also be in the house of Belshazar?"

"I've heard the name, though not in many years," Ellizar replied. "It was one ov my ancestors' names, it has a long history. My own name is a derivative of the ancient name. My name is Ellizar."

"A pleasure to meet you," the Dwarf said bowing. "My name is Mashtruesi. I do not know how you came to be here, but I am glad for the company. There are many strange things about this room, the first being that it seems to only be visible to people with ancestorial ties to the house of Belshazar, for it is also in my family line. I have watched from the doorway, as people over the ages have come down and walked right past without noticing or even turning a glance in this direction."

"How long have you been down here?"

"Nearly five hundred years!" the Dwarf exclaimed. "As far as I can tell anyway. It does get a little hard to keep track of time when you're stuck in a mountain."

"I suppose it does," Ellizar said.

"What is it that you're looking for?" the Dwarf asked. "There are many texts here that would prove to be most educational and informative."

"I can see that. What occupies your studies currently?"

"This most interesting text about the *Sword of Narahune*. It's an ancient legend and I daresay that the writer is a little off his rocker, but it still makes for an interesting story don't you think?"

"I'm familiar with the Sword ov Narahune, but I must say that I think there is far more truth in the story than fiction."

"Perhaps a difference in our point of view," Mashtruesi said. "Fact or fiction, it doesn't matter in the end."

"I say it makes a great difference!" Ellizar exclaimed. The Dwarf looked slightly annoyed.

"Again, a difference in our point of view. But never to worry, we would certainly both agree whether fact or fiction, it is a great literary work. For if it was not such a great work we would not have interfering opinions. In fact, we wouldn't remember it at all."

"I suppose that is sound logic," Ellizar said, a feeling of unease growing in him.

"When you've read as much as I have my friend, things make much more sense." Ellizar didn't reply. "So what is it you're looking for? I'm sure I could easily produce it. I know this place like the back of my hand."

"I'm not exactly sure what it is I'm lookin' fer, but if I might look around fer a couple ov minutes, perhaps I'll see somethin' that catches my eye."

"Yes, please do," Mashtruesi replied. "Let me know if you need anything."

"What did you say your name was again?" Ellizar asked.

IDOLS & TRINKETS

"Mashtruesi," the Dwarf replied.

"It sounds familiar to me."

"Seeing as we're both from the house of Belshazar I wouldn't be surprised. It is tradition to keep old names going. Mine can be traced back to the earliest Dwarves in the far distant Imuh Mountains."

"It's a good history," Ellizar said. He turned and headed into the shelves of books, keeping a watchful eye towards the other Dwarf. Ellizar scanned the shelves and bookcases; his unease growing. Something about this place was wrong.

As if in an answer to his prayer a peace came to him and with it certainty and discernment beyond what Ellizar could comprehend. He moved quickly towards the center of the room where a large table lay. In one corner was a stack of old maps. Some were made from parchment, others were made of animal skin among other materials.

"Ah! I see you are a lover of topography. I was never too big on the subject back in my day, but I've become quite versed in it lately. From what I can gather these are maps from the far north, which is an area I know little about. It's said to be the home of some ancient races and civilizations or something like that. Who knows really? There could be nothing up there but empty space."

"Why are there so many maps?" Ellizar asked. Mashtruesi paused for a moment as though he was trying to recall something from memory.

"This is where I have become well-versed in Topography," Mashtruesi started. "If you'll notice each one of these maps, appears on first glance to be completely identical. Look closer and you'll realize that not only are there subtle differences in the location of landmarks, but also the positioning and names of cities are different.

"There are different seals on the reverse side." He flipped one over to see. "Each map is different. Now either they are all real maps and depict the same area changing through the ages, which would explain the different material they're made out of, or five of them are fakes. I for one can't think of any good reason to make a fake map in the first place. Knowing that we must further investigate the seals on the maps to determine which one is the real one.

17

"I have read much, and have ruled out the ones that are on the bottom of the pile. If they have any validity then they are from ages long past, when it was much less common to make a map in the first place. Through my research I have narrowed it down to these two maps." He pulled them from the stack and laid them in front of Ellizar. "This is the symbol of Poju. Kingdom from the North that at once was said to cover the entire area. The symbol on this map is the symbol of Ter. That kingdom still exists today, at least as far as my reading down here is concerned."

"So you're sure that this map." Ellizar pulled the last map and set it on top. "Has nothing credible about it?"

"Nothing that I can tell," Mashtruesi answered. "It contains some markings that look real enough, but I cannot for the life of me find any kind of scroll, parchment, text, or reference with a matching seal."

"Then why does it exist?" Ellizar asked. The Dwarf looked confused so Ellizar continued. "According teh what yeh yourself said, yeh could think ov no reason fer anyone teh go teh such lengths teh make a fake map, because what would that gain them? But if a person like yeh was purposely placed here teh show me fake maps and tell me that the real one is a fake, then I'd say it must certainly have somethin' ov interest on it that yeh don't want me the know about." The Dwarfs' smile faded and instead, his eyes became filled with a powerful venomous stare.

"Furthermore, yer name Mashtruesi has no dwarvish heritage as yeh would like me teh believe. In fact, that name is Elvish in origin! Yeh see, unlike others ov my kind I have become quite versed in the Elvish writings! In my studies, I have found that no matter what tongue yer vile name is spoken or translated to it means the same thing... 'Deceiver'. Yeh may be able teh pull the wool over my eyes fer a moment, but Lathon has given me much understandin'. Yeh fool no one Merderick, reveal yourself now!"

In an instant, the room changed and Ellizar was standing in a dark damp room in the cave. In his hand, he still had the map. The Sorcerer stood in front of him, glaring.

"Well played Ellizar of Jermin. I can see if I'm going to get you to trip up

I'm going to have to work a little harder."

"Yeh might just give up," Ellizar said. "My soul is secure, go haunt someone else."

"Everyone has a point at which they will do what I want. I want you to leave that map right here and say you never found it. What do you say to that?"

"I'd say its all the more reason fer me teh continue with what I'm here teh do." Ellizar moved past the Sorcerer until once again he appeared in front of him.

"Perhaps I didn't make myself clear!" the Sorcerer boomed. "You will give me the map or I will make sure that you feel pain and suffering like you never imagined. Perhaps if I threaten to kill your wife…or your children? What do you say to that?"

"I'd say I have a hard choice teh make, but there is in reality only one choice that I can make and it would be fer me teh keep walking."

"You would risk the life of your wife and your kids?" Merderick taunted. "That's not very loving is it?"

"Yer a fool Merderick. Always have been, and always will be. When one does not place their treasures here on the earth, one has a different perspective on life."

"Fine!" Merderick exclaimed, clearly getting frustrated. "Then maybe I'll kill you!" He drew a sword, but Ellizar didn't reach for his. Instead, he stared at the Sorcerer in front of him and held the gaze. They remained silent for several moments, neither of them wishing to concede the contest.

"Maybe I'll just call my friends from outside," Ellizar challenged. Merderick scoffed.

"They can't get down here. I made sure that whole was big enough for only one person."

"I'll take that bet," Ellizar said. Merderick looked taken aback. "Yeh know Aiden is outside right? I'm sure he could get down here mighty fast if he needed teh." Merderick held his deadly glare, but Ellizar could tell beneath the surface Merderick's resolve to maintain his threats was weakening.

In an instant, a flash filled the room and when Ellizar's sight returned to him, he found himself back among the dark shelves of the library, map still in hand. Ellizar swiftly moved to the tunnel and began climbing out. Finally, he was pulled from the tunnel and set on his feet.

"Well done Mr. Ellizar," Aiden congratulated. "That's exactly what you needed to get."

"Glad to hear that," Ellizar replied. "Don't know how long I was down there but I was beginning to get discouraged. Who do I hand this teh?"

"I think Isabel will be needing it in the future, but for now keep it for yourself. I think the map will require attention that only a Dwarf can provide," Aiden replied.

"Sounds cryptic," Ellizar said. "I'll have a closer look once we're out ov these blasted mountains! How are we goin' teh get out ov here? Is the fightin' still goin' on outside?"

"Yes it is, and it won't likely stop until we get there," Aiden said. Without saying another word they started through the confusing maze of tunnels and corridors and secret rooms. Ellizar watched the surroundings carefully, noticing that as they went, more people, similar to the strange riders who had been with Aiden, began joining them. By the time they reached what Ellizar thought might be the end of their journey, the company numbered almost sixty.

"Wait here for a moment," one of the men said. Ten of the men followed him ahead into the darkness, while the rest of them waited.

"Good job today," Aiden complimented again.

"Thanks," Ellizar replied. "I saw him, the Sorcerer, down there. Why did I see him there?"

"Physically he's dead. But his spirit lingers in the dark parts of the world. He tested your resolve, your faith, your commitment, your character and you passed all tests with flying colors."

"Could he have appeared any time he chose?" Aiden nodded. "Then why did he choose teh appear at that moment."

"Because you were alone. A person who is alone is the perfect target for him. If you're alone, your friends can't keep you from faltering. Also, you were tired, and by his wisdom should be easier to trip up because of it. However, you were not stressed which is another trait he looks for when picking out those he wishes to deceive." Silence fell over them.

"So, the spirit ov the Sorcerer is still as potent as ever."

"Always. He tried to conquer everything in physical form but failed. Now; now his game has changed. He drives for the heart, to not just conquer but control, from the inside. In many ways, it's a game that's much more dangerous because he will be *unseen* by many." The conversation was pushed to the side as the ten men who had gone ahead returned.

"It's as good of a time as any," the first man said. "The amount of people have doubled in the past hour alone."

"Goodness! How many unsavory people did this woman know?" Ellizar asked.

"Far too many," Isabel said. Ellizar did a double take, hardly recognizing her. Isabel noted his confusion. "Don't worry, it's just a disguise, see." She pulled a black bracelet off her wrist. In an instant she changed back to the Isabel he knew. A moment later she turned back to her new appearance.

"Please promise me once we're out of here you'll be your normal self," Morgrin stated. "I'm not sure I could stand to look at an Enya lookalike for the rest of my life."

"Don't worry, I don't want to stay this way any longer than I have to."

"So this is what Enya looked like?" Ellizar asked, and they nodded. "Gives me the creeps. I assume this has something teh do with how we're going teh get out ov here?"

"Watch and learn my friend," Isabel said, stepping forward, pausing and for the first time Ellizar could remember she looked nervous.

"Don't worry, we'll be right behind you," Aiden encouraged. "Just act the part, we'll take care of the rest." She nodded and walked into the darkness, the rest of them followed quietly behind. The sound of fighting and war became louder until a light appeared on their left, offering them a glimpse of the outside world.

They walked until they were nearly at the end of the tunnel. Ellizar feared that they would all be spotted, but he soon cast that fear to the side. Everyone

21

outside the cave fought viciously, stepping over their dead as they tried to take their claim on the treasures or horrors of Enya's halls.

"What are yeh waitin' fer?" Ellizar asked. Isabel studied the area intently, as though she was seeing something everyone else wasn't.

"I need your help Ellizar, but you're not going to like it."

"As long as I live teh tell the tale, I'll do whatever you want."

"Good," Isabel said, grabbing him by his shirt and pulling him along. Ellizar grasped for footing, but Isabel in her strength managed to keep his feet only just dragging on the ground. No one took notice of her immediately, despite Ellizar's repeated cries to let him go.

With surprising strength, she lifted him up and threw him to a pile of bodies. She faced him, a look in her eyes he had never seen dominated her expressions.

"I've had enough of you! I've had enough of all of you!" Isabel screamed. Her voice was magnified and changed and if Ellizar hadn't known any better he would have said it was Enya speaking.

Quickly and abruptly the fighting and yelling stopped. Everyone stared at Isabel with faces that clearly showed their surprise. No one moved or spoke, they just stared at Isabel, disguised as Enya.

"Well, well, well, what do we have here?" Isabel asked. "Thugs, lowlifes, royalty. commoners; you are a very interesting group!" She paused and began walking closer to them. They backed away, frightened. "I'm not dead you imbicles!" Everyone cowered and began to retreat to their own people. "Perhaps all you rotten pieces of morality would like to become subjects of my newest experiments!" The people cowered more.

"Let me tell you how this is going to go! I'm going to count to three and if you're still here then you will be tortured, starved, fed to wolves, slaughtered like the miserable pieces of flesh you are!" Isabel's voice boomed, shaking the entire mountainside.

Ellizar looked to the tunnel they had come out of, able to see Aiden and his host of men, ready to spring into action. Off to one side was the main entrance of Enya's house. Ellizar drew his weapons as did everybody else.

"One!" no one moved, but Ellizar thought he saw movement on the mountain behind Enya's house.

"Two!" Isabel's commanding voice boomed. The people's faces began to wash white, fear beginning to take hold of them.

"Three!" Silence followed and everyone watching relaxed and began to laugh.

"Nothing here but a good bluff!" a man shouted. The crowd laughed starting to advance towards Isabel. A moment later the mountain trembled violently. Ellizar watched in wonder as Elohim and Aspen had both crept down the mountain and mounted the great tower and roof of Enya's stone house. Fear filled everyone and froze them in place. Isabel's appearance changed and their fear and surprise became even greater.

"Witch?" someone stammered. Isabel smirked at them.

"I warned you." She twisted and let a knife fly and strike the first man in the chest. He dropped to the ground. Aiden charged forward and everyone else let out a cry.

The people panicked and began fleeing, but didn't get far before the Taruks took flight and landed in the forest, setting it ablaze. The flustered enemies turned and attacked the wave of soldiers that had come out of the caves.

Ellizar ducked the blade of one man, spinning and collecting the man with his axe. The Taruks closed in on everyone, unaffected by the flames and the heat as they strode through their own fire to further devastate their enemies.

Aiden's men moved with a speed and ferocity that Ellizar had never seen. Isabel and Morgrin fought as well as they ever had and somehow seemed to be fighting with more determination than he had seen previously. Ellizar only had a few moments to ponder the notion.

Ellizar found the battle harder than it should have been, but the reason why was lost on him. It had only been a few months since the attacks leading to the Sorcerer's defeat. Still, he felt sluggish and had to be saved more than once by Aiden's men.

Three hours later the last enemy fell to the ground, joining their comrades who had already passed into shadow. Everyone fell to their knees, exhaustion threatening to overtake them.

"That was a lot harder than it should've been," Isabel said. Ellizar felt his spirits rise.

"Glad teh know I wasn't the only person thinkin' that," Ellizar replied. "It's the presence ov the Sorcerer isn't it?"

Aiden nodded.

"Yes it is, and it's one I'm not going to put up with anymore. Be gone!" Instantly they felt their bodies revive and more life returned to them.

One of Aiden's men approached them and stood silent for a while as everyone looked at the carnage that had been created. Small blazes still burned in the forest. The Taruk's moved through the forest hunting down any other survivors. The tower and house were mostly unaffected, though in places there were gaping holes where the Taruks had latched onto it.

"So much death and destruction," Morgrin lamented. "They destroy each other and then are destroyed."

"That's all the Sorcerer can do is destroy," Aiden said. "The ability to create was not given to him, but to mankind. He is trapped by his own inabilities."

"What was in all these tunnels that everyone wanted teh have so much?" Ellizar asked.

"Things that cannot be allowed to be taken from this place," Isabel answered. For a long while she stared at the ruins, weariness and sorrow on her face. "I know me coming here as a child has been made good through the will of Lathon, but I cannot fathom how we can destroy everything in her caves and halls. Some items in my own shop, I've tried everything I can think of and still they have not been destroyed."

"That is about to change Isabel!" Aiden exclaimed. Even as he finished speaking, the noise of a great host of carts pulled by horses could be heard clamoring their way through the mountains. The Taruks flanked the main path, bowing their heads as if they already knew who was coming.

Ellizar watched in wonder and amazement as cart after cart, each filled to capacity with wooden barrels came and stopped in the clearing before Enya's house. They stood and turned their attention to the driver of the first cart who dismounted. They bowed before him and in his heart, Ellizar knew why. The man had a great long beard and a great staff, inlaid with veins of gold. The top of the staff was sprouted with almonds.

"You have done well my daughter!" the man exclaimed, motioning for them to rise.

"I don't feel like it," Isabel replied.

"Ah, that's because you can't see from the view of beyond," the man stated. "From the view of beyond, never have I been prouder of you than I am right now!"

"Who is this man?" Ellizar asked.

"It's not that hard to figure out Ellizar," the man said. At the mention of his name, Ellizar understood. "I am, who I always have been." The conversation continued but Ellizar was in a daze, pondering the man's words and feeling more blessed, happy, and content than he had in ages. The man's voice was comforting and soothing, but Ellizar always knew it could be terrifying and deadly if it needed to be.

"Now, let's get all these barrels unloaded and in the tunnels and rooms. I've brought enough for one barrel per room of tunnel." Then as the man commanded, they began unloading the barrels and rolling them down into the deep depths of Enya's fortress. When finally the job was done the carts were driven away as everyone made their way to the Taruks.

They all climbed aboard and flew into the sky, leaving the man with the staff on the ground. They watched as he stood before the menacing ruins and held his staff to the sky. A great blinding flash came from the staff and struck the ruins.

At the moment of impact a light and sound greater than any that Ellizar had ever seen erupted from the mountain. Fire lept into the sky and rocks and carnage covered the mountain. When finally the fire and smoke cleared, they could see only an immense crater carved into the side of the mountain.

The Taruks turned and left the smoldering mountainside behind them. Ellizar rode atop the Taruk, new life flowing through him. He pulled the map from his pocket and stared at it in wonder. What had once been confusing, now seemed clear.

Chapter 3

FELLOWSHIP

Horns trumpeted their notes all throughout the city. Though Drake and a few of his men were nearly a league away from the city of Avdatt, the notes were heard clear and plain to his ears. Despite their best efforts to get into the city unnoticed, they had been discovered.

"Sorry, Your Majesty," Matthew said. "Someone blew our cover."

"So much for going cross country and avoiding roads," Drake replied. "Though I feel like it was an accomplishment to get this far without being noticed."

Despite Drake's best efforts to have a low-key wedding and party, the Governor of Avdatt had insisted on having the greatest party the city had ever seen.

It was considered by most, both unusual and odd for a king to get married anywhere but his own kingdom, and even in all his years he couldn't remember such an occurrence. Strange as it may seem there was more than one reason he and Rachal had decided to have the wedding here, versus in Rhallinen.

Drake allowed himself to drown in his thoughts as they walked under the shade of Baccata trees. To their west, the sea opened to whatever lay beyond. Ahead, though still distant, were hills and mountains. Many memories came back to him of the last time he had been in this city and the journey that had followed soon after.

The journey had brought more than just a few changes to his life and lifestyle. As Drake rode towards the forest edge, he began to understand that the Drake that had entered the city so many years ago, would not have been able to do what he and Rachal were going to do in a few days.

IDOLS & TRINKETS

It was only five days until he and Rachal would finally be married. It seemed surreal to both of them and in some ways it was. It was still unknown to them why Drake had been allowed to lose his memory in the first place, but at the very least Drake and Rachal, both trusted that there had been some divine reason for it.

What it was, Drake couldn't wager a guess, and a part of him didn't want to. Lathon had a plan, and that plan involved bringing both of them to the point where they finally were totally surrendered and loyal to Lathon. Even if it had taken very different steps for each of them to get there.

The city grew larger before him, the walls coming into plain view as they left the forest. More horns bellowed through the air, and Drake could already hear the city alive with excitement. Drake let a smile come to his lips as he rode down the slope.

Matthew rode close by his side, five other men flanking them as the gates of the city were opened. "Hail the king of Rhallinen!" the Heralds announced.

"Hail the king!" the crowd replied.

They entered with the thunderous roar of the people. In the distance, Drake caught a glimpse of a white speck in the sky. His spirit soared, despite growing more nervous.

Drake waved and smiled as he and his men were paraded through the streets for some time. Finally, they reached the end where they were brought before the governor's mansion. The governor and all his top officials came forward as Drake and his men dismounted.

"Greetings my Lord!"

"Greetings are returned Governor, although I thought I distinctly specified that I wanted a low-key entrance into the city?"

"Indeed that is what you said, but never to worry I got your message just an hour ago. Besides, you are so famous and well-loved by the people after your battles against Megara that it is hard to not give you a kingly welcome."

"I appreciate the sentiment," Drake said. "Though we both know that I had little to do with it."

"True, but Aiden isn't here is he?" the governor teased. They both laughed and then shook hands. Drake scanned the faces of the officials behind the governor, noticing a few that looked familiar. "Will you do us the great honor of joining us for the evening my Lord?"

"It would be a great honor indeed, but I'm afraid I've already made arrangements for tonight's entertainments, though if I could use a bed of yours until the wedding I would be greatly indebted to you."

"We will see if we can find a bed worthy for you!" the governor said.

"You will give me no more than a mat on the floor!" Drake said, laughing as he did so.

"If I may interrupt my Lords." They turned to see a robed man coming forward, a great white beard on his face. Drake bowed to him as he approached.

"Cornelius," Drake greeted. "A pleasure to see you again."

"You two know each other?" the governor asked. Cornelius nodded.

"We have met on several occasions, though I don't believe we've yet had the privilege of being friends," Cornelius started. "My house has many rooms and I would willingly and with pleasure lend one of my rooms to you, Mr. Thomas. It is close to your old home, which I believe is where the rest of your party is residing until the wedding is it not?"

"Indeed it is. If it's not an inconvenience."

"Not at all, you'd be among friends."

Drake studied the man in front of him noticing there seemed to be a different light in his eyes than when they had met previously, though whether it was a good light or a bad one, Drake couldn't tell.

"Then I will see you later tonight," Drake said, extending a hand. Cornelius shook it.

"Nickolas knows where my house is. The door will be opened no matter what time you knock on it!"

"Very well I will see you then, and I'll see you sometime tomorrow governor."

Cornelius quickly vanished from the scene.

"Would you like us to put up your men and horses?"

"That would be most appreciated, though Matthew will be staying with me."

IDOLS & TRINKETS

They dispersed, leaving Matthew and Drake to go their own ways.

"More than a few interesting things going on in this city," Matthew said. "Is this the Cornelius you've told me about previously?"

"It is," Drake answered.

"And he wasn't friendly then correct?"

"That's right."

"You'd better watch yourself carefully if you're going to reside with him for the time that we're here. We both know you didn't send any word for a big entrance."

"Right again," Drake said. "If I had wanted a big entrance I would've brought Destan. People recognize him from ten leagues away. Someone's trying to mess with me."

"We had some men in the city yesterday, they were probably watching the gate. I'll see if they've seen anything unusual."

"Sounds good, first though I need you to come with me to the house."

"Why?" Matthew asked.

"Just come along, you'll see."

"I'm not liking the sound of that."

"It's nothing to be worried about, but something might happen to me between here and there, and you're job is to keep me safe right?"

"Yes, but I can smell a secret."

"Just come along and all will be revealed," Drake stated.

The city although it was much the same as it had been when Drake had lived here many years ago, had undergone some subtle changes. The buildings had become taller and also the wall around the outside was much more foreboding than it had been in the early days.

War had ravaged the nation and especially the city of Avdatt for several years after Drake had left. Always though, Avdatt and Rhallinen had remained friendly and had often done trade, as well as supplied aid and troops when one nation was under attack.

The distant peaks of the mountains towered over the walls. Within the mountains, Drake knew the Taruk stadium still stood, getting used several times a year. Drake hoped for old time's sake he would be able to see it one more time before they left the city.

His old street stretched out before them and as he and Matthew turned the corner Drake had to fight back the emotions and the memories that still lived in this city. He and Gwen had lived a beautiful life here and even though he had thought he had successfully moved on, he was still bitterly reminded of the love they had shared. He had been to this city many times since Gwen's death, but somehow this visit was bringing another wave of emotions that he hadn't expected. Sorrow, happiness, regret, thankfulness. His life had changed in more than just one way when he had lived here.

"Drake Thomas!" a woman's voice yelled from behind. They turned to see Isabel skipping her way barefoot down the street. "My most favoritist son-in-law!"

"Isabel! How's everything going?" Drake asked. "I must point out that technically I'm not your son-in-law yet."

"You were married to Gwen."

"Who wasn't you're daughter?" Drake asked teasingly.

"Close enough, besides you're going to marry my real daughter in a few days anyway. So you *are* my son-in-law." Matthew chuckled.

"Very well I concede."

"Good, it's useless to argue with a woman the age I am."

"I find it hard to think of you as the age you are," Matthew replied. "You certainly don't look like you're old enough to have a grown daughter. Let alone you're skipping barefoot down the street."

"The joys of strange enchanted items and Lathon given protection. The unfortunate side effects of having to use disguises for your entire life like I have," Isabel replied. "However I was thinking, Drake, as my son-in-law you wouldn't mind helping your dear mother-in-law with something would you?"

"I'm growing scared of what that might be," Drake said.

"I left the house and there's a Dwarf named Ellizar inside who no doubt has prepared some childish trap for me upon my return. Be a good son-in-law and go up to the door first," Isabel said, flashing an innocent smile.

"No way! I'm not getting in the middle of you guys and your games. I like to watch them, not be in them. Besides you don't know for sure that he did anything."

"Drake, it's Ellizar; of course he did something," Isabel said. "Spare me."

"I have a better idea, why don't we pull a fast one on Ellizar and neither of us gets caught in his trap."

"I'm listening," Isabel said. Drake looked at Matthew and smiled childishly.

"You're joking right?" Matthew asked. Silence lingered, while Drake tried to come up with some excuse. "You can't pay me enough money. Isabel, I've met you a few times but I've heard for years of these *pranks* that you and Ellizar pull on each other and I'm not doing it."

"Really?" Drake asked. "What if I beg you?"

"Nope."

"What if, as your king, I commanded it?"

"That's cheap! Seriously cheap!"

"I'm sure Isabel has some wedding details that she needs to tell me, which is why you're going to the door first," Drake said. Matthew rolled his eyes.

"I like this plan," Isabel said.

"So do I."

"Alright your *Highness*, I will be a good second in command and go to the door."

"Thank you, Matthew," Drake said. "I'll give you a bonus for this."

Drake and Isabel watched Matthew go up to the door and knock. The door opened and a moment later he stepped inside. "There you go mother-in-law, you are safe to enter the Thomas mansion."

"Good to know!"

Drake and Isabel walked up to the door, with Drake falling behind as they went up the steps. Isabel paused and looked back at him. "Is there something wrong Drake?"

"No," Drake managed. "I was just admiring this lovely rose plant you gave us; grew over this archway very nicely don't you think?"

"Yes, lucky I found it too, the vendor only had that one plant left. You're in on it aren't you?"

"Better not wait any longer!" Drake yelled. Instantly a white cloud fell from the archway and billowed around Isabel's feet. Laughter and cheering ensued from the house. Isabel was covered from head to foot in flour.

"Drake Thomas!" Isabel cried. The door opened and Ellizar proudly stepped out onto the doorstep. "After all these years, all the pranks; I was bested by a Dwarf with a bag of flour?"

"That's right!" Ellizar exclaimed. "It's the simple tricks that are the best don't yeh think?"

"Now you actually look your age," Matthew retorted from in the house. Isabel scowled while unsuccessfully managing to hide a smile.

"Don't draw any more attention to yourself, Matthew," Drake replied. "Good work though." Ellizar pulled a small wad of cash and handed it to Matthew. "Consider that your bonus."

Just then, Morgrin came walking up the steps."Where can I find my wife?"

"Right here!"

Morgrin looked at Isabel and jumped. Silence followed as he tried not to laugh.

"Ellizar?"

"Yep," Isabel said, turning her glare to the Dwarf who was still smiling proudly. "This isn't over."

"Blasted elf-kind!" Ellizar cried.

They broke into laughter and they entered the house. Matthew remained outside and talked to a couple of people that they had sent in as spies.

Drake was greeted by many of the friendly faces that he had met over the past ten years, as well as people that he had never met before.

Some names came to him instantly, others remained at large and vague, leaving him to fake his way through the conversation as he had been trained to do for many years now.

"How's my favorite cook!" Drake greeted. Shavrok towered over him, beaming from ear to ear.

"Quite well. Right now I'm working on a secret recipe from the northernmost tribe of Gog's. It's a special dish only served at weddings. Care to sample?" Shavrok held a plate out to Drake who looked suspiciously at the food prepared for him.

"What is it?" Drake asked, inspecting carefully.

"It's called *Dervunai*. Not sure what it means; it's a word that has been lost to our language. It's got North Remu trout, mixed with…I can't remember what I mixed it with, I had to improvise as you showed up on short notice."

"You only live once," Drake said, eating it. He gagged and spit it back out. "Do everyone a favor…don't serve this at the reception."

"Sorry," Shavrok apologized. "I'm sure I'll be able to tweak it enough in the next couple of days to serve it."

"Doubt it," Drake said. "Have you tasted it?"

"Not yet." Shavrok took a bite and spit it out a moment later. "Ugh! That stuff is nasty!"

"You're telling me?"

"Northern Gog's must have no taste buds left if they like to eat this stuff."

"My thoughts exactly," Drake said. Shavrok disappeared to the kitchen as Drake was greeted by everyone who was present. "Anyone seen Rachal?"

"She's out with her brothers, picking up some things for the wedding," Nickolas said.

"Aaron and Jacob are here?"

Nickolas nodded.

"Saul here too?"

"He'll be here tomorrow I think. Aiden's supposed to be here today, right?"

"Yeah, I saw his Taruk in the sky as we approached," Drake said. "Rachal and I are supposed to meet with him soon."

"She was planning to meet you at my restaurant," Isabel said. "That is where you were meeting Aiden right?"

"Yes indeed," Drake answered. Matthew slipped into the house and motioned for him. They both stepped outside where their other men were waiting for them. "Anything interesting?"

"Perhaps my Lord," one of his men on the right said. "We didn't see anything unusual going in or out of the gates earlier this week. But today there was a man on a horse that went through the gates at incredible speed. We think he was the one who carried the message about a big arrival. But it seems to have only been a diversion because a ragged, disgruntled-looking man slipped past the guards after you entered the city. We don't know what he might want, but we'll be keeping an eye out."

"In the meantime, we probably should have someone with you all the time," Matthew said. "For your own safety."

"If you insist," Drake said. "Just do me a favor, you sometimes freak me out when you're just stalking me everywhere. Follow me close, but not too close. If this guy does show himself, he will do it when it appears I'm by myself." They all agreed and Drake and Matthew went back into the house, while the other two men vanished.

***

An hour later Drake stepped out onto the front porch of his house and began walking down the crowded city streets. His sword was strapped to his side, should he need it. Drake marveled at all the people who made up this great city that had been a part of his life for so many years.

He turned from the main street, choosing instead to travel by the back alleys. Some were empty, others were filled with women and children, all of whom needed a little extra help. Drake reached into a pack he had brought with him, making sure to drop a small bag of coins at the feet of everyone he passed. Some thanked him, some didn't pay him a second thought, but Drake didn't care.

He stole a glance behind him, vaguely seeing a person in tattered clothes dart from view. Drake loosened his sword in its sheath and entered again into the crowded streets, but out of the corner of his eye every time he looked back he felt like he saw something for just a moment.

He wandered for a few minutes, going through the thickest crowd he could find and when the opportunity presented itself, slipped into another empty alley. Drake walked slowly, faintly picking up soft footsteps. He turned around but saw nothing.

Drake stayed where he was, taking in everything. When he turned back he saw a man standing in front of him. His beard and his hair were overgrown. Despite his appearance, it didn't take long to notice that he was a strong burly man. He was dressed in tattered brown clothes, an expensive chain and medallion hung from his neck.

The man didn't speak, or move, choosing instead to stare at him from underneath his overgrown hair, his eyes barely visible. Drake rested his hand casually on his sword but didn't draw it.

"You're the one who gave me a good welcome today no doubt, now name yourself!" Drake declared.

The man let out a cackling laugh that filled the alley.

"Don't you recognize me?" the man asked. His voice was thick and deep with a strange accent. A strange light was in the man's eyes which didn't give Drake any comfort.

"My question first, I demand it!" Drake said forcefully. He drew his sword and held it to the man's neck. Behind the man, Drake could see Matthew and a few other men carefully moving up the alley.

"I'm afraid I can't answer you Mr. Thomas!" the man said, letting a laugh tainted by sheer pleasure escape him. "Not when men are coming up the alley."

By the time Drake had swung his sword, the man had twisted out of the way with astonishing speed. Matthew and his men rushed forward, equally surprised by the speed of the man. He twisted and jumped furiously, dodging all the attacks that Drake and his men could throw at him.

The man once again twisted away from Drake's sword and darted to the edge of the street, where he pulled his sword from the dust. Drake and his men rushed in, engaging the man in battle, but the man was up to their challenge and hardly seemed to be challenged.

Drake swung the sword one last time and this time the man's sword was knocked out of his hand. Drake and his four men surrounded him, backing him up against the wall.

The man started laughing again. A pounding, combined with burning light began to fill Drake's head as he looked at him.

"You should have answered my question," Drake taunted.

"No," the man said. A moment later, before any of them knew how, the man had escaped them and was sprinting through the alley, quickly darting into the city streets.

"Get after him!" Drake ordered. Everyone except Matthew took off after the man.

"What's wrong?" Matthew asked. "All the years I've been your Captain you've never given up the chase, even when I told you to. What's going on?"

"I'll tell you later if I figure it out. Let's get after him." Matthew led the way, Drake followed shaking his head and hoping the pounding would go away. In the distance, he thought he heard strange voices, familiar but strange. He strained his ears, unable to make out clearly what the voices were saying.

They entered into the streets and the sensation stopped. Drake and Matthew studied the streets, noticing commotion further up. Drake and Matthew quickly strode to two men walking their horses.

"No time to talk. I'm the king of Rhallinen. We're taking your horses, we'll return them later if we can!" Drake motioned and Matthew pulled out a couple of small packs of coins and dropped them in the men's hands. They took the reins and jumped on, sending the horses as fast as they could through the streets with all the commotion. They quickly caught up to his men, one of whom stopped the chase long enough to talk.

"He slipped away from us. He ducked into that alley on the left; runs nearly straight through the rest of the city."

"You guys keep coming from behind, enlist the help of Avdattian guards. This should help." Drake pulled off his signet ring and handed it to his men. "No one will question you now. Matthew, you and I are going to get him from the other side." The man took off; Drake and Matthew turned their horses and went north.

"How are we going to get in front of him? We don't know where he is?" Matthew asked.

"Trust me I know these streets!" Drake exclaimed. "That alley runs clear to the other side, with three other alleys that join to it from this street. He will not double back, he'll keep running. If we get to the other side he'll be trapped."

"Seems like a stupid design."

"It is until you can funnel an attacking army into it and pick them off from the rooftops."

They wound through the streets eventually coming out where Drake had wanted. They turned their horses down the alley, his men and some Avdattian guards could be seen nearly a half mile down the tunnel.

"Looks like you were right," Matthew said, "but where is the man?"

Drake didn't get a chance to answer as two men jumped from the rooftop and knocked them off their horses. Drake and Matthew scrambled to their feet, swords drawn. The man from earlier stood, smiling with his sword, while another man, who looked a little more put together was watching Matthew.

The two men engaged them in swordplay, both pairs seeming to be perfectly matched. Matthew cried out and was knocked to the ground, his sword lost from his grasp. He was quickly bound by two more men who appeared out of the shadows. Then they retreated, leaving just the one man standing over him with a sword.

Drake and his assailant seemed equally matched as they swung, dodged, and blocked the attacks of the other. Finally, the man threw his sword behind him and put his hands in the air.

"You are a much better fighter!" the man exclaimed. Letting out another cackling laugh. He grabbed the golden chain and yanked it from his neck. He threw it at Drake's feet. Drake stared at it and then at the man. The man stood perfectly still, the shouting of Drake's men was growing nearer.

"Call them off!" the man urged.

"Tell me what I want to know!" Drake cried.

With a quick twist and leap the man jumped to a ladder and scaled to the roof. He vanished from sight and the ladder was shoved to the ground. The man holding Matthew vanished in an instant. Drake untied him as his other men caught up.

"This is not normal," Matthew said, getting to his feet. "We chase, we catch, and he gets away. Repeats; capture me but not kill me, what is this guy's game?"

Drake picked up the golden chain off the ground, looking towards a large diamond in the middle of a single medallion. Etched into the diamond was a crest of some kind. Three stars were at the top followed by a sword pointing up and below that a very detailed picture of a city. The etched lines in the diamond glimmered a pale green. Around the edge were strange markings of a tongue that Drake didn't know. Light and searing pain filled his mind for a moment.

"If he meant to kill us he would've. He's a friend of some kind, who got spooked with your swords. He'll show himself again I think. This time if you catch him, use no weapons and put him in Cornelius's house and hold him there until I can question him tonight."

"Are these your orders sir?" Matthew asked. "What are you going to do?"

"Meet with my fiancé and Aiden in Isabel's restaurant. Go do as I ordered. Once I'm there I will be more than protected. Aiden and Rachal are both good with swords and Isabel long ago told me the command for the vines."

The men dispersed. Matthew hesitated for a moment and then followed Drake's command. Drake walked to the horses and whispered in the Elvish tongue for the horses to return to their owners. The horses snorted and trotted through the city. Drake looked at the necklace and then slipped it into his pocket.

Isabel's restaurant, The Taruk's Pub, didn't look any different than the last time that Drake had been here. The flowering vines, (which by now had become her trademark in his mind), still covered all of it. The whole place looked beautiful and not nearly as old as it actually was.

Drake stepped onto the porch and opened the squeaky door noticing how the inside had changed. Where once this had chiefly been Isabel's dwelling, with outdoor seating for customers. Now the entire area had been given tables and chairs, including all the other rooms down the hall.

Isabel had recently cleaned out all of her relics and strange items and surprised everyone by selling the restaurant to new owners. Though she had left specific instructions for any family members of hers to not be charged for anything that they wanted.

"What will it be today?" the woman at the front asked.

"Perhaps a cup of ale for me, my fiancé, and one other guest that will be joining us."

"Coming right up. You're Drake Thomas right?" the woman asked. Drake nodded. "Pick whatever seat you wish, Isabel's conditions upon buying this place."

"I'll take the seat over in the corner by the window."

Drake moved into the light and airy corner and waited anxiously. Finally, a brown-haired woman entered and after spotting him, made her way over to Drake in the corner.

"There's my beautiful fiancé!" Drake greeted, standing and pulling a chair out for her. Rachal smiled shyly and sat down. She was dressed in a dark blue dress, that Isabel had made for her, and true to Isabel's fashion, the trim on the dress would change colors every so often, though not nearly as frequently as Isabel's changed. "I'm glad to see you."

"As am I."

"How are you feeling?"

"Nervous," Rachal admitted. "Excited to be getting married and starting our life together, but nervous because it's a very big and very public wedding and we have no idea where we are going afterward."

"I understand," Drake said. "I'm told it's going to be the wedding of the century."

"I guess the important thing is that Lathon has finally brought us together, and that's what really matters."

"I quite agree."

"So this is my mother's old place?"

"One of them. She's had four or five that I know of. Her decision to sell this place is a surprise. I've never come to fully understand her."

"I'm sure she has her reasons."

"Let me ask you, what was it like growing up with her? Obviously, you didn't know she was your mother until recently, but she seems to have been a friend of the family. Was she as strange to you growing up, as she seemed to me when I met her?"

"She was just always there," Rachal said. "Strange as she might seem to other people, she never seemed strange to me and we had a lot of good times. She was like another family member, an aunt, or a long-lost stepmother. Looking at it now I'd say she was in some ways a role model for me. There were some times it was hard because she wouldn't say when she was coming. She would just show up, but it was part of her charm.

"When she first told me that she was my mother I was more confused than ever before. However, as I've had time to think about it, I've come to understand her situation and truly am thankful for everything she did for me when I didn't even know it." Silence lingered for a moment. "How was your trip here?"

"More eventful than I would've liked. Ended up with a grand entrance that I didn't ask for, got attacked in an alley by a huge strong, crazy guy. You know, the normal."

"I'm glad you're okay, did you catch him?"

"He got away. He knew who I was, and something about him seemed familiar to me, though I can't place what it was."

"What else happened?"

"Some more memories returned to me. I don't know what they mean yet, mostly it's just voices, conversations that I've apparently had and am now meant to remember. Also, the guy I was fighting threw this at me and then vanished." Drake pulled the medallion out of his pocket and handed it to her. She cautiously took it, almost as though she had seen a ghost. "Does it look familiar?"

"Isabel and I found of these in your northern house when we were packing everything last week. Exactly the same, the etching on the outside is a little different. You got this off some weird crazy guy?"

"Yes," Drake said. "You said I have one of these?"

"I'll have to dig through some boxes to find it, but it's the same. I wonder what it means."

"Perhaps I can shed some light on this mystery." They looked up to see Aiden standing at their table.

"Good to see you Aiden!" Drake said. They both stood and embraced him.

"Likewise my friends."

"It's been a while."

"Indeed it has, the kingdom of Lathon doesn't wait for anyone. There is always pressing work to be done. That being said a little rest and the wedding of two people who are very dear to me? I wouldn't miss for the world."

"That is why you're so awesome," Drake said. Aiden half laughed. "You are going to take care of the drinks at the wedding right?"

"I'd like to say no, but I'll do it for you guys." Drake gave a thumbs-up while Rachal remained silent for a moment.

"I feel like there's a story that I don't know about," Rachal said.

"Allow me to explain for you, my dear!" Drake started. "It was shortly after I was appointed as leader of Rhallinen, we attended a wedding in a small town near Aiden's parents. We were just guests, but during the reception, they ran out of wine. His mother told him about it and Aiden's famous reply was '*What am I supposed to do about it?*'

"Well, his mom clearly thought he should do something about it, so he had some jars filled with water and they all turned to wine. It was no doubt the best wine I ever tasted. Never seemed to run out either."

"The whole ordeal was quite annoying really," Aiden said. "But I shall gladly do the same for your party's refreshments because I like you."

"We'll take it!" Rachal exclaimed.

"Have you two given thought about what you are going to do after the wedding?" Drake and Rachal looked at each other for a moment, reading each other's thoughts.

"We've decided to follow where you lead. Point us in the direction you want us to go and we'll try to make you proud," Rachal started. "We've already sold the northern house Drake had once built for us and we plan to do the same with the one here in Avdatt before we go."

"Excellent," Aiden said. "How do you feel about it?"

"Scared out of my mind," Rachal admitted. "I've never really ever gone on an adventure before. I always pictured getting married and settling down and having kids in the town I grew up in. Isn't that what all girls dream about when they're growing up?"

"I wouldn't know because I'm not a girl," Aiden replied. They all shared a chuckle. "But I can understand the sentiment. How about you Drake? How do you feel?"

"Equally as scared, but I've trusted you before in a situation like this and ultimately it brought Rachal and I together again. I'm your willing servant, who is ready to go east."

"I'm proud of you both. You're willing to lay aside everything you have and everything you might have and pursue what Lathon wants you to do. It makes my heart smile."

"Though there are a few things I might like to know," Drake said.

"Understandably so," Aiden said. "What are your questions?"

"What's going to happen to Rhallinen?" Drake asked. "It's been my home for a long time and I love the people there. What are they going to do without a king?"

"I'll be staying in Rhallinen for a while, but I would like you to appoint a successor. Someone you think would be most suited to do the job, even if they're not perfect at the beginning."

"Tough job; I'd say Matthew would be a good candidate."

"I'd concur," Aiden agreed.

"He's in favor with the people and has seen enough of my screw-ups that he might be able to avoid them himself. If you're okay with it that's who I'll appoint."

"Very well. Like I said I will be staying in Mera Runa for a while and can coach him until he is ready to fully take the reins. Next question?"

"Where are we going?" Rachal asked. "Out of all the things that's been burning in my mind, this one has been threatening to drive me over the edge. How far is it? What's it called? How should we get there?"

IDOLS & TRINKETS

"The nation is called Rinevah. It lies far to the east. A remnant of a once greater nation. Great troubles came on it years ago and it's never fully recovered. It's going to be quite a trip, probably at best take a month. I haven't done much scouting to tell you how you should get there, but I would not recommend taking any Taruks as they are heavily hunted and worshiped in some of the neighboring nations."

"The name is familiar," Drake said. "Some memories are coming back to life in my head."

"Yes, you might find it like that from now on. It might be hard to understand, but your memory is meant to come back to you in pieces. You might see someone and it sparks something, or you might hear a name or a place and it sparks something else. There are reasons for it, but it is for Lathon to reveal, not myself."

"Speaking of that, can you tell me what this is?" Drake put the necklace and medallion on the table. Aiden picked it up, studying it carefully. "Rachal said she found one just like it in our northern house."

"This bears the royal crest of Rinevah. Three stars for the three kings who came to Masada to find me one night long ago. The sword represents the word of Lathon, stronger than any double-edged sword. Below is the city. If this isn't yours, where did you get this one?"

"Off a man who challenged me this morning."

"Did you trust this man?"

"He attacked me," Drake reiterated.

"Yes, but why? Who drew his weapon first?" Aiden asked. Drake fell silent. "He may not be the bad guy that you think he is. There are a hundred different possibilities for why he did what he did. Always make sure to find the right one before concluding your judgment."

"I'll have to do better at that," Drake admitted.

"It's okay I'm here to help, encourage, and give a swift kick in the pants if I need to." They all laughed.

"What is this place like?" Drake asked.

"I will have to be incredibly annoying and not answer that question...only

43

because I know someone who can answer it much more deeply than I can in our brief time. Before you two make your final travel plans I would like you to go see Queman."

"Queman?" Rachal asked. "The same Queman that I've known all these years?"

"The same one. You will find that he has recently left his herds in the hands of your brothers and now resides not far from this city. He has quite a knowledge about things that are long past. There is much you can learn from him. Also, Ellizar has recently become well-versed in old texts, together they are quite a powerful combination. I would highly encourage you to find them and learn what you can before you set out."

"We will certainly do that," Rachal said.

" Again, I'm proud of both of you for your choice to go east. Long and hard the road might be, and even more so in ways you do not expect, but at the end of your life if you remain faithful to Lathon and myself you will be able to see a greater story and legacy that will far outlive you."

They talked long into the afternoon before returning to the house where everyone was staying. Whatever troubled hearts they had been burdened with when the day had started vanished as quickly as they had come.

The night grew deep as they enjoyed the company, and reminisced about their adventures together, and imagined about what life in the future might hold. Drake watched everyone as they interacted together, sad that after this week ended he might never see any of them again.

Matthew joined them after a while having come up empty in their search for his attacker, but not without being extremely close a couple of times. A couple of the men had gotten roughed up during the last confrontation, but unfortunately for everyone he had escaped. At length, they said their goodbyes, and Matthew and himself stepped out into the cool starry night. They walked in silence for a while.

"What are you thinking Drake?" Matthew asked.

"This is a strange week for me. The beginning, yet also the end all in one."

"I wouldn't worry about it too much," Matthew said. "We'll get back to Mera Runa and it'll be just like normal, except this time you'll have a beautiful wife to share your life with."

"I suppose you're right," Drake said. "Except that I'm not going to be returning to Mera Runa. At least not as king."

"Two questions: What are you talking about? And Are you sure this is a conversation we should be having in the middle of the night?"

"Sure as anything I've ever done. I've put it off long enough and nearly paid for it. Rachal and I have thought long and hard about this, but Aiden has asked us to go east and it's hard to say no to him. You are the first one to know besides the two of us, and I thought I would tell you now because I plan to appoint you as King of Rhallinen." Matthew stood, dumbfounded. "Aiden thinks you'll make a great ruler and he will stay with you until you are ready to lead without him. I know this must be a shock, but it's what Lathon wants."

"Shocked is an understatement. I've never thought of myself as King Material."

"None of us are; not unless we're open to the leading of Lathon. You have the heart for it, even if you don't think that you do. You've stood by my side through many trials, mishaps, and good times. The way I see it, there is no one else worthy of appointing.

"Rachal and I will come back of course, for a little bit, long enough to say our goodbyes and see the people. Then we will appoint you and we'll leave. I think it's safe to say that I don't know if we'll ever see you again. I'm still not exactly sure where we are going or what we're going to do."

"I'm not sure what to say."

"You've done well Matthew; you've become like a brother to me. Regardless of whatever happens between now and when we get back, enjoy the moment."

Chapter 4

AN UNINVITED GUEST

Silence came over them as they continued walking to Cornelius's house. Drake felt more relief now than in the past three months. While Drake may feel like he was the only one Lathon was asking to step out and be bold, it was what every follower of Lathon was called to do.

Finally, they knocked at the door of Cornelius's mansion. The doors were opened silently and they were greeted by a large vaulted ceiling and marble floors. Countless candles and chandeliers illuminated the great space. They were led through the mansion until finally, they entered a small study on their left.

Bookcases went from floor to ceiling, and the room was filled with beautiful furniture, but somehow seemed lackluster compared to the grand and glorious look and feel of the rest of the house. Behind the desk in the center, Cornelius sat reading a scroll. He took note of them and quickly stood to his feet, his eyes beaming as they approached.

"I am so honored that you accepted my request and allowed me to put you and your men up while you are here!" Cornelius greeted. Any suspicions Drake had held back about him earlier, were almost immediately pushed from his mind; a fair change in his demeanor was obvious. "I hope everything is well tonight my Lord?"

"Yes everything is quite fine indeed," Drake said, bowing as was courtesy.

"Well please, please, if there is anything unsatisfactory let me or one of the staff know and we'll gladly go and get it for you. You have no idea how happy I am to see you, my Lord! Please do me the great honor of joining me for tea by the fireplace. I know it is late, but I tend to find that time is shorter and shorter and one must make use of every moment they have."

"I will gladly join you for some tea," Drake said.

"Splendid!" Cornelius beamed. "Go ahead and find your rooms, wash up if you wish and when you're ready I'll be waiting for you with some fresh hot tea. Would you like anything to eat at this hour?"

"No thank you," Drake replied. "We ate earlier."

They took their leave and were led through the vast halls and chambers until they came to a large, spacious guest room. Basins of water and fresh towels were brought in and they cleaned themselves up.

"Do you think it would be incredibly rude if I just went to bed?" Matthew asked. "I've spent all day chasing some weird guy through the city and am weary."

"Get your rest it will be just fine."

"Be careful about Cornelius."

"Strangely, I'm not worried about Cornelius," Drake admitted.

Matthew didn't say another word and climbed into the bed prepared for him. Drake stepped into the hallway and made his way to the room that was prepared. Cornelius was already waiting, a tea kettle and cups sitting on a small table. Cornelius stood and poured the water and soon they sat in silence.

"I'm grateful for your hospitality Cornelius."

The old man shifted in his seat and smiled. "I am most certainly glad to provide. You must be wondering what it is that I want, or what I seek to gain from this. Seeing our past."

"Thoughts have crossed my mind, but they don't seem to stick. The air around you is filled with sincerity, not suspicion. I somehow think we are meeting here as friends, long separated, as opposed to thorns and old wounds in each other's sides. How has life been for you?"

"Better than I deserve let's put it that way," Cornelius said. "After you and Aiden left this city nearly six years ago, I had long plotted a way to kill you, destroy you, and ruin your legacy. I made all those plans and got so close to carrying them out, but then one night about a year ago, I had a dream.

"Aiden visited me in this dream, but he did not look at all like I knew him.

In this dream, he looked like a king. A king more glorious and humble than any that had ever walked the face of the earth. He came up to me and put a hand on my shoulder and said in a gentle voice that I was pursuing the wrong things. I laughed and quoted some random bit from one of the ancient scrolls. I don't even remember what it was I said, but in that moment the words I had spoken seemed emptier than any unused tombs.

"The vision changed and Aiden was on the balcony of a great castle. Before him, I could see everything in the world, animals, plants, beasts, and every person that walks the face of the earth. Everything and everyone there was bowing to Aiden. Even the trees and plants seemed to be bending towards him. It was incredible and no matter what happened in the vision after that, I could not speak. I was overcome with so much emotion.

"Then at the end, I lost my sight. I was told afterward that it was three hours that I *claimed,* (as my staff tells it), that I couldn't see. I heard a voice talking to me. Clearer and more pure than any sounds I've heard in all my life. The voice told me *I, Cornelius of Avdatt, was to take the message of Aiden and Lathon to the people of Erithia.* I do not know where that is! Have you ever heard of Erithia?"

"Can't say I have," Drake replied. "But I think you had best find out and go there. Lathon doesn't like to delay because people won't do what he wants, though that is often what happens."

"I've said all of this to tell you, Drake Thomas, that I am forever indebted to you and Aiden for coming into my life. I can see the light now, I know that I acted horribly to all of you, including hiring a man to kill you. Can you ever forgive me?"

"Of course, I can forgive you," Drake answered. "We all have things we regret. Thoughts, emotions, and feelings that we don't tell anyone else. But they don't go unseen, do they? I've learned the hard way that holding a grudge of any kind or choosing not to forgive is like drinking poison. Only one person dies, and that's the person you see in the mirror." Cornelius fell silent for several minutes.

"You said the nation Lathon told you to go to was Erithia?"

Cornelius nodded. "Do you recognize that name?"

"Perhaps, but only a little. My memories return in little bits and pieces. The name sounds familiar-"

"It should sound familiar," A voice said from behind them. Drake whirled around and looked at the darkened figure standing in the doorway. "It is a small, but rapidly growing country in the southeast sea, also known as the Sea of Cordair. Beyond the maps that exist here. The only way Mr. Thomas knows of its existence is that Ariamore, at one point in their history, did trade with Erithia. They wished for gold and wool, which are in plenty in Ariamore but in short supply there. Ariamore in return got many expensive spices and herbs that are hard to come by anywhere else in the known world."

"Hello James," Drake said. Through the darkness, he thought he could see the man in the doorway smirk.

"So you do remember me?" The man stepped forward, revealing himself as the man who had attacked Drake earlier in the day. He came and took a seat on a large sofa across from Drake and Cornelius.

"Not really," Drake said. "Your name came back into my mind about five minutes ago."

"I had heard that a man named Drake Thomas had lost his memory," James said, studying Drake with hard and intimidating eyes.

"You've been standing there for the whole conversation. You heard me as clear as Cornelius. My memory comes back in pieces." James and Drake locked eyes, both determined to outlast the other one. Finally, James' stern face cracked, and from it, a cackling laughter echoed through the mansion, as it had in the alley earlier in the day.

"Without a doubt, this is one of the best days of my life," James said. Drake puzzled over the man sitting in front of him, unable to conjure up any more memories or familiarity with the name.

"The best day in your life? From what I hear you were chased all day through the city. I certainly hope that whatever guise you've worn recently, your goals in life are higher than this."

"Most certainly my Lord, but you do not completely understand the situation. If you'll allow me, I'll fill in some of the pieces that you're missing." Drake and Cornelius exchanged glances and then nodded. James sat up straighter, seeming to lose the rough ragged character that Drake had thought he was. He carried himself in a way that was proud and sure. Confidence flooded into the room and a sense of familiarity came to Drake. Drake now noticed that the man was Elvish.

"First of all, I would start by complimenting you on employing some of the finest guards that I have ever seen. They have been well trained, and to say that I escaped from them would be nothing short of a lie. An escape was made quickly, but they chased me all day and despite my best efforts to lose them, I failed every single time. In the end, when I was getting tired of the games I roughed them up a little, to discourage them from tracking me any longer. I meant no harm to come to them, and no permanent damage was done. Ask them tomorrow and they will tell you how until that last confrontation I did not harm a single hair on their head!

"As for you Drake Thomas, I have been searching for you for ten years. You did what I had thought was impossible and completely disappeared from the face of the earth! My father was furious with you. I was the one who told you to flee and stay hidden for a while, but if you ask me going so far east was a bit excessive.

"After you had gone, about six months passed before I asked my father to grant permission for you to return in safety if you so desired. He granted this request, and it was my job to find you. I searched everywhere in Rinevah to no avail. From the far reaches of the Rinevah shipping routes to the Caves of Seredath. It seemed you had become a ghost.

"Then I heard voices over the winds, strange they were, but I followed them. I cannot ever fully explain what these voices were, or what they sounded like, for they spoke in a language that I did not understand. They seemed strange to me, but amid all of it I heard one name I recognized and that was the name Drake Thomas.

"I traveled east, planning to search the mountains of Nargaroth for any sign of you. When I got there I was ambushed and captured and for the next five years, I remained a prisoner in the nation of Nargaroth. The last time I had crossed those mountains I had never seen a single soul, so to be captured was a bit of a surprise."

"I'd imagine it's always a surprise," Drake said. James laughed.

"It appears they have been rebuilding and fortifying the mountains since their defeat. Their numbers are great, and for the first year, I sat in the prison cell wallowing in despair. I plotted escape a dozen times, but never tried out of fear. If I gave them any reason I knew they would not hesitate to kill me. As I lay there in the darkness of my cell, strange things came to my ears, from the guards. I was summoned several times to answer questions that concerned ancient things as well as what they called a 'growing threat' in the southwest. Eventually, your name came up in the discussion. Then I knew that it was time for me to escape.

"Years later I managed to do it. Until six months ago I was trapped in those very mountains, unsure of how to get out. With great effort, I finally got past the guards to the desert beyond and walked further than I could even comprehend.

"I reached the site of a great battle. A few nomads similar to myself were there, and I asked them what had happened here. They spoke of a man named Drake Thomas who conquered someone known as the Sorcerer. Upon further conversation with these men, they revealed that they knew many things about you, including the fact that you couldn't remember your past. I hoped harder than ever that this would be true.

"I made it out of the desert and eagerly searched for you. It seems everyone has heard of you, and you have lived in many places. And now at last I have found you and we have indeed been reunified! Even greater is my joy to hear from *you* that your memory is not complete. For that means you have done no wrong and have not intentionally abandoned our people."

"That is quite a tale," Drake said. "I wish I could take credit for everything people seem to think I did, but I'm afraid that I didn't kill the Sorcerer. Aiden, Sherados is the one who was leading. I was merely doing my part."

"Wait! Did you say Sherados, the heir of Lathon? He's here?"

"Yes, he's been with me for the past ten years, or I with him."

"You are certain?"

"Yes," Cornelius replied, breaking his long silence. "I, over the past couple of years have done plentiful research, traveling, interviewing, and found that not only does he live among us, but he has fulfilled all the prophecies about the coming savior. I was a skeptic at first when I began looking into it, but the evidence backed up his claim."

"This is amazing! Everyone back home has to know this," James exclaimed, beaming from ear to ear. "Another night perhaps I must know everything that has transpired in this part of the world, concerning Sherados…what do you call him?"

"He goes by Aiden, but his true name is Adonai," Drake answered. "I look forward to also sharing this news with Rinevah. I feel like that's part of my purpose when I get back."

"So you mean to return?" James asked.

"Yes, I will be returning, though there are a few things that must be sorted before we come. It may be a couple of months before we set out."

"From the people on the street, I hear you're getting married in a few days!"

"That's right."

"Tell me, who is this woman that you're marrying?"

"It's kind of a long story. I was apparently running from your father and I wound up working for a person named Queman in Laheer. Rachal lived there and over the course of several months, we fell in love and intended to marry. Strange things happened to me, including me being abducted on the eve of our wedding and losing my memory. It's been a long road for us, but now at last we are excited to start our life together."

"I'm glad to hear it! The tidings we have shared and learned tonight have already made me glad to have suffered for so long in trying to find you. If you'll have me Drake, I would very much like to attend the wedding, but soon after I must be on my way back. Who knows what my father has done these past ten years with both of us missing? He will be more than happy to see us than we can comprehend."

IDOLS & TRINKETS

"Not only can you attend the wedding, but you will be the guest of honor, after Aiden that is. As for you heading home, what accommodations do you have?"

"To be truthful, in only recently learning of your existence, I hadn't yet thought that far ahead."

"If I may," Cornelius interjected. "I am very well connected with a lot of people who could help you get wherever you need to go. I humbly propose a trade, you tell me everything you know about Erithia and I will arrange a safe way back to Rinevah, supposing you can tell me where it is on a map."

"We have an accord," James said, extending his hand. Cornelius shook it. They talked long into the night before finally disappearing to their beds and falling into a deep restful sleep.

Nothing short of amusing had been the reaction of Matthew when he had come down the stairs in the morning and seen James sitting at the table. James told Matthew his tale and hard as Matthew tried to believe otherwise, everyone agreed that the tale was true. As the morning went on, Matthews's suspicions were subsided and soon it was clear that if they had the time they would certainly become good friends.

The next few days leading up to the wedding were nothing short of a blur to both Drake and Rachal. Even though Drake had hardly thought it was possible, more and more tall ships came streaming into the harbor. Many of them Drake recognized as nations that Rhallinen did trade with, but there were just as many he didn't know or recognize. They stretched up the coast of the city for nearly a mile and the population of the city seemed to double.

Saul and all of their friends from the east (Rachal's family included) arrived in style and ceremony, escorted by fifty strong soldiers and horsemen. Drake's house soon became a busier place than he wanted as everyone tried to make sure their part of the wedding festivities was under control.

Isabel and Rachal did a lot together throughout the next couple of days, but hardly any of their time was spent planning the wedding details. Drake often would find them on the back porch talking as though they had been best friends for years and had only just discovered that they were related.

He marveled at the both of them. Drake tried but failed to imagine what it would be like to leave your daughter with friends and never be able to tell her the truth. Or to spend your entire life not knowing that the long-lost family friend was actually your mother. He smiled to watch them as they seemed to be catching up on lost time.

In the few moments of solitude that Drake managed to seek out, he spent most of his time puzzling over his past and the memories that were slowly starting to resurface. They were still distant and still vague, and a large number of them made no sense to him.

Some were good, others were painful, and others still were filled with loathing and hatred. What the future held, and what his memories could foreshadow, neither Drake nor Rachal had any clue. The only thing they were certain of was that they were supposed to go east, and they would be obedient to that call.

Aiden stayed with them for much of the time in the days approaching the wedding, but now and then he would go out into the city looking for people to help in addition to teaching down at the temple. Drake hung onto every word that came from Aiden's lips. The truth and authority that he spoke with amazed the people and it became nearly as hard for Aiden to get away from the crowds as it was for Drake.

Nonetheless, every night when Drake went back to Cornelius's house they would sit and talk for several hours with James, Matthew, and Aiden. As much as Drake wished to sleep he forced himself to stay awake because he knew he wouldn't have this time much longer.

Each night they talked longer than the rest, enjoying the company and sharing great stories from all their travels. Cornelius listened with delight and curiosity, having never traveled before, he was now starting to make his own plans on how to travel to Erithia.

"This is a great day," Aiden said, breaking the silence that had fallen over them.

"Tomorrow will be better," James said. "At least that's what Drake's thinking, right Drake?" They laughed.

"Yes, though I must admit that I'm nervous."

"Why?" Matthew asked.

"Last time I was going to marry Rachal, I was kidnapped." Drake laughed. "In reality 'nervous' is not really the right word...maybe I should say 'anxiously excited?' After the wedding, everything changes. I'm going east, James is going east. Cornelius is going somewhere in a somewhat easterly direction and Matthew is going to be appointed as the king of Rhallinen. It's a lot to take in."

"Indeed it is, but change is not bad," Aiden reminded. "Regardless of what does and doesn't change, the one thing that remains is the love that we have for Lathon and for each other. He has blessed each of you immensely, perhaps even more than you're aware. He rejoices to see the change in all of your hearts over these past few years. I can see that it's real. Cornelius can tell you firsthand how important it is to see sincere change. You are all about to set out on a journey that will carry you to very different places in your life and may force you into uncomfortable situations. Choices will be made, either they will bring glory to Lathon, or they will bring you to destruction. It's perhaps the hardest lesson to learn, but in the end, even if Lathon did choose you, even if *I* chose you, you must always stay alert. You will be accepted if you do what is right. But if you refuse to do what is right, then watch out! The Sorcerer is crouching at the door, eager to control you. But you must subdue it and be its master. Be strong and courageous, do not be afraid. Lathon goes before each of you and he will not forsake you."

"Comforting words, but I'm not quite sure what you mean," James said. "I have lived many years on this earth. I have seen many things from my father's house. I have read all the ancient scrolls. I was told that the Sorcerer was defeated, yet you speak as if he is still among us? And I know you are the heir of Lathon, but didn't Lathon live thousands of years ago?"

"Yes he did, but there is more than one force that roams the earth. Lathon still walks the earth, watching over everything. Many do not believe and therefore they have made him invisible. I was sent so that people's faith may be renewed and one day all can be united with Lathon. As for the Sorcerer, physically he will not reappear again, but his spirit has lost none of its potency. He will be dealt with, but at the proper time and by the father not by me. Until then I expect that he will deceive many and in a last feeble attempt twist things into hideous forms of creations that were once good and perfect at the dawn of creation; in fact, he is already at work in the world. The temples all over the world, to *other gods* are only the beginning. You have yet to see the full power of the Sorcerer's deceit. He failed to gain control physically, so he will seek to gain control spiritually."

"I'll believe that," James said. "I've spent a lot of time in Nargaroth, and the things I've seen and heard are enough to make me think that the entire nation is built over the pit of Hell."

"Darkness exists, but the light is greater," Aiden said. "The light is what pushes back the darkness. Action, offensive. That is where the battles are won, the one before you is no different. The light of Lathon will be with you and may your life be a display of the hope that you possess."

The sun rose and already the excitement of the day's celebration was thick in the air. The birds fluttered through the treetops and sang their songs, seeming to be more animated about it than they usually would be. Then again perhaps Drake was only imagining things.

Although still groggy from the late-night conversation they had all shared, Drake quickly dressed and prepared for the day. Everyone else did the same and soon stepped out into the already busy streets. Warm soothing rays of sunlight were cast down on everything, illuminating the colors of the flowers, banners, and decorations that now covered the entire city.

"Drake, what kind of flowers are these?" Matthew asked, staring at one of them intently. "I would swear that this was a red flower just a second ago, but now it is orange and I'm starting to think it's actually a blue flower."

"Perhaps you had too much to drink last night," James jeered. They chuckled, but Drake didn't reply. After a moment James too was enthralled by the strange flower.

"Still want to make fun of me?" Matthew asked. James shook his head.

IDOLS & TRINKETS

"What kind of flower is this?"

Drake shrugged. "You'll have to ask Isabel when you see her. Things like this have been a staple in her shops and houses for as long as I've known her. It does my heart good to see them as I haven't seen them myself in many years."

"I thought you might appreciate them," Isabel said, walking up the street. Her hair was unkempt and she was without shoes, but seemed not to care.

"You've outdone yourself this time," Drake said, motioning to the city all around. She shrugged.

"A woman does what she can. Besides I've waited over ten years for today to come, I'm going all out!"

"Well, the odds are looking to be in our favor. I haven't been kidnapped yet."

The rest of the morning was a bit of a blur and overall Drake kept to himself and watched everyone else with joy. The city hadn't seen this much positive excitement in many years.

A great chorus of horns sounded from outside the wall, grabbing the attention of nearly everyone in the city. Large carts, loaded to capacity began entering the streets. Banners covered the numerous boxes that were loaded on the back. The banners were burgundy red with gold thread, proudly displaying the crest of Rhallinen.

Drake and James watched the people, whose minds were already filled with anticipation and ideas as to what the carts contained. For nearly ten minutes cart after cart rolled through the front gate and the city eventually departing through the north gate to the great tents that had been set up for the celebration afterwards.

"A gift from the King of Rhallinen I presume?" James asked.

"A little token of appreciation...for everyone in the city," Drake replied. "This wedding is turning out to be much larger than I anticipated. We wanted a small wedding but when you're a king that's pretty much impossible. Therefore I should at least be grateful for the love and support of all my people, especially those in this city who have no reason to be loyal to me."

"You are a wise man, Drake Thomas," James said. "You would make a fine King of Rinevah."

"Ha! Don't say that with your father around or we'll be outcasts for sure!"

"True enough my friend," James replied. "I'm not one to get in the way of Lathon, though I can't speak for my relatives."

"I'd ask you how your family is but I don't think you would know much more than I do."

"It has been long since I've looked on their faces," James agreed, seeming to be overcome by a wave of sorrow. "But Lathon knows I wish to see them again. Even my father, who as you know can be an interesting sort."

"That's putting it mildly," Drake retorted. They chuckled. "Did Cornelius help you find some means of getting back home?"

"Aye, he was very helpful," James said, staring off into the northwest. "He found me a ship to the small island of Ruya. It's not exactly where I need to be, but I know I'll be able to get to the port of Lanarka from there. Incidentally, my ship leaves tomorrow afternoon so I won't be seeing you again until we both get back to Rinevah."

"I'll be there as soon as I may," Drake stated. "I have a few things to wrap up here first. If it wasn't for the fact that we couldn't take Taruks we would be there a lot faster."

James laughed.

"Something funny?"

"You just mentioned Taruks as if they exist," James answered.

"They do exist," Drake said. James laughed again. "In this part of the world, they are plentiful and tame. We even race them for sport!"

"You're not serious are you?" James asked. "We're talking about *Leviathons!* Mythical creatures from the ancient scrolls. They can't be real."

"The scrolls are real why wouldn't Taruks be?" Drake asked. James still looked confused. "Allow me to show you!" Immediately two great Taruks dropped out of the air and landed in front of them. James jumped back in fright and was speechless for several moments.

58

IDOLS & TRINKETS

"Taruks?" James uttered in disbelief. "They're real!"

"Of course they are," Drake replied. "The racing circuit is in the southern seas right now, which is why you probably haven't seen any of them. This here is my Taruk, Destan, and this Taruk is Rachal's, her name is Ezion. Rachal calls her Ezzie."

"You have two Taruks?" James asked in disbelief. "How did that happen?"

"It's a long story."

"I'm beginning to believe there's no such thing as a short story with you." They laughed. "Though I think that's true of anyone who lived. Truly magnificent."

"You should ride one," Drake said. James looked at him blankly.

"You're serious?" James asked. Drake nodded. A giddy smile came over James as he looked at Ezzie. "How do you ride one of these?"

"Just climb on," Drake sat atop Destan and James carefully crawled onto Ezzie. James looked as though he was sitting on a cactus, while Ezzie was amused by the awkward person on her back. "Just sit back and relax. Grab onto the leather straps that go around her body."

"How do you steer?" James asked.

"You don't. Taruks do most of their communication in thoughts. Think what you want them to do and they will. I've carried on many conversations with these two over the years. Since it's your first time, I'll give them the commands, and don't worry...I'll make it a nice relaxing ride." Ezzie and Destan both stirred with amusing and somewhat sinister thoughts. Drake thought for a moment, considering the options. A moment passed and James, who had appeared ready, relaxed.

"What a nice ride this is!" James mocked. "Oh yes, I'm-". Drake laughed as Ezzie shoved up into the air at breakneck speed. The morning hustle and bustle for a moment was disrupted as everyone looked to see the source of the screaming that came from the sky. Destan gently pushed up into the air and after a minute or two, flew up alongside a terrified James and an amused Ezzie.

"Now my dear friend, you do look a little terrified," Drake said with a laugh.

"People race on these things!" James exclaimed. Drake laughed again. "I suppose I have you to thank for that lovely takeoff I experienced?"

"To be fair, it was Ezzie's idea," Drake said. "Don't worry she won't do anything else unexpected. Enjoy the view, it is a lovely morning." They flew over the city and beyond the great walls. To the northwest, the Mezutor stadium towered. To the northeast, a sea of great tents with lavish designs dominated the landscape.

"I assume this is where the great party will be afterward," James said. The Taruks slowly descended out of the sky and landed in an open field. They disembarked and James hesitated as he took another look at the creatures. "They are magnificent creatures. I am glad to know they are not myths as everyone back home says."

"There is a good deal of things back home that people don't know the way I've come to know them."

"I have much to learn, but most of all I am glad that you are my friend Drake Thomas, and I'm glad at last we're reunited."

The rest of the morning and into the early afternoon passed slower than any day that Drake remembered his entire life. Eventually, he withdrew from the outside world and found himself immersed in a sea of books in the private library in the palace.

"Let me get this straight," A voice said. Drake turned to see Ellizar walking towards him. Aaron and Jacob followed him on either side. "This is yer weddin' day and here yeh are readin' a book?"

"Good to see you Ellizar," Drake said. He embraced all of them as they took seats next to Drake. "I'm glad you could make it."

"I wouldn't have missed it fer the world," Ellizar said. "I'm glad to stand by yer side on a great day such as this."

"How's Lily?" Drake asked.

"She won't be makin' it to the weddin'. But she's here in spirit. Just make sure yeh stop in and see her before yeh leave to go east."

"I definitely will," Drake replied, turning his gaze to Aaron and Jacob. "How are you doing today?"

"We're as right as rain. As Rachal's brother, well, adopted brother, I must tell you she's going to look quite well when she comes down the aisle."

"I look forward to seeing her for myself," Drake said. "She's an extraordinary woman. Time has been good to her and somehow sitting here now with you three I feel as though I am the luckiest man alive."

"I'm not sure luck has anything to do with it," another voice said from the doorway. Aiden stepped forward. The four of them stood to greet him.

"Why doesn't luck have anything to do with it?" Jacob asked. Aiden looked at Drake knowingly and Aiden motioned for him to speak.

"Luck speaks of coincidence. Which nothing happens by. Lathon is not a God of coincidence. He takes our mistakes and mischances and can use them to glorify the goodness that is he. Though moments in life may arise that are unexpected by us, he has foreseen it and has already planned for it, supposing we surrender ourselves to his will."

Aiden smiled. "And on that note, I am most glad to tell you that it is time."

Drake followed Aiden, with the others close behind. They made their way to a large courtyard where a carriage was waiting for them. They rolled through the streets until a large building appeared on their right. They were quickly ushered inside where they changed into their dress clothes and waited behind grand doors. Aiden stepped outside and moments later the doors were opened and they descended a large staircase to a platform that had been prepared. The platform was covered in deep red, and golden flowers encircled the perimeter. A grand arch had been constructed over the entire platform, with flowers of deep purple and red, covering the entire thing.

The city square was filled beyond what Drake could have even imagined. Every possible place a person could stand, from the street up to the highest of the rooftops was filled with people standing shoulder to shoulder. In the front, several dozen chairs had been reserved for family and friends.

Drake stood waiting at the front with everyone, for what seemed like an eternity. One moment faded into another. Finally, trumpets echoed through the skies as Rachal appeared.

DRAKE THOMAS

***

The sounds of music and joyous celebrating were heard long into the night as the nation rejoiced and celebrated the wedding. After far too long, Rachal and Drake managed to break free of the crowds and leave it all behind them. Destan and Ezion quietly landed in a field far away from the party.

Drake and Rachal took to the sky, the lights of the city fading and the glow of the moon and the stars growing brighter. Finally, the Taruks descended to a modest tent and a campfire that was easily started thanks to the Taruks. Drake and Rachal both gazed at the Taruks, enthralled by the wisdom that they held within their eyes.

"Have you ever felt that the Taruks know far more than we are aware?" Rachal asked. "I look into their eyes for a moment and I feel like there's unfathomable knowledge and power behind them."

"Taruks are by far the most amazing creatures I've ever seen," Drake replied. After all these years I'm not sure I'm any closer to understanding any of them. Nonetheless, it cannot be denied that as assuredly as I know Lathon still watches over all the earth, and Aiden walks the earth; Elohim seems to command as much of a presence as either of them. They seem united, the three of them. A perfect trinity, helping the believers of Lathon and Aiden to do things they normally couldn't."

"Do you think that's why the Elves have always been able to do what is called 'Elvish magic'?"

"Perhaps, but I'm not sure it'll stop with the Elves anymore."

"I'm not sure I understand," Rachal said.

Drake shrugged his shoulders. "I'm not sure I do either. But maybe if we understood everything about Lathon and his nature, then he wouldn't be important."

"You can say that again," Rachal said. Taking Drake's hand and leading him to the roaring fire. She slipped out of her shoes and stared up at the stars. Her white dress sparkled in the starlight. Drake took her in his arms and kissed her deeply.

"What is it about that dress?" Drake asked. "I've been thinking all day that it

62

sparkles, but then I think it looks completely ordinary."

"My mother's touch, need I say more?" Rachal asked. Drake smiled. "It's a special powder she put on it, makes it sparkle like diamonds. She put the same stuff on my hair. Do you like it?"

"Of course I do," Drake replied. "You should keep it your hair all the time."

"Maybe I will Drake Thomas," Rachal said. They lay down on the blanket, looking up at the stars.

"What are you thinking about Mrs. Thomas?" Rachal smiled.

"I'm glad to be married to you. It may have been an unusual road for us to get here, but we've grown so much and come so far since we first met. I truly feel peace about everything that happened. In a way that I haven't felt before."

"Me too," Drake said. "And now we live happily ever after right?"

"Now, my dear husband, we live." They kissed each other in the night. The stars growing all the brighter.

Chapter 5
MANY PARTINGS

The smell of salt water overwhelmed them. Wave after wave crashed onto the docks and rain came down in sheets. Drake and Rachal grabbed onto a railing as another massive wave crashed into the break-wall to their left. They were nearly swept off their feet by the power of the water.

"How much further is it?" Rachal asked above the roar of the wind and waves. Drake looked at the ships thrashing in the water, studying each of them closely.

"I'm not sure," Drake answered. "Usually he's right on schedule. He should have made port a week ago." Black clouds and torrential rain had covered the city of Avdatt since they had returned from their honeymoon nearly a week ago. They resumed their search, looking at every ship they passed carefully. A man carrying a lantern came down the docks and made directly for them.

"Are you Mr. Drake Thomas?" the man asked.

"Depends on who's asking," Rachal answered. The man studied them both intently for a moment.

"My master, captain of the *Sargon* has seen you wandering around the docks from the building on the south. He sent me to bring you to him."

"What is your master's name?"

"Barnabas, my lord," the man answered. Drake nodded and they followed the man. Five minutes later they stepped into a warm and well-lit building. The halls were lavishly furnished and they were hastily rushed through the masses inside to a small, simple room on the side of the building.

They entered into a darkened room, the only light coming from a fireplace and a few candles on either side. The curtains were drawn and the room remained silent as they were led towards a man in a deep armchair near the fireplace.

"Master, I present Mr. Thomas and his wife," the man said. The man in the chair, as if pulled out of his deep thoughts, smiled and stood to his feet. His eyes sprang to life.

"Thank you Renma. Please return to your post," Barnabas ordered. The man bowed and moved to a dark corner of the room. "Come my friends, have a seat. There's soup on the fire and I can send for some tea water if we so choose."

"That's very kind of you," Drake said. Barnabas held a hand out to Drake but Drake embraced him instead. "Good to see you, my friend."

"Good to see you too." Barnabas turned his attention to Rachal. "You must be the enchanting woman that Drake told me about? I'm sorry I couldn't attend your wedding, there were rough waters and hard sailing for several days. We were nearly a week late, due to having to stop in Revly to make repairs."

"It's quite alright," Rachal replied. "Drake speaks very highly of you. We are fortunate that you saw us on the docks. We were looking for you."

"And I for you," Barnabas said. "Your letter was most intriguing. You wish to go east?"

"That's quite right," Drake said. "Are you familiar with the waters to the east of Ariamore?"

"I once had a trade route to Ruya. Southeast of Ariamore about two hundred miles. It's been years since I've traveled so far. I know a few other sailors who have traversed those waters, but I'm not sure where they might be right now. Do you have any maps or idea where exactly you're headed? In your letter you wrote about a friend; which way has he gone?"

"He didn't think he'd find a ship that would know where he was headed; he boarded a vessel for Ruya just after our wedding. He assumed from there he would be able to find his way," Drake said. "He said he was headed towards the port of Lanarka. My memory has not been jogged by that name, but I am sure it is not on Ruya."

"It doesn't do any good to me either," Barnabas said, dishing them some of the soup and then relaxing into his chair. "You might as well be speaking another language, or making it up entirely. I've sailed the seas for nearly thirty years and I've never heard of it."

"None the less we need to get there as swiftly as can be managed," Rachal said. "Our first choice was to take the Taruks, but we've been warned against that."

"I'll agree with that advice," Barnabas said. "Sailors do hear strange tales on the seas, whether they be true or not who can say? I presume you wish to hire one of my ships?"

"That's right," Drake replied. "We can pay you well. I will be selling my house in Avdatt. Name your price."

"I won't charge you anything Drake," Barnabas said. "We've known each other far too long."

"Much appreciated, but we insist on paying you something," Rachal argued. "We won't take no for an answer."

"How about I just give you a very good deal?" Rachal nodded her agreement.

Barnabas smiled at the two of them. "You've got a strong woman Drake Thomas."

"Will we be taking the Sargon then?" Drake asked.

"The Sargon's too old for a trip like that. She was ten years old when I met you. You can do the math. I don't use her for anything more than coastal runs. I've got newer, stronger ships on the waters, but the one I have in mind isn't likely to be back in Avdatt for at least a month."

"Sounds agreeable," Drake replied. "We have a few things left to do before we depart anyway."

"That settles it. I'll be the Captain of the *Evin Lador*, Elvish name, came with the ship. I don't even know what it means."

"It means 'Morning Light'," Rachal said. "It's one of the titles for Sherados in the Ancient Scrolls. Though I believe in ancient Elvish it's pronounced *Lattar*."

"You are a wealth of information," Barnabas said. "A deep knowledge of the language of the Elves is uncommon, especially when one doesn't appear to be

Elvish."

"My mother is part Elvish, and she knows many things," Rachal said. Barnabas studied her for a moment. Seeming satisfied with her answer, he turned to Drake.

"Let's say the fare to be fifteen percent of whatever you fetch for your house. We'll plan to meet in Avdatt in about six weeks, and hopefully set sail a week after that. If in any way possible you happen to come across a chart or map of the waters we'll be in, I'll be much appreciative. No doubt such an item would make our travels easier and swifter."

"I can't make any promises, but we'll do what we can," Drake stated. "We may have to find Lanarka after we get to Ruya."

"So be it," Barnabas said. "I leave in the morning, but this room will be yours for as long as you want it. Let us now talk about other, lighter things and cheer ourselves before we depart."

The storm passed and the next morning they set about their separate ways. Barnabas boarded his ship and Drake and Rachal took to the skies. For the moment their cares and troubles were gone. By the end of the day, they had covered half of the distance between Tyre and Mera Runa.

Another night came and went and before meal time of the second day, Mera Runa could be seen glistening in the brilliant sunset. Drake stole a glance over at Rachal who looked on the city with wonder in her eyes. She had never seen the city before.

"It's bigger than I imagined," Rachal said. Trumpets sounded throughout the city and countryside as their Taruks were spotted. "I'm assuming we'll be getting a royal welcome?"

"I'd bet on it," Drake replied. "There's no escaping it this time." They both smiled and began their descent to the ground in front of the city. Everything had been prepared for their coming. Within moments of their landing, a group of five horsemen rode from the city to greet them.

"Long live the king!" the men exclaimed, quickly dismounting. "We have prepared much for your coming my lord, a great feast will soon be prepared.

Everyone in the city is very eager to meet their new queen!"

Without saying another word they mounted the empty horses that had been brought for them. The Taruks took to the sky and vanished to the wilderness, while the horsemen went ahead of Drake and Rachal announcing their coming with horns. The city roared as they were paraded through the streets and led up to the great palace at the summit.

The grand lawns that led up to the palace were prepared with great tables and seating for thousands and Drake had noticed that many other such courtyards in the previous levels of the city had also been prepared in similar fashion. They rode up to the palace and dismounted.

"What do you think?" Drake asked.

"I think I feel utterly insignificant next to this glorious city," Rachal answered. Before they could talk further the great doors of the palace were opened and Matthew came out to greet them. They embraced and went inside as the crowds began preparing for the great feast.

"I'm glad to see the two of you," Matthew said once they were in private quarters.

"And we are happy to see you," Rachal replied. "Are you ready for everything that's going to happen?"

"Everything is arranged and prepared, though I don't feel particularly *ready* to be king."

"A good leader is always learning more."

The tables and seating were filled and the celebration of their coming went long into the night. Drake and Rachal, though they wished they could leave the party, stayed until the last person had gone home. Matthew, Drake, and Rachal stayed up, talking until nearly dawn when finally sleep overtook them.

By the time they woke, they found that it was nearly mid-afternoon and Aiden had already arrived and was waiting for them in the south gardens. By then it had become well known that Aiden was in the city. As planned Drake and Rachal, mostly stayed away from the crowds for the next couple of days, letting Matthew handle most of the affairs, but offering help if he asked for it.

IDOLS & TRINKETS

As a result of their absence, the rumor mills in the city were working overtime, having heard whispers of big changes that might be coming. Drake and Rachal were particularly amused by some of the rumors that resulted from people guessing, though none of them were correct.

Some said that Drake had not been himself and was therefore going to be kicked out of the city by Aiden, while others thought that the food served to their king and queen the night before had been poisoned and they were in their chambers withering away. And still others said they had already left the city and had been seen flying away in the middle of the night, never to be seen again.

Nonetheless, the word was sent out to everyone that a new king was going to be appointed to lead the nation as Drake and Rachal would be going away to the east as Aiden had asked of them. Excitement filled the city and great celebrations were planned as the coronation grew nearer.

The day of the coronation came and the city was alive with life and excitement. The ceremonies went off without difficulty and there was much celebrating both for their new king and for their former king who was being sent out into the world. Drake watched the crowds and studied the people and their reactions, surprised by the positive reaction that their departure was creating.

After another two days, they said farewell to everyone in the city and vanished into the sky, unlikely to see the city ever again. Drake grew quiet as they flew. Rachal looked his way and smiled at him.

"It's a strange day for me," Drake admitted. "I've lived in that city for so long, and learned so much, and now I may never see it again."

"I may have only lived in it for a week, but it was a splendid city if I do say so myself."

Two days later the city of Avdatt once again appeared on the horizon. They were greeted by a small, modest gathering, which was much to Rachal and Drake's approval. They made their way into the city, once again boarding with Cornelius as the preparations for selling Drake's house got underway.

To say that the next week was anything but relaxing was a bit of an understatement. As King, Drake had often overseen sales of property for people, or at least heard about them after the fact, but never had he really been involved in one. Even when they had just started with preparations, the word had slipped throughout the city, and by nightfall, they were hounded with so many requests and offers that they could hardly keep things straight.

To make matters even more complicated, Drake and Rachal had decided not to only sell the house, but to sell everything within the house separately. After that, *everyone* wanted in and was trying to get something. Finally, the governor of Avdatt sent soldiers to help secure and watch over the mansion while everything was made ready.

There was much grumbling from the people, but within a couple of days everything was in order and they began the tours of the house. The showings were on a first come first serve basis, which greatly irked many of the Farsees who thought that being friends with Nickolas or Cornelius would get them in first, or perhaps a private showing.

Nonetheless, tours were started every ten minutes and upon exiting the people could place a silent bid on any item or items as they wanted. The house was then sold afterward at a public auction, held in the governor's court.

Under Drake's insistence, all members of the city who could afford to bid on it were allowed to attend, regardless of their societal rank.

When all was said and done, the auctioning of everything had made more money than any such auction before. Drake and Rachal carefully counted out the amount they had agreed to pay Barnabas and kept an equal share for themselves. The rest of the money they largely entrusted to business owners and other associates Drake had come to know and trust. They were under strict orders to use the money to help someone in need when it was least expected. When the entirety of the money was in the proper hands, everyone breathed a sigh of relief as they sat within the walls of Cornelius's mansion.

Both Cornelius and Nickolas had come under fire from the Farsees as they had, willingly and without being threatened, taken in all of the house guests that had been staying with Drake and Rachal, who had yet to leave the city. Drake sympathized with them and shook his head at the frivolous side of the Farsees.

Still, within the walls of Cornelius's house, they all became the best of friends, despite the varying backgrounds or cultures that they came from. Nickolas after much thought had decided to join Cornelius on his journey to Erithia. Isabel and Morgrin and most of Rachal's adopted family were also guests of the house. They would talk and laugh long into the night before they would finally slip off to bed.

Another week passed before everyone dispersed to their separate affairs. Isabel and Morgrin were to stay in the city for another couple of days while Drake and Rachal left the city behind them and traveled up the coast for two more days. The city vanished and even roads became somewhat seldom and at times hard to travel. The hills grew steep, but the horses easily picked their way between trees that were strange and different.

They grew tall, but not straight like other trees. Where most would have been straight this forest grew in twisted patterns that had no sense of order at all. The wall of the forest seemed almost to have been made that way on purpose, as from the outside you could hardly see within the woods.

They traveled for another day along the edge of the forest until finally, a single arched opening appeared on their right. They led their horses through, entering into a dark, moist forest.

"This feels old," Rachal said. Drake nodded his reply, finding it hard to speak. Finally, a light was seen in the distance. When they reached the end, they saw a small village spread out in a lush green valley. Buildings dotted the countryside, at first glance it was maybe a town of three hundred people.

The smell of salt water drifted towards them. It was only then that Drake and Rachal realized they were on a small peninsula. Far across the valley, the land lay open border by the ocean a mile later. Kids played in the streets and the people of the town were plainly dressed and went about their business, almost unaware of the arrival of guests. An elf finally took notice of them and came and bowed before them. After a moment he stood and spoke in a strong clear voice.

DRAKE THOMAS

"You must be Mr. and Mrs. Thomas?"

"Yes indeed," Drake replied. "Who do we have the honor of speaking to?"

"Irn. Irn of Helfazi. Please forgive our lack of perpetration, for we did not know when the day of your coming would be!"

"You did not know, because we did not say," Drake replied. "Still one could make the point, that we never do know the day of The heir of Lathon's triumphant return, and had best be ready at any time."

"The point is well made Mr. Thomas," Irn said. "I apologize but my master is not at home currently, but I can take you to his house as I was instructed to do."

"Can't argue the master now can we?" Rachal asked. The man smiled and turned, mounting his horse. He led them through the small little town which was filled with life and the smells of the upcoming supper which were being prepared.

Ten minutes later they had left the town, following the main road which lazily wound through farmland until the ocean greeted the shoreline. They turned off the path after some time, rising up a steep embankment to a fair-sized house with beautiful flowers bordering a long-covered porch that was painted white.

"Drake and Rachal Thomas madam, as requested!" Irn announced. The woman, who sat in the shade on the porch stirred and stood to her feet, but seemed to struggle to do so.

"It has been far too long Mr. Thomas!" the woman cried. Drake ran up to the steps as Lily was now making her way down. She wore a long plain blue dress, and her hair, though it had clearly been done earlier in the day, was now wind-blown and tangled. She embraced Drake and then she turned her attention to Rachal. "So Drake, who is this beautiful woman? Ellizar told me she was beautiful, but he didn't exactly do the term justice." They laughed.

"This is my wife Rachal. Rachal I'd like you to meet Ellizar's wife, Lily! We've known each other for many years."

"It's a pleasure to meet you," Rachal said. "This is a beautiful home you have."

"Thank you," Lily said. "Took a lot of work to get it looking this way, but the best things take a lot of time I think." She turned to face Irn. "Thank you for bringing them, you may have the rest of the day off!" Irn nodded his thanks and then left. "Well, come on in and we'll have some tea and chat. I'd love to give you a proper tour of Car-mun, but it seems I'm having a little more difficulty doing things these days. I hate that I wasn't able to come to your wedding."

"It's okay. We're glad to come and visit you," Drake insisted. Having to help Lily up the stairs.

"It's a charming little town," Rachal said. "How long have you lived here?"

"The short answer to that question is about one year. We lived in Cos when you were rescued from the Sorcerer. However, I had bought this place just before I met Ellizar, before all the adventures with Drake. I had always wanted to live here, but life happens. So finally, we decided to come make this our home. Unfortunately, these days I feel like my health is waning, and I cannot enjoy it nearly as much as I would like to."

"I'm sorry you're ill," Drake said. Lily shrugged her shoulders.

"Part of life," Lily said. "You can fight it or accept it. I find the latter brings more peace and pleasure."

"Well said," Rachal replied. "Where is everyone else?"

"Celine and Timothy are in town getting some last-minute things for the meal tonight. Ellizar is at the library with Queman. He's been quite puzzled by a map he got on an expedition with your mother a few months ago."

"She's never idle for long is she?" Rachal asked a smile tugged at all their lips.

"No, but sometimes I think it's better that way," Lily said. She paused and grabbed at her chest for a moment, wincing from pain. "Sorry, never know when it's going to be a problem." She drew a deep breath.

"At times my lungs burn with fire, and other times I can hardly get my breath, no matter how much air I breathe. My limbs burn and I nearly pass out if I don't take many breaks.

"As I was saying, to an extent I think a healthy amount of staying busy or doing something is good. I've watched many people achieve a great feat of one kind or another, and then they marvel at that. Deceit, lust, and half-truths arise in their minds and hearts. It doesn't take long after that for it to leak from their hearts and poison the *perfect* world they've made. People become unfaithful and untrustworthy, their very character is corrupted by idleness. I'm sure Drake has seen the same thing."

"Far too much I'm afraid, even I was guilty of squandering what I had been given for a while," Drake admitted, the memories playing through his head as well as Lily's. "Everyone has their demons don't they?"

"Half the time we create them," Lily answered. "Still, even though you squandered much, Lathon has returned to you tenfold what you had! And brought back the woman you love."

"And for that, we are both eternally grateful," Rachal said.

Chapter 6

THE TOWER OF IMRAHUNE

The night had been filled with laughter and camaraderie, the likes of which neither Drake nor Rachal had enjoyed in some time. When the sun woke the next morning Drake awoke to the sounds of the birds chirping in the trees. He looked at the space next to him, noticing that it was already empty.

Drake quickly dressed and headed down the stairs finding Rachal sitting on the porch swing that looked out to the town and countryside beyond.

"Good morning beautiful," Drake greeted. Rachal smiled as he sat down. "Sleep well?"

"Not really," Rachal said. "After so many years in Enya's chambers, I suppose I'm probably doomed to a lifetime of bad dreams."

"I'm sorry," Drake said.

She shrugged. "It is what it is."

Silence fell over them for an unknown amount of time. Suddenly it seemed as if everything stopped. The birds stopped chirping, and the sound of the distant ocean even seemed to grow silent. A deafening silence filled the air until a voice from somewhere in the town pierced their ears. It was distant, but Drake listened to the voice that was singing.

Lost and Found
Day and Night
All that is hidden shall see the light.
Though stars have fallen, all shall see
The origin of the things that be

DRAKE THOMAS

There was a land, I saw it once
We were young and so was it.
In the midst of all, there stood before thee
A large and luscious Vemroliet tree.

In the darkness, it would shine,
Alive and well in the darkest time.
Great were its limbs, long was its reach
Frightful and strong did it seem.

A spirit of strength, but also humility
Did this tree stand ever so diligently?
It watched the land, it made its mind
It would be here until the end of time.

Oh Vemroliet tree, how I wish I had known
Of the great sorrow that came upon that morn.
When the world, made as it should be,
Was destroyed by greed. Oh, Vemroliet tree!

Cursed is the land in which now it lives.
Whispers echo in the hillsides faintly.
They speak of life and death and pain
And even hope, though it seems little remains.

Its secrets are lost, and forgotten by time.
The Vemroliet tree still stands by and by.
The whispers are fading, they are barely heard.
Will they survive the dark?

Oh Vemroliet tree, untouched by time
Its beauty is veiled and cast aside.

76

IDOLS & TRINKETS

Still, whispers speak to the hearts of Men,
Hope returns only then.

"Tell me you heard that," Rachal said, as the voice faded and the sounds of the world returned.

"I heard it, but I have no idea what just happened," Drake replied. "It was like all time stopped. That was strange."

"Indeed it was!" A voice yelled across the field on their left, they turned to see Isabel and Morgrin walking towards them. Rachal jumped from her seat and ran to her mother, embracing her and Morgrin. Drake smiled as he joined them.

"I'm glad to see you," Rachal said.

"We're glad to see you too," Morgrin said.

"Now, since you are now officially my son-in-law, you are required to give me a hug."

Drake embraced Isabel. "Should we go back to the porch?"

"Why?" Isabel asked, sitting down on the wet grass. They followed suit.

"So you heard the song?" Rachal asked.

"Indeed we did," Morgrin answered. "Though it is not the first time we have heard it."

"You've heard it before?" Drake asked. Isabel nodded.

"Shortly after the Sorcerer was defeated the first time those words echoed through the air, though in that instance I think we were the only ones who heard them. I was unable to remember the words afterward, but the tune stuck with me. It's been of interest for many years because my father would hum the same tune when I was a child. Now my heart wonders why we've heard it again and what it might mean."

"You mean you don't know? All these years I've known you, it seems you always have the answers when the rest of us are confused."

"As much as I might know Drake Thomas, I don't know everything. It's a big world out there."

"We came to tell you goodbye," Morgrin said.

"You're leaving?" Rachal asked.

"Yes we're leaving, though Morgrin might have made it sound a little more sudden than it will be. We don't plan to leave before you set out on your travels."

"Where are you going?" Drake asked.

"We're not quite sure," Morgrin answered. "We are called away, somewhere far to the north. Aiden has said that we should go there. Ellizar is currently working on decoding a map we found a couple of months ago. Once we see that, we'll know where we're headed."

"Did Aiden give you any clue as to what you were supposed to do that far north?"

"No, but we trust him," Isabel said. "I have a few things I'd like to look into, and I can do my research just as easily from the north as I can from the south."

"What are you working on now?" Rachal asked. Isabel reached into a small bag that Morgrin had been carrying and pulled out two cloths.

She set them on the ground and opened up the one on the right. Before them was revealed a small box, each side two inches wide. Grey in color, yet with hints of green and even red and blue. It glittered in the light, mesmerizing them. Drake reached out his hand and picked it up, surprised by the weight that it held.

"It weighs nearly five pounds," Isabel said. "Shake it."

Drake did, surprised that something rattled inside. On the outside, there were no hinges, or locks of any kind. Small holes, some barely big enough to see, covered the outside faces. Drake handed it to Rachal, who studied it with as much fascination as Isabel.

"It feels like rock, doesn't it? It may surprise you to know that this is anything but rock. I've tried to open it for years, but never even put so much as a scratch on it."

"What is this and where on earth did you dig this up?" Rachal asked.

"I have no idea what these are called. We had three or four of these sitting on our mantel when I was a child. I thought they were just for decoration, then again I'm sure there are things my parents didn't tell me at that age. I found this one in Maurivian Tower, it's an abandoned stronghold of an age long past.

IDOLS & TRINKETS

Among the ruins, there are many things that a person like me could find interesting. I found it at the top of the highest tower by itself, right in the middle of the floor. If I have to give these a name I would call them Maurivian Blocks, because that's where I found the first one."

"What's in that cloth?" Rachal asked, handing the block back. Isabel covered it and carefully uncovered the other one. An identical block was revealed, except that it was all black and looked like it had been through an intense fire. The air changed, becoming heavy and oppressive, even pushing their thoughts to where they began to despair.

Faint whispers echoed through their minds and through the air around them. Drake felt an urge to touch it and extended his hand. His finger touched the surface and it felt like fire burned through all of his body for an instant. He jerked his hand back. Isabel covered the block and the sensations and heaviness of the air vanished in an instant.

"Is this some dark art?" Rachal asked.

"One that we have never seen before," Isabel said. "I found this one in the heart of Korinth. The Dwarvish city that was conquered by the Sorcerer's armies on his second rising."

"How did you happen to learn of it and how did you acquire it?" Drake asked. Isabel shrugged her shoulders.

"I have a knack for finding unique things Drake, you of all people know that," Isabel answered. "Near seven years ago I discovered it when I was visiting Korinth. Strange place, but full of mysteries and things that fascinated me. Morgrin and I stayed there for some time."

"How did you even discover Korinth? Even in Ariamore, I don't think Atruss had knowledge of a surviving Dwarf city until four years ago."

"As you'll soon find out, Queman has quite an extensive library of strange and forgotten scrolls. This block was mentioned in one of them, so I went there to study it. They were welcoming to us, as we were the first people to visit the city in twenty years, and I wished to know more about the block. They were eager for this also. They had found it deep in the mountain when they were starting to mine a new tunnel and discovered, quite by accident an even older

79

tunnel that had been sealed off. They discovered it and were afraid of it, they had the tunnel sealed, and never set foot in it until we arrived.

"The history of the block is muddled to me, even with all of the surviving lore and records in the scrolls that I looked at. When they were crafted, and for what purpose they were crafted I cannot rightly say. In ages past, it seems as if they may have been given as a token of love or friendship. But this I am certain of, they are not made the same as the Maurivian Blocks. The Maurivian Blocks have small holes in them, these have slashes. Small difference, but that's how I was able to discern that this one matched the description in the scroll.

"There is a curse upon them as you might have noticed, but from my research, I would say they were not always cursed. Surviving scrolls from nearly three thousand years ago, indicated that the leaders of Korinth began to grow fearful of the block and likely they were the ones to seal it up in the tunnel in which it was found. At some point, they were changed or tampered with, or perhaps their true nature was finally revealed."

"Life with her is never boring is it Morgrin?" Drake asked. Morgrin smiled.

"Indeed not, but like my wife, I do have a fascination with history. I'm more than glad to sit with her for hours, reading strange scrolls. I'm glad for the moment, war is over and I have time to do that with her."

"But enough with the strange dark stuff," Isabel said, putting the items back into her bag. "How about some presents?" Drake and Rachal smiled, unsure of what to expect as Isabel pulled two small cloth-wrapped items. She unwrapped the first one and revealed a large dark ring. The metal was colored black and on the front of it was a single, large red ruby. "This is for you Drake." Drake studied it for a moment, looking intently at the red ruby, noticing a strange insignia etched into it.

"Where did you get this?" Drake asked.

"Found it at a marketplace in Yerma five years ago. This is just one of the reasons why I love markets so much. You never would expect to find family heirlooms in such a place as that."

"Heirlooms?" Drake asked. "My family?"

"Mine," Isabel said. Drake and Rachal both looked at her blankly.

IDOLS & TRINKETS

"The etching on the ruby is the family crest of Isabel's family," Morgrin said. "I have a ring as well. He pulled one out of his pocket, the stone in his shone a vibrant green. The etching was plain to see. "It hasn't been safe for me to wear it until now, but we're done hiding."

Instantly Isabel's disguises that she had worn for so many years vanished. Her hair turned white and she looked much older.

"No more disguises?" Drake asked. "This will be strange to get used to."

"It's time to let everyone see beneath the mask. That ring bears my family crest on it because it belonged to my father. How it survived the explosion that killed my father I cannot guess, but stranger things have happened. I saw it in the marketplace and I knew instantly. My father claimed it had other qualities about it that made it the most valuable item in our house. I was young at the time so I thought he was joking. Still, I've studied it for the five years since I got it and I think there *is* some hidden quality, but I haven't been able to find it."

Isabel reached behind her and unveiled the other item. A necklace filled with diamonds and expensive jewels flickered in the dim light. Drake and Rachal were both taken aback by its beauty. A large red ruby pendant hung in the middle, bearing the crest of Isabel's family.

"I don't know what to say," Rachal said, mesmerized by the sparkling necklace. "It seems like it's too expensive to wear!"

"Go ahead and try it on," Isabel said. Rachal slipped it over her neck amazed when it shrunk to the right size and vanished. "No one can steal what they don't know is there. Unless you or Drake remove the necklace, no one will ever know about it. You can still feel it around your neck right?" Rachal nodded. "If there's deceit being told to you it'll turn cold."

"Thank you," Rachal said. She hugged her mother, who smiled. Drake marveled to see the two of them side by side.

"Now, for one more thing," Isabel said. This time she pulled out a small metal flask, which was dull and unattractive. "I warn you right now that this flask is for your most dire need only. It may have drastically bad consequences if you have too much of it at once, or use it needlessly. It's a drink called *Hanyta*. It's a drink from an ancient time."

"And you just happened to find it?" Drake jested. "Or knowing you, you just happened to find some ancient piece of bark that had the recipe on it?"

"Exactly," Isabel said. "Seriously though, this stuff will kill you if you drink more than is necessary. No more than one sip, and you'd better be an inch away from death when you use it."

"So where did you find this concoction?" Drake asked, smelling the liquid. Drake gagged as an overwhelming smell of sweet, but tainted with harsh sour odors moved through his lungs.

"My dear son-in-law; I'm without my disguises, I look as old as I am. I can't give up all my secrets in one day."

"We have one thing we would like to ask of you," Rachal said. Isabel and Morgrin both waited patiently. "Everyone seems to think that it would be unsafe to take our Taruks to Rinevah. Whether that is or isn't true I guess time will tell. Would you be willing to look after them for a while? It might be quite a long time. We want them to be safe and if they can't go with us, I want them to go somewhere they'll be needed and appreciated."

"We would be honored," Morgrin answered. "Though I do not doubt that if you are in dire need the Taruks will come to your rescue no matter what the distance. A Taruk's heart is always loyal to those who are worthy."

The morning passed slowly but happily as they sat and talked for several hours in the grass. They were later joined by Lily and Ellizar and their kids. When the sun was high, Ellizar led the four of them away from his house, walking for several minutes until they reached a large canyon that was delved out of the earth. Within the canyon, a small dwelling sat next to a large and glorious building.

Following Ellizar closely, they started on a steep narrow path made of rock. The path moved down the great canyon until they were finally able to rest their feet on solid ground. Drake and Rachal walked in silence, each of them for the moment absorbed in their own internal thoughts.

The large glorious building they had seen from the top of the canyon was three stories high, and rising above those three stories, stood an even taller tower with a large bell on it. Beautiful gardens surrounded the structure and a large well-kept lawn had met them as soon as they had stepped on the canyon floor.

"I can say I expected this," Rachal said.

"This place has been kept this secret for a very specific reason," Ellizar said. "Until recently, I was not aware of its existence either."

"You lived right next to it and somehow you were unaware of it?" Rachal said. "That sounds about right."

Ellizar gave an amused look.

"He did not know of it because he did not need to know about it until he turned up with that map!" They turned to see Queman coming up the lawn behind them. "Though I am most glad to reveal it to you today!"

"Good to see you again Queman," Drake said, shaking his hand. Queman bowed and took Rachal's hand.

"And I am glad to see all of you, but come along! There is much to talk about and my old tired legs would very much like to sit in a comfortable chair while we talk. For we may be talking quite a long time."

They followed Queman up to the large house and were ushered in by a few housekeepers who spoke little. The floors were beautifully finished. an unfamiliar marking burned into the wood in the middle of the floor.

"Beautiful design," Rachal commented. "I've never seen the insignia before. What is it?"

"The symbol of Ariamore. The old Ariamore. Outside of this canyon, you'll have to look far and long in the world to find any scrolls with that marking on it," Queman said. He motioned that they should follow him.

Ellizar led Isabel and Morgrin away down a hall to the right and were lost from sight.

They entered a large room facing to the west and climbed a set of spiral stairs until they came upon a large room filled from floor to ceiling with books and scrolls. A large grand table spanned the center of the room, but they chose to sit in large cushioned chairs next to a set of open windows that looked out over the vast canyon. Far within a green field, a small lake lay undisturbed.

"Make yourselves at home!" Queman said as they sat down. "Would you like anything to eat or drink?"

"Maybe some tea?" Rachal asked.

"You shall have it!" Servants were summoned into the room and took their requests, vanishing somewhere to prepare it.

"It brings me much joy to finally see you two together after all these years; many years have I prayed for you to be reunited as you should have been. My apologies for not being in attendance at your wedding, it seems as if my age has finally caught up with me and I'm not quite as good at traveling as I used to be."

"We understand perfectly," Rachal said. "There were a lot of people, far more than we would've liked."

Queman chuckled. "I'm sure."

Silence came over them for a moment.

"If I am reading your thoughts correctly, you are unsure what to say because neither of you have ever really known me as a scholar. Am I correct?"

"Yes," Rachal said, as the three of them broke out in laughter. "You've lived in Laheer as long as my memory goes back and I never knew you to have a library."

"Well...I had one. Not too many people came into my house," Queman said. "If you had entered into my basement you would have discovered many things about me and my younger days that would've surprised you. Just another reminder to always look beneath the mask that a person wears."

"So, were you wearing a mask?" Drake asked.

Queman shrugged. "To an extent, but it was for the good of everyone else. I always had a love and respect for animals, hence my herds. My love of history and lore was better kept to myself for the most part."

"Why's that?" Rachal asked.

Queman held up a hand. "In due time my dear. We'll get to that question later, but I'm sure many more questions should be answered first. What would you like to know? About any subject!"

"What is this place?" Drake asked. "I've gathered that the town doesn't know about it."

"No, they do not. Herfon is a lovely town to live in, but the people themselves are exceptionally ordinary and do not have much imagination or curiosity about the outside world. Spend just one night with them in the town square and you'll soon realize that many of them have not been off this peninsula, and some of them have never even passed through the tree pass that you entered through! As such, they are very set in their ways and are creatures of habit, routine, rules, and customs. You understand."

"All things that drive me crazy," Rachal said. "It's a wonder that Lily and Ellizar were even allowed to buy land here."

"Indeed," Queman said. "She has some ancestral ties to this place; far, far back mind you. That is why she and Ellizar were allowed to build here. If you notice though it is far from any other house."

"Interesting dynamic," Drake said. Queman nodded.

"The citizens do not know I exist."

"What about the servants?" Rachal asked. "Aren't they town people?"

"No," Queman said, motioning for them to lean closer as he spoke under his breath. "There is more than one mystery about this valley. In my youth I discovered this building; these people were here when I arrived. It is because of this oddity that I can tell you the history of many things, starting with this building, with unfailing certainty and conviction. Care to know the history?"

Rachal and Drake both nodded and again relaxed into their chairs. They remained silent for several minutes as their tea was brought to them. Queman didn't stir until they had left, instead staring off into space as though he was trying to organize his thoughts.

"This is called the Tower of Imrahune. It is the only surviving building from a great city called *Perin*. At one time it was the second largest city in the nation of Tracshef; a large and powerful empire at the time. The entire peninsula was a city. It was considered a strategic position to hold because of its proximity to the neighboring empire of Cedon.

"As you can imagine, this city was always at war and fought over. First, it would be controlled by one nation, and then the other. It was a horrible life for the citizens, and in the end, the city became rather destabilized. Suddenly one night the city was set ablaze. A great war followed as both kingdoms blamed the other. The ruins of *Perin* were a battleground for nearly fifty years.

"The war only ended when the Cordellians, who saw an opportunity, came from the north and with their might and their strength, crushed both the Tracshef and Cedonian empires. After their victory, they deserted the place and never came back."

"Why not?" Drake asked. "I've never ruled an empire, but I would think that if you conquer one you take control of the region as your own."

"Sound reasoning would agree with your logic," Queman agreed. "But the little that I've learned of the Cordellians suggests they're more sadistic than that. They came, they conquered and then they killed every living person and animal they found. They plundered the land of wealth and food and left.

"Three hundred years later, a captain of a Cordellian naval ship got caught up in a storm and shipwrecked on these shores. Their boat had been shattered by large reefs that sit offshore and all their charts and navigation equipment were lost in the storm. Two hundred men were with him and they quickly built shelters as winter would soon be approaching.

The captain's name was Ipirus and in his journal, he tells how a strange and different sort of people came to them and helped them set up their towns and told them where they might get supplies. They also offered the knowledge of this very building, which amidst all the fighting over the ages, had not been damaged or destroyed.

"Why it was not destroyed Ipirus could not discern, and I can only in retrospect form my theory that this building is needed and special in many ways, that perhaps I don't even realize. When the spring came they chose not to build or seek any kind of vessel, but instead stayed on this peninsula and restored life to the lost city."

"How do you come into the story?" Rachal asked.

"I was a young boy, my family lived here for about five years. One day I suffered a leg injury while picking some apples on the border of the valley. I was trying to make it home, but I had hit my head and became disoriented. At last, I collapsed on the ground.

"During the night I was awoken by a person who said I needed to follow him immediately. I did so without delay. In short, they brought me here. They healed my injury and revived my spirits. I began to inquire about the large number of books and they showed them to me and said I could come and read from them anytime I wished.

"I spent all my spare time in this library of sorts, taking in everything I could get. It was then I fell in love with history, and knew that I would need this building in the future. Ipirus knew about this building, but his journal says that none of his men could see it. He seemed to think they were blinded from it.

"It remained my secret for many many years until I brought the three kings of Ariamore to this valley and they too could see the building!"

"The three kings?" Drake asked. "The ones who knew of Aiden's birth?"

Queman nodded. "The very same three."

"How did you know them?" Rachal asked.

"I had become a scholar in the nation of Ariamore and was within their trusted circle of advisors. They were very educated about the history of the world and were familiar with the prophecies concerning the birth of Sherados. I consulted with them many times before they sought permission to go in search of him."

"One thing I've always wondered about is why did Ariamore have three kings?" Drake asked. "Ariamore is not that big of a nation."

"In those days the nation of Ariamore was the largest and most powerful nation on the face of the earth. Its borders stretched from the Ariamore as you know it, all the way to Rinevah where you are headed. It was a massive kingdom. The governing of such a nation required three districts of sorts, and together the leaders of those districts ruled the nation. The capital city was the city of Merisyll"

"Why is it so much smaller now?" Rachal asked.

"When the elf kings arrived at King Erode's palace they requested to search the city for the heir of Lathon, who they found. Despite Erode's sinister plan they escaped and returned to Ariamore unharmed, but it was not without consequences. Bitterness and anger festered in Erode's heart. He went on a rampage, first in his own nation, killing every baby boy under the age of two. When he was satisfied with the blood and death in his own nation, his heart was hardened and turned towards Ariamore.

"His leading advisors told him that he could not let the elf kings get away with humiliating him in such a fashion. They told him it would certainly bring down the king's own nation in due time. After much digging, I discovered who the main proponent of this thinking was."

"Rohemir," Drake said. Queman nodded.

"For many years, in confidence, Isabel and I pondered what he had been doing there. Finally, years later we are certain of our suspicions. He turned the king, who was already enraged, to action. He summoned nations, near and far. Nargothians, Nashurians, Bazarran, Osh, Venyania. Strange, dark nations. Unexpected in the night, a year after the elf kings had visited him, their attack was unleashed.

"It was a horrible attack from every side. Overnight it seemed Ariamore was brought to its knees. When it became clear that the attack would likely destroy the nation, we made a plan.

"The three brothers and I went on a last crusade, to preserve all the knowledge and ancient scrolls that we could. We ran ahead of the advancing armies, taking whatever we could find and hiding it. The three kings eventually went into hiding and I over the next few years, spent my time running back and retrieving everything that we had hidden. I brought everything to this library."

"The people of Ariamore were scattered, carried off to other nations like a prize in a contest. Some banded together and they are what formed the current nation of Ariamore. The rest were persecuted, killed, and enslaved. The worst things you could imagine happened to these people."

"Did the three brothers tell them what they found when they had traveled east?" Rachal asked.

"Yes, though not all believed. In the world, you will find many who say one thing but secretly believe another. Many of the Farsees didn't want to hear about the heir of Lathon being born, because that meant he would be greater than them. I'm sure you haven't encountered that thinking." Drake laughed. "Some of them believed, but when Ariamore was attacked and destroyed, they lost faith and grew bitter towards Lathon.

"It was six years until a man came forward, seeking to unite the Elvish people and regain the land that had been taken from them. He, more than any others at the time, believed in the prophecies, he believed what the three brothers had told the people. He knew that nothing ever got accomplished, by sitting in the shadows.

"His name was Jeoshssan. He marshaled the Elves together from the lands that captured them and set out to conquer their enemies. They reached the shores of what had once been Ariamore, finding things much different than when they had been taken captive. Walls around all the cities were higher, spies were everywhere. Many were intimidated but Jeoshssan stood firm and his faith strengthened the people.

"It was plain to see that Lathon's blessing was with him, for many miraculous things happened as they overthrew their enemies against all odds. The sun stood still for an entire day so he could finish conquering their enemies in one battle. Large hailstones were thrown from the heavens, crushing the enemies in another battle. Long and hard was their fight, but Lathon was always with them.

"Once they had regained much of their land it was time for a king to lead. Jeoshssan consulted Lathon and Lathon sent the prophets out to seek for one who was worthy of being a leader."

"Jeoshssan didn't become king?" Drake asked, a few memories returned. Queman shook his head.

"Many wished for it to be so. Still, Jeoshssan was resolute in his decision. He said 'I have done my part and have run my race, as surely as Lathon lives I am not the one to become a king to the people. His words couldn't have been truer as he died five days later."

"Who became king?" Rachal asked. Queman looked at Drake, a light in his eyes.

"Do you remember?"

"I can see his face, but his name is still lost to me. The prophet who appointed him was named Sarule right?"

"Very good Drake Thomas," Queman said. "You're memory has improved drastically from the last time we talked!" Drake smiled. "The prophet Sarule came to Zebethar and appointed him to be the leader. It was two years after they had completed the campaign to retake the land."

"Was he a good king?" Rachal asked.

"Partly," Drake said. "He started good, I think."

"Depends on your definition of good," Queman said. "On the day of his coronation, they couldn't even find him. He was hiding, afraid to take the throne, despite Lathon's guidance. If he had listened to Lathon every step of the way he would have been an amazing leader. But many times he would only do half of what Lathon wanted. This is why Lathon eventually removed his favor from Zebethar and sent Sarule once again to find the next king."

"Me," Drake said. Rachal's face showed surprise.

"You never told me that years ago."

"There's a lot of things I should have told you years ago, but it seems as if I too was running in fear. Zebethar had become quite troubled in the mind. He denied it, but everyone could see it."

"What happened?" Rachal asked.

"He tried to kill me," Drake answered. "I've never understood though, why his mind became troubled. Seems like a cruel thing for Lathon to do."

"That's because you're thinking of it wrong," Queman started. "*You* were appointed to be king. Lathon's favor has clearly been removed from Zebethar, but he won't give up the throne. I tend to think that Lathon never inflicted Zebethar with evil spirits because that would not fit with his nature. More so, Lathon removed the protection that he had given Zebethar from things of this nature."

"Did people like that Drake was appointed? It's an Elvish nation and he's not Elvish."

"Opinion was divided. But the truth of the matter remains that Drake *was* chosen by the prophet Sarule to be the leader of Rinevah. That's how you got that mark on your hand."

Drake looked at the scar, which he had almost completely forgotten. He stared at the mark on his hand, suddenly aware of the presence of Lathon coming upon him. It was a strange feeling and at first, Drake didn't quite understand what it was. It came over his soul, giving him courage and certainty. Fear and doubt still lingered in his mind, but now they seemed distant and their power lessened.

Chapter 7
HOPE AND DESPAIR

Salt water misted through the air as the bow of the Evin Lador pushed through the waves. Drake and Rachal could feel the adrenaline of a new adventure flowing through their veins, but more than anything, they felt relief. Glad to finally be underway after nearly two months of waiting.

They had found Barnabas and the ship in Avdatt as they had agreed on and preparations had begun immediately. Drake, at first had been overwhelmed by the sheer size of the ship, being almost the biggest ship he had seen in any waters, save the Gog ships.

Barnabas had laughed at their reaction when finally he had led them to the great vessel, but he was certain that he was only going to take the strongest ship in his fleet into waters he didn't know.

The Evin Lador towered over the sea beneath it, pushing effortlessly through the waves that were thrown at it. A hundred and fifty men crewed the ship and despite Barnabas's best efforts to keep Drake and Rachal from working with the crew, the crew had been very welcoming and taught them everything they could have wanted to know about sailing. It didn't take long before Drake and Rachal were working regular shifts alongside everyone else.

The first day had passed without incident. They left the port and mostly stayed within sight of the coastline, preparing to make way. Thanks to past experiences, Barnabas had chosen to pass by the island of Calamar on the left. The unsettling nature of his last trip through the Sea of the Spirits still lingered in Drake's mind like it was yesterday.

On the morning of the third day the coast had vanished from their view and they slowly began heading more southeast where Barnabas knew there were faster currents and generally stronger winds that would speed their journey. Thanks to Queman, Drake and Rachal had produced a map that (at the very least) gave them an idea of where they were headed.

The fifth day brought high winds and rougher seas, making it harder for them to keep the ship on its course. They fought with the wind and the waves all day, but altogether felt like they had made no progress. The night had come and only then did they begin to have a sense of despair. The stars had changed drastically since the night before, meaning they had been pushed off course more than they had initially thought with the rough seas.

The sixth day brought no relief, only doubt and confusion as they pressed forward battling the high winds and rough waters, eagerly searching for any sign of land so they could regroup and get their bearings once again. Drake and Rachal found themselves in the crow's nest for much of the morning.

"First time I've ever sailed before…and here we are lost at sea," Rachal lamented. The skies had grown steadily grey, furthering the feelings of vanishing hope that was now being revealed in the crew.

"At least we still have a ship," Drake said. "The first voyage that I remember we were shipwrecked and had to walk for nearly a week until we reached our destination."

"Have you sailed much since then?"

"A few times here and there," Drake answered. "As you know Rhallinen was mostly a landlocked country. Using Destan was more practical for me to get around. But I knew Barnabas and he would bring in goods to the Belvanor port. Some would then be ferried up the river on smaller ships, while the rest would be loaded on carts and taken to their destination."

"Sometimes I feel like I've done nothing compared to all the great things you've done," Rachal said.

"Have no doubt, I've screwed up just as much as I've succeeded, and the only reason I've succeeded at all is because of Aiden and the grace of Lathon.

You, on the other hand, did something unthinkable. How many years were you held captive and tortured in Enya's house?"

"More than I care to remember," Rachal said.

"I pity the enemy that ever tries to capture you and get you to talk. You'll be the toughest prisoner they've ever had."

"I suppose that we both learned what we needed to through those experiences. Though it may not be for many years until we can see the lesson."

"I agree with that," Drake said. "That seems to be the way of it though. Some things are better revealed in retrospect."

"Why do you think that is?"

Drake fell silent for a minute. "I think understanding comes in that moment that we are finally quiet enough to listen to what we've learned, or been through. In the moment we're in the story, but afterwards, we better understand the story and can see the lessons; the hand of Lathon moving. However, we were unaware of it at the time. After all, we're just living our part of a greater story. How easy it is to forget that it's not about us."

"I wonder what the rest of the story will look like. The real story."

"I'm curious to see what our part of it holds."

They fell silent for several minutes, both of them scanning the horizon. After some time Rachal stood at attention straining her eyes to the south off their starboard side.

"There's a ship out there," Rachal said. "Maroon flag."

"Are you sure?" Drake asked. Rachal nodded and pointed to the place where she saw it, but Drake was unable to find it. They climbed down to the main deck, quickly making their way to the stern where Barnabas sat eating his lunch.

"How are the crows doing today?" Barnabas asked.

"There's a ship off our starboard side. It has a maroon flag if that sounds familiar," Rachal answered. Barnabas moved to the railing and pulled out his eyeglass and with much effort, found the ship that Rachal had seen.

"Aye, there's a ship of some sort. The fact that you saw it without an eyeglass is no ordinary feat! Even now I can barely make out that it even has a flag on it."

"Is it maroon colored though?" Drake asked. Barnabas was silent for two minutes studying and straining to confirm it.

"Aye, there's a maroon flag," Barnabas said. "I've always heard that Elves had great vision, but this is ridiculous. You're not even Elvish, for crying out loud."

"Part Elvish," Rachael reminded.

"I can't make any other details on it." Barnabas handed the eyeglass to Drake and then to Rachal who studied it closely.

"It doesn't appear to be a coastal vessel. Its masts are large and numerous. it's certainly designed for the open ocean," Rachal concluded.

"You truly are incredible my dear," Drake said as she handed Barnabas the eyeglass. "Should we see if it's friendly?"

"I'm not sure," Barnabas replied. "I'm going to say no. We're in strange waters, with no clue where we are. It could be a trading route that I'm not familiar with. If that's the case then we should head in the general direction of the ship but not close enough to arouse any suspicion. With the weather doing what it is right now I'm not sure I want to take any chances."

The orders were given out and the ship's course changed only slightly. Slowly but steadily keeping the ship with the maroon flag within Rachal's sight. Drake joined her in the crow's nest now and then, but for the most part, he worked with the crew on their various tasks.

The wind seemed to be working in their favor now, though Drake could tell that something was making Rachal uneasy. Her expressions were hard and focused beyond what they normally were as she studied the horizon intently. The day wore on and turned to night.

Finally, Rachal came down to the deck, unable to see anymore until the morning would come. Rachal didn't speak at supper and the crew was also silent, a spirit of unrest falling over them. The crew dispersed, some to their sleeping quarters, while others went to their posts or kept watch on the dark waters.

"Something is not right!" Rachal exclaimed once they were in their room at the stern of the ship. "The ship that I saw this morning, I never saw it again after we turned our course. I'm positive that I've seen five different ships over the course of the day, all bearing the same flag."

"Why didn't you tell Barnabas?"

"There's something strange about these ships and it seems familiar to me. Whether it's folly or a leading of Lathon, I didn't feel that we should change course, even if I'm wary of where they might be taking us. A whisper came over the winds to me, it was soft and faint, but it said

'Do not despair, this is the road that you must travel.'

"I am going to hold to the course these ships set for us to whatever end. Though I fear what tomorrow will bring."

"I'm with you and support you all the way," Drake said. "Similar feelings have plagued me. Let us not tell Barnabas our suspicions yet. He seems to have a growing fear in his mind. It's clouding his vision. If we say anything I fear that he would turn and run."

They sat in silence for a while. The night moved slowly, neither of them able to sleep as they felt a presence creeping through the dark. The wind grew stronger and dark clouds moved in, blocking out the stars and the moon.

When daybreak came Drake could hardly tell it was day. The clouds above were dark and oppressive. Everyone scrambled around the deck, doing whatever they could to keep the ship on course. The winds grew more fierce over the course of the day and seemed to switch direction nearly every half hour. The ship was pushed off course and hope was fading in their hearts with every wave that crashed into the ship.

Through it all Rachal stood in the crow's nest, yelling back what way they needed to go. Whether she could see ships on the turbulent waves, or not Drake couldn't begin to guess, but they pressed forward, trying to ignore the wretched feelings that were growing in their hearts.

By the seventh day of the storm, it was all any of them could do to keep the ship in any reasonable heading. A heaviness was in their limbs, making it harder and harder to carry out the orders that were being given. Despite all the efforts of the crew, little progress had been made, and the crew in the last efforts to do something to help them had begun throwing things overboard to lighten the ship.

"I have no idea where we are!" Barnabas exclaimed. Fatigue and anger tainted his voice. Drake and Rachal closed the door behind them, sealing them off from the water-drenched world they had been immersed in for some amount of time. Whether the whole day had passed or just a couple of hours, they didn't know. "I hate to say it Drake, but I've gotten in a bit over my head, and in all my life I've never seen a storm like this one!"

"We have a map!" Drake exclaimed. Barnabas threw it at him. They stumbled for a moment as the ship was tossed around in the ocean.

"The men are despairing! As you know, we've resorted to lightening the ship to make it easier to keep afloat. I'm doing all that I can your *highness*, but we're going to be up against a rock and a hard place real soon unless our fortunes change fast. If the ship goes down we'll have to pile in the lifeboats and hope for the best. Though that will be a dark moment as there aren't enough boats for all the people."

"The ship will not go down and not one single soul will lose their life as long as they hear my words and believe them!" Rachal stated.

Drake and Barnabas were both taken aback by the authority that had come in her voice. Drake smiled and nodded his approval, while Barnabas, clearly taken aback, remained silent for a minute.

"So that's it then?" Barnabas asked. "Who died and made you a prophet? It is foolish to claim something like that when you know nothing about the seas!"

"More foolish is it, to turn away truth when it stares you in the face; to slap the hand that seeks to encourage and give out hope. I do not speak these words to merely make you feel better for a moment, I speak them because I feel I must. As surely as Lathon lives, those words came from him. To speak against them is blasphemy."

"Forgive me, my lady," Barnabas said, his expression softening. "On the seas, we seldom hear or use the name Lathon, and in anger and frustration, a person can say many things they regret. I am grateful for the hope your words offer, but the circumstances are weighing on my soul and I am afraid."

"I forgive you, Barnabas. This ship will not go down, and no one will die on it. This storm will pass."

"I now sense the truth in your words," Barnabas said. "What are we to do? We can't continue sailing like this forever. The ship, as strong as she is may not last much longer without a chance to make some repairs. We need to find somewhere to hole up and rest."

"I can't make heads for tails where we are on this map either," Drake said. "But if we make it through the night then perhaps our fortunes will improve."

"How about this," Barnabas started. "We'll make it through the night and the early morning, but the first island that we see, we need to head straight towards it. I don't care if we get stranded there for the next five years, it's better than sinking to the bottom of the ocean."

"Agreed."

The morning came without relief as the weary crew continued to battle the waves. Rachal had again taken to the crow's nest, calling down any information that was useful to them as they tried to navigate the turbulent ocean. During the night many supplies had been thrown over, and afraid that the ship was going to break apart, the crew had managed to wrap ropes around the hull, trying the ship together to make it stronger.

Drake braced for another impact as they broke into another massive wave. They were soaked in cold water, but by this point, they had become numb to it. Two men sat on the wheel, holding it in place while Barnabas stood alongside ordering the sailors about.

A couple of the large sails had tears in them. Thankfully, despite all the water washing up on the deck of the ship, below it was mostly dry.

"Land Ho!" Rachal cried from the crow's nest. Drake stood up, his spirits soaring at the mere mention of land. Rachal pointed to their port side just ahead of their bow. In between the waves and wind, Drake spotted a small piece of land. Drake ran back to Barnabas.

"Land on the port side!" Drake announced, even those within earshot were encouraged by the words. "What are your orders?"

"The winds too strong to give her a good docking. Do we know if there are any signs of life on the island?" Drake quickly scaled to the crow's nest and looked at everything there was to see before heading back to Barnabas.

"No signs that we can see," Drake replied.

"Draw up the sails, let the current push us in. We'll drop the sea anchors to slow us. Hopefully, it's a deep bay and we can run aground without much effort. We'll take the boats to land and wait for the storm to ease."

Everything was carried out as Barnabas had ordered and soon they found themselves rushing towards the island that was now large in their view. The anchors were dropped, digging into the sea bed, and slowing the ship as they continued to be pressed forward by both wind and waves.

"Shallows just ahead!" Rachal yelled. Drake and Barnabas both looked to the horizon, seeing the crest of the waves earlier than they had hoped.

"Too late to do anything about it now!" Barnabas exclaimed, cursing. They held their course and struck the shallows, the ship was jarred and came to a slow stop as the anchors sunk into the sand. Rachal climbed down from the crow's nest, and all the sailors let a breath of relief escape them.

The bay was surrounded by a large beach made of a mixture of rocks and sand. Past the beach was a large ring of sheer cliffs. As far as they could tell the rock face had no cracks in them at all. In fact, they were completely smooth as if they had been recently carved and carefully and skillfully maintained. The rocks shimmered in the pale light, and seemed to consist of several different kinds of stone.

"Ellizar would love this place," Drake said to Rachal who nodded her agreement. The ship was secured the best that they could hope, and then they went ashore in the long boats as planned.

They stepped onto the shore, greeted by large cliffs. They found many openings carved into the cliff. They entered inside, finding the rocks slick and slimy. Large shafts were cut through the cliffs, ascending straight up letting in light from above.

"We'll have to find better shelter than this," Barnabas said. "It'll work for now, but I'll be willing to bet that when the tide is in this place is flooded."

"At least we know we'll be able to get the ship out when the time comes," Drake said. They exited the cavern and walked along the shore, discovering one more archway on the far south side of the bay. It entered into a rock tunnel, which had a staircase carved out of it. Though the stairs were wet and covered in algae, they could see dry rock further up. They continued until they came out into the daylight after several minutes. They stepped into their new surroundings, realizing they had scaled the entire cliff and were now seated on top overlooking the bay, where their ship sat motionless.

The top of the cliff was covered in grass and strange flowers, some were red and others were black, but all of them were no taller than two inches. A large open field stretched out before them, and at the end of their line of sight, they could scarcely see tall green spikes of evergreens.

"This will have to do for the night," Barnabas said. "We won't get flooded and we won't sink. Count your blessings, men. I want some men to stand watch over the camp. A couple of men go scout as far as the forest and report back your findings. Others go looking for food. No fires for anyone tonight. We don't know if this is a friendly island or not, but if we can avoid being seen, then all the better."

The night was long and cold, and despite the fatigue that Drake knew he should be feeling he couldn't sleep. Rachal lay next to him, also awake and staring up at the stars.

A sound came over the air, like that of an enormous Taruk. The sound was distant and muffled, but still, it came. Drake focused his mind, listening to only the Taruk. The Taruk's noise steadily grew, the waves of sound striking his ears in a new way.

Suddenly it seemed as if it was a loud, resounding roar. The whole island shook with the voice of the Taruk. Drake trembled wondering if anyone else was feeling what he was. Another earth-trembling roar shook the island. Drake looked towards the sounds, gasping as a vision overtook his mind.

A great white Taruk, Elohim was before him. Two other figures could be seen further back, One, he assumed was Aiden, but the other was clouded and mysterious. The Taruk held his gaze for what felt like an eternity, warmth and life flooding into Drake's soul.

In an instant, the vision faded, but still, the roar of Taruk lingered in Drake's mind. As if a veil had been lifted from his mind, memories, clear and fresh came into it.

"Any memories of where we might be?" Rachal asked.

Drake remained silent.

"Give me a minute to sort through some new memories that came to me."

They fell silent while Drake puzzled over the memories.

"I know this place," Drake said. "The visions that are playing out in my head about this place aren't nice ones."

"Where are we?"

"We are in a place called Tuthar," Drake replied. Frustrated he sighed heavily. "I wish Aiden was with us right now."

"I think he is," Rachal said. "In some way at least."

Chapter 8

LUMAFLOR

Isabel woke with the sun in her eyes as it rose over the distant eastern mountains. She sat up, casting off the large blanket that she and Morgrin had slept under the night before. Heavy dew covered everything and a light cool breeze out of the north chilled them. Soon they started a fire, eating their meager breakfast in silence.

The sun rose higher and the Taruks began to stir, taking to the sky and enjoying the freedom of being able to fly anywhere they wanted without being seen. Isabel had seen a lot of places in her lifetime, but she never remembered being in such a desolate place.

The landscape was that of a desert, a few tumbleweeds and strange desert plants dominated the plains almost as far as the eye could see. The furthest settlement of any size wasn't to be found until you reached the mountains in the east and they were at least eighty miles from here. To the south, the desert spanned nearly five hundred miles occasionally dotted by a few nomadic tribes, but they were seldom and small.

There were no other signs of life until you reached the borders of Goshen, and not far from that, you would find Drake's northern house. It had been generously purchased by Saul and was often used as his vacation home for him, his wife Alexandrea, and their three young children.

To the west a rocky coastline had emerged, wrapping itself around the farthest edges of the Dead Mountains and then continuing almost straight north. Now, they could see only the faintest sight of blue if the elevation was right, but at this distance, even Isabel was unsure if they were seeing everything clearly or not.

IDOLS & TRINKETS

Isabel started heating some water from their canteens. She reached for her pack and unfolded the map that they had acquired in their venture into the Dead Mountains several months ago.

Morgrin quickly packed up the few belongings they had brought with them. Finally, he dropped some of their tea leaves into the now-boiling water and greeted Isabel with a kiss.

"Good morning beautiful," Morgrin said. Isabel smiled.

"Beautiful?" Isabel asked, half-jokingly. "Have you seen my grey hairs without any disguises on? They somehow went curly. In short, you're going to be married to an old grey frizz-head."

"Fine by me. I think it's neat you're going to be a grey frizz-head."

"Whatever," Isabel joked.

"You look good to these eyes," Morgrin said. They sat in silence, both lost in their thoughts until their tea was ready. Morgrin poured the tea into two wooden cups and handed one to her. "Do you know how much of this desert we have left to traverse?"

"My best estimate, if Ellizar's notes are correct; we're about one hundred miles from the northern coast and a settlement which may provide some last-minute supplies before we go over the ocean."

"Ellizar's certainly become quite a scholar over the person I met eleven years ago," Morgrin said. "I can't believe all the things he found on the map."

"He is good at what he does, that's for sure. He's a good friend. I feel sorry for him though with Lily's health unstable," Isabel lamented.

"Do you think that the medicine you gave him will help?"

"Can never be sure. I've not usually dealt with lungs before. It's my best idea for medicine and the rest will come as may." Isabel paused, lost in thought. "It does make one realize just how fortunate we all are. I've been hiding and running all around here and there for as long as I can remember. Somehow through it all I've lived to tell the tale."

"And here we are together continuing the tale," Morgrin said, raising his cup as if to honor her. "You never know? Perhaps in hundreds of years some descendants of ours will be huddled around a great campfire listening to our great adventures and everything we learned along the way."

Isabel smiled. "It would be a grand thought my dear, but I would much rather hear about other more important things going on in the world, as opposed to some strange old lady who went on gallivanting around the world."

"You are far too modest my dear," Morgrin complimented.

"There's only one stage I want to see my story told on and that's when I walk through those pearly gates. Because that's the only time that it will be complete."

"I hope we get to walk through those pearly gates together someday. And if, Lathon forbid, I should die first, I will pull up a bench and wait for you." Isabel smiled, reminded of why she had fallen in love with him. Another bout of silence fell between them as they drank their tea.

"Does the map speak of any surprises ahead of us today?" Morgrin asked. Isabel quickly shuffled through some papers to find the notes that Ellizar had made. The nature of the map had both surprised and intrigued all of them. It had seemed like a simple enough map at first glance, but it appeared different to each race that looked at it.

Certain names would be written in different languages. Isabel who could read Elvish fluently saw many of the names in Elvish. Even with that, the Elvish, or Dwarvish often would be written in an ancient dialect, which required study and hours and hours of pouring through books and scrolls to find the right one.

"His notes don't speak of any great surprises," Isabel answered. "At least not between here and the sea. He has a lot of notes in here about strange ocean currents and wind patterns around certain islands on the map. He also mentions a number of irregularities, where the wind and ocean currents seemed like they should be going around something, but there was nothing to be found."

"Someone must have tampered with it?" Morgrin asked.

Isabel shrugged.

"That's my great theory right now. Perhaps those islands and information are written in an entirely different language and that's why we can't see it. I should've had Shavrok look at it before we left. The wells are well marked and as long as they're not dry we should be in good shape." She paused for a moment collecting her thoughts. "Presently though it looks like we shall have a most mundane and boring hike across the desert today, and probably tomorrow as well. The town we're looking for is Nain. It's literally the only town on the coast."

"Then it should be easy to find!" Morgrin exclaimed.

They hastily ate a few flat cakes that they had brought. They didn't hold much flavor, and at times tasted like nothing at all. But they provided an energy that would last them throughout the day. Finally, they picked up their packs and began their trek across their desert.

They talked frequently during the early morning hours, but as the day went on both of them grew steadily quieter. Isabel looked at the new landscape with curiosity, wishing she had more time to spend in this desert. The skies were clear, and though the hot sun beat down on them mercilessly, she saw the beauty. Far to the east, they could see the snow-tipped mountains, and to the west a distant sea churned. The wind swept across the plain, kicking up clouds of dust that would occasionally block their sight.

Over the course of the day, it became clear they were almost completely alone. No animals were to be found, save a stray shrew that quickly darted into their underground burrows once they were spotted. The only things in flight were the three Taruks who often stayed high and traveled far during the day.

It was midday before the desert landscape gave way. Smoke drifted lazily through the air. They turned towards the smoke and came to a small village. The roughly made wood buildings had been burnt and still smoldered. Isabel and Morgrin looked at the sight, sorrow filling their hearts as they noticed several bodies lying on the ground. Vultures circled overhead.

"Foul play happened here," Morgrin said. Isabel nodded. "Is this place on the map?"

"Yes," Isabel replied. "The name on the map is Encatar. Elvish name, meaning life." They walked in silence through the desolate town.

"This was not a small raiding party that caused this carnage," Morgrin said.

"There are tracks enough for at least a hundred people. On horses."

Isabel stooped and picked up a small book from the middle of the street. She flipped through the dirty blank pages, before putting it in her pocket. "Nothing about this place strikes me as important enough to get such attention."

"Perhaps they were just raiders, out to steal everything they could get their hands on?" Morgrin suggested.

"You think so?" Isabel asked. Morgrin shook his head and slipped into his thoughts.

"An attack like that would not leave the place like this. Raiders would've carried off all the women, not left them dead in the streets. This was an intentional strike, meant to devastate everyone, but for what reason I'm not sure."

They carefully walked through the ruins and sea of dead bodies. They were silent nearly the entire time, each of them trying to put together the pieces of the puzzle. After a while Isabel slipped away, easily locating the well, three hundred feet from the last building.

The well was made of stone, with a small roof protecting it from the sun. Isabel looked down the well, finding no rope or bucket. It didn't take long to realize that it had been dry for some time. She returned to the ruins and spotted Morgrin, who immediately looked in her direction.

"Well's dry," Isabel stated.

"The mystery deepens," Morgrin replied.

"We'd better get moving," Isabel said, sorrow tainting her voice. "With this well dry, we have to go another five miles to get to the next one."

"Can't we give these people any kind of proper burial?" Morgrin asked.

"I wish," Isabel lamented. "It would take too long and whoever did this could return at any point. We have to keep moving."

They continued north heading into the wilderness again. They spoke little, too overcome with sorrow to say much of anything. The sun beat down on them mercilessly as they trudged through the desert. Isabel studied the plants as they slowly and steadily seemed to have more and more white on them. She stooped down and ran her fingers along the now-white vegetation. To her surprise, the white was a crusty and crystallized substance, that was rubbed off even as she touched it.

"What do you think it is?" Morgrin asked.

"I have no idea," Isabel said. "But I think lingering would be a bad choice." They began walking.

"Isabel?" Morgrin asked. She looked back to see him. "I normally wouldn't ask such a question, but is there a logical reason why we're traveling on foot as opposed to enjoying a nice leisurely ride atop the Taruks?"

"No."

"Really? We're walking across this desert for fun?" Morgrin asked. Isabel laughed and smiled at him.

"I've never been in this part of Lathon's creation. I'd much rather see it with my own eyes." Isabel stopped and grabbed a strange nine-pedaled flower from the ground. She studied it intently. "Like this flower for example...I have no idea what kind it is...I'm taking it with us." She stuffed it in her pocket and continued, with Morgrin close behind shaking his head.

By mid-afternoon, the next well appeared on the horizon. Unlike the previous well, there was no town to contend with this time. They lowered the bucket and soon brought up fresh water. They quickly drank it and lowered the bucket again. Soon the next bucket full of water sat on the edge of the well. The sound of hooves grabbed their attention. To the east they could see a line of horsemen, sending a cloud of dust into the air.

Morgrin and Isabel exchanged a look as they waited for the horsemen to reach them. The ground shook as they approached and within a moment the entire well was encircled, cutting off any hopes of escape. Morgrin and Isabel remained where they were, passing the bucket back and forth and helping themselves to the fresh water.

"What is your business that you should be so far in this forsaken place?" a man asked. He was young, but a quick look at the well-armed man told them he had the authority to make something happen if he wanted it to happen.

"Getting a drink," Isabel answered, handing the bucket to Morgrin. The men around them exchanged glances, almost as if they had never heard that kind of reply.

"A drink?" the man asked.

"It's kind of hot out here," Isabel replied. "Kind of happens in deserts."

"You dare insult my intelligence?" the man asked.

"If you had any I would," Isabel remarked. The men were dumbfounded, while Morgrin was trying his hardest not to laugh or smile.

"If you knew who I was, and the authority I have-"

"Then I'd be frightened?" Isabel asked mockingly. "Let's look at a few facts. Five miles back the way we had come, there was a small village burned and all the citizens were dead. You surround us in great numbers but nowhere on any of your horses or wardrobe is the crest of a king or anyone. On top of that you are harassing two people who are just trying to get some water. Seeing the evidence the only question I have for you is why are you harassing us?"

"I do not need to answer your questions, nor will I. I am Halar of Tyriam and it is my sworn duty to kill all who wander this desolate place! Now state your names this very second or I shall have you sliced from head to toe, and leave you to be eaten by the vultures."

"I can give you three good reasons why you should turn and head back the other way," Morgrin said, breaking his silence. Halar sat up taller in his saddle, seeming interested and annoyed. A few seconds passed before Halar gave an amused expression.

"Are you going to tell me what these reasons are today?" Halar mocked.

"Look behind you," Morgrin said. The men all looked behind their leader, their eyes wide with fear. While everyone had been keeping their attention on Isabel and Morgrin; Aspen, Destan, and Ezzion had gently landed and walked up behind the horsemen, having gotten so close that the riders nearest the Taruk were within three feet of the circle.

The men panicked and all at once everyone scattered, riding their horses as fast as they could. The Taruks chased everyone over the countryside, leaving them alone by the well.

"That went better than it could've," Morgrin said. "I have a feeling though that we haven't seen the last of them."

"Probably not, but for now we can continue our trek through the desert, to the sea, and beyond.

The rest of the day passed without incident as they walked until sundown. They stopped for the night and started a small fire, enjoying the cool night air. Sleep overtook them. Isabel woke to the sensation of leaves against her face, making her jump in surprise. She sat up immediately, noting that the sky was filled with an iridescent green light.

She looked at the ground, alerting Morgrin from his slumber next to her. He awoke groggy until he saw the same things that Isabel was seeing. In front of them as far as the eye could see, the desert was filled with green flowers that appeared to be glowing.

"This is new," Morgrin said. Isabel quickly jumped to her feet and let out a joyous yell as she happily skipped through the flowers. She stopped and looked at Morgrin, who was smiling at her.

"You have no idea how great this feels."

"You're right...what are these? They're beautiful."

"In Elvish, they are called *Lumaflor.* Moonflowers as I call them," Isabel said. "I wasn't fully aware that they actually existed. I've come across them in my research over the years but until now they've seemed to be just lore that might not be real. Lore says that each color has a different effect. Supposedly the green ones give you more energy, blue is supposed to cure headaches and I can't remember any more at the moment. They are a rare thing to find, and to find them in a desert of all places!"

They looked to the horizon and could faintly see other colors glowing in the distance. Each flower had nine pedals, all neatly arranged. They glowed brightly and seemed to sparkle and shimmer. Isabel picked one and smelled it, the scent was crisp and pure, unlike any that she had ever smelled before.

"Things are starting to make sense now," Isabel said after a while. "This is why these towns exist. They must harvest and sell the flowers." Isabel reached into her pack and pulled out the book she had taken from the burned-out village earlier in the day.

Where once the pages had been blank, now they were filled with color and life. The first page was written in the common tongue, and the words glowed like fire. All the other pages contained a language she didn't know, the words on these pages were a color she couldn't place. Seeming to change to a different color as soon as she thought she had it figured out. She handed it to Morgrin who looked at it with as much fascination and wonder as she had.

"It says that the green ones *do* give you lasting energy, like you thought," Morgrin read. "Orange; gives you a sugar rush as though you've eaten too much candy. *Yellow*, cures a headache. Purple gives you a heightened sense of merriment. Pink can heal any injury if properly boiled. Red is poisonous. The list goes on. I'm willing to bet the men who surrounded us earlier thought we were after their fields."

"I think, there's unsavory business happening in this area."

"You couldn't be more right!" A voice echoed from across the field. They looked to the sound, seeing a tall dark shape with a flowing cape and a purple ring that glowed, coming nearer to them. His identity remained veiled until he was near enough that their fire revealed his identity.

Rade.

"Let's have a seat," Rade said. "There is much to talk about!"

***

"It's been a long time," Morgrin said. "I don't think we've really seen much of you since the Sorcerer fell the first time."

"You're quite right," Rade said. "I was not as active in the second attack against the Sorcerer for reasons that must remain secret. Still, I was there and now I am here."

"How has life been treating you and how did you come to be up here?" Isabel asked. Rade studied them both curiously.

"Life has been very good to me, but the great Lathon and his son Aiden have been far more gracious than I deserve. After the Sorcerer was defeated the second time I wondered greatly what on earth I was going to do with my life. I had been trying to thwart and undermine the Sorcerer for far longer than you two could imagine and now I had nothing to do except wander the earth as a cursed soul.

"Despair would've had a strong foothold on me, but I was met in the wilderness by an old man with a great wooden staff. Our first conversation nearly drove me over the edge. He would hint at something and then say he couldn't tell me. It wasn't until the third day, with this man following me every step of the way, that I finally figured out whose presence I was in.

"Once I knew it was Lathon, I kind of let him have it. Attacked him in every verbal way that I could think of. I suppose in my drive to undermine the Sorcerer I failed to realize who had made me in the first place. Nevertheless, my anger took center stage as I accused him of conspiring to kill me, and then I demanded to know why I was made to suffer as I had for countless years.

"Still, no matter how angry I got and how frustrated I was, and how many threats I swore to harm the heir of Lathon....he didn't flinch. In fact, he hardly showed that he was surprised by my reaction. He sat there listening like I had never thought possible.

"Finally my will and my stubbornness broke like a wave upon the shore. I wept at his feet and begged for mercy and forgiveness. I didn't even care if I was healed of my 'Spiritness', I just wanted meaning. To know that I was loved. To know that I was important. That I was cherished at the level that only the creator of the universe can provide.

"The old man smiled at me and then told me that someone was coming who would be able to heal me and set me free of everything that I had been carrying around. He assured me that out of all the things I had ever done, the greatest was yet to come.

"He left and it wasn't until the dawn of the second day that Aiden showed up. I had always heard he was the heir of Lathon, but for the first time it sunk in and I marveled at the infinite genius of Lathon. I had been fighting against the Sorcerer, but I had never considered that I should be fighting with someone.

"I bowed before him and confessed every bad thing I had ever done and asked if there was any way to forgive such a person of the crimes they had committed. He smiled and said there most certainly was. A great change took over me. I was cured of my 'spiritness'. He then proceeded to tell me that I was to come up here and get acquainted with the town called *Encarta*."

"So, you're a completely normal person now?" Isabel asked.

Rade beamed. "Yes. After all these centuries I can finally live. However, with all the things that Aiden cured me of, I can still." He paused for a second and held his arm out, hand upward. A small ball of flame appeared in his hand. A moment later it vanished. "He left me with that party trick, though it has been kind of fun to amaze everyone with how well and how fast I can start a fire." They chuckled. "I suppose ultimately the ability was left to remind me of my story."

"Some people hate their story," Isabel commented.

"I hated my story for years. I walked around beating myself up for my transgressions. I now understand the difference between remembering the past but not being consumed by it."

"Well said," Isabel complimented.

"Until just today I wondered what on earth I was supposed to do up here. Encarta was destroyed and I would be lying if I said my heart was not troubled by this. Then I received a note that you had passed by our town and would be here tonight. I left at once, and came to find you here."

"Some great mystery has brought us together," Morgrin said. "Who delivered a note to you? We certainly didn't know you were here."

"I'm not sure who it was or where he came from. I was staring at the campfire and then, as if he came out of the darkness itself, he was there. *Poof!* He disappeared in about the same fashion."

"Curious."

"I have lived in this area for quite a while, I will gladly answer any questions that you have."

"Tell us everything," Isabel said, sitting forward to listen. "How about you start by telling us about Encarta and what happened there?"

"There's a nation of people called Cladhach which live in the mountains to the east. They have quite an impressive mining operation and have certainly not become poor in their exploration of the mountains. The wealth and power of the

Cladhach people has grown over the centuries and within the last five years, they have started to look to the desert. At first, it was just raiding farms and fields, but within the last year, they've started wiping out the farms and small settlements, like Encarta.

"When these thugs move into a town or near your town, you have two options. Do as they say and ask no questions, or be killed. My town stood up valiantly against them, but only a handful of us made it away. Survivors are in hiding until I give the okay. My village was destroyed because we refused to side with the thugs that do their dirty work. A man named Halar is the right-hand man of Gravv of Moki."

"I believe we had the privilege of meeting Halar earlier during the day," Isabel commented.

"What would they gain from taking over small towns and pillaging crops?" Morgrin asked.

"This desert is a prime place to grow *Lumaflor.*"

"Moonflowers," Isabel said. Rade nodded.

"It's a lucrative industry," Rade explained. "The people of the desert have become very good at it. They harvest it and sell it at the ports. The people of Cladhach, have also become very good at it. The majority of their clients are less than reputable. The Sorcerer having been among them."

"So they've been running out the locals and taking the fields for themselves?" Morgrin asked. Rade nodded.

"They've taken over nearly half of the Lumaflor fields in the past year. This desert is the perfect place because they need hardly any water to grow, and they're invisible during the day."

"Certainly this entire region must have some kind of defense?" Morgrin asked.

"People in this part of the world have been left untouched for centuries, the idea of people invading and fighting them is foreign. I've been working for some time to convince them to form an army of sorts, but it's not easy."

"Doesn't anybody see the concern?" Isabel asked.

"A few," Rade replied. "The regional governor, Ramun, has begun to see the light. He ordered walls to be built around the strongest cities and commissioned thirty warriors to be trained for each city."

"Thirty?" Morgrin asked.

"To these people, it is a lot. I was recruited to train them. They were good students, and attentive. Caught on quick. Just not many of them."

"So what do you anticipate Cladhach's next move is?"

"I know what it is, because they've already started. Gravv and a small force, of one hundred men captured the town of Nain."

"Nain's a port city isn't it?" Morgrin asked.

"Yes. By getting the port they don't have to haul the Lumaflor by cart to their cities. They can ship them directly from the city."

"Any survivors?"

"It's unclear," Rade admitted. "It was taken swiftly though. My thirty well-trained troops would've been nothing to these trained warriors. I fear they are dead."

"What of the city?" Isabel asked.

"Most likely the majority of people are alive but bound by fear and Gravv is having a run of the place."

"You want to go after Gravv?"

"I've been considering it for a couple of months. When he took Nain two days ago I knew I had to do something."

"Is that why you are here?" Isabel asked.

Rade thought.

"I think it's why *we're* here. You may not have known I was here, but I was given a note saying *you* would be. Seeing recent events, I think there's something greater at work here."

"I'm beginning to think the same thing," Morgrin said. Isabel nodded her agreement.

"You said the city has a wall right?" Isabel asked.

"Yes."

"So it's defensible if we should get it back?"

"I believe it is," Rade answered after a moment.

"If this Gravv took the city, what timeline are we looking at? No doubt after he took it he would likely have sent word for more reinforcements," Morgrin asked.

"It's a five-day trek to the mountains. If we get there in two days, we would in theory have at least three days until extra help would come. Isabel and Morgrin exchanged looks, knowing what the other was thinking.

"We're in," Isabel answered for the both of them. Rade smiled as though he had won a prize. "Do you have a plan?"

"Partially," Rade answered.

"Who is Gravv?"

"Do you recognize the name?"

"Yes."

"Good. How?"

"My former husband spoke of him often," Isabel answered.

"Good. If that's all you know he will probably have no idea who you are. Gravv is Elvish, tall and ugly. I have met him once before in negotiations with the Sorcerer. He's powerful though, darn powerful. He's got a lot of pull in the nation of Cladhach. If you're going to strike him you need to do it swiftly and silently."

"Any weaknesses?"

"Yes," Rade said with a smile. "Word of southern lands like Grimdor move very slowly if they move at all. No one in these parts could tell you where to find Grimdor. That being said...that means he doesn't know Grimdor, as he knows it, has fallen, and that's where we'll get ahead of the game."

"What's your plan?"

Chapter 9

NAIN

The next morning they left at the crack of dawn, riding by horseback and letting the Taruks fly free. The Taruks, at this point, would catch the eye of too many people if they were right about their suspicions. They now rode by horseback and made much better time. Rade had left them during the night only long enough to bring what remained of the people of Encarta.

In total, they numbered fifty as they set out across the desert. They listened and talked as the people of the town lamented about what had transpired. Finally, everyone fell into silence, lost in their thoughts.

"You okay?" Morgrin asked. Isabel nodded.

"I was just thinking this is the first time I've ever heard Rade ask for help."

"Bad or just different?"

"Different. For years I've been harboring secrets and surprising people at the opportune moments. This time however I feel like I'm the one who is in the dark."

"I'm very curious to see what we find as we go north," Morgrin replied. "As a child, I heard strange tales of the lands up north. I'm just not sure if I should believe them."

"I've heard my fair share of tales and myths as well," Isabel said.

Morgrin chuckled. "I'm sure you have."

They rode for some time, coming across another town that was decimated in the same way Encarta had been. They rode in a somber silence for the rest of the day until they made camp when the light would not allow them to go any further. Rade took the first watch and let everyone sleep.

Isabel woke suddenly, haunted by her dreams. She took a deep breath and noticed everyone else was asleep. Rade sat keeping watch, staring straight ahead.

"You okay Rade?"

Rade looked at her as if pulled out of a dream. "Yes, I'm fine. I suppose I'm just afraid."

"You afraid?" Isabel asked. Rade smiled.

"When you think about it...this will be the first time in centuries that the possibility of dying, is a possibility. Up until this point I was a Spirit, then I was a cursed Spirit and now I'm healed. I'm grateful that I am healed, please don't misunderstand, but I'm not sure what the next few days are going to be like. If I die during the battle...that's it? Nothing else?"

"I understand your fear," Isabel replied.

"How have you done it all your life?" Rade asked. "You never seem to be afraid of anything."

"If death is the end then Lathon is powerless, but it is not the end. Trust me, I've been plenty afraid, but I have found peace through Lathon."

"I wish I had your confidence," Rade said.

"Just always remind yourself that nothing is about us. Everything is for Lathon and his glory. That's why we ride into battle with courage! The end is already determined, though evil may appear to have the upper hand it will never win the war." Silence passed between them for a minute.

"I'm scared for Temperance," Rade admitted.

"Temperance? That's a lovely name," Isabel said. Rade smiled for a moment. "Who is she?"

"Ramun's daughter. I'll make it no secret that I've grown rather fond of her."

"I assume you got to know her when you were training the soldiers?" Rade nodded.

"We became good friends. Only now when I fear she may be dead do I realize just how I feel. I haven't told her any of my past, as far as being a Spirit is concerned."

"Why not?"

"I suppose I was afraid she would look at me differently if she knew.

"If she loves you even a little I'm sure she'll be more than understanding."

"I suppose," Rade said.

"Do you think we'll make it to Nain tomorrow?"

"We've made good time in our travels today, so I would suspect by noon we should arrive at our destination," Rade said. "Everyone with us is ready to do their part and hopefully we can pull off ours."

"Or die trying."

***

Isabel and Morgrin led the company slowly over the plains. The town of Nain was in the distance. Even from a distance, they could make out a few small shapes taking notice of them. Rade rode in the back of the company, with the remaining fifty people fanned out to either side.

They all wore swords at their sides and were dressed in armor that they had raided from dead soldiers in another town. Isabel took a deep breath knowing that they didn't have time to make any other plans.

Clouds had rolled in, blocking out the sunlight and casting everything in dark grey shadows. The smell of salt water could now easily be distinguished. On the north side of the town, the sea churned. Isabel breathed in deeply, a strange sense of familiarity coming over her.

Morgrin rode alongside her, munching something out of a bag. He rode beside her as if he didn't have a care in the world. A giddy smile across his face. Isabel watched him carefully for a moment.

"I'm surprised you can eat at a time like this," Isabel said. Morgrin smiled.

"I could eat these things all day," Morgrin replied, chuckling to himself.

"What are you eating?"

"The purple flowers," Morgrin replied, with a light laugh. "These are the flowers that give you energy right?" Morgrin asked holding a purple one out for her to see.

"How many of those did you eat?" Isabel asked, grabbing the bag from him. He shrugged.

"I didn't bother counting them," Morgrin answered. Trying not to laugh. "Is something wrong?" He laughed joyfully into the desert air.

"Just a little," Isabel replied. "You've just eaten a whole bag of flowers that have the power of merriment." Morgrin chuckled. "Rade!" Rade rode forward and she showed him the empty bag. Rade took one glance at Morgrin and knew immediately.

"He ate the whole thing?" Rade asked. Isabel nodded. Morgrin laughed.

"I didn't get a chance to finish!" Morgrin exclaimed.

"How are we going to pull this off now?" Rade asked. "For this to work I can't be on the front lines."

"We'll have to improvise. Morgrin!" Morgrin looked in her direction. "You are not to speak to anyone and please don't laugh!" Morgrin laughed uncontrollably for a moment before getting a hold of himself.

"I'll try," Morgrin said, looking as though he was trying to hold back more laughter.

"Lathon help us!" Isabel exclaimed.

Horses rode from the gates of the city. Rade slipped to the back and Morgrin sat up trying to look more pulled together than he was. They were met moments later by a group of twenty horsemen. Behind them, on the city walls, they could see archers watching and awaiting orders.

"Speak now your name and your business!" the horsemen demanded. Morgrin burst out laughing. The horsemen exchanged looks, suddenly seeming unnerved.

"I come representing the people behind me, and the people of every other town that you have butchered. I seek the head of Gravv of Moki on a platter," Isabel declared. The guards laughed at them. Morgrin also joined in their laughter, unable to contain himself.

"Come back another day," the horsemen taunted. "We cannot fulfill your request, but we could send Gravv your head couldn't we?"

"That we could," another of the horsemen jeered. Isabel lunged forward and punched the man in the neck. He fell off his horse, grasping his throat. No one else moved. The soldier stood up and sputtered loudly.

"Perhaps I didn't make myself clear!" Isabel said more forcefully. "You thugs have secured and emptied the land, but you have not looked beyond your borders. I assure you that in less than one hour, a legion of soldiers will arrive and take this city from you! Now you will lead us into the city and take us to Gravv do you understand?"

The leader took a moment, before finally agreeing. A messenger came forward.

"What name shall I give my lord?"

"Isabel of Grimdor! I come under the authority of Rohemir of Grimdor, now see it done!" The man cowered at the names and the tones in which they had spoken. A messenger was sent into the city. A dozen soldiers surrounded them until the messenger returned and stood before them.

"Lord Gravv is more than ready to welcome you as a guest of Grimdor," the man said. "But he will speak only with Isabel of Grimdor. Is this agreed?" They nodded and they were escorted into the city. Isabel dismounted her horse. Rade had pulled his horse up next to hers.

"Be careful," Rade whispered.

"You too. Be ready for anything and keep your eyes open." Rade nodded. Morgrin erupted in laughter. "And please make sure my husband behaves himself the best that is possible seeing the situation and makes it out alive should something go wrong."

"I'll do my best."

She turned and strode to the guide who then proceeded into the building. Immediately they turned to the left and walked for a couple hundred feet before they reached a heavy wooden door. The door was opened and they entered into a darkened room with only a fireplace for light.

Isabel puzzled over the fire burning in the great fireplace. The air was far from cold and to her, it seemed warm, muggy, almost to the point of being uncomfortable. A large desk was sitting at the far end of the room. In the seat behind, a broad-armed elf with long flowing white hair awaited her. He smiled as she was escorted in, giving Isabel pause for just a moment.

"We finally meet!" the elf exclaimed. "My name is Gravv and it's an honor to meet you."

120

"The honor is all yours," Isabel said, slightly taken back by the friendliness of his greeting.

"Please come and sit, I can send for a cup of tea, or anything you'd like. I own the town, so literally you can have anything you want." He chuckled to himself and Isabel struggled to remain in character and stay composed. "I was told nearly a week ago that you were traveling through the desert and I hoped that you would pay me a visit if you were in the area."

"You knew I was coming?" Isabel asked.

"Of course I did. You, as well as your husband, cannot possibly come this far north without half the vagabonds and lowlifes who wander this country running for the hills."

Isabel pondered his words, wondering what they meant. Somehow everyone seemed to know that they were coming. Now, Gravv seemed to indicate that he thought she and Rohemir were coming. Either she was being played or Gravv truly didn't know anything that had transpired in the past decade.

"The very nature of your arrival has me intrigued. You say you come with the authority of Rohemir, but what brings you so far north? I haven't seen Rohemir in well over a decade, and in all those years I never knew him to send a woman to do his bidding."

"I came seeking to help those you've chased out of their towns."

"Chased is such an ugly term," Gravv replied. "The way I see it is...they broke the deal. The deal when I move into any town is that the people answer to me and me alone. If they break that trust I can't afford to have them around. It's not a very happy thing, but it's what must be done if order is to be kept. I'm sure you understand."

"I understand completely." Isabel paused. "I cannot say that I disagree with your tactics either. The problem of the matter is that Rohemir and I were planning our own excursions into this far northern wasteland and you have now ruined our prospects and vision."

"If I had known that Rohemir was planning anything of the sort no doubt I would've stayed away," Gravv said, thinking for a moment. "As it is, it is far too late to reverse my plans now. I have my fields clearly marked and they will be planted by tomorrow. You must understand that to move mature Lumaflor is no easy task and therefore I am unlikely to do it again."

"Perhaps I wasn't clear! You can and you will remove your presence from this forsaken place or Rohemir himself will come and remove you, and he is likely to come destroy all your other fields out of spite."

"Would Rohemir really seek out a war?" Gravv scoffed.

"What war would there be?" Isabel asked. "Grimdor has fallen, it is simply him versus you. What it would come to then is brute force. If you think your men are so great because they can kill defenseless women and children then, by all means, try our hand. But you will only find yourself joining your followers in a shallow grave."

"You speak boldly; almost too boldly. I was not aware that Grimdor had fallen," Gravv said, seeming to think and choose his words more carefully. "At any moment I can call for aid from the Cladhach Mountains. If Grimdor truly has fallen as you say then what can you possibly have up your sleeve to deter me from my plans?"

"Rohemir suspected you might say that. He sends me with a rather valuable resource, which he said would help you change your mind." Isabel pulled out the notebook she had picked up in Encarta.

"I've never seen that notebook in my life."

"I believe you," Isabel said. "But in this matter. it is important to remember who *could* read the book?" Isabel paused, noting the concern that was beginning to appear in his eyes.

"Do you know what this book is? Of course, you don't. But Rohemir and I do. For a number of years now we've had people following you, some of them right in your ranks. They have carefully cataloged everything you have done here and abroad for the past five years. All your crimes, all your sins. It also provides detailed instructions on where to find you and anyone associated with you."

"You're bluffing," Gravv said.

"Try me." Gravv reached for the book. Isabel pulled it away. "That comes with a price."

IDOLS & TRINKETS

"I suppose that price is me leaving the town?" Gravv asked Isabel nodded. Gravv settled back into his chair for a moment or so, stroking his beard. "I would like to make a counteroffer, one that I have no doubt Rohemir would approve of. Please come this way." Isabel stood and they exited the building. They entered a tunnel and after a few minutes came out on the shores next to the ocean.

"Feast your eyes my lady, on a sight that would truly impress Rohemir, or for that matter any ruler of any nation of the earth," Gravv exclaimed. The shoreline in front of them was covered with large cages each one filled with a Taruk. "Is this not an impressive sight?" Gravv asked again.

"Among my other trades and interests, I have spent much time in the realm of Taruks. I have finally figured out the secrets and mysteries of Taruks and their breeding. I know what you are thinking! I know the eggs aren't supposed to hatch unless the Taruks likes the person, but I have discovered many methods and ways to force the Taruks to hatch whenever *we* want. I humbly suggest that you and Rohemir join my promising industry and split the profits, fields, and Taruk's alike."

"This is most certainly something that Rohemir would approve of!"

"Of course agreeing to this enterprise would mean that I will be staying in control of Nain."

"And I suppose you want the journal?" Isabel said holding it in plain sight.

"As a sign of our peace and partnership, I would like you to destroy it right now. I would gladly welcome Rohemir to this city as a prince would be welcomed into his castle."

"Then I believe we have a deal," Isabel said. They shook hands and he handed her a candle and the book was promptly burned without Gravv even looking to find out that there was nothing inside.

Gravv smiled. "I am glad to have a new business partner! Let alone the famous Isabel and the infamous Rohemir. I'm sure the three of us will get along perfectly. Now let us go and talk over finer matters in great detail."

***

Rade stayed in his place at the back of the procession, his instincts telling him something was wrong. A few people peered at them through their windows, but everywhere else in the city, it was completely silent. Even the wind had stopped. The guards stood without speaking, staring intently as if trying to bore holes into their heads. The only sound that could be heard anywhere in the city was Morgrin sitting at the head of their company, quietly chuckling to himself.

Rade grew restless as the seconds passed into minutes. The silence was broken by the sound of a guard cautiously approaching from the rear.

Rade turned to see a man dressed in a Cladhach uniform. Rade noted that the soldier was one of the thirty men he had trained. He gave a nod to Rade who did not return the gesture for fear of being seen. The man came alongside Rade, who was still atop his horse.

"Rade," the soldier whispered. "What's going on?"

"Trying to get the city from Gravv," Rade whispered. "Be ready for anything. And can you get our laughing friend up here something that will clear it up?" A few minutes later the man returned with a flask and slipped it into Rade's saddle bag.

"What now?" the soldier asked.

"Wait for our signal."

The guards stepped away and Rade casually grasped the flask and undid the top. He sniffed it and was pleasantly surprised to find that it smelled good and that he knew what the mixture was. He carefully moved his horse to the front, not looking any guard in the eye as he pulled up next to Morgrin.

"Thirsty Morgrin?" Rade asked. Morgrin burst out in a fit of laughter, which lasted longer than he would have liked. "Here, drink this!" Morgrin took a drink from the flask. He screwed up his face and blinked hard as though he was waking out of a dream. He looked at Rade, questions filling his eyes.

"I'm not quite sure what came over me," Morgrin said.

Rade smiled. "Tales for another time. Good to have you back. Stay alert, something's not right."

"Where's Isabel?"

"With Gravv, or so I think," Rade said. "He has not shown himself yet." They fell silent, watching, listening, and waiting for something to happen.

Several minutes passed, putting them all on edge.

"Rade?" Rade looked in Morgrin's direction. "It seems my mind is a little clearer now."

"And what are you thinking?" Rade asked.

"How is your skill with a sword?" Morgrin asked. "I think it's time that we use them." Without speaking Morgrin drew his sword, causally appearing to admire the blade. The guards watching them shifted uneasily, glancing over their shoulders. He laid the sword across his lap. Morgrin looked directly at the Cladhach soldier in front of him.

"Every person puts their faith in something. They may say that they don't, but that's hardly the truth is it? For when you put that faith to the fire, to test it...their true colors are revealed for everyone to see. A person can change their colors but it takes work, which sadly some people never want to invest in.

"What I'm asking you son is what side are you on? There comes a time when everyone has to choose. I know Gravv has threatened you greatly, and I cannot guarantee that if you help us you will live. But in the end...the real end, when the sorrows of this world fade to dust and every hint of sadness seems like a fading memory; when you stand before the very presence of Lathon...how will your choices be seen? Will you live in fear or stand boldly for what is right and good, regardless of the circumstances?"

"I have never heard of this Lathon," the soldier said, looking at the other men. Rade noticed each of them standing taller than they had been, already giving them hope. The soldier moved close to both of them and then looked around at his comrades receiving nods.

The soldier looked back to Morgrin and in a whisper said "Let this be the hour we draw our swords together!"

**

Isabel followed Gravv, who now walked briskly. They walked down a large flight of stairs and entered the streets. Morgrin and everyone else still stood in the street. At the moment Rade was nowhere to be seen.

"Listen up all you filthy dogs!" Gravv yelled, sure to be heard by anyone. "I have myself a new business partner and I am putting her in charge for a couple of days. If you think I'm a piece of work, just know that this woman is far worse! She has my full authority to do whatever she pleases, in the manner that she chooses to do it in." Silence followed but all the guards could be seen nodding their reply.

Gravv moved ahead of her but turned back to face her.

"If you have any problems with these rats feel free to throw them to the Taruks. Taruks do love to eat."

Gravv turned and began walking towards a horse that was waiting for him. He grabbed the reigns but was never able to mount as Rade cried out and charged his horse directly at Gravv.

Gravv was promptly tackled to the ground as Rade leapt from his horse. Gravv threw Rade off and jumped to his feet. Within seconds Gravv was flailing on the ground, having been struck in the gut by a woman's heel. She was a young elvish woman with long red hair.

None of the guards in the city moved to defend their leader. Instead, they watched, with a look of indifference on their face. Gravv cried out but never got a chance to do anything further as Rade jumped on top of him. Rade pulled something small and purple from his pocket.

His fist struck Gravv and the world vanished. They were blinded by a flash of purple light. Thunder rumbled and smoke rapidly spread through the entire city, moving between buildings.

When the smoke cleared it became evident that Gravv was dead. Rade lay several feet away, his eyes vacant and his body rigid. The young elvish woman stooped over him.

Isabel joined the woman at Rade's side as she frantically searched for a pulse, while Isabel searched his body for the cause of whatever had just happened. The people, who suddenly found themselves unafraid, cautiously came to watch.

"Can you do anything to help him?" the woman asked. Isabel looked at her sorrowfully.

"I can do many things, but I cannot stop death," Isabel admitted. The woman burst into tears, lost in her sorrow. An hour passed and she refused to leave

Rade's side. Isabel motioned everyone away while she tried to comfort the woman.

"What's your name?" Isabel asked. The woman looked up and wiped the tears from her eyes.

"Temperance," the woman answered.

"He mentioned you before we came." Temperance's expressions softened. "How long have you known him?"

"I met him a couple of months ago and we had become very good friends. To say that I hadn't hoped for something more would be a lie. He had a kind soul, and only now when death is between us do I begin to understand how much of my heart he had captured."

"I have no doubt you have the same heart that he did. The heart of a servant." Temperance smiled and nodded. A few more minutes passed as they talked.

"I'm not doing that again!" a voice exclaimed. Both of them jumped back. They watched in disbelief as Rade slowly began to stir. He groaned and tried to sit up. Temperance rushed to him, looking as white as a ghost. He leaned into her embrace.

"How is this possible?" Temperance asked.

"Take this!" Rade said, hastily pulling a glowing purple ring from his finger. Isabel reached out and grabbed it, inspecting it carefully. Her hands trembled as she looked at the trinket.

"Is this what I think it is?" Isabel asked, almost in a whisper.

Rade nodded.

"You have a Gagnsae ring?" Isabel asked in disbelief.

"Never thought I would use it."

"You were dead!" Temperance exclaimed. Isabel could see the conflict in her eyes as she wasn't sure whether to express sorrow or joy.

"I was," Rade said. "But now I am alive. By the power of Lathon, I am alive."

"So if you were dead, what did you see?" a soldier asked.

"Let me rest first. Then I will explain many things."

With Gravv gone, everyone else who had been a supporter of his pledged an oath of loyalty to the elders of the town and were given a clean start. Within an hour they sent armed soldiers throughout the desert, ridding the area of any last supporters of Gravv.

Slowly the the town of Nain began to pull itself back together and mourn those that had been lost under the tyranny of Gravv. The city was repaired and presentable in record time.

At Isabel's suggestion, the entire town threw a small celebration to remember their victory. It was nothing fancy, everyone brought whatever they had to eat. They arranged some torches in the town square and several people brought out musical instruments of various types.

Rade joined the party too, though he was still weak after everything he had been through. For the night he seemed content to be where he was, which was something that Isabel hadn't seen in him before. He smiled happily, seeming to take joy in Temperance who was quite determined to help him in any way she could. When the day was done everyone drifted off to sleep, while Isabel sat up late, reading her map with wonder and excitement.

The next morning Morgrin and Isabel found Rade sitting by the fireplace in the chamber they had been given. He had a dark blue blanket wrapped around him. His eyes smiled at them as they came and sat down across from him.

"You're looking better," Isabel commented. Rade smiled.

"Better yes, but not good," Rade replied. "I still feel weak and frail."

"You're alive though," Morgrin said. "Despite the situation, I'd say you're nothing short of a miracle."

"It is truly a humbling thought that I died."

"What did it feel like?" Morgrin asked. "Surely you must have known something had happened to you."

"I did," Rade said. "But death did not feel like how I thought it would. In an instant, I had gone from the desert to a place so beautiful I could never describe it. The veil of this world was torn off and I saw things far beyond the imagination. Merely standing there brought me to my knees. After what felt like only a moment I heard a voice talking to me, saying that my time was not yet done on this earth. Then I woke up."

"Incredible," Morgrin said. Rade nodded.

"After this, I have no doubt in my heart about the words of Lathon or his promise of life after death. Though they seem silly to others around the world, how can I deny that which I've already experienced?" They fell silent, each of them lost in their thoughts.

"How did you get the ring?" Isabel asked. "Best research I have says these rings are easily three thousand years old."

"I've been many places and done many things. I took the ring into my care long ago. The ring was made by evil hands. The ring can only destroy-"

"Shapeshifters," Isabel said. Rade nodded. "How did you know he was a shapeshifter?"

"His eyes. Shapeshifters have triangular pupils," Rade said with a chuckle. "I'm just glad he didn't have time to shapeshift."

"How does it destroy them?" Morgrin said.

"Shapeshifters are not natural, it's something they create within themselves. It's far too dark and twisted for me to care to explain further. That being said when the ring touches the blood of a shapeshifter, it uses the very evil that they used to turn form, against them. Evil cannot stand evil. A house divided against itself cannot stand. Which is why he disappeared. The ring more or less, traps victims inside."

"So now I'm the proud owner of a strange dark ring? You gave this ring to me?" Isabel asked. "What do want me to do with it?"

"In all my years, which are plenty, I've never been able to be rid of it. Destroy it if you can. If you can't or don't have time for it, there are numerous caves along the coast. They already have many interesting things in them, one more certainly won't hurt." They fell silent. Temperance quietly slipped in and moved to Rade's side.

"How are you feeling this morning?" Temperance asked.

"Better, but not quite back to myself yet."

"I'll help you with anything." He smiled at her. Just then a young man popped his head into their tent.

"My lady, the assembly wishes to speak with you."

Temperance sighed heavily and turned to leave but Rade grabbed her hand.

"What is it, sir?" Rade asked.

"My Lady's father was killed by Gravv. We are without a leader. We were going to nominate her to be our new Governor."

Isabel watched Temperance carefully, noting anxiety and fear were all over her face.

"Please give us a minute," Rade said. The young man withdrew and he looked Temperance in the eyes.

"Are you afraid my dear?"

"Yes," she answered. "I'm not my father. I know nothing about running a city, let alone a country."

"Let me help you."

"How?"

"I've lived a long time, and have lived through far worse than what we faced yesterday. Let me speak to the assembly and see what I can do. Just give me a moment with Isabel and Morgrin and then I will go with all of you."

She smiled and embraced him. When she left Isabel turned to Rade.

"She seems like quite a fine young woman," Mogrin said.

Rade tried to hide a smile. "Yes, she is."

"I could see a fine marriage to a woman like that."

"I have never really considered marriage before this," Rade said. "But perhaps there may be something to pursue."

"I've seen her eyes," Mogrin said. "There's definitely something there."

Rade looked into the fire, losing himself in his thoughts.

"What's your plan?" Morgrin asked.

"To help keep everyone alive. The three of us have lived long enough to know what the city of Nain will be up against in the coming days, but these people don't have a clue."

Together the three of them joined Temperance outside the tent, heading off to where the assembly was gathering.

Chapter 10

THE HALLS OF JERMIN

Drake and Rachal both fell into an uneasy sleep and didn't wake until the sound of horns bellowed through the air. Hooves thundered over the ground and within a few seconds Drake, and Rachal had jumped to their feet and searched the horizon for their visitors. The other men jumped up, drawing their swords.

"Stand down sailors!" Drake commanded. "Do not fear these men just yet! They gave us warning, let us give them a chance."

"I'm the captain!" Barnabas cried, getting to his feet. "Defend yourselves, men!" Barnabas gave a great cry and sprinted out into the field in front of them, sword in hand. Many of the other men gave a great cry and followed their captain, the rest stood with Drake and Rachal.

"He's a rather rash person isn't he?" Rachal asked.

"So I'm learning."

More horns bellowed through the air from in front of them, but there were also answering horns from behind. The horsemen clashed with Barnabas and his crew.

Drake and Rachal looked behind, seeing a group of nearly fifty horsemen behind them. They circled Drake and his group and once they saw that Drake wasn't going to raise any challenge, half of the men left to aid the other group in their defense. Within a couple of minutes the challenge Barnabas had mounted, failed and their weapons were taken away and all of them were forced to start a slow, defeated walk back to Drake and Rachal.

"You are a rash people! We offer you peace and you repay us in steel. Perhaps we should give you a taste of your own steel and watch you beg for mercy!" A man rode through the ranks, his horse taller and seemingly more proud than the others. He wore a helm which was colored blue. His armor was the same with a white mountain over a moon engraved on the front. A few of the men riding with them carried flags and banners with the same symbols. Some of the horsemen also bore white flags

"You must forgive my Captain," Drake said. "He seems to have been at sea for so long he's forgotten how to behave in public!" Barnabas winced as the man's eyes pierced him and then turned to Drake.

"You speak with authority above your captain? Audacious or foolish I cannot yet guess," the man said. "Nonetheless your Captain's actions were not wholly a surprise, it is our custom as a nation to slay uninvited guests without question."

"A bit harsh don't you think?" Rachal asked.

"It is clear you do not know the ways of the forests. This piece of land is split between us and those that are far more dangerous than we are. We do not take chances. However, in this matter, we came first to seek you and then determine whether you are to be killed."

"We hope you reach a just decision," Drake said. "To whom do we speak?"

"I am Prince Afador, heir to the throne of Tuthar under my father, lord Imun, King of this land. Your fate lies at the edge of my sword. Your coming was foretold, which is why I ride with the white flag and not a quick sword. As you can see none of your men were hurt, as a token of good faith. I seek a man named Drake Thomas of Merisyll and his wife. If I'm not mistaken I believe I have found them."

"You have indeed my Lord," Rachal said.

"Mr. Thomas and his wife are to come with me for questioning and other matters. The bulk of my men will stay with the crew and your captain. When the high tide comes they will help you sail what's left of your ship to the Caves of Feitlen on the North side of the island. There your ship will be mended and repaired the best we can. Any failure to comply with these commands, or any attempt to slay my men and your own will suffer in acts of self-defense."

"How do we know this isn't just some elaborate trap?" Barnabas asked.

"You have a skeptical heart," Afador replied. "In anticipation of this request,

I have the following."

Afador motioned to his men, and a young woman with long tangled brown hair was removed from a horse. A young man was also brought down off a horse. Their hands were tied and they looked no older than the age of ten.

"These are my children, which you are to hold as captives until I return Drake and his wife to you. Keep them well and do not harm them, or else there will be severe consequences. If I fail to return Mr. Thomas and his wife then you may kill my men and do with my children as you see fit." Some of the crew started to raise their voices but Drake held up a hand.

"This is their soil, it is their right to set the terms," Drake said. "We will gladly come with you and no harm will be done on our part." Drake looked towards Barnabas who was clearly angry. "Give me just a minute to speak with my captain before we depart."

"Yes of course," Afador said. His men drew their horses back as everyone huddled close to Drake and Barnabas.

"I don't like this!" Barnabas said. "We don't have a clue who they are."

"No, but they said that our coming was foretold, which means it is out of intrigue that they likely wish to speak with us," Rachal said. "Have a little faith, Barnabas. It'll be alright."

"Faith I have. It just doesn't seem as if I have as much as you. What's to be done with his children, if they *are* his children?"

"Treat them as if they are and even better. Do not give us a bad name. Everyone must show them the most respect that they can muster, or else they are to not speak at all," Drake said.

The men within earshot shook their heads in agreement and Drake knew that they would be true to their word. Without speaking another word Drake and Rachal walked away from the group and to the two horses that had been previously occupied by Prince Afador's children. The children were led forward where they were welcomed by Barnabas and the crew.

The prince turned and spurred his horse forward, leaving his children to watch him ride away. Drake and Rachal followed everyone else, soon surrounded by ten of the horsemen.

IDOLS & TRINKETS

Two hours passed before they reached the nearest landmark. No one had spoken in that time but Drake and Rachal had observed enough to make a few educated guesses.

Out of all the men that were riding in the company the only one who had looked in their direction at all, was the prince himself. As the ride had continued they had gotten the impression that Drake and Rachal were feared by many of the men that were with them.

At one spot they had passed through what had turned out to be a narrow pass in the forest. A large gully, with a small stream and trees towering on either side of them. Even in that moment Drake and Rachal had both sensed a presence that weighed their spirits down and seemed to bring thoughts of despair and hopelessness. The riders that were around the prince doubled during that stretch, which probably lasted no longer than ten minutes, but felt like an eternity.

Once they left the trees, the spirits of everyone were lifted and the sun shone on them brightly as they continued on their way. They had traveled inland, leaving the shore far behind. They passed through countless villages and towns, the people listening to the Herald who issued a command to make way for Prince Afador.

After a while, they stopped at the base of a large lone mountain in the middle of a great plain. The mountain was covered with trees, but unlike the forest they had passed through earlier, this forest didn't dampen their spirits despite their hearts warning them there was danger.

"The trees of the forest are strange here," Rachal said. "They're familiar to me."

"How so?" Drake asked. A few of the men turned their heads.

"I've heard of these trees before. They're called Imartis Trees. In the springtime, they would be covered in flowers from trunk to limb."

"Sounds beautiful," Drake said.

"Deadly. Their flowers are poisonous."

"How do you know about this?" Drake asked, noticing the men looking at them and listening closer to their whispering.

"Enya spoke of them," Rachal finally answered. "This is a dark island."

"There are many dark things on this island," one of the guards said in a whisper. "But take some advice and do not mention the name you just spoke in front of the prince."

"Our apologies," Drake said. "We are in a strange land and don't know much about it."

"You won't get in trouble from me," the guard said. "But others may be quick to turn you in for any reason they could find, true or false."

"Who do I have the honor of speaking with?" Drake asked. The man straightened, suddenly tall and proud.

"I am Remus of Jermin. Lieutenant of the Circle Guard of Prince Afador."

"Pleasure to meet you." Drake and Rachal both shook his hand. "Is it okay to talk? I haven't heard anyone speak a word since we left the coast."

"It is custom to ride in silence when we're not in a city or village. Spies could be everywhere and we must be cautious in these dark days. We are nearing the city, and we are away from the main party a little bit, speaking a quiet conversation is permitted at this point."

"Why are we stopped?" Drake asked.

"You must perform a ritual to the gods if you are to pass through the tunnel of Gewnik."

"Dare I ask what it is?" Drake asked again. Remus shook his head.

"I will not speak of it, it is detestable in every way. Unfortunately, it seems all the gods require such rituals."

"If the ritual is that detestable, I hold little faith in the god it supposedly honors. Don't you agree?"

"It is not safe to speak of such heresy among others," Remus said, whispering and leaning in close. "But to foreigners, I would say that I would agree with that sentiment. Already your presence brings something that I've never felt before. The other men feel it too. It is plain to see in the way they are carrying themselves, though they will not speak of it."

"Why not?" Rachal asked.

"We are a proud people, who take pride in self perseverance. In addition, it is punishable by death to denounce, privately or publicly, any of the gods." A few of the men suspiciously glanced in their direction.

"What can you tell us of Tuthar?" Rachal said in a whisper.

"I fear I have said too much already. People will grow suspicious if I speak with you anymore at the moment. I must apologize but I hope you'll understand once we're in the city."

They said no more and let the silence linger, instead choosing to study their surroundings and watch the men more closely. Although they were believed to be in a place of safety, none of the men looked relaxed. Instead, they looked worn and traveled, wearied with age as though it was all the strength and energy they could muster to stand.

The prince and several dozen of the men disappeared into an archway that was carved into the side of the mountain. During the time that they were in there, no one spoke at all. The entire company was silent as if they were waiting to head to their deaths.

Drake and Rachal listened and observed as hard as they possibly could. Rachal closed her eyes and seemed to be feeling pain of some kind. Drake moved closer to comfort her. He went to speak but Remus held up a hand, signaling that they should remain quiet.

An hour passed until finally everyone returned to the camp and seemed satisfied with whatever had happened in the mountain. Within a minute the order was given and they mounted their horses and galloped into the mist.

The path started wide but soon became narrow and steep, starting to climb its way up the side of the mountain. They rode two abreast as they climbed higher and higher, following the ever-winding trail.

At times it rose steeply and at other points, it would drop suddenly for a couple hundred feet. Now and again they would turn into the mountain, following a well-carved tunnel for about a thousand feet before they would return to the side of the mountain.

As far as Drake could see there was no particular reason the path would have to veer off like it did, but it happened again and again as they rode for nearly two hours. Prince Afador reached for his belt, pulled a golden horn, and let a loud clear note ring out. An answering horn echoed from somewhere in front of them.

Now and again the prince would blow on the horn again, and the horn would be answered by another. Drake and Rachal grew nervous as time wore on. By now the path had climbed nearly six hundred feet and was steadily becoming steeper and narrower.

They came to a sharp turn in their trail and they once again passed into a tunnel. This one was bigger than the previous tunnels and had a rock bottom on it, making every step the horses took seem like the loudest noise they had ever heard. Finally, the heralds took their positions and blew loudly on their horns. A dozen horns blared their response.

The light grew at the end of the tunnel, until finally they rode out of the darkness and into light, which was now a warm sunshine. They entered onto a long stone bridge that towered over a valley below, leading them towards a great city in the distance.

The city was built on either side of the valley, and all the buildings, streets, and structures were made out of stone. Drake and Rachal were mesmerized, unsure if the city had been built out of rock or if the rock had been built out of the city. A swift river rushed through the gorge below them, dividing the city down the middle.

Mist from the gorge and a great waterfall on the north side of the city floated through the air. The sunlight sparkled on all the droplets and off the bridge and walls of the city. The bridge and the walls of the city looked like they were on fire with crystals as they reflected the sunlight, illuminating the valley further. The company slowed to a walk as more horns announced their arrival.

"Welcome to the city of Jermin," Remus said in a hushed whisper. The large gates at the end of the bridge opened and at once they were joined by fifty other riders.

Drake and Rachal studied their new surroundings as quickly as they could but mostly found it difficult to conclude anything for certain as they didn't slow down. The city was a nation of men, with no other races found among the people. They entered the city, turning to the north and heading along the raging gorge that separated the two sides. Their attention was pulled towards nooses that hung over the side of the railing, each of them with a mangled and deranged body rotting.

A few minutes later they turned to the left, leaving the water behind. Everyone brought their horses to a halt at a large gate, built of bronze and gold.

The prince spoke in their own language and the doors were opened. They swiftly passed through the gate and the massive courtyard that lay before them.

The courtyard was arranged into rows, with large monuments in between all the rows. As they walked Drake and Rachal became aware that these were their gods. Some of them looked human, while others still had three heads or tongues of a snake.

When Drake thought that he could look no more, he lifted his eyes, noticing a small monument built directly in the middle of the large courtyard. It bore no image or name. As they passed it by, only one piece of writing in a language Drake couldn't read could be seen on the great monument.

At length, they exited the expansive courtyard and rode through another street, this one lined with great mansions and houses. Slowly the street began to rise as they turned towards the gorge. They reached another set of gates and were immediately ushered through.

They entered into a courtyard that spanned the entire gap of the valley. Below them, the water churned and noisily made its way through the valley. To their left a large palace stood, rising high above everything else. The prince stopped and dismounted, and everyone else followed suit.

The prince vanished inside with a couple of the captains and Remus followed. The rest of the men slowly dissipated, leading their horses to tunnels that led to underground stables. Remus reappeared at the stairs and came down to them.

"It is my orders to lead you to your sleeping quarters for the night. You are to be given anything that you ask for and I am at your disposal. We may talk more freely now if we so choose. Please follow me."

They both followed as they entered the large doors, which were noisily pushed inwards by three of the guards who were nearby. Inside, the light of the world was blocked out. Curtains were drawn over all the windows, leaving only a few torches to illuminate the vast hall they were in.

The floor was made out of a strange red tile, dull and worn from years of use while the walls of the palace seemed to alternate between brown and black stones. Heaviness fell on Drake and Rachal, their spirits quickly became depressed and weary.

Drake looked to the shadows, thinking he saw strange cloaked shapes at every corner, watching them as they passed. He looked harder, his mind coming alive and perceiving things clearer than he had moments before. Drake stared through the darkness into the eyes of the beasts and creatures that lurked in the shadows.

As if in response to him, or to something greater than him, each of the shadows seemed to cringe and then whither further away. It happened on every corner that they were led by.

They both watched Remus, noting that he seemed to not see or sense the figures in the corners. Still, as each one withered away into the darkness, they could see that Remus was standing a little straighter as if relieved of some great burden that he didn't know he had been carrying.

Doors were opened on their right. They entered into a large spacious room, the roof of which was made of glass. The walls were dark gray, with small flecks of crystals every so often. Furnishings were made of polished wood and the floor was made of white stone. A large fireplace roared in the corner

"These are to be your quarters while you are here," Remus said. "I know you might not like to stay long but early reports about your ship and its conditions say that it may take two weeks to fully repair the ship. Your ship and all its crew have arrived at the Caves of Feitlen an hour ago. We will gladly escort you there tomorrow so that you can see your captain and crew, as I'm sure you are eager."

"What is to happen now?" Rachal asked.

"I will have seamstresses sent to take all of your measurements. While here, your entire crew will be clothed in the finest fabric that we have available. Whatever you wish shall be done. If there are any specific colors or symbols you wish to have on them it will also be done. You may stay here or linger anywhere on this floor of the building. It is requested that you not go to any other levels at this time."

"Certainly, we can respect that," Drake said.

"At supper, we will send for you. The prince wishes to see you both accompany him afterward to his private dwelling where he hopes to have further discussions."

"Thank you for everything," Drake said, shaking Remus's hand. Remus smiled.

"Thank you, Mr. Thomas. Already the air seems to have cleared a little bit, though I know not why it is."

"I hope soon things become even clearer than you say they are," Drake replied. Remus and his men turned and exited the room, closing the doors behind them.

"What are you thinking Drake?" Rachal asked, moving to the only window in the room. It looked out over the courtyard and to the mountains beyond.

"I'm thinking, spending a few weeks here may be a very interesting experience. I've lived in Avdatt for years, which is known to have a few different *gods* that they worship, but never have I seen a place with this many, nor a place with this dark of a presence over it. The spirit of the Sorcerer has had a hold on this city for many years. I think your leading on the ship was right. We are supposed to be here, but to what end and for what length of time? I'm not sure. I don't think this is a city built by men?"

"What makes you say that?" Rachal asked.

"The level of craftsmanship of rock displayed here is far beyond the skill of men. Only Dwarves are so skilled in such things. Long ago Ellizar told me he was from Jermin, but I've seen no signs of any Dwarves as of yet."

As Remus had said, seamstresses came and took all their measurements and requests, hoping to have the garments finished in time for the evening supper. They left, leaving Drake and Rachal to be by themselves. Soon after, attendants came and offered them food and drink, which they gladly accepted.

Two hours passed and they grew restless. Occasional footsteps were heard and sometimes they imagined faint whispers spoken in the hall outside, but none ever entered the room. Rachal took to pacing nervously and staring ahead.

"Something's making me uneasy!" Rachal said. "I wish these people would just come in instead of stand outside and do nothing!" Drake thought for a moment, a feeling of dread coming over him.

"I don't think there's anyone out there," Drake said. "When we were led here I imagined I had seen dark shapes lurking in the halls of this fortress. Perhaps I wasn't imagining, but instead seeing something that isn't supposed to exist?"

"Like Spirits?"

Drake nodded. "Something like that, agents of the Sorcerer. He may not be physically here but Aiden was sure that his spirit would prove all the more potent."

"So what's the best way to defeat this darkness?" Rachal asked. "I feel as if we're going to be crushed if we have to leave this room." Drake thought hard for a moment.

"Let's get some light in this place," Drake said. Drake and Rachal strode to the hallway and grasped the heavy curtains that sealed off light from the outside world. Sunshine poured in, chasing the darkness away. One by one Drake and Rachal pulled all the curtains back until the entire hall was filled with brilliant light.

Whispers echoed through the chamber. A foul-smelling wind struck them, leaving them unable to move. The light was extinguished and the curtains were blown shut by the wind. Drake and Rachal could see nothing for several minutes until finally the whispers stopped and the foul wind dispersed.

"Do you really think you're going to win this?" Drake taunted. The darkness lingered, but everything was still and silent. "You might win against us, but there's someone greater who *can* keep you at bay! You scoff at me for saying this, but your days of ruining this city are nearly at an end. You know the name that can keep you at bay. The name that will strike so much fear into your soul that at the mere mention of it, you will run for the hills. The name of Lathon is the one whom I serve."

There was silence for a moment, then followed by faint and distant speaking. In the darkness, the voice scoffed at them and insulted them in every way. Every second that passed felt like a hundred hours. Their spirits were crushed, thrown into depression in an instant.

Then a change came, a slight breeze fluttered through the air for only a moment. In that moment Drake and Rachal felt their resolve grow and their confidence increase. They stood tall and proud as the darkness pressed against their mind and souls.

A loud cry came from the darkness and they were pressed up against the wall, held there by an invisible force. Drake focused hard, able to make out shapes that were holding them. Time faded and seemed to go on endlessly, but still, their spirits remained strong, undeterred by the darkness.

A flash of brilliant light filled the hall and with it the sounds of a thousand voices crying out, as if they were a great army rushing headlong into a battle. The curtains were opened, and the darkness chased away. A strong wind swept away the foul stench that had lingered. Rachal fell to the floor, released from their captors.

Drake and Rachal both tried to clear their heads before searching the area for the person who had intervened and saved them. None was to be found. They fell to the ground and gave thanks while trying to collect their thoughts.

"This city is definitely immersed in darkness," Drake said.

"Yes, but at least now they have hope."

Chapter 11

HEALING OF HADASSAR

Time passed slowly and evening approached before they heard footsteps of any kind coming down the hall. Drake and Rachal listened intently, noting that the footsteps were coming at irregular intervals. At times they would stop for a minute, then they would go for only a few seconds before apparently stumbling over themselves.

Drake and Rachal stood and strode towards the hall, looking to their right. Remus and the seamstresses walked cautiously and looked uncomfortable with each step they took.

"Is everything okay Remus?" Drake asked. Remus jumped as though he was startled by the sound. Remus fumbled for words for a moment before getting his thoughts.

"I think so," came the reply. "Is everything alright?"

"Don't be afraid Remus. Everything is just fine," Drake said. "We just decided to let in a little light."

"How?" Remus asked, wonder in his eyes. "My father's family moved here over two hundred years ago and never in that time have we been able to keep the windows open! But now somehow in one afternoon, you have managed to do such a feat?"

"We aren't trying to cause any trouble, we apologize if we have," Rachal said. Remus broke down, tears threatening to come down his cheeks.

"You do not understand yet what this means! For this to be possible?..." His voice trailed off and for a moment he wept. Drake and Rachal gathered around him and prayed. "I'm sure you will better understand my emotions after you speak with the prince tonight."

IDOLS & TRINKETS

At that, he spoke no more about the wonder and emotion he was feeling. The seamstresses came forward with the clothes that had been made for them. To everyone's surprise, they fit perfectly.

They had been made with silk, colored dark blue with white lace trimming to compliment it. Their hair was done up and when finally they were considered presentable they left the room and followed Remus.

The sunset poured in through the windows, casting everything in brilliant orange light. The mist in the air was also illuminated, making it look like a swarm of sparks was rising all around them. They entered into the cool night air, where a large carriage drawn by two horses waited for them.

They climbed in and started through the city, passing through another gate that they hadn't noticed earlier. It was smaller than the rest but still wide enough for four horses side by side. The road on the other side gently and easily ascended upwards.

To their left, a sheer cliff fell to a large ravine where the water had churned for the last thousand years. To their right, a tall wall of rock, also sheer, rose above them.

After several minutes they reached the top and entered into a great courtyard, larger than any they had seen so far. In the distance was the citadel which overlooked the great city. They drew nearer, passing through yet another gate and several beautiful gardens.

Lamps and torches of every size lit the path as well as the gardens. Finally, they came to a stop in front of the enormous palace, which was built into a mountain. Drake and Rachal were taken aback by its beauty. Remus opened the door of the carriage and motioned them forward. They slowly made their way to the great stone doors at the head of the wide stairs.

"Don't worry Mr. and Mrs. Thomas, your Captain and crew are receiving just as much respect and care as you are tonight. You and your wife shall sit at the right hand of Prince Afador, a seat of high honor, and your crew have been clothed as you have and are also present and seated in *Ketium* Hall."

"Ketium? Isn't that a Dwarvish word?" Drake asked. Remus shrugged his shoulders.

"I'm not accustomed to learning the ways of Dwarves. Dwarves built this great city, but the last of the Dwarves left when I was a small boy. I know nothing of what has happened before then."

"You said your descendants had lived here for two hundred years. Sure you don't know anything?" Rachal asked.

Remus sighed heavily and turned to face them, taking them off the main path and out of sight of the guards at the top of the stairs.

"I know many things," Remus answered. "But there are many I wish I did not know. I will not speak of this anymore. You may ask Prince Afador after supper if you wish."

They returned to the path and climbed the stairs to the grand doors, which were promptly opened. Trumpets echoed inside and every person in the room stopped what they were doing and rose to their feet. A large pathway of black polished stone led to the front of the room, where a long table was prepared. The prince and members of his house were there, including his two children. Remus cleared his voice and the entire hall fell silent.

"Your Majesty. Lords and Ladies. It is my honor to present to you, Mr. Drake Thomas and Mrs. Rachal Thomas. Visitors and guests of the highest honor!" The trumpets blared again and everyone in the room raised their glasses and cried out.

The feast went quickly, compared to others that Drake had been to. And soon, one by one the guests started filing out, making their way to the carriages that had brought them. The prince and his children at last rose and turned to Drake and Rachal.

"We are very honored by your presence Mr. Thomas," Prince Afador started. "Please forgive me if I have seemed cold or acted strangely since you've gotten to the city. There are many things I wish to discuss with you but first please follow me to my living quarters."

They followed the prince through a large door in the wall directly behind the table they had been sitting at. They entered into a long, torch-lit passage. The only outside light was the moon which shone through small openings in the roof.

IDOLS & TRINKETS

Soon they were surrounded by darkness as they went deeper into the mountain. At the tunnel's end, they stood in a large clearing, with the roof a hundred feet above them. The air instantly became chilly and tainted with a hint of moisture.

At this point, the prince's children parted ways, led by men back to their quarters. They remained behind the prince, who walked without talking. Drake watched him closely, noticing that his steps appeared to be labored and his breathing was hard.

At length, they came into the prince's dwelling. Drake and Rachal followed Remus into the large spacious room that almost made them forget that they were in a mountain at all. A roaring fireplace was on either side of the room, and the walls were made of red polished rock, while the floor was white.

Lavish furnishings filled the room, displaying the wealth and prosperity of Jermin. Remus motioned for them to sit on a large silk sofa next to one of the fireplaces, while the prince sat across them in a large chair.

"It is truly the greatest honor I have ever beheld to sit and talk with the two of you today," the prince started. "That may sound strange when you seem to have only come to this great nation of ours by accident, but it is in every way the truth. I have told you that your coming was foretold and it most certainly is true. It was foretold two years ago by a prophet named Gerdint from this very island. Strange we thought it at first, for he often spoke of many strange things and strange faraway lands, but never before had he spoken so specifically about the time and matter of your arrival or of specific names for that matter. Even my wife had dreams about a man of great wealth coming to Tuthar.

"Great wealth?" Drake asked, taken aback. "I'm sorry Your Highness, but it seems you're going to be greatly disappointed. The wealth that I had previously acquired, I either gave away or invested." The Prince's face clouded over as though a part of his heart had died. Then a moment later it returned as if a new dawn had come in the dark chasms of time.

"Perhaps wealth was a poor choice of words. You must forgive me, for my wife is Wyn and as a result, speaks only her language. Perhaps a better phrasing in the common tongue would be 'great wisdom'. From what people of the lower levels of this city tell me, you have already done some amazing things, which quite frankly are beyond my comprehension. But enough of me for now, I'm sure you must have many questions for me, about life, the city. Any questions you have I am more than glad to answer."

"For starters what is the history of this place?" Drake asked. "I have heard of the city of Jermin on only one occasion before this and it was from a dear Dwarvish friend of mine who said he was from here?"

"You two are a most fascinating couple I must say," Afador reflected for a moment. "You are mankind and your wife is an elf, and you have a Dwarvish friend?"

"I'm only part Elvish," Rachal interjected.

"I see it in you though," Afador replied. "Strange these tidings are, for never in any of my family's history have Dwarves and Men lived in peace. My ancestors were mariners from lands long forgotten by my kin. They were employed to search the seas over for riches and new land. When my ancestors arrived here they quickly noticed this land had much to offer. When they returned to the land of my ancestors it was determined that we *should* occupy the island. For the entire month, my ancestors were scouting the island; they had found no other person to stop us.

"It was in the tenth year of King Buriius's reign that a fleet of thirty ships was commissioned, with everything that would be needed to successfully inhabit the island. A month after the fleet arrived we discovered that we were not the only people with that idea. Nearly fifty ships full of Dwarf warriors stormed the settlement. It was all but destroyed. A small handful of men escaped and they captained one boat that was not destroyed and made it back to the southern land.

"Within a year, a plan had been formed, and to make things simple we'll say that my *"grandfather"* led the entire campaign of nearly four hundred warships to the island, and stormed the beaches as the Dwarves had done a year earlier.

My grandfather was a cunning man and unknown to all but a few trusted officials, he had come up with a different attack plan. He fought not to kill all the Dwarves, he only wished for their service. They captured all the Dwarves on the island and gathered them into camps. Their gods were destroyed and our gods were established and we made them our slaves. That is why this city looks like it was something that was built by Dwarves because it was.

"The generations to the total of five thousand years passed and this great city was built. Our contact with our homeland became sparse and scattered, until finally for whatever reason they ceased entirely. There has not been a ship from our homeland since the days of my grandfather. Some say it is a curse for what we have done to the Dwarves, while others say, there is some new power ruling the seas. Either way, we are alone, as few maps of those waters exist. To make it complicated we are not alone on this piece of land, the woods are full of strange things and we must be cautious at all times.

"So my Dwarvish friend said he was from Jermin. I met him a very long way from this island. How do you explain that?"

"My father, the king, loathed the Dwarves his entire life. When he became king he executed all the Dwarves, but to show mercy, shipped all the children on one-way trips all over the world. I couldn't tell you where for I was just a young boy at the time. I've thought all along that the ships never sailed that far. But just threw their bound captives overboard. If your friend says he is from this place then perhaps he was taken to an actual city. If I ever could have the honor of meeting your Dwarf friend, then I would like to do so. I have thought for years that my father was a cruel cold hardhearted murderer. Perhaps he is, or perhaps someone acted on the Dwarf's behalf. Though I can't imagine what would have compelled him to do so."

"Is your father here now?" Rachal asked.

"No, thank goodness he is not! When I began to seriously ponder the foretelling of you coming, I needed to make sure that he was not here. He is currently away to the south on some official business. It is well understood that everyone that is seeing and interacting with you will keep quiet or else I will make sure they are quiet permanently if you understand me."

"I understand fully," Rachal said. "Forgive me for asking, but is your wife well? I sense that she isn't, for you spoke of her earlier but I haven't seen her."

"Indeed you haven't," Afador said, his face becoming softer and more tormented. "Your senses are great indeed. In fact, I do not understand them. It is in part why I believe you were sent to us. My wife has gotten deathly ill in the past two weeks. She's had a high fever for the entire time. She sweats constantly, eats little, and drinks little. She's almost always asleep. I'm afraid that she won't get better. I've sacrificed to all the gods, trying to appease them and convince one of them to remove this curse from her, but I have failed. I am at the end of myself and I do not know what else I can do."

"All due respect your Majesty-"

"Please, call me Afador. I very much wish us to be friends."

"As you wish Afador," Drake started. "I've come to believe that when a person finally comes to the place you are, the end of themselves…that is when true change and miracles happen. When you have no other choice but to trust something beyond yourself.

"As we were approaching our quarters down below, we passed through a large courtyard filled with shrines, who I'm assuming are your gods?" Afador nodded. "I quickly noticed that you are a very religious people. As I was looking, I saw a plain, almost boring-looking, shrine in the middle of the vast courtyard. I'm not familiar with your tongue so I could not read the inscription on it. What did it say?"

"I know the one you talk about," Afador answered. "In the common tongue, it reads *'to the unknown God'*."

"Tell us about it," Rachal said. "How can you have a god and not know who it is? What's the history?"

"According to lore, shortly after my people conquered the Dwarves, a great plague came over our nation. It started in the mainland, killing thousands and then it came to our shores as well. We exhausted all our options, sacrificed to all our gods and nothing would stop it. In a last effort, we had heard of a man named Epirius far to the north. He was known for having clarity and perhaps, as we thought, an idea on how to end the plague. Perhaps there was a god that we didn't know about.

"As quickly as we could manage he was brought to the mainland, and then to this island. We asked him what to do and for a day or two he didn't know.

Finally, he came to us and he said we were to take two dozen sheep and starve them for two days, then we were to release them outside the city gate.

"We did as he said. Once they were released, Epirius watched them intently. To everyone's wonder and amazement, the sheep did not run for the grass. Instead, they ran inside the city and made their way right to the middle of our vast courtyard. They lay down peacefully. Epirius concluded that it was surely a sign of an unknown god because only God could have made a hungry sheep rest instead of eating, after being starved for two days.

"My people built an altar and turned to Epirius and asked *'what name and image do we put on the altar?'* to which Epirius responded. *'I have no idea, but there is an unknown god that is at work. Sacrifice the animals on the altar, but put no further inscription.'*

"We did as he said and on the third day after we sacrificed the sheep, the plague stopped and we have never had such a plague again. All through the mainland as well as several other places around here, such alters have been built as a reminder of our great humility. Do you have any insight about such a god?" Silence lingered for a moment, Drake looked to Rachal who smiled with a light in her eyes.

"We know the God you are looking for, and he can certainly save your wife from death and do many things far greater than that," Rachal answered. Afador let out a deep breath.

"What do I have to do?" Afador replied. "I do not know the ways of your God. How am I supposed to get his attention?"

"You already have it," Drake said. "Lathon walks the earth and will hear your prayers any time of the day."

"But does he always grant you what you pray for?" Afador replied. "I cannot live without my wife?"

"He doesn't always answer your prayers, but in this case I believe I can heal your wife of her illness, hence answering your prayers," Rachal said. Afador wept for a moment and then wiped the tears from his face. "Take me to your wife, and she will be healed."

They were led through the massive dwelling place of Afador to a large and spacious bedroom in the back. A woman lay on the bed, her golden hair wet with sweat. Drake and Rachal struggled to walk into the room, feeling instantly fatigued and weighed down, the room filled with the same stench that had occupied the hall below earlier in the day. Afador hurried to his wife's side, the servants looked at the ground.

"We're sorry my lord," one of the servants said. "She's gone."

"How long has she been gone?"

"Twenty minutes." The prince wept.

"Can I sit next to her?" Rachal asked. Afador looked up at her, sorrow and regret written over his face. For a moment Drake thought Afador was growing angry as his facial expressions sharpened and became more focused. The wind swept through the window, taking the foul smell away. Afador's expression lightened and he came to himself.

"Yes you may," Afador said. He stood and moved aside and Rachal took a seat on the side of the bed. Rachal touched the woman's skin, surprised at how cold and wet it was.

"She's beautiful," Rachal said, smiling at Afador. She turned and gazed into the woman's lifeless face. The wind grew stronger but only Drake and Rachal could feel the wind that was whirling around the room. Rachal took the woman's hand. "What's her name?"

"Her name is Hadassar." The wind grew more fierce in the room. Rachal looked Hadassar in her sleeping eyes and bowed her head. The wind slowed and nearly stopped. Then a great roar echoed over the wind.

"Hadassar. In the name of the unknown God, I command you to wake and be well." Everyone listened in amazement as Rachal closed her eyes and spoke in a language that they had never heard before. A moment later she stopped and Hadassar's eyes fluttered open. Afador held his breath, watching in wonder and amazement. Rachal motioned for Afador to come and sit next to her. He did so trembling.

"My love?" Afador finally managed. Hadassar smiled weakly and looked at him.

"Many nights of darkness did I hope to hear such words again," Hadassar replied speaking clearly in the plain tongue, as opposed to the Wyn tongue she had spoken in all had all her life. Everyone else fell silent in amazement. "Now it seems that my painful sleep is over and my prayers were answered."

"Yes my love, they were. By two people that are as kind as angels, and will always have a place of honor in this house?"

"It wasn't me who healed your wife," Rachal said. "It was someone far greater."

"Tell us about him."

Chapter 12

GOVERNOR OF NAIN

Isabel and Morgrin filed into the assembly area and found a seat as Temperance and Rade both walked to the center. The assembly area was certainly not large with only enough seats for fifty people, one for each of the villages in the surrounding desert. It didn't take them long to notice that a third of the seats were empty.

Surprise showed on everyone's face as Rade stayed with Temperance even after they had reached the center of the room. Rade was now able to walk mostly on his own, though he still held a staff for support when he needed it. Together they stood before the assembly. A man dressed in a dark red robe strode to the center.

"Welcome My Lady!" the man said. "I am Umar, mediator of the assembly. I'm sorry to meet you under these conditions, but as your father has been killed, we are in need of leadership. It is your duty and right to take up his position if you so choose."

"I understand, however, I decline the position," Temperance said. The assembly gasped and murmured to themselves. "Though, if it pleases the assembly, I wish to nominate Rade of Encarta for the position." Again a murmur went through the crowd. "He may not be known to all of you, but he is the only reason any of us have lived to be here today. He is experienced in the ways of defense and war and will be better able to direct our course than I would. I choose to serve in whatever role is asked of me, but only if Rade is Governor."

For a moment there was a great commotion among all the people of the assembly as they all cried out their support in one way or another. Isabel and Morgrin studied the scene closely. Finally, Umar held up a hand to silence everyone.

"I move to make a motion-"

"All due respect Mr. Mediator, but we don't have time for motions," Rade said.

"What do you mean?"

"How many more seats would you see empty in this hall? You forget that Gravv was not just a lone man acting on his own, but a high-ranking official of Cladhach. If he suffered a defeat, it will not go unnoticed. Having met Gravv in the past, I know that if he had, by accident or on purpose, easily taken control of *any* port city he would have sent for more men to secure it and enslave its citizens."

The room became deathly quiet as everyone pondered the implications.

"I'm not asking you to appoint me Governor. I'm asking for the chance to help you stand against these vermin. I cannot guarantee victory and I cannot say we will escape as one big happy family, but if you'll let me, I will do what I can to protect you and maintain our freedom."

"What exactly are we up against?" another assembly member asked. "This kind of thinking is new to us, this you know, and now I seek to beg forgiveness for brushing you aside so much this past year or two."

"We can make a stand, but it'll take cooperation between all the villages and towns, cities."

"Everyone in the nation of Luma must come together!" another assembly member exclaimed. His voice was joined by a chorus of agreement.

"Yes, we must!" Rade agreed. "But we must also seek out the help of Dengar!"

A chaotic commotion arose from the assembly.

"Why should we seek out a nation who has not spoken with us in two hundred years?" several voices asked.

"It's easy enough to defend against a battle on one side of the city, but have you forgotten about Halar?!"Rade exclaimed. "He has killed many in Gravv's name. He will certainly show his face if he learns of this. Also what about the sea? Cladhach has a great navy that they could use to land ships on our port and infiltrate that way. If Gravv sent out word for reinforcements two days ago, then we have at most three days until they return. We will need the aid of Dengar before this is all over!"

A commotion consumed the hall and didn't die down for several minutes. Isabel and Morgrin closely watched Temperance and Rade, who both were still standing tall and resolute in their decision to do this together. Finally, Umar held a hand up and called to the assembly.

"Gentlemen! I beg of you to think not of yourselves in this!" Umar cried. "Unity will make us stand against this foe, not pointless bickering. Whether you think good or ill of Dengar, My Lord and Lady are right!"

Again commotion ensued and this time it lasted so long that Rade and Temperance joined Isabel and Morgrin on the sidelines.

"How are you doing Rade?" Isabel asked.

"I'll survive, I think," Rade said, then he leaned close to Isabel for a moment. "Though they're lucky I'm not a Spirit anymore."

She held back her own chuckle as they watched the assembly go back and forth. Finally, Umar was able to regain control.

"Perhaps, for the sake of everyone here, I might suggest a compromise? It seems a battle is imminent and we do not know what we're doing. What if we were to appoint Rade and Temperance to lead us-" The crowds started to speak but they were silenced. "But they are forbidden to seek the help of Dengar? We have but one choice...stand together with Rade and Temperance both as our leaders or trust in our own judgment and take on the storm ourselves."

Some shouts of praise echoed through and for the next ten minutes, it was a constant flurry of back and forths, yelling, interrupting. Just when Isabel thought all hope was lost the assembly allowed Umar to speak to everyone.

"If we agree on nothing else can we at least agree that we need help and these two will be the ones to help us?" The assembly fell silent, though a great number of them shook their heads in agreement. "All who choose for the appointment of Rade and Temperance to lead us say, "Aye.""

A moment of silence passed before the first of the council members voiced their approval. And then as if some kind of spell had been placed on the assembly everyone agreed with the decision.

Rade and Temperance were invited up to the center once again, but only Rade stood to speak to the assembly.

"How do we counter the Cladhach nation?" Umar asked. Rade faced the assembly.

"I require two things before I get started. I need to have Isabel and Morgrin from the southern lands given the ranks of lieutenants to assist me. They are seasoned warriors in their own rights and I need to have people in those positions that I can trust."

Umar studied the faces in the assembly. "Any objections?" When there were none he motioned for Rade to continue.

"I need all of the thirty warriors from each town to come to this city."

"But what about our homes and fields?" Some of the members asked.

"What good are they going to be if Nain falls? It is this city Cladhach wants, once they have it they will not be content until they have taken over all the villages and settlements. You will be enslaved within a week," Rade said.

The room was silent now.

"Is there any armory, ancient or new?" Everyone thought.

"I believe there is a special entrance in my father's room," Temperance said. "He always said it was to be used only in an emergency."

"Every person who is old enough to use a sword is to be trained to fight. If they are going to take this city, then they will not get it without a fight that will be remembered for years to come.

"Bring with you any supplies that could bolster our defense. Wood, Coal, Food. Those who cannot fight will be placed in the Caves of Exo five miles north of the city. I know those caves to be well stocked with provisions."

The rest of the day was filled with tedious meetings and planning. Finally, by the time supper came, everyone had come on board with Rade's plan, and all the assembly members were sent back to their respective towns.

The four of them had searched the room of Temperance's father extensively and had at last found a trapdoor beneath his bed. It led to a single staircase that went down to an armory that had been left untouched for generations. The armor was old, but it would do the trick.

They talked long into the night, warmed by the heat of the fire.

"How can we serve you Rade?" Isabel asked. He looked at them knowingly.

"I'm almost sorry I insisted that you join me. It wasn't exactly a fair thing for me to do, volunteer you for a battle you didn't create."

"Rade you know we would've helped you no matter what," Morgrin said. "We are very good at finding trouble when we're not looking for it."

They all laughed.

"This I know to be true. Morgrin I would like to place you in charge of the wall defenses."

"Consider it done."

"What can I do?" Isabel asked.

"What can you do about the ships?" Rade asked. "I'm sure Cladhach will send some naval presence to our shores. Keep in mind that I don't think we have much to defend the port. This is a shipping port, not a ship-building port."

"I understand," Isabel replied, slipping into her thoughts for a moment. "Gravv had some Taruks in crates on the shores...maybe they can be used against the ships. I've got two days, if I can get them to follow Aspen, I'm sure we can mount an offensive.

"Good. The only place that I want an attack to be possible is from straight on because we will have the advantage," Rade declared. "Temperance and I will take care of incoming supplies and people tomorrow. I'll appoint people to help with training and the fitting of armor.

"What do you wish the scouts to do," Temperance asked. Rade thought for a moment.

"Double the guards on the wall and the number of scouts that get sent out. They ride in groups of two from now on. If war is coming to us then we should be ready for it!"

"I've never been in a battle before," Temperance stated.

"I've been in plenty and I'm haunted by the many things that I've witnessed. I hate war."

158

"Why does it always have to come down to war?"

"Because the Sorcerer will listen to nothing else." They fell silent for several minutes before Rade spoke again. "Temperance, why is everyone so against seeking aid from Dengar? I did not understand that."

"It's a long complicated history," Temperance started. "We were good trade partners at one point. They traded us supplies for Lumaflor."

"What race are they?" Morgrin asked.

"They're Elvish. At least so I've heard. No one has set foot in their land for two hundred years."

"Why?" Rade asked.

"Fear. Even now there are few villages to the west of us. Eventually, as the years went by the people of Dengar became estranged, starting to sway from the Elvish beliefs in Lathon.

"We learned that they had begun doing trade with The Dead Mountains, and nothing good comes out of those. Eventually, Luma refused to do trade with Dengar. By this point, they hardly agreed with us on anything. They had rejected Lathon and had become a brutal people.

"They did unthinkable acts to prisoners and foreigners alike. We refused to even acknowledge them. In a final act of defiance, they attacked our western settlements and killed everyone, people and livestock alike. Then they set them ablaze. They retreated into their borders and swore to kill any Lumian who stepped foot into the nation."

"Did anyone do this?"

"Yes, several throughout the years several have wandered too far. Typically, their heads were stuck on spikes at the border. Never seen it for myself, but that's the story."

They talked longer and eventually Isabel and Morgrin retired themselves for the night, too tired to talk anymore.

The dawn of the second day since their victory over Gravv also brought the first of the settlements to the walls of Nain. The notes of the horns bellowed through the air alerting everyone to their presence. Rade and Temperance met the people at the front gate and directed them on what to do next. Supplies were brought in and placed throughout the cities as they tried to prepare for every scenario.

***

Isabel quietly walked down the steps that were carved into the cliff. Slowly and steadily she made her way to the shoreline, greeted by the smell of the ocean.

She stopped and looked at the ocean wondering what else could possibly lay to the north. Aiden had asked her and Morgrin to come north, but just how far were they supposed to go?

As far as the eye could see was an ocean bigger than any she had ever laid eyes on, and certainly bigger than any she had ever tried to pass. For a moment fear consumed her.

She turned and walked down the coast and finally came to the same place Gravv had shown her the Taruks. They still remained in their cages, all six of them asleep. She marveled at the amazing creatures. She walked towards the first crate but was startled when a man appeared against the rock.

"Don't be afraid," the man said.

"You just startled me that's all," Isabel replied. "I thought I was here alone."

"You're never alone," the man responded. A silence fell between them. They both looked at the Taruks who slept peacefully.

"You're curious about them." The man said.

"Yes, I've always found Taruks to be intriguing. Wouldn't you agree?"

"Yes, I would."

"Who do I have the pleasure of speaking to?" Isabel asked. The man thought for a moment.

"Michal. You may call me Michal."

"Pleasure to meet you, Michal," she greeted. "My name is-"

"Isabel, of course," Michal said. Isabel fell silent unsure of what to say or feel. She should be alarmed but there was something different about his tone and his appearance that she couldn't place. Surprisingly she found herself comforted by his presence.

Turning her attention back, she slowly reached out to one of the Taruks.

"I know you have a curious heart," Michal said. She pulled her hand back. "But do not bother these Taruks. They have suffered greatly and rest would do them better than flying up the coast to attack some ships."

Isabel's mind reeled. "Who are you?"

"Michal," he said again. He stood and came next to her, looking at the Taruk. "It's rather horrible what some people can do to Taruks...or each other for that matter. Taruks are not meant to hatch unless they choose it. These ones had no choice."

"I have thought about that," Isabel said. "All I want to do is help them, I thought if they could fly with Aspen and the others it might be just what they need."

"By most wisdom that would be true. But sometimes healing is different from what one might think," Michal said. "Please take my advice and do not trouble these Taruks again. They will be well again someday in the future."

"But what about the ships that are likely coming up the coast?" Isabel asked. "What am I supposed to do about those? Are they not coming?"

"Ships are certainly coming, but on the day you go to them you may not use these Taruks." Isabel was taken aback by the man's audacity and she thought about arguing with him but decided against it. Something about the man seemed to have an authority that she couldn't place. The longer she held the man's gaze the more a suspicion filled her heart.

"You can take better care of them than I can," Isabel said, pulling herself back from the Taruks. "Of that, I have no doubt."

"Thank you dear one," Michal said. "I'm sure you know, they will be in the best care."

"I do," Isabel replied, her heart filled with hope. She took one final look at the Taruks and then walked back to the shoreline. Michal joined her as she looked out to the sea.

"What lies to the north?" Isabel asked. "Do you know?"

"Aye, I know," Michal answered. "The ocean is large but there is land further north."

"I was told to go north," Isabel said.

"Afraid?"

"A little."

"Why?"

"I'm not sure," Isabel admitted. "Usually I'm the one rushing into the unknown with all the answers. I don't even know why I'm supposed to go north."

"But still you go?" Michal asked, conviction drenching his words.

"Yes."

"That's a heart Lathon is proud of!" Michal said. Isabel smiled at the mention of the name. "Wherever you are in life, trust in the name of Lathon above all else." She only nodded, unable to speak. A sense of strength washed over her. She thanked Michal and walked back up the steps and into the city. That same evening she returned to find that Michal and all the Taruks were gone. As though they had never been there.

***

The day wore on, and it only got busier. Morgrin immediately set to work improving the defense of the wall and instructing the incoming soldiers on the best strategies and techniques.

More timbers were added to the gates of the city, and in front of the city they erected hundreds of poles that reached ten feet into the air. It wouldn't stop the army from getting to them, but it would discourage the use of any siege towers or things of that sort.

They also assigned large portions of men to dig as many trenches and pits as they could. Making sure to cover them with straw mats and dirt when they were done.

In record time Catapults were constructed and tested, and the armory became the busiest place in all the city as anyone who could fight was conscripted into the army.

Scouts were sent out in groups of two as talked about the day before and the reports that they returned, along with what the Taruk's had observed were less than comforting.

IDOLS & TRINKETS

Coming on the mainland was an entourage of nearly two thousand people. How many of the people were soldiers, none of them knew for certain, but the scouts supposed the number was likely fifteen hundred. The others were surprised, but it was exactly as Rade would have guessed.

The day wore on and to everyone's disappointment, the number of settlements arriving dropped dramatically. By day's end, only twenty-five of the thirty-three settlements who had been present at the assembly had arrived.

"Where do you think they are?" Temperance asked.

Rade sighed heavily. "I fear that they either chose to ride out the storm themselves or they were wiped out by Halar." A somber silence filled the room. "Has anyone been able to spot Halar? Scout or Taruk?"

"No," Isabel said. "Wherever he's hiding it's somewhere secure and not within the twenty miles of lands that's been searched."

"There's no telling how many men he could have with him," Rade lamented.

"What are you thinking Rade?" Isabel asked.

"I'm not sure we're going to have the numbers to pull this one off. If Halar shows up with any number of people we will be overrun," Rade said. "It seems of the thirty warriors I trained for each village, they have dwindled in some places down to twenty. We have more people who have been conscripted, but they are not warriors. What of the Taruks and coastline Isabel?"

"I was met by a man named Michal." Rade seemed to stand straighter as he heard the name. "He said that I'm supposed to attack the ships that will be coming up the coast, but I am not allowed to use the Taruks that Gravv had."

"If he said that, then I trust him," Rade said with certainty.

"You know him?"

"If he is Michal of the White Ships, then I would not doubt anything he says."

"What are the White Ships?" Isabel asked. "I've not heard of them."

"He didn't tell you?"

"No," Isabel answered.

"It's a sailor tall tale or myth," Temperance explained. "Some sailors have claimed to see the White Ships appearing at strange times and taking down sailors without warning. They are considered cursed ships because there is never a crew on the boats."

"Empty ships sailing the seas and wreaking havoc?" Morgrin asked.

"So the tales go," Rade said.

"Any basis to the claims?" Isabel asked.

Temperance shrugged her shoulders. "I'm not a sailor, that's just what I've heard."

They fell into silence for some time.

"What should we do tomorrow?" Isabel asked. "If the scouts are right Cladhach could be here by late afternoon."

"Let everyone rest tomorrow. Anyone who's not defending can be taken to the caves to ride out the battle. If Lathon is with us we will see the light of day."

"Numbers don't win a war," Morgrin reminded.

Rade shifted uncomfortably. "I know. Forgive my momentary lapse in hope. This battle is affecting me differently from the others."

"Why?" Temperance asked. Rade hesitated.

"Because I can die in this battle," Rade said.

"Dying? What! No!" Temperance exclaimed. "You can't die Rade. What would I do without you?"

"This might be hard to explain, but in the past battles I've been in I haven't been able to die."

"I don't understand what you're talking about."

He looked to Isabel and then to Morgrin.

"Please give us a chance to talk privately," Rade said. "I need to explain some things that I have yet to explain to someone I love very much."

At once Morgrin and Isabel got up and left the two of them alone.

***

To say that Temperance had been surprised by everything Rade had explained to her would be an understatement. They had talked for nearly an hour and afterward, Temperance left to somewhere else in the city. It was almost midnight when Morgrin found her standing atop the wall looking to the west.

IDOLS & TRINKETS

"Penny for your thoughts," Morgrin said. Temperance stirred as if pulled from whatever thoughts or visions were haunting her.

"It's a lot to take in," Temperance asked. "I suppose you never truly know someone unless you know their story, but with all Rade told me and all that you three have done I'm not sure I could ever measure up."

"No ones asking you to," Morgrin said. "I understand if you feel overwhelmed though."

"That's an understatement!" Temperance said sharply. "I'm not sure what to do with most of it. Put yourself in my shoes. I just found out that I've fallen in love with a guy who's a thousand years old or something like that!"

"And you find it hard to believe?"

"Don't you?"

"No," Morgrin answered.

"He doesn't even look like he's a thousand years old, he looks like he's in his twenties." Temperance turned away for a moment. "Then he tells me Sherados is here, among us...as an Elvish person in an Elvish town I am thrilled by the idea. Nonetheless, that doesn't displace my confusion about why he came into the world as he did. He should have rode in on the most grand and majestic stallion and slaughtered his enemies in the blink of an eye. Yet Rade says he sits idle?"

"Not idle, just waiting. Do you not believe Rade?" Morgrin asked.

Temperance exhaled quietly. "I want to."

"It's no harder to believe Rade is who he says he is than the Heir of Lathon being among us," Mogrin argued.

"Yes it is," Temperance replied. "What am I supposed to do? I've made a fool of myself-"

"Let me just stop you right there," Mogrin started. "Before you actually make a fool of yourself. Now, whether we're talking about the heir of Lathon being among us, or about Rade having been cured of a strange curse that most could not have endured, it *is* the same. It all comes down to the heart."

"The heart?" Temperance scoffed. Mogrin ignored her tone.

"Yes, the heart. You want to know why Aiden, the heir of Lathon, came the way he did?" Morgrin asked. "To test our hearts. To see which one of us would choose to follow him. The choice to follow him comes with a price. Are you willing to pay it? And as far as Rade is concerned I say this in reply.

"I've been married to Isabel for a long time, but I haven't always been. She has a lot of demons in her past, a lot of things that most people would count against her. But beneath it all, when you strip away all the frivolous things that are a part of life, it's the heart that matters. Isabel, demons or no demons, has a heart for serving Lathon unlike any other I've ever seen. Freaks me out sometimes, but it always pushes me to become a better person, to become more like Lathon. Whether Rade is a hundred years old or twelve I ask you what is his heart like. You'll live with that much longer than anything else in this world."

"I know," Temperance replied. "I know that Rade's heart is pure and I will be alright, but right now I need some quiet, just so I can process everything."

***

The next morning came faster than they had hoped, and the mood in the city was somber. Everyone said their goodbyes as the last of the civilians were sent out of the city and the gates were sealed. Scouts were sent out in groups of two, bringing back reports of the approaching people.

Rade and Temperance stood atop the wall, looking out to the horizon, dreading the battle that was coming. They had talked more in the evening and now, she found herself looking at Rade in a different light. Even though her head was still trying to catch up with everything she had learned, she realized that Morgrin was right.

"I've never been in a battle before," Temperance told him. "I've never killed anyone before. I'm not sure I want to." A tear trickled down her face. Rade wiped it away and took her by the hand.

"I'd be concerned if you did want to kill someone. War is ugly, but I promise we'll get through it together."

She smiled softly at him. "What if we don't?"

"Then I'll be glad to walk with you through the pearly gates, in a world free from the sorrows of this one."

166

"I'm afraid to die," Temperance admitted.

"Death comes to all my dear, but it is not the end," Rade said. "If this is all there is then we are doomed. The fact is we did not choose to start our lives therefore it can only be concluded that we are created. If we are created, then there is a creator...and that is what you'll see after death. The glory of Lathon! Unveiled. Unhindered. Unspoiled. As it was meant to be so long ago in Erathos."

Temperance seemed to relax as she heard his words.

"Doesn't sound so bad," Temperance admitted.

"No. No, it's not." Rade pulled her in and gave her a gentle kiss on the lips. "I'm with you to the end."

"And I with you," Temperance said, her heart soaring. "But I have an honest question to ask you?"

"Ask away."

"Do you think we have the numbers to win this battle? Honestly?"

"No," Rade admitted. "The scouts warn the army of Cladhach is just hours away. Aspen spotted a black mass to our southwest. I fear that Halar will come with many soldiers once he learns of our treachery. And if Isabel cannot stop the Cladhach ships from arriving..."

"I will ride to Dengar," Temperance said. "I wish to summon them for help."

"I can't let you do that," Rade said.

"I know. But I need to do it. No one else in the city will go near them. I know it'll make some people mad, but if it keeps us alive?"

"You can't go by yourself," Rade said, concern written on his face.

"Then assign some people to go with me. No more than five," Temerpance said. They looked into each other's eyes and in that instant, both of them understood what had to be done.

"Are you sure?" Rade asked.

"Lathon will be with me. One way or the other. I have to try."

"How long will you be gone?" Rade asked.

"Two days each way. Maybe an extra day in there for negotiations."

"Five days?" Rade asked, thinking aloud.

"I need to have your blessing for this."

"And you shall have it!" Rade declared.

Fifteen minutes later Rade and Temperance stood at the west gate of the city. A large crowd gathered around them and Isabel and Morgrin were at the gates to see them off. Five other soldiers were on horseback, looking more nervous than he had ever seen them.

"Be careful my dear," Rade whispered. He kissed her again.

"I will."

Rade handed her an envelope, containing a letter to the king of Dengar. Temperance mounted her horse and tried to keep her own emotions in check as Rade stepped back from the horses.

"Open the gates. She rides for Dengar!" Rade announced. Murmurs rippled through the crowds and then a somber silence came over them as the gates were opened to the desert beyond. Without hesitation, Temperance spurred her horse forward, followed by five other soldiers.

***

Rade watched as Temperance and the others faded into the horizon a tear slipping down his cheek. He turned to the sea of faces watching him.

"I can see in your eyes that you do not approve of what happened."

"Is she really going to Dengar? Or are you just trying to save her for yourself?" a soldier asked.

" I will not lie to you! She rides for Dengar," Rade declared. The tone in his voice, caused everyone else to shift uncomfortably.

They knew he was telling the truth.

"She rides to Dengar because nobody else would! Pay careful attention to what that woman is doing! Temperance is not going off on her own to be safe. She is risking and very likely laying down her life for every one of us! Even if we don't deserve it. It is as Sherados, the heir of Lathon, will do in the days to come."

"Why should we not just run?" another soldier asked. Rade looked at the man.

IDOLS & TRINKETS

"Would you see your home destroyed? Your heritage left to rot? We fight now because we must," Rade declared. "This is our home and I will not see it destroyed because we were too lazy or so detached that we chose to do nothing! I cannot guarantee that we will live. Nor can I guarantee that Temperance will return! But together we can do far more than we can by ourselves.

"If this scares you and you wish to leave, do so now! But you will not be allowed to enter the caves with our people. You will face this battle on your own! Choose now, men!" He paused for a moment, but he could see their resolve returning to all of them.

"Our enemy will likely try to kill us, but our will and determination and love for those around us is worth far more. Right men?" A great cry rose from the city.

Their celebration was short-lived as a scout came galloping through the city and dismounted his horse in record time.

"They come, my lord. The main assembly is one hour away! They are not staged for battle, but they bring with them an armory and more than enough men to fight us."

"Thank you. Go rest while you can," Rade said. The scout vanished into the city. "The rest of you, man your stations, and may Lathon be with us all!"

Chapter 13

THE LIFTING OF CURSES

It wasn't long before word of the great miracles that were being performed, escaped from the palace walls. Soon people everywhere were coming forward from every corner of the mountains to see everything that had happened. To say the prince had been grateful was more than an understatement and to some extent, it was difficult to deny the many numerous gifts that he had wanted to bestow upon them.

Of all the things that he wanted to give them, Drake and Rachal would only accept a few. His eternal friendship and fine garments to take with them when they had gone. They were made the same as his. except lined with silver was the crest of Rinevah as they had requested.

The crew and the ship were repaired far better than they had expected and in nearly half the time it was predicted. The ship had been outfitted with new sails and lumber where it was needed. In addition, Afador had ordered that some of their gold reserves be taken and the railing of the ship all along the outside was covered with gold.

The ship was fixed in full within a week and a half, but still, Afador and his wife Hadassar insisted that they remain with them just as long as they were able. It was expected that the king would not return for many days and he always sent riders two days ahead to ready the city for the glorious entrance he always demanded.

The days went faster than they had wanted and even faster than they had expected. Each day it seemed like they were taken to another great sight of the city and nation and when Drake and Rachal thought they could not see anything more beautiful they were proved wrong. Sparkling caves, rivers of gems, waterfalls nearly a thousand feet high were just a few of the things that they, along with Barnabas and the entire crew of the ship, had been allowed to enjoy.

Remus also became a great friend to them and was always allowed to join the four of them every night as a friend, not just as the prince's personal attendant. Drake watched carefully, concluding that something like that had never happened in all the years before.

Drake marveled to see all the changes in the people in such a short amount of time. Hadassar and Rachal had become best friends and they did many things together. Hadassar who had her whole life been only able to speak a dark and hideous language that had origins that they could only guess, picked up the common tongue fluently and amazed the people at the eloquence of her speech.

The people of Jermin, though originally shy and skeptical of the transformations of the hearts and minds of the prince and princess, seemed to find a new life and energy that the prince was unable to explain. Drake and Rachal smiled to themselves, trying to teach them as much as they could before they left.

It was the fourth day of their stay at Jermin when many strange things happened, concerning the courtyard and all the monuments of the gods that they worshiped. They had risen to find a commotion in the great courtyard. The prince and his men were called at once and Drake and Rachal were also urged to come.

Inside the courtyard, every statue, every monument that had ever been erected for them to worship had fallen, tipped, or seemingly been pushed off in the middle of the night, and all of them lay face down on the ground. The only monument not affected in any way was the monument to the unknown God.

The people were confused and conflicted about this at first and made an enormous effort to fix and restore the monuments by day's end. Early the next morning it was discovered that the same thing had happened again. Once again the monuments were fixed and set a right.

That night Drake and Rachal had been staring up at the stars, enjoying the night when their eyes had been drawn to the courtyard. There stood a shadow of a man with a great staff. He walked slowly, seeming to stand and look at each of the monuments as if he knew the great history of each one. After nearly an hour of surveying them, the man held out a single hand and pushed each one of them off its pedestal where it clanged and crashed to the ground. When finally the last one was pushed to the ground, the man walked a few steps and then seemingly vanished.

In the morning the concern from everyone was even greater than the day before. Dismayed at the great statues being toppled yet again, they were fixed with great vigilance and the prince ordered an armed guard around the entire courtyard with permission to kill anyone who entered it during the night.

The night came and the soldiers were commissioned. Still, Drake and Rachal saw the shadowy figure walk around, seemingly unseen by the men keeping watch. He pushed them off the pedestals once again and none of the men even seemed to notice the sounds.

The next morning the furry of the people was more than Drake could have predicted. During the night all the men had fallen asleep, overcome with a drowsiness they could not explain. Again the statues were fixed, this time many of the citizens took up arms and joined the soldiers in watching that night.

But the next morning brought the same thing, with each and every statue lying face down in the courtyard. The people began working and laboring to repair the statues but were overcome with great boils that spread through the city at a speed that was unfathomable.

By noon every citizen of Jermin was covered in boils from head to foot, the only ones who were spared were Drake, Rachal, and the crew of their ship. Afador and Hadassar called for Drake and Rachal to sit in on a council meeting, eager to figure out a solution.

"What is going on?" Afador asked. "I have traveled many places in the world and seen many things, both terrible and great! But this is beyond all explanation. How is it that the courtyard is trashed every morning and that the guards always fall asleep and see nothing? What sort of dark wizardry is this?"

A man stood to speak, his hair black with flecks of gray in it.

"Let us not beat around the bush! There is only one explanation for this and we all know that this is an elaborate attempt by the Munda people to weaken and then conquer us!"

Several voices joined in agreement, and others started arguing with them. After a moment Afador was able to regain control.

"I know there are many who wish to see the end of the Munda people, I among them, but what proof do we have that they have done anything! Unless their gods have become greater than ours!" Again an uproar ensued.

"No gods are above ours!" a person on the left said. "If this is what the Munda think, let us go to war right now and wipe them out. I care not what their sorcerers would do to me if I could take a few of them on the way down!"

"Gentlemen, Gentlemen, please. I urge caution. We can't just start a war while my father, your king, is gone. Merited or not, this kind of talk will have to be started before his ears. I ask basic questions in this matter. Have our gods fallen subject to their gods? I think not, and if it has happened then I daresay our doom is inevitable. What other possible explanations could there be?"

"Perhaps our gods have gone to sleep. It is said in the ancient days that the gods were silent and did not wake for nearly a thousand years."

"So it is said," retorted another man. "Perhaps we have made the gods ashamed. Perhaps something we have done has embarrassed them beyond hope and they now lay on their faces in shame?"

"If we have caused them this much shame then perhaps we have angered the gods to the point that they will disown us, inflict us with disease and we will now surely die," Afador said. A hush fell over the room.

"You will not die," Rachal said. "But I daresay you *have* angered a God; but not the one you would think."

"You speak that we have angered the unknown God?" Afador asked. Drake and Rachal both nodded. "How is this possible? What have we done to deserve such treatment when we have only become aware of him now?"

"The unknown God, Lathon, ruler of all, brought us to you and healed your wife. You have seen things that go beyond comprehending, yet you ask us this? Can any of your gods heal so quickly and assuredly?" Drake asked. Silence lingered for a moment. "Lathon is the one and the only God that can save you, and he has. But why should he rejoice or bless you further when you scorn him with worship and sacrifice to your other gods? At the very least, Lathon has done what your gods could not do, your gods *should* throw themselves down in shame."

"Lathon is a jealous God, this I am beginning to see," Hadassar said. "What is to be done then? Are we to endure this testing?"

"Lathon asks us to lay aside many things if we wish to follow him and this is the greatest. He asks everyone to give up something and if I may be so bold, I would recommend that you destroy the entire courtyard and all its idols, saving only the altar to the unknown God."

A long silence followed and Drake and Rachal grew nervous as the minutes passed. Finally, with a single glance from Hadassar, Afador spoke again. "You have not led us astray so far and we will once again trust you and Lathon. Remus!" Remus came forward from his spot in the corner. "Send word to all the citizens far and near, every idol, every shrine, every place of worship except those that now honor Lathon, must be destroyed immediately. Refusal to carry out this order shall result in the highest penalty, which of course shall be death if we do not carry this out."

"I'm sorry to say this Your Majesty, but doesn't something like this require your father the king to give his consent to the order?"

"I care not about politics right now Remus," Afador said. "If this continues, my heart warns me that we will be dead by the time my father returns. Everyone in this room listen well! Do not worry about yourselves, I will make sure that only my family and I will be held accountable should something go wrong. You will not be blamed for anything that you do under this order. Now do as I say."

"It shall be done according to your word."

Less than an hour passed before Remus stood before a great gathering of people and gave out the orders that Prince Afador had commanded. The people, shocked and surprised, went about the work amazingly fast and by noon, had cleared nearly the entire courtyard.

IDOLS & TRINKETS

Citizens of every shape and size participated, using whatever tools they had at their disposal. The statues were pulled down or toppled over by horses and then smashed into pieces with hammers and other objects of blunt force. The pieces were then carried and thrown over the great falls, lost to the immense foam and water at the bottom of it.

Even by noon improvements of the boils could be seen clearly, and by nightfall, they had disappeared entirely.

Evening came and the nation celebrated as every town and city who destroyed the idols were healed of the boils instantly. Drake and Afador walked down by the gates of the city, looking over the top of the waterfalls.

"I can't thank you enough for what you have done," Afador said.

"I've hardly done anything, I've simply pointed out to you what was already there."

"My family's history is tainted by darkness, this now I see. I have only learned about this god Lathon, but I feel as if he brings life and not despair. We sacrificed to our gods out of fear, but fear of what I cannot say. It was just tradition. You were right earlier when you said that our gods do not heal quickly. Never has such transformation been seen. I can only conclude that your God is truly alive and involved in people's lives, whereas ours have been shown for what they truly are."

"I daresay you came to the right decision in the end," Drake said.

"Anything you wish to know?" Afador asked. "I feel as if you've given us more than we deserve, there must be something that I can tell you about." Drake thought for a moment.

"Tell me of the Munda. I heard many interesting things in our meeting earlier, but I am unsure of what they are. Are they man, or beast, it was suggested that they have some sort of magical abilities."

"Come see for yourself."

Drake stood and followed Afador who led them out to the courtyard. Their horses were soon brought for them and they rode to the left side of the palace where they came to a large metal gate in the side of the mountain. A torch burned to either side of the entrance and ten soldiers guarded it. At once they were allowed to pass, entering into the dark abyss.

"The nation of Tuthar is uniquely positioned in a bad place. We are stuck between the Munda and the Bazarran. Both deal heavily in the dark arts, which even our own people think badly of. The chief difference between the two nations is that the Munda only appear to strive to alter natural things storms, the environment, etc. whereas many Bazarran have been said to have unnatural abilities. There is something down here that I wish you to see."

They rode through a confusing maze of twisting caves and tunnels until finally, they entered into a shaft that there was no exit from. Ten soldiers stood in front of a heavy iron gate, and beyond Drake could vaguely see a shape strung up to the wall in chains. They entered the cell, the man staring blankly at Drake. Instantly a feeling of dread and confusion came over Drake.

"Who is he?"

"A man named Jeklym. He claims to be one of the Munda. The first night you were here he came to our gates wishing to seek an audience with you and you alone. I took the liberty of intervening and found him to be a character of suspicion. This has been weighing on me greatly."

"He showed up the first night?" Drake asked. "That's quick."

"Too quick. I had him imprisoned then. We've been interrogating him and he claims that he was hired by a prince of Rinevah. He said he had given this prince passage to *Merisyll*, and was told to do the same for you."

"Did he speak the name?"

"James, Prince of Rinevah. Does that name mean anything to you?"

"I know James and, indeed he was to go ahead of me." They left the prisoner and began riding their horses back through the caves. "What do you discern the truth to be?"

"I think he most certainly did give passage to your friend, but it seems to me a trap. Under normal circumstances it's unlikely the Munda would have any interest in a person like your friend; seldom do the Munda care of the affairs of the world beyond this island. He does not strike me as a Bazarran, for they are rash and strong with their might. That being said, they might have a sinister interest in your friend and yourself. I feel though that the man we just saw is a middle man between the two nations. It is my belief the Munda and the Bazarran are working together. I suspect the storm that you came through was a storm created by the Munda. Once again the supremacy of your God is brought to the forefront of events, I think they meant you to crash on the other side of the island. Despite their best efforts and all their strength, your God defeated them as you crashed upon our shores and not theirs."

"Any guesses of what happened to James? If a partnership is underway as you think, and he was taken by the Bazarran, what do you think happened to him?"

"The Bazarran do not keep captives long, they either kill them or sell them. Important prisoners go to the highest bidder. I fear either way your friend is likely dead. Why were you not traveling together?"

"He was a very dear friend of mine. He sought me out when I had been lost and long thought dead. James had to leave earlier than I did for personal reasons. My road home has not been easy. I am grieved to learn that he might be dead."

"The death of a friend is never an easy thing," Afador reflected. "I have maps that can help you avoid the detection of Bazarran on your way to Merisyll."

"We would be indebted to you."

"No Drake Thomas, it is we who are indebted to you. I was wondering if I could make one small request."

"Name it," Drake said.

"I wish for your map of where you come from. I know much of these waters, but we have not been allowed to do trade with the rest of the world for many years."

"Why not?"

"My father has forbidden it. He always told me that it was for the safety of the people. He seemed to be afraid of the Dwarvish nations of the world rising up and seeking vengeance for everything that had been done. Only recently have I begun to think there's something deeper behind the fear."

"You can certainly have our maps, and perhaps in the future our nations can have a peaceful existence together."

"You are a man of great hope Drake Thomas and it is refreshing. Before you leave you shall have a feast thrown in your honor and it will be celebrated every year as long as I live. It will be remembered as the day that a man of the living God came and restored our nation. The great and glorious ways you have saved this nation will be made into song. My heart is freer than it has ever felt and somehow even the air feels better to me and lightens my spirit."

Their last night in Jermin came sooner than they wished. As the prince has said, a great feast and celebration was thrown in their honor, celebrating the great deeds that had transpired since their arrival. The celebration lasted long into the night and went far beyond the great halls of the prince. They had once again been adorned in the finest clothes and placed in seats of honor next to the prince as they ate. At long last when the feast was over the prince stood to speak.

"My fellow citizens and friends. I have gathered us all here in celebration. Not only for the wondrous deeds that the living God has done among us; but because for the first time, I feel a hope and a joy that I cannot explain. It seems as if a darkness has been raised from my eyes, as though I see better and sharper than I did before. I can only conclude that this too is a sign from Lathon, the God of Drake and Rachal Thomas. So everyone raise your glasses for a toast." Everyone raised their glasses. "Hail!" Everyone echoed the words and then drank from their cups.

"Furthermore this is a day that shall be celebrated annually throughout our country. Never has such transformation been seen but now may the same power that transformed us even a little over these past few weeks, transform us further in the days to come! Now listen one and all to a song that has been prepared to help us remember our great humility." The prince sat and a young singer stood and in a clear, strong voice addressed the crowd.

Hail the King! Hail the King!
The one who reigned before us.

IDOLS & TRINKETS

Though in darkness we wandered far,
You never did forsake us.

Our hearts were dark, our blood was cold
We were asleep, unable to hold.
Still, we clung to the gates of death
Nearly taking our last breath.

But then it happened, oh yes it did.
A dream you gave and came true it did.
On the shores, we found a clue
It was he who told us what to do.

Standing now, we've paid the price,
We've found the grace, we've found the light!
Guide us now in days to come,
And every day till kingdom come.

Hail the King! Hail the King!

Later, they once again sat with the prince and princess in an open courtyard. The stars were high above them, shining like diamonds. The only other sounds that could be heard were drowned out by the noise of the great falls.

"I am most saddened that this is your last night," Hadassar said. "These past three weeks have seemed to be something out of a dream for me. Never in all the years that we have been married, has there been such joy in the air. You have certainly, as my dream said, been of high worth."

"Thank you," Rachal said. "It is an honor to have met you as well. You have treated us very well, better than we could ask for. You will always be welcome at our house no matter where that may be."

"I only wish you could stay here and dwell with us forever," Afador stated.

"Indeed," Drake agreed. "But alas, it seems I have been away from my home for far too long and am needed there, though I know not what for."

"Even so, I wish you and your wife all the blessings we can give. Perhaps one day far from now, we will be able to sit down and tell each other the great tales that have passed since we parted."

"That sounds like a good idea to me," Rachal said. Hadassar's eyes changed, displaying fear instead of joy. "Is everything going to be okay?"

Hadassar's eyes showed fear, but a quick look of encouragement from Afador softened her expression.

"We will be. One of my father's most cherished spots in this city was the Garden of the gods. He will be most enraged to see it destroyed." They sat in silence for a moment. "He will not be happy with the changes while he's been gone. I care not what he thinks. I've seen and had enough. I will not bow to any other idol or statue that is carved. Remus!" Remus stepped forward. "Tomorrow morning please escort my wife and kids to the Makkura and make sure they are safe. It is quite likely that we will need their aid."

"What are the Makkura?" Drake asked.

"We're not exactly sure. Makkura is a strange term. It cannot be translated into any language that I know of. They are a race that is not so different from us, but they're not Elvish and they're not Mankind. They are different, and I'm not even sure I can find the words to describe them. Even if I was given ten years to write down everything I could hope to learn from them I fear it would take much longer.

"The shorter answer is that whoever they are, they have watched over me since I was a child. They live deep in the mountains and talk to no one except myself. They have taught me and Hadassar many things. They have been a source of joy in my life and have always been very kind to me.

"They discovered me when I was nine. I had gotten lost and it was nearly dark. I had fallen down a steep ravine and was unable to climb out. I had just laid down, thinking that I would die there, when a bright light appeared on the top of the ravine.

"I cannot begin to describe what the light was like or how it was different from the sunlight, but it was. One of them lowered a rope to me and I climbed

180

out of the pit. They took me to their camp for the night. It was an odd camp and hard as I tried I have never been able to find that place again.

"Still they considered me a friend and have offered me, Hadassar, and our kids protection if ever it is needed. There is one spot in particular they said that we could meet, as it turns out I believe it is not far from one of the alters to the unknown God. Perhaps there is a connection there that I had not thought of until now. I have given them Remus's name, so he will be safe when he reaches them. If things go ill for me here, I would like to at least know that my wife and children are safe."

"No matter what happens. If it turns out that you need safety and protection, in the future, please seek us out. We would be more than willing to help you or your family if it is in our ability," Rachal offered.

"That is comforting to hear," Afador said. "A man needs friends, perhaps once you have come into your own, our nations will share a better relationship and can do great things for the world."

"I hope for the same, though we do not know how long it will be until we're in any position to seek you out."

"I understand entirely," Afador said. "It may prove to be the same here, depending on how things go with my father." They both laughed and the silence lingered for a moment. "It has been an honor to meet and spend these last three weeks with you, but alas the night is getting deep and it will soon be time to see you off to your ship." Drake and Rachal were seen to their rooms and they once again sat outside looking up at the stars, pondering and thinking deeply about everything that had been said.

The dawn came too soon for all of them, having been up so late the night before. The sky was faintly colored, with the first rays of light threatening to rise above the peaks of the mountains. Remus led them out to the courtyard once again where the entire crew and the prince's men waited on horses.

Drake and Rachal mounted, and they immediately rode through the silent and dark streets. Barnabas rode beside them, while all three of them rode behind the prince and his banner. Loud horns were trumpeted through the city as they exited, heralds crying out all along the way that the honored guests were leaving and that they would be remembered forever.

They rode into a large tunnel in a mountain and were immersed in darkness, save the torches that Afador's men carried with them. After a while the tunnel descended sharply, nearly becoming too steep for horses to carry them. A few minutes later the path leveled and the smell of salt water greeted them. They entered onto a large rock formation that encircled the entire ship.

Down below sat the repaired ship looking even better than it had before they had left at the beginning of their travels. They followed the path, which entered into the rock formation and led them to the floor of the strange cave which was dry. The ship now loomed over them, a single rope ladder hanging over the side. They dismounted and the crew immediately began climbing aboard, getting ready to make way.

"Thank you for everything," Drake said. Afador smiled.

"It is I that should be thanking you," Afador said. "Best of luck on your journey, may Lathon, who you've taught us so much about, protect you in every way."

Without speaking another word they climbed the ladder. Once everyone was aboard, the prince and his men mounted their horses and rode away, back up the path the way they had come. When they reached the top of the formation they stopped and faced the ship, bowing low and then raising their hands, which they had learned was a way of showing high respect for someone or something. Horns blared, and the sound of water rushing came to their ears.

At the mouth of the rock formation, near the sea, the walls of rock were cracked open, allowing the water to rush in. The doors were opened further as the dry floor filled with water and lifted the ship off the supports. The sails were loosed and a strong wind came from behind and pushed the ship through the open doors.

They entered into the seawater, listening to the chorus of horns from the shoreline. They let loose notes of their own, waving goodbye. Before long they had faded from sight as the men went back to their work. Barnabas stood at the rear of the ship smiling like Drake had never seen.

"How are you doing Barnabas?" Drake asked. Barnabas laughed.

"I'm doing just fine, glad to be out on the open seas, and for once Drake Thomas I can't complain about anything. We all made it off the island alive, this ship is the best it's ever looked. I still can't believe the prince laid gold over the rails."

"He was very kind to us," Drake said. "And now we have a map, so it should be smooth sailing from here to Merisyll. We just need to keep clear of Bazarran waters and it should be smooth sailing."

"I'm still surprised everything worked out the way it did," Barnabas said. Rachal laughed.

"Is your faith a little stronger now? I'm not sure I've ever heard you this positive."

"Perhaps it is improved," Barnabas said. They all went about their business as they sailed further and further away from the island.

-

Chapter 14

TO THE HIGHEST BIDDER

The first day of their voyage was one of the best that Barnabas had ever sailed in, (or so he said) and went without any difficulties. At any rate, it was one of the best that they had experienced on their voyage. The wind was strong and from a direction that allowed them to make faster time than had expected.

The second day the favorable conditions continued as they were able to travel much of the day without seeing any other ships, despite being near a major shipping route.

On the third day, the winds changed slightly, turning into more of a headwind, forcing them to adjust their sails. Reluctantly they had to turn more towards the west, though they had been cautioned against doing so.

"I just checked the charts and with the navigator," Barnabas said, stepping out from his cabin. "It appears we're still right on track, even with having to turn west. If we can hold our course we should arrive within two days."

"Where are we in relation to the shipping channel?" Rachal asked. "I perceived a couple of hours ago we lost it."

"Lost for now, but not for good," Barnabas replied. "We're no more than three miles off it right now and we'll make sure that we don't drift any further."

"How can one be sure of that?"

"Got to admire her Drake," Barnabas asked. "She sure speaks her mind." Barnabas moved on, handing out orders and calling to the crew.

"He's interesting," Rachal said. "Not sure if he's arrogant or just overconfident."

"Perhaps a little of both."

The day wore on and faded into night, the sun dipping below the horizon.

IDOLS & TRINKETS

Up above a million stars shone down on them. Drake and Rachal sat atop the deck, enjoying the silence that came with the night. Several men kept watch and kept the ship on course. The rest, by now had fallen asleep.

"Drake," Rachal said, sitting up suddenly. Drake shook his head, trying to rid the wave of fatigue that had come over him. "Do you see something out there?" Drake searched the dark horizon.

"It's dark, it's hard to see fifty feet in front of us, where are you looking?"

"Starboard side, near aft." She pointed in the direction. "The water seems to be changing colors." Drake strained his eyes desperately. "Do you see it?"

"Indeed. It seems at times as if the water is a deep purple color. Strange, but rather beautiful if you ask me."

"So I thought an hour ago, but look off the bow and tell me what you see." Drake looked.

"Green. Dark murky green, almost like a glowing moss."

"And now off the port-side?"

"Orange, bright orange." A sinking feeling came over both of them as they watched the lights for the next few minutes. They seemed to flash only ever so often, but usually in sequence as if they were in some way trying to communicate with each other. Also, they seemed to be getting closer. Drake searched for any sign of a ship when the lights flashed, but no ship was ever seen.

Suddenly the lights moved a great distance. Now were within easy eyesight of any of the men who were watching. A few of them took notice, pointing it out to everyone else. Drake called for one of them.

"Get Barnabas out here at once! Tell him it's urgent!" Drake ordered. The man made for the captains' quarters. Only a couple of minutes passed before Barnabas stumbled out of his cabin, more asleep than awake. He found Drake and Rachal quickly.

"Don't you two ever sleep?"

"Not tonight we don't," Rachal said, pointing out the lights to him, which had now moved closer, only a couple hundred yards off from their ship. Barnabas's face turned white.

185

"About face! About face! Turn this ship around now!" Barnabas yelled. Drake and Rachal were unable to get a word in edgewise as he yelled out orders, including for everyone to wake up and call to arms.

"What's going on?!" Drake yelled. Barnabas paid them no mind, frantically looking at the lights that still closed on them. Men scrambled out of the hold, weapons at the ready, though many of them clearly didn't know what they were awakened for.

Barnabas sprinted to the wheel and shoved the man aside, wheeling to the right. Fear instantly gripped all of them as they immediately looked at the long side of a ship. Barnabas cursed and yelled out more orders.

"What's going on?" Drake asked. Barnabas refused to answer. Despite a desperate attempt to change course, within seconds ropes and grapples were thrown onto their ship and a mixture of Gog's and Men poured onto the deck. Everyone fought the boarding party, but within a couple of minutes, they were defeated and rounded up into the middle of the deck.

The Men and Gogs went below deck, bringing up a few other sailors who had either tried to hide or had still been sleeping when the attack started. The lights that had been surrounding them on three sides were now all around the ship, They had become brighter, lighting everything up in the strange rays of color.

The men circled around Drake, Rachal, and their Captain, doubt and fear in every one of their eyes. Finally, the last man was thrown into the circle and the Gogs and men closed off any chance of escape. Drake studied them carefully, the Gogs were similar to the build and stature of Shavrock, but if it was possible they were taller with numerous piercings and strange markings covering their bodies from head to toe.

The men were much the same, more unkempt than Drake was accustomed to seeing, even if they were at sea. The minutes passed and the silence lingered. Drake and Rachal both became aware of strange noises echoing from beneath the ship. Finally, an entourage appeared on the deck of the other ship.

Ten men, all dressed in black, came forward bearing torches. Swords were strapped to their waists as well as large sapphire horns. They circled the group and faced the great sea, blowing into their horns. No noise was heard, but the strange noise from beneath the ship increased as if in an answer to the call.

Finally, another man appeared at the head of the other ship. He stood tall and proud, walking swiftly onto the deck of the Evin Lador.

A foul stench overwhelmed them as the man approached. His appearance was rough and ragged, his face and skin covered with dirt and grime. He looked towards the group of people that were rounded up like a herd of sheep. In an instant, his eyes changed. One became vibrant green, while the other turned black and was seemingly lost from his face.

One at a time the crew members were brought forward and presented to the man. He watched and studied them intently and would either order that the person be thrown overboard, or tied up in chains. Whenever a man was thrown overboard, a horrible heart-piercing screech would ring into the night, replaced a moment later by men screaming and being lost to whatever was surrounding them.

Drake, Rachal, and Barnabas were pulled from the middle and dragged before the man. He studied each of them. He didn't speak, but the longer he looked the more pleased he seemed. Finally, laughter escaped him, joyful laughter, like one who has just opened a great gift, given to him by a friend.

"Gentlemen and creatures!" the man started. His voice was deep and raspy and had a quality about it that alarmed their hearts in an instant. "This is a moment I've been waiting for. We shall certainly become rich off the great things aboard this vessel!" The Gogs and men let out a single shout, as the man turned his gaze back towards the three of them. After a moment he focused in on Drake.

"I can see that you do not know who I am fine sir," the man stated. "But, I know who you are; you are the legendary Drake Thomas are you not?" Drake didn't answer. "I'm sorry, where are my manners, I've most certainly frightened you no doubt. My name is Rodum, admiral of the Bazarran navy. I'm sure Barnabas has mentioned me in a prior conversation?"

"Can't say as he has," Drake replied. Rodum smiled slyly.

"I can only say that I'm a bit shocked and honestly a little put out. Then again everyone has their secrets, don't they? Barnabas here knows who I am better than anybody, though if you asked him I'm sure he'd deny it." He paused and looked at Barnabas. "You do go by Barnabas these days don't you?" He laughed and turned back to Drake. "Last I knew this vessel was stolen out of a port in Hareshat was it not?"

"I bought the vessel fair and square and yes I would swear by it!" Barnabas said. Rodum smiled again.

"I'm glad to see that you have not gone mute in your years of running like a coward and a thief."

"Care to explain what's going on here?" Drake asked.

"Stories for another time Drake, I know his business and it won't wait."

"To correct my old friend here," Rodum started, pointing out towards the strange lights beneath the water. "*They* won't let business wait, so we really must keep things moving. In short, the details you need to know are that the lights are created by something we call *Sefult*. Very deadly kind of sea creature. They emit light and are drawn towards food sources. Usually, the bigger ones catch their attention quicker.

"My job is to catch ships and determine if there are any people on it that will pose a threat to the Bazarran nation and its interests. If they are, then we take them to our capital and turn them in. If they are not of any great worth, they are thrown overboard for the Sefult to consume as they will.

"Now old Barnabas here is not worth too much to me, but there is a matter of that tribute he failed to pay as a young lad. I will keep him alive and present him to the king, plus I have a few special things in mind for him." Rodum chuckled to himself. Drake watched the two men exchange glances.

"You Drake, are a very special man. And are worth a lot of money, I will gladly present you before the king, and may the highest bidder obtain your soul to do with as they will." Finally, he turned to Rachal. "Now you, my dear-"

Everyone, even the creatures in the sea fell silent as Rachal spoke forcefully in a language Drake didn't recognize. Drake and Barnabas were taken aback by her fury and rage, and the look of surprise on Rodum's face was a welcomed sight. Rodum responded in the strange language and after a minute or so Rachal nodded in agreement, as one who had just won a great contest. Rodum opened his mouth to speak but never got any words out, as if fear had consumed him. An awkward silence fell over them until finally, Rodum managed to speak.

"The Lady may do as she wishes, you are to give her anything she demands. I can see there is no one of value left on this ship. Throw them overboard and let's get going, there are still more ships to raid before morning. Lock Mr. Thomas and his friend into the hold."

The Gogs and other sailors forced the rest of Barnabas's crew off the deck of the ship and into the water. Screaming and cursing filled the night air and within a couple of minutes, a heavy silence had filled the area. The lights faded and then disappeared, leaving the two ships floating in the darkness.

As Rodum had ordered, they were led below deck and locked in the holding cell. Rachal walked with power and authority and didn't change that stance until finally the last of their captors went back up to the deck and they were alone.

"Full of surprises your wife is," Barnabas said.

"Aren't you also?" Rachal pointed out. "My part is easy to explain. I heard the crew speaking the language and I knew it. Enya used to speak it and I had more than enough time to pick it up fluently. It's a strange language. Depending on your class you speak differently. I spoke in the highest form I knew how and it was enough to momentarily convince the man that he shouldn't mess with me."

"Good work," Drake complimented. "Hopefully he's fooled better than you thought."

"Time will tell," Rachal said. "I doubt my speech will hold up once we get the king, but at least we'll have a little peace until then. Now, how about you Barnabas?"

"Me?" Barnabas asked stammering. "I grew up in these parts."

"Interesting place to grow up," Drake stated. "What else do we need to know?"

"Nothing," Barnabas said. "I've worked hard to erase the memories of my life long past, I'm not going to talk about it now."

"What of the stolen ship Rodum spoke of?"

"I don't know what he's talking about. I've never stolen a ship in my life. Most likely he's conjuring up some false report to accuse me with. Make me worth more money. That's what he does best."

"I'm sorry this journey's causing you such pain," Rachal said.

"It's okay," Barnabas said. "I've been running from the pain for so long, maybe it's time I face it."

"Seems like wisdom speaking to me," Drake said. "We will have to be extra careful about what we say. No telling what we'll be up against."

"I can tell you exactly what we're up against, and I can also tell you there's only one way we can save ourselves from what lies ahead and that's a whole lot of money, we don't have with us."

What had been predicted to be a one-day trip to the capital, ended up being two days, and not before several more ships were boarded and the valuable prisoners put down below with Drake and Barnabas.

The days passed slowly. Rachal who was free to move about the ship as she wished, spent most of her time above deck, trying to learn as much of their language and culture to hopefully be able to get them all out alive once they arrived. The night would come and the crew would sleep and then she would come down and talk to them for as long as she dared.

The little food that they had been given was stale and bitter and on the second day, no food was provided. When the dawn of the third day came a great horn bellowed from the deck above and an answering horn came from the east. The ship made port and the prisoners were marched off the boat in irons.

Rachal stuck as close to them as she dared, insisting that she wished to buy Drake and Barnabas for her own purposes. Drake marveled as he watched Rachal speak and talk in a language that he had never heard, while doing it flawlessly. The day grew long and Drake and the other prisoners were led to the dungeons deep within the city.

It was the middle of the night before Rachal was able to come to them. She entered the prisons bearing no torch and managed to get past the guards unnoticed.

IDOLS & TRINKETS

"How the blazes are you still alive?" Barnabas exclaimed as she woke them.

"By the grace of Lathon and nothing else," Rachal said. "Rodum gave me his guest house for my own while we're here, so I'm well looked after. This is a most interesting place. Your 'trial' before the king will be tomorrow afternoon. There, they will assess how much you're worth. Drake is worth more money than I could ever imagine to a nation called Nargaroth. There are a few other places that want him dead, but Nargaroth is going to be the winner I'm sure.

"Barnabas is likely going to be purchased by Rodum himself. He is quite insistent on having you serve in his household as a slave."

"I hope that moment never comes."

"So do I," Rachal replied. "I'll try my best to get us all out of here tomorrow. I might have to do a little bluffing about how much money we have."

"I'm sure it'll be forgiven this time," Drake said. "It seems that they trust you."

"Well enough for the moment. Tomorrow will be the harder test."

"I have faith in you and I know you can do it," Drake said. Rachal smiled.

"I'm glad you're my biggest fan because I certainly don't feel confident right now,"

"That's what I'm here for."

Chapter 15

BATTLE FOR NAIN

Rade sat at the front of a small group of horsemen. Morgrin sat beside him and behind were two soldiers and a flagman. He held up a large spike, bearing the flag of Lumar and a white flag. Their horses shifted uncomfortably, They could see the large mass moving towards them step by step.

"The scout was right. They do not appear anywhere near prepared for a battle," Morgrin said.

"True, but there's more than enough of them to put an end to us."

"If they're not ready, then they won't dare attack us right now," Morgrin said. "Not with them?" He motioned behind to where they had hastily assembled everyone either on the wall or on the ground in front of the city.

"I'm glad you're here alongside me," Rade said.

Morgrin smiled. "Ironic in a way. I'm now your advisor."

They both chuckled.

"It is ironic. Let's face it, if I was still a cursed spirit I could obliterate the entire army in a matter of minutes. This kind of a battle, in some ways, is very new to me."

"You're doing good so far," Morgrin said. Rade smiled. "You already passed the biggest test in my books."

"What test is that?" Rade asked.

"You gave up something dear to you. You let Temperance go, for the sake of the bigger picture. I know it wasn't easy for either of you, but some people wouldn't have been able to do it."

"That means a lot to me, my friend," Rade said. A few more minutes passed before the host in front of them stopped and made no sound. A couple of uneasy minutes passed before a group of six horses could be seen coming across the plain.

"Here we go!"

Rade took a deep breath. The men behind them shifted uneasily as the six horses came and stopped in front of them. "I am Rade, governor of Nain and Lord of Lumar. With whom do I speak? Name yourselves!"

"Where is Gravv?"

"Names first, information later!" Rade declared. The men exchanged looks.

"I am Amor, son of Tamar, son of Mekul. General and Captain for the sixth legion of Cladhach. My company and I were promised that this city was ours."

"You were misinformed!" Rade exclaimed. "Gravv no longer rules this city, nor this nation. He had fallen into shadows and people like him have no place in this city."

"Perhaps we didn't make ourselves clear," Amor retorted. "This city is ours as declared by Gravv of Moki. I will not hesitate to slaughter every man woman or child who stands in my way. According to our laws, even animals who are ridden by contrarian filth must be killed after the battle. The gods demand it."

"Mine doesn't," Rade said, staring into the eyes of Amor. The contest lasted several seconds. "Why don't you leave and go home?!"

"You are standing in our way. We were promised this land-"

"By one who did not own it!" Rade retorted. "Gravv is dead, you have no claim here."

"So you force us to do war upon a town that is ours anyway."

"I don't force you to do anything," Rade stated. "But I make this deal with you. If you do your worst, we'll do ours, then we'll see who comes out on top. "

"So you will not remove yourselves from our path and lay down your arms?" Amor asked.

"I will not!" Rade said.

Amor glared at them for a moment.

"Fine, if this is how you will have it then I shall make sure my blade is the one to sever your head!"

"So be it!" Rade declared. Amor cursed and turned his horse, galloping away from the site. When they had gone, Rade and Morgrin both let a sigh of relief come over them.

"You're scarier than I remember," Morgrin said.

They chuckled and slowly led their horses back to the city. The flag bearer blew three short notes on the horn, ordering everyone into the city.

Rade and Morgrin were the first to enter and the gates were closed and barred behind them. The giant locks fell into place and an eerie silence covered the area.

"I want eyes on them at all times. Men are to be ready to report at any moment!" Rade yelled out. Orders were repeated and Morgrin led the way to the stables.

"It is late in the day, they will not attack before dawn," Rade stated.

"They were not expecting to fight us, that much is clear," Morgrin said. Isabel appeared in the doorway and quietly joined them.

"Have the Taruks been able to spy anything else from their high seat in the sky?" Rade asked.

"They've spotted another group coming from the mountains. They are a days march behind," Isabel said. "Best estimates are an additional six hundred men." Silence came over all of them.

"Twenty-six hundred men, all of them able to fight," Morgrin stated. "It wouldn't have taken half of that to secure the city before we got here. Gravv must have had some greater plan for the city of Nain. I shudder to think what it might have been."

"Most likely he wanted to take all of Lumar."

"I suppose it is a good thing we're here and putting up a fight," Isabel said. Rade nodded his agreement.

"Now comes the hard part," Rade said. "We need the defenses and the people to hold for five days, and hopefully after that, we see Temperance on the horizon with aid."

"We will do the best we can Rade, I promise you that!" Isabel said. They turned and left the stables, heading back to their quarters. They all tried to sleep, but no one in the city was able to as the Cladhach army made camp a mile from their walls.

The morning came too soon and when they woke they looked out to a grim sight. Amor's army was now spreading out and covering the entire perimeter on their three exposed sides. The soldiers of Nain watched with anticipation.

By noon the entire horizon was filled with a sea of black uniforms and armor. Beyond that, the army did not move and they hardly even heard a sound. For a long time, no one in the city talked, for fear of being heard.

"They're not going to do anything today?" one of the men asked. Morgrin nodded in reply.

"Take it as a good omen," Morgrin said. "If they had come prepared for war of this kind they would've attacked us by now. But instead, they wait. Because they know they're vulnerable." Rade walked up at that moment.

"It's almost worse than attacking as far as morale is concerned," Rade noted. "Far worse."

They left the wall for the moment and went down to their private quarters where Isabel was casually sipping a cup of tea.

"How long do you think they'll sit out there and do nothing?" Isabel asked.

"They have the means and resources to request anything they want, or pillage it from towns and villages," Rade said. "They could stay out there indefinitely."

"I'll bet in that other convoy that is coming they have the supplies they need and they're going to wait until they get here," Morgrin said.

"And don't forget that Halar is still out there and doing who knows what," Rade pointed out. "Eventually they will try to attack us, the question is when."

"In better news, they really don't have the time or numbers to keep the attack going through the night," Isabel said. "If they do attack it'll be either all in one day or they'll be stopping for night."

"True, but we need to think of ways to stretch it out," Rade said. "I know that these walls are not the most impressive, it's only twenty feet high, but we need to think of unique ways to keep them at bay."

"Any ideas?" Morgrin asked.

"I have a couple, but they will take some time to set up and I'm not sure they'll work."

"Either way it would be good to give the soldiers something to do," Isabel said. "Otherwise they will go insane waiting for something to happen. Dark thoughts will soon fill their minds if we don't do something."

"What of the caves where the rest of the citizens are?" one of the guards by the door asked. They looked towards him and he shrunk in shame, knowing that he shouldn't have spoken.

"I share your concern," Rade said. "Fact is, we are cut off now. We can't do anything to help them. We just need to have faith that Lathon will look after them." He turned back to Isabel and Morgrin.

"Isabel, why don't you take the Taruks up the coast tomorrow and see if you can find the fleet that's supposedly coming down the coast. If you can successfully take that out perhaps the Cladhach army will be slightly unnerved."

Isabel nodded and for the first time since Morgrin could remember she looked nervous, almost afraid. They talked with Rade for a while longer until the sun vanished from the sky altogether. The campfires of their enemies lit up, circling the entire city.

"You going to be okay tomorrow?" Morgrin asked. "You looked a little nervous earlier."

"I am," Isabel said. "I will gladly attack these ships tomorrow, but something about this battle is haunting me. I have three Taruks, against an entire fleet of ships..."

"My dear, I do not doubt that we were meant to be here for this moment and for whatever lies beyond. Aiden wouldn't have told us to go north for nothing."

"I know," Isabel said. "I just wish you could come with me tomorrow."

"I could.-"

"No. Stay here and help Rade. That's more important at the moment." Morgrin nodded in understanding and for a while they stood looking out at the campfires. He kissed her deeply and she smiled.

"I love you Morgrin, no matter what happens."

"I love you too."

IDOLS & TRINKETS

***

Isabel walked barefoot along the shoreline enjoying the feel of the water as it swept over her feet and ankles before being pulled back into the ocean. The birds of the sea soared through the sky, completely unconcerned about the battle that was looming. Isabel marveled at Lathon's creation.

She came to the small cove that the Taruks had taken a particular liking to and Aspen raised her head to greet her. She rumbled in pleasure standing to her feet, her large neck now jutting up into the sky.

"What do you say, Aspen? Should we go show some people how Taruks fight?" Aspen rumbled with pleasure as Ezzion and Destan rose from their spots, ready to follow their leader. Isabel climbed atop Aspen and they pushed off the ground and quickly soared above the clouds.

The ground passed rapidly underneath them for many hours and still, there was no sighting of any ships. Aspen descended as both she and Isabel intently studied a large river branching off of the ocean. A smile stretched across her face.

"That's what we're looking for Aspen!" Isabel exclaimed. "That river runs right towards the mountain. I'll bet that's where the ships are." Aspen and the other Taruks climbed back up into the sky. The trees were no more than specks on the ground. Far away to the east, a brown mass could be seen. They made for it, but still kept high enough to not raise suspicion. Finally, an impressive amount of ships could be clearly seen on the horizon and still, they seemed unaware of the Taruks in the sky.

"Gravv sure doesn't mess around," Isabel commented. Aspen rumbled in agreement. "There must be fifty ships there." A minute or two passed until they were nearly on top of the ships. Isabel checked her sword and took a deep breath.

Without saying a word, Aspen, Ezzion, and Destan threw themselves into a nose dive. Isabel clung on as they plummeted towards the ships and it was plain to see the commotion on deck as the crews now noticed them. In a moment arrows with large nets were fired into the air, they narrowly avoided being ensnared.

197

Aspen leveled out and streaked past the first ship, crushing the bow of it with her tail. The next ship she grasped onto the port side, her claws piercing the planks and letting the seawater in.

Isabel was slightly taken aback, having never seen Aspen in such a rage. Destan and Ezzion were following Aspen's example in every way performing similar antics and leaving a great number of ships sinking into the river.

Isabel flinched and ducked for what little cover she could as Destan spewed fire into the cargo hold of a ship. The ship exploded, sending chunks and pieces of wood sailing through the sky. Isabel's world went dark for a moment as she was knocked off Aspen's back and was submerged into the cold dark waters.

She pulled herself back to the surface, sputtering and gasping for breath. She grabbed hold of a wood plank and was quickly spotted by another ship. The ship pulled alongside and she was brought on deck. Isabel coughed and sputtered for a moment before looking up to see an old man standing before her.

The man was thin and tall, with a grey beard and hair. He was dressed simply, but the way he walked indicated that he was someone of importance, it also indicated that he was much older than he appeared to be. The man smiled, though his eyes held a sinister glare. An armed soldier came on either side of her.

"Don't worry lads, I think we'll be quite safe now!" the old man exclaimed. Isabel was pulled to her feet. "I was wondering if and when you would ever show up. You see, not all of us were convinced of what we were told years ago!"

"And what were you told?" Isabel asked. The old man smiled but said nothing.

"It matters not. What now matters is that you are here on *my* ship! My truth that I have clung to in the dark places of my heart are proved to be correct."

"So the truth is a matter of perspective?"

"Indeed it is," the old man replied. "One's truth guides one's life. And everyone's truths can be their own. For perhaps I was brought up by a heathen but I believe my truth can be different from your truth." The old man chuckled to himself and came a little closer.

"It seems you were brought up by a heathen after all," Isabel agreed. The crew mumbled and tried not to laugh.

"Do you really intend to mock your captor?" the man asked.

"No. Only to show your faulty logic and help you see clearer."

"I have said my view on truth and it has suited me well all my life. Why should I change now?" the man asked. "But in light of all of this, why don't you take a moment and defend your ridiculous statement."

"It's simple. You are using the wrong term. Look up the word truth in any dictionary in the world and you will find it is defined as *that which is true, or in accordance with fact or reality.* And that is where your argument fails. For surely if my truth is a different truth than yours they cannot both be right. Perhaps your truth is actually the correct truth and I am ill-informed? But the greater question is shall we continue this conversation further to seek out which truth is in fact greater?"

"Nay," the man growled. "I have no time for idle talk. I have work to attend to."

"Avoiding the challenge?" Isabel taunted.

"Do you know who I am?"

"Misdirecting the challenge? Wonderfully played! As to your question, which matters little to the one I asked you, I have absolutely no idea who you are. I would have played my cards the same, even if you were the greatest king of the earth."

The old man turned to the crew.

"My lads, we are graced by the presence of the most amazing traitor and backstabber in our history, Isabel!" the man said. The crew gasped and then hushed themselves. Isabel's mind froze wondering how this man knew her.

"Don't you care that your ships will be destroyed?" Isabel asked.

"Destroyed by what? You? Your Taruks?" the man fired back. "I'm not afraid of them. And they may take down a few but they'll drown in the water, same as you in the end." Isabel quickly looked to the sky noticing that none of the Taruks were to be seen anywhere. Her heart was flooded with questions.

"Now if you're as good as I've heard...since we know who you are, but you claim to not know anything about us. Who do *you* think we are? I'll bet you can make a few good guesses. If you're as good as your reputation." Isabel paused and whispered a prayer, as if in response a deep soothing calm flooded over her.

"You are mercenaries, hired not to protect the other boats or to keep them safe, but to carry something they do not. The boats are here to protect your ship from attack because this one is carrying something far more valuable." The old man seemed to smile at her.

"It seems your intellect is indeed what rumors and stories have suggested," the man came nearer, malice in his eyes. "Now how will your intellect explain that I know your name? Who am I, oh great Isabel?"

"I have no idea," Isabel replied. "How should I know you?"

"You shouldn't!" the old man exclaimed. "I am Agram. And let us make one thing clear dear *Isabel*. I know who you are, and where you come from. I have heard of you much, though only as an omen of destruction and death. Once, I made a good living working for a well-known Sorcerer named Merderick. It seemed that he fell into ruin and your name kept popping up again and again. At first, I thought it impossible, but then I realized that there *was* a chance you had somehow lived. Does any of this ring a bell?"

"No," Isabel admitted. "I'm intrigued by the notion that you have some knowledge of me and that I have incurred such a reputation when I've never set foot in this part of the world until now." The old man scoffed.

"You've got too much of your mother in you, the impure beast she was." Isabel felt her anger rise at the use of hurtful words about her mother.

"You are very bitter," Isabel said in reply. The old man glared at her.

"Make no mistake I am a very old and cranky man," Agram agreed. "And you misjudge my bitterness. It is not so much bitterness as it is disdain." He paused, caught up in some thought that only he knew. "There are some things in this world that should not be allowed to live."

"And who are you to decide that?" Isabel asked. Agram stared at her and then turned away. Isabel's mind reeled, wanting to keep this conversation going. "I'm guessing you' are making some vulgar comment about my mother who you knew at some point in the past?"

"Thankfully not for long. Your father was a little more agreeable when he was in his right mind."

"My family is dead. What is your point in all this?"

Agram grunted.

"The point is, I get to kill the great Isabel...and no one's going to help you. No one is going to save you. Where are your Taruk's? Looks like they're visiting the bottom of the ocean." He spat on the ground in front of her.

"Not everything is as it seems," Isabel said.

"Can you see the Taruks anywhere?" Agram taunted.

"No," Isabel answered. "But I see them." She pointed to the horizon where seven White Ships were coming towards them. Fear instantly covered the faces of her captors. Within a moment they forgot all about her. Agram yelled orders relentlessly and all the other ships panicked just the same. They turned wildly as everyone strove to get away from the White Ships which were approaching with astonishing speed.

By the time Agram had managed to turn the ship about the White Ships reached the first of the fleet who had been ahead. The ship was reduced to splinters as though it had run into a cliff.

The next ship sunk in a fashion that it appeared to have been pulled beneath the surface by a hand. Another caught fire and was left to burn. Isabel strained her eyes, unable to clearly identify the crewmembers aboard the White Ships. A sense of wonderment came over her and then fear.

One by one the ships fell and no matter what Agram did, the ships only came closer. The sailors cursed and several jumped overboard hoping to go unnoticed by the White Ships. Isabel never saw what happened to them.

At that moment the men cried out and were thrown to the ground as the ship shook and shuddered. Aspen, Destan, and Ezzion were all perched on various parts of the ship. Isabel grabbed onto the railing and watched in amazement and wonder as the three Taruks latched onto the sides of the boat.

They roared mightly and then in unison extended their wings.

They beat their wings furiously and slowly the ship began to rise out of the water. The men cried out and several of them threw themselves overboard as the ship raised a foot or two out of the water. Isabel grew nervous as the ship creaked and wood began splintering.

Agram clung to the center mast, his face white and almost expressionless as he seemed to be caught up in a vision that only he could see. In an instant he fell to the ground, frantically searching for a place to hide as small streams of fire began coming from the Taruk's mouth. Isabel clung tight to the ship as it was carried towards the shore. Isabel looked at Aspen and knew her thoughts. In an instant Isabel threw herself off the ship, plummeting to the water, which was now twenty feet below. She was submerged in the icy waters and surfaced only long enough to hear a thunderous crash.

***

The morning offered no relief to the city of Nain as everyone was awakened by the sound of a Cladhach horn from the east. Against the bright sunrise, they could only see another sea of black coming to the camp. None of them had to think hard to know that it was the second mass that had been spotted by the Taruks the day earlier.

The day was slow to pass and saw a small group of three hundred soldiers waging very small movements. They came as close as they dared and then pulled out as a volley of arrows was sent forth. Several men were struck. After that happened several times Rade ordered the people of Nain to refrain from shooting arrows as much as possible because arrows would be hard to come by once the battle actually began.

They studied the enemy's movements carefully, posting a watch every second of the day and the night. Behind the enemy lines, they could see catapults being hastily constructed.

Every second felt like an hour and each hour seemed like a lifetime as they sat waiting for something to happen to change their fortunes. By the time nightfall came, Isabel had still not been heard from.

By noon on the fourth day since Amor had arrived, it was clear that something was going to happen soon. Halar had arrived with the dawn and with it, he brought an unknown number of soldiers.

"Where do you think he managed to find all those people?" Morgrin asked.

"I've suspected for a while that they've been taking over towns and settlements. For all we know they've been moving their soldiers into the nation for months."

"Makes you wonder what Gravv had up his sleeve," Morgrin said. Rade nodded his agreement.

"I'm glad I don't know," Rade replied. "But we may be thrown into the frying pan real soon!"

Even as he finished speaking a bone-chilling sound of a Cladhach horn filled the air. At once, soldiers began assembling. Over the next hour, soldiers came from their camps and formed ranks of soldiers.

An hour passed as the mass of soldiers grew thicker and thicker until at last another blast of a Cladhach horn announced they were ready.

"To your stations!" Rade ordered. The wall became a bustle of activity as everyone took their place, ready to deal with whatever was sent their way. Morgrin took his place, on the south wall, while Rade would command the east, and the west wall was captained by a trusted friend.

***

It was still another hour until Amor rode to the front of the army and stared at the city of Nain. He caught Rade's eye and gave him an icy glare before turning to his army, yelling something to them.

He rode this way and that, no doubt giving one of those speeches that leaders gave to their men before marching into battle. A great cry went up from the Cladhach army.

A moment later another cry came from the Cladhach army. They still hesitated, sending up another great roar that Rade could tell was rattling the nerves of his own men.

"They will not be getting this city today!" Rade yelled, his voice carrying farther as though something was helping it be heard. No matter where a person was waiting in the city, the words resonated in their hearts and they were filled with courage and hope that they hadn't known before. "Stand your ground!

Fight for your family, your friends, and above all else Lathon! Let's send these demons back into the abyss!" Rade yelled. A tremendous cry went up from within the city as the Cladhach army began to move.

The approaching army slowly picked up speed. Rade studied their movements carefully, noticing a mass of archers in the middle of the coming group. He also saw a number of boards and battering rams with them.

Finally, the army reached the poles that they had set up as a deterrent and the soldiers were forced to maneuver around it.

"Archers ready!" Rade yelled. The command was repeated by others who were each in charge of a certain section of the wall. The archers fitted arrows to their bows.

"Hold your arrows!" Rade yelled. "Hold your arrows!" Everyone followed his orders, watching the army snaking their way through the poles.

Finally, a number of the soldiers fell into the pits that they had dug and covered with straw and dirt. Men cried out as they were impaled by the many sharp poles that had been put in the bottom.

"Fire!" Rade yelled. The order was repeated and each group let a volley from their bows. Many of the distracted soldiers were struck and they fell to the ground. Their relief was short-lived as the archers within the Cladhach army, fired a volley of arrows into the city. A number of the men near Rade were struck. The others were embedded into the wall.

"Give them another!" Rade yelled. A moment later more arrows were released into the army who had now passed through their deterents and raced towards the walls. Another round of arrows came from the Cladhach army, but to their surprise none of them were aimed at the soldiers.

Instead, the arrows struck the wall and embedded themselves deep into bricks. Everyone waited and watched in confusion as another volley was sent into the walls. Rade rushed towards the edge and looked down.

His heart dropped as he noticed that the arrows were arranged in perfect rows and at different levels. He stepped back, narrowly avoiding an arrow aimed at him.

***

IDOLS & TRINKETS

"What the blazes are they doing!" Morgrin exclaimed. He had seen large amounts of wood and bowmen coming up to the wall, but after that, he had seen nothing. Even the rest of the soldiers had stopped, allowing them to be easily peppered with their arrows if they slipped between the armor.

He looked over the wall seeing nothing but shields covering the heads of the soldiers. Gregthan came up to him.

"What is it, sir?"

"I don't know. Fire some catapults at them. Might break their momentum. They're constructing something under the shields."

"Anything you want to try?" Gregthan asked.

"Start with the catapults," Morgrin answered. Gregthan immediately hollered out orders and the catapults were made ready.

Men bearing torches came forward towards the wooden boxes that they had built for their own catapults. They had built the boxes the day before and then had lined them with whatever leather materials they could find. Then they had been filled with oil. The oil was carefully lit and then the catapults were released.

They flew through the air, dumping burning oil on everyone who was underneath. When the box finally hit the ground it burst into flames cutting off the next troops from coming forward.

"Gregthan! How many rounds do you have?" Morgrin asked.

"We have twenty projectiles for each catapult sir!"

"Send no more than five. Also, send a message to Rade! Ask if there are men working on his side of the wall!" Gregthan left for a moment, finding a messenger. Projectiles flew from the south side of the city, landing in the middle of the troops that were waiting.

Morgrin quickly and skillfully made it to the edge of the wall and looked over, noticing that the shields were now higher and to the left of where they had been.

"Oil!" Morgrin yelled. "Get me a barrel of oil and a torch!"

***

Rade stepped forward, another volley of arrows flying through the air, again seemingly aimed at him. He jumped back, letting them strike the top of the wall. He grabbed one of the arrows that was now embedded in the top of the wall. He dropped it instantly as it grew too hot to handle, when it hit the ground it turned into a strange orange smoke and was blown away by the breeze.

He quickly inspected the next one, noticing it was three times as thick as a normal arrow. He touched it and this one remained cool but would not be removed from the place where it had landed.

"Lord Governor!" a messenger said. "Morgrin wishes to know if anything strikes you as unusual about this attack."

"Much is unusual!" Rade exclaimed, coming down off the wall for the moment. "I'm not sure what it is, but if he has any idea how to deal with the strange things at the wall. I'm open to suggestions!"

***

Morgrin peeked over the wall again, noticing the shields were higher and again to the right. Confused and alarmed he looked out to the west watching the setting sun.

"Sir! We have oil!" several men yelled from below. He ran back to them.

"Get it up here!" The barrel of oil was promptly raised by a hoist to the top of the wall. Then they rolled it to the edge and pushed it upright. As he expected the arrows from the Cladhach army quickly peppered it with arrows.

He raced forward and motioned one man to grab a torch and follow. He quickly plucked the arrows from the outside of the bucket. Oil began raining down on the shields beneath them.

"Light it up!" Morgrin ordered. A man came forward with a torch and lit the oil as it poured from the barrel. The fire soon cascaded down onto the sea of shields.

"Sir, do you think that's a good idea!" Gregthan asked. Morgrin immediately understood what he was talking about. Together they shoved the barrel over the edge. As it was falling the flames caught the barrel. An explosion lit up the area beneath the wall, shaking it and sending a large shower of rock and dust into the air.

"That was not my brightest idea!" Morgrin exclaimed.

"Started well though."

They scrambled to their feet and looked over the edge. The sea of shields had been destroyed and were scattered on the ground far below. To Morgrin's wonder and confusion, the arrows that had been fired at the wall were unharmed and there were still boards stretched across them, almost like scaffolding at a built site. More troops rushed towards the area, quickly rebuilding the sea of shields.

The hours blended together as Morgrin and Rade led the defense as best they could. Already they could tell their soldiers were tiring and the assault on the wall was gaining momentum. While no one complained, they could tell the soldiers were concerned. As of yet no enemy soldier had made it onto the wall, which was now heavily damaged by well-placed shots by the Cladhach catapults.

The battle for Nain continued until it was dark and then the soldiers were called to retreat with a single note of a horn. The people that had scaled the arrows and boards that had been set up, stayed where they were, hidden under a layer of shields.

Guards were posted on both fronts.

Morgrin stepped into Rade's quarters collapsing into a chair. Rade soon came in with Tero, the commander of the west wall, behind him. Morgrin sat up and the three of them took their seats around the table.

"So how was your day?" Morgrin asked. The three of them broke into grins.

"Oh you know, just doing the normal business," Rade replied. "But the important thing is we're all here and still alive." They all agreed to that. "What news of the west wall?"

"The west wall is holding up okay, we've had some bad damage from the catapults and we've been dealing with a large number of Giants who are involved in the battle. I've lost twenty men to injury, I just confirmed that nine have perished."

"Morgrin, how about you and the South wall?"

"I've lost ten, but have you seen strange things happening?"

"More than I wish to acknowledge," Rade said. "I fear that they have something else hidden behind enemy lines that we don't know about."

"What do you think it is?" Morgrin asked.

"I suspect they have a Mage amongst themselves."

"A Mage?" Tero asked. Rade nodded. "I've only heard of them in stories."

"Nothing to be trifled with," Rade warned. "Everything I saw today hints at a Mage, but I'm not sure, and until we do know for sure we should not tip our hands. There's no telling what an angry, enraged Mage could do to us."

"They're probably going to try and destroy the gates next. Halor and his men are waiting. On the edge of their camp, but have not made any movements."

"As soon as the gate is down he could run right into the city, with little resistance," Tero added.

"What if they couldn't?" Rade asked.

"How is that?" Morgrin asked. "We can't build new ones overnight?"

"What if we did?" Rade suggested. "Think about it, if at first light we gather whatever scraps of wood we can find throughout the city and then we use it to block the alleys and streets once they get in. They would break down the gates and run right into a kill box of sorts."

"Never seen that one done before," Morgrin replied, "But it sounds like an idea that might get us some time."

"We just have to last much longer for Temperance to arrive," Rade said. "She should be back tomorrow as it is the fifth day since she left."

"I hope she does come," Tero replied. "If she doesn't I fear that our people will falter and we will be overrun."

"Then let us trust that Lathon will bring Temperance back to us!" Rade said. From the way he said it, Morgrin could tell that he was worried about her even if he was trying not to show it. "We need these defenses to hold until she can get here."

"They will."

Morgrin was woken by Rade shaking him urgently. Morgrin sat up and instinctively reached for his sword, but Rade motioned for him not to. Morgrin pulled his hand back.

"What's going on?" Morgrin asked.

"A visitor," Rade said. "Strange visitor."

"Can't it wait until morning?"

"No, I can't," a woman's voice said. Morgrin looked up to see Isabel standing at his feet. He smiled to see her. Her frizzy grey hair was a mess and she looked as though she had been swallowed by the desert. He stood and embraced her.

"You look terrible." She laughed.

"Maybe you should look in a mirror!" Isabel jested. Morgrin kissed her, but came away sputtering as her lips were covered in dirt and dust and then burned as though they were on fire. Isabel laughed.

"So, what have you been up to?" Morgrin asked.

Isabel shrugged. "Oh, you know...stuff. It's been interesting."

"So I've noticed."

"What have you been up to?" Isabel asked.

Morgrin smiled sheepishly and shrugged. "Oh, you know...stuff. It's been interesting here as well."

They laughed again and Isabel laid down next to him.

"She got some very interesting things to tell," Rade said. He turned to look at her but was immediately met by the sound of snoring as Isabel fell into a deep sleep. They both exchanged an amused look.

"What do I need to know?" Morgrin asked.

"What you need to know is that we agreed that as long as there's the possibility of a Mage we can't use the Taruks. If he knows anything about them we're toast for somebody's breakfast in the morning."

"Agreed," Morgrin said. A silence fell over them. "I've only ever faced the Sorcerer. I've never seen a Mage before.

"They have similar qualities, like where they get their power. But they differ in that the Sorcerer is always playing the long game to get you because he's after your soul...that's not how Mage's work. They are quick, fast, and wicked deadly."

"Anything else?"

"Yes, but that's for her to tell you in the morning. She will join Tero on the west wall," Rade said as he turned to leave.

"Rade?"

"Yes."

"If they do have a Mage, how do we defeat it?"

"I don't know."

***

Isabel struggled to wake up as Morgrin shook her vigorously. Eventually, she sat up and stumbled to a small table where he sat down. Two mugs of coffee waited for them.

"I made it extra strong for you," Morgrin said.

"Good. I am going to need it," Isabel said taking a sip and showing her surprise as she realized just how strong Morgrin had made it. "Whew! You weren't kidding about strong, were you? My mind is awake now!" Morgrin laughed.

"Good. Rade wants you to take over command of the west wall. Tero will be your assitant."

"Better drink this fast. Is it daylight yet?"

"No, daylight won't be for another hour," Morgrin answered. "I suspect Cladhach will not wait long after sunrise to begin their assault for the day."

"Probably true," Isabel replied, taking a sip.

"I'm really glad to see you alive," Morgrin said.

"I'm happy to be alive," Isabel replied. "About fifty ships were coming up the river. They're all gone now. The coastline is secure."

"Good work my dear."

"Thanks, but I feel as though I hardly deserve credit for accomplishing the goal. The White Ships that Michal spoke of...appeared."

"So the White Ships aren't just a myth, they're real?"

"I was captured on the deck of one of the other ships when they appeared and within minutes the entire fleet was sinking to the bottom of the river."

"What about the ship you were on?" Morgrin asked.

"The Taruks lifted it out of the water and dropped it on land." Morgrin nearly spit his coffee out at the revelation.

"Are you serious?"

"Very. Freaked me out too!"

"I can see why!" Morgrin exclaimed.

"I had already figured out that the ship I was on was holding some kind of precious cargo, but I never would have expected to find these." She quickly crossed the room, grabbed an object folded in a cloth, and brought it to the center of the table.

She pulled away the covering and brilliant green light flooded the room. They both had to shield their eyes and after a second or so the light dulled to an amount that was easy to see the object in detail. Morgrin looked at it dumbfounded, much like she had done when she had first picked it up.

"A Maurivan Block?" Morgrin asked.

"Yes." Both of them stared in wonder at the small box that was exactly like the one she had shown Drake and Rachal before they had left.

"It's glowing?"

"There were thousands of them on this ship."

"Are these the same as the one you have?"

"Except for the glowing. Yes. They were scattered all along the coastline. Once I got to the shore I had quite an ordeal convincing any of the crew that they didn't need to kill me."

"How'd that go?"

"I'm alive, they're not," Isabel said. "It was ugly, as fighting always is. When the last one had fallen Michal again appeared to me. He told me to bury all of them and come back for them after the battle was over. The Taruks were spooked by something, so they were little help in the way of digging and flying back. I walked most of the way. Finally, they came to their senses and came back to me yesterday." They fell silent for a moment.

"Isabel. Just what do you suppose Michal is?"

"I can't be certain."

"But you must have a guess?"

"Yes, I do."

"Do you think?..."

Isabel nodded. "Yes, I do."

Chapter 16

THE BURNAKS HEIGHTS

The morning came with a swift sunrise and before long the city was bustling with people going about their business. Rachal and Rodum came with a dozen guards and chains and led them out of the caves. Drake and Barnabas were loaded up in a large crate that was atop a wagon.

They started down the streets getting hardly any attention from the people. Drake and Barnabas both got the impression that the sight of prisoners being led through the streets was nothing strange. Drake listened as closely as he could to what Rachal and Rodum were saying but it was all gibberish to him.

Just then a tremor passed through the ground. It shook Drake and Barnabas to the floor of the crate. They gained their bearings and stood once again but found that no one else seemed to have noticed the large tremor. Whispers echoed through their heads for a moment, strange voices. The feeling passed and they were shocked to hear everyone speaking in their own language.

"What's going on Drake?" Barnabas asked, looking as white as a ghost. "I can understand these people as clear as day."

"Me too," Drake said. "I think there's only one explanation."

"Lathon?"

Drake nodded.

"I've never heard of this kind of thing happening before."

"I haven't either, but I'm not surprised. Lathon is with us and that's all we need to know, at least now we can understand what's going on."

They remained silent, listening to the people around them and learning all that they could, given their new ability. A while later their cart came to a stop at large gates made of rock and steel. They were a dull grey, showing signs of wear from the moist, salty fog that often plagued the city.

Rodum spoke with the guards' and they were soon allowed to enter. Inside Drake and Barnabas were nearly overwhelmed by the sights that awaited them. People were chained in lines, nearly one hundred people long. At the head of the great courtyard, a host of rich businessmen looked out on the people.

"Slave auction?" Drake asked.

Barnabas nodded. "It's a big business in some parts of the world."

They passed the auction and headed further into the courtyard until they reached a large building nearly as big as any castle that Drake had ever seen. Guards were everywhere. People of great wealth walked the courtyards, seeming to gather at the steps as their cart was brought to a stop.

Rachal and Rodum climbed down from where they had been sitting and waited by the cart until twenty heavily armed guards approached them. Rodum turned to Drake and Barnabas with a sly smile on his face.

"Welcome my dear friends, to the throne of the great King Tethelas. For peoples of importance, such as you Drake Thomas, your case will be presented directly to the king." He turned towards the lead guard.

"Watch him carefully. If anything happens to him or if he escapes, you and your family will be slaughtered by nightfall. Do I make myself clear?" The guard nodded, fear flashing through his eyes. Rodum turned back to Rachal. "And I'm sorry my dear Enya, but you will have to wait outside. The king does not entertain women unless it's late at night if you take my meaning."

"I'm not staying outside. I have an interest in these two men. I wish to reason with the king myself and have no middleman."

"But my Lady-"

"Is that understood, or do I need to draw your sword and cut it into a thousand pieces and feed you to the vultures." In an instant, Rachal had pulled Rodum's sword and held it to his throat. The guards were at a loss.

"As you wish my Lady, you shall speak with the king," Rodum said. Rachal handed the sword back to him. After a moment, Rodum turned to the guards. "I think this will be the most interesting meeting. Bring them, but keep them bound." The guards did as they were instructed, leading Drake and Barnabas with the chains that were bound around their hands.

They entered into a great hall, filled with very few people. A large throne sat at the head of the room, empty. To either side were six lesser chairs all filled. Drake and Barnabas were pushed up to a half wall, guards coming on either side of them. Rodum and Rachal moved ahead to a large table and stood waiting. A slave dressed in nice clothing appeared at the head of the room and everyone stood to their feet.

"Please bow before The King and Lord of this land, Lord Tethelas!" A large man entered the room, standing nearly eight feet tall. A lavishly decorated crown of gold was set upon his head, and a sword was strapped to his side. He strode in and everyone except Drake and Rachal cowered. The king studied Drake for a moment, before taking his seat. Everyone else soon returned to their former positions.

"Begin," Tethalas ordered. "Who have we captured this time Rodum? Unless my eyes cheat me, this is a very valuable man!"

"Your eyes do not deceive you, Your Majesty," Rodum started. "This is none other than the famous Drake Thomas of Rinevah; also I have brought to you today a former Bazarran, who was in your service many years ago. Barnabas.

"I remember very well. His services were high in praise and the beauty of his wife was well renowned and most certainly pleasing to my eyes." A quick look at Barnabas revealed years of hurt and grief suddenly coming back to the surface and threatening to burst out in anger. "As I can recall, there is no bounty or interest at all in Barnabas. Is there some other reason he has been brought here?"

"He was found to be captaining the ship that Mr. Thomas was aboard. I would wish to purchase Mr. Barnabas for my own use and interests if the law allows such a thing."

"As much as I would enjoy seeing Barnabas as your personal slave for the rest of his life, as would be just; it is not within the laws of the nation to do such a thing."

"My next suggestion was to ship them off as a pair and by chance get more money for them."

"I'm sure we can easily fabricate some charges in connection with Drake that would make him valuable. Who's the woman with you Rodum?"

"My name is Enya of Mariuvan Tower of the Dead Mountains my lord and I'm here to petition that both of these captives be released into my care and custody. I was on the same ship with them and they were doing my bidding, I know they may be valuable to you but they are indispensable to me. I have many more experiments that I require them for."

"Do you now?" Tethelas asked, breaking into laughter. "First things first. I know you are not Enya because I have personally met Enya, in fact, I have had many dealings with her and everyone associated with the Dead Mountains. I see through your veil! You are beautiful beyond compare, that is obvious. Guards would you kindly move *'what's her name?'* over with the others. I'll deal with her after I finish with Drake and Barnabas." Rachal was dragged away. "Who wants the most for Drake?"

"Mr. Thomas is wanted in four countries currently." The king gave an amused look.

"My, my, my, haven't we been busy? Tell me more."

"Osh is willing to pay nearly twenty thousand for him, dead or alive. Before he went missing ten years ago he had killed one of their greatest warriors a giant named Iratha." The king thought hard for a moment. A searing light filled Drake's mind as the memories of that moment returned to him.

"He was indeed a great warrior and many myths were born out of that incredible feat. But all of this and he is only wanted for twenty thousand? It seems as if the memory has gone cold. Osh cannot be where he is sent. Next."

"Nashurra also has interest in Mr. Thomas," another council member started. "As you are aware my lord, Nashurra has a long and drawn-out history with the nation of Rinevah, most of which involves war of some kind. They at one time promised one hundred thousand but haven't changed it in many years. They may have assumed that he is dead."

"If this is what they think, then let them continue to think such a thing. Next."

"Vonlaus has a contract out on his life for nearly three hundred thousand-"

"That's a number I like, what is he wanted for?"

"He's actually wanted by the King Ervinule of the Dead Mountains. Drake Thomas and his companions destroyed an entire city in a matter of seconds and violated other sacred sights beneath the mountains."

The king laughed.

"I can see I'm in the company of a very smart woman," Tethelas complimented, turning his glance to Rachal. "You know our language extensively that is clear, but it was the copied dialect of Enya that I picked up on. Whatever the history between the two of you is I cannot guess, but you must know of Ervinule wanting Drake dead in order to claim that you wanted to take him for your own?" Rachal gave the king no reply, but Drake sensed that he had guessed right.

"To make things easier, King Ervinule is only interested in the head."

"Vonlaus just may get it. Was Mr. Barnabas with them?"

"Not that we know of, but we could easily fabricate that and likely get another hundred thousand."

"Very good. What are the other options?"

"The last nation is Nargaroth and they are willing to pay seven hundred thousand for him, alive. You know their customs and ways better than anyone, so you can imagine what they might do with him. He is wanted for destroying the nation of Megara and its ruler, who was rumored to be Merderick, a great Sorcerer of some kind. Nargaroth had many dealings and interests with Megara."

"Seven hundred thousand for a two-day trip by boat?" Tethelas taunted. "I think we can accommodate that. How about Barnabas?"

"Not wanted, but I think perhaps he was a spy within Megara who helped Mr. Thomas with the demise of the nation. I think also we could make it appear that he was working with Mr. Thomas to bring down Nargaroth. I'm sure we could easily get a great amount of money for them."

"Then Nargaroth it shall be!" Tethelas ruled. "Rodum will escort the two men back to their cells for the night and you shall depart tomorrow morning at dawn."

"What shall be done to the pretender?" Rodum asked. "Is she to be taken to Nargaroth as well? More fabricated charges could make her valuable."

"She's already valuable Rodum. One look at her tells you that. It is the beauty unveiled that I am interested in. She shall be taken to the *Burnaks Heights* and inducted to the house. She will live a lavish and wonderful life, serving and entertaining me and my household for the rest of her days."

They were immediately dismissed and dragged out of the room. Rachal and Drake fought their captors, trying to break free. Finally, all the procession was stopped and Rodum stepped in between.

"Hope you've enjoyed knowing each other. I see now there is a connection here deeper than I had first thought. I shall enjoy the next few minutes." Rodum turned to the guards holding Rachal. "Take her away." Commotion ensued as Rachal struggled with them and Drake and Barnabas tried to get free from their captors.

"In the name of the Lathon, Adonai, and Elohim, any person that should touch even a hair on her head with ill intention will be struck dead on the spot!" Everything stopped. Rodum and the guards laughed.

"I do not fear the words you speak!" Rodum declared. "Evidently your faith is so childish you can't decide which god to call upon to protect her. Hear me now! You can't save her. Your god can't save her. Your god does not exist in this place." Rodum began moving away.

"We'll see about that."

"Actually I'll see you tomorrow at the ship. I hope you enjoy your time in the prison cell tonight. After a couple of days in Nargaroth, you'll be begging to be killed, or to be brought back here, and I can assure you that will not happen."

The night passed without rest for Drake and Barnabas. Their cell had turned out to be a wagon with a metal crate on the back of it, which was promptly placed in the middle of the town square. A great mob surrounded them for most of the time, all the while cursing them and throwing objects, most of which noisily clanged off the metal bars.

Drake heard the people and was filled with sorrow realizing now why Aiden had been sent to the earth in the first place. He looked at the faces and conviction overtook him prompting him to stand to his feet. At this gesture the people fell quiet, stunned almost.

"Ladies and Gentlemen! Lords and Ladies! All within earshot of my voice please listen to what I have to say!" Drake paused for a moment. "The leaders of your nation have condemned me and my friend to the nation of Nargaroth, which I gather is the equivalent of a death sentence. Knowing this, why do you display such anger and hatred towards two condemned men?

"I look at you and I see people who have no idea why your actions are such. Lay down whatever pretenses you have about us. We are no criminals or dangerous adversaries; as you may have been led to believe. We are people of integrity who only wish to help in this world of hurts. Lay down your anger, your hatred, and your hard hearts, because soon someone is coming to you who is far greater, they will bring good news to you and I pray that your lives may be transformed by the greatness and glory of Lathon-"

Drake was unable to continue speaking any longer as the crowd exploded in fury. Drake continued standing but Barnabas shrunk back into the corner of their cage. The mob grew more and more deadly until finally the guards were forced to move the cart into a protected courtyard which was promptly blockaded. After that, they were left alone with not even the guards in view of them.

"I don't think your little speech back there improved our situation any," Barnabas said. "Lord knows how many people you just ticked off. I'm sure the king won't appreciate all the commotion."

"Tethelas wants his money and he's going to get it," Drake replied. "They won't be nice to us sure, but they aren't going to kill us." They were silent for some time. Drake finally sat down cross-legged in their cage.

"You're different than what I remember or expected Drake Thomas. When I shipped things for you before I can't say I remember you being this outspoken and bold."

"I wasn't for a long while. I should've been though. I squandered what was given to me the first time. Now with Lathon's help, I won't sit idle again."

"So I notice. What of your promise that someone else is coming? Do you know something I don't?"

"I have no idea who that will be, but now the people cannot possibly claim ignorance. I have spoken out in faith and I'm sure Lathon will grant my requests and send someone here."

"What about your wife? Aren't you concerned about her?"

"Yes, but I trust that she'll be okay. I swore an oath in the name of Lathon, he will protect her."

"Your faith is far greater than mine."

"I find it bodes better to speak about the power of one's God, versus the danger of the moment. Perhaps the coming of the dawn will open your eyes and your heart."

The night passed slowly and uneasily for both of them. The air grew cold and damp as the wind shifted out of the west, bringing in the chilly sea air. The courtyard was silent, save for their own breathing, and as much as they hoped to see the coming and going of a guard now and then, they were grateful for the silence. In the silence, a calming peace came over both of them and they felt their spirits lift.

At first light, they were woken by a commotion of a dozen soldiers marching towards the cart. Rodum led the way. The dawn was only starting to illuminate the sky and all the men carried torches. The soldiers threw open the doors of their cage and dragged Drake and Barnabas out, placing them on their feet. Rodum stepped forward, studying Drake with an icy glare.

"Word of caution Drake Thomas, one does not do the things you do and get away with it. Bring him." Rodum began walking while the guards covered their heads with towels.

They were dragged for a while and then finally allowed to walk. The guards spoke mostly in their own tongue, though they would insult Drake and Barnabas in the common language. Drake in some sense was amused, knowing that they still didn't realize he could understand what they were saying.

After an unknown amount of time passed, they were stopped and their blindfolds were taken away. A great iron gate was in front of them. Rodum pulled out a key. A few servants and attendants appeared on the other side of the gate, further up the path a large and lavish mansion could be seen. Rodum opened the gate.

"Welcome to the *Burnaks Heights*," Rodum said, motioning them through the gate. "For reasons you do not need to know the soldiers are not able to continue any further. The attendants will lead us to what I wish you to see and explain. Any move to escape will mean sudden death. The path borders the ocean; one quick shove and you would be gone. We also have marksmen covering the entire path. Their aim is good if you care to try anything."

They started up the path, hardly hearing anything over the sound of the ocean. The path climbed steeply and steadily with a number of well-adorned cabins along the ascent. Finally, they reached the great mansion, which on second glance looked more like a palace. Rodum knocked on the door and a man answered. He was clean-cut, but thin and rather scrawny, striking Drake as strange. Even the attendants escorting them looked as if they would have been able to hold their own in a fight, compared to this guy.

"Name and business," the man said.

"We're here by order of the king to see the Enya would-be." Rodum handed the man papers and after a moment they were let inside. They entered into lavish marble halls. A great stair was on the far side across an open courtyard which was filled with gardens and exotic plants. They passed by several great pools inlaid with gold. A gentle stream flowed through the entire area, filling the pools and nourishing the plants.

They climbed a staircase and turned to the left entering a passage that was filled on either side with room after room. Each one appeared fit for a king. As they walked by each one Drake became aware what this place was. About halfway down the hall, they stopped outside a plain door.

"I'm under orders to kill the person inside, I thought you might be interested to see what's been going on here," Rodum said. They stepped inside to see Rachal sitting quietly sitting in a great chair reading a book. Her bare feet hung loosely off the floor. Nearly fifty men lay face down on the floor, all of them dead. "We're not sure exactly how this happened. I can assure you that not all fifty men were sent in at once. Somehow she managed to kill them all without spilling any blood. When a person in *Burnaks Heights* gets out of hand, the king gets quite upset and orders the death of that person and any involved. The king has ordered her execution for good reason."

Rachal looked up and flashed a smile at Drake.

"Normally, we'd send her swimming in the ocean. I have a better plan though. I'm going to keep her alive and sell her to Nargaroth as well. She'll be gone, the king will be happy. What the king doesn't know can only make me rich, and the wife of Drake Thomas I'm sure will fetch a pretty price. That being said we're a little hesitant to touch her. If you would just come this way you won't be shot." Drake smiled and Rachal jumped to her feet. They were led out of the palace and down to the docks where they were swiftly loaded onto a ship and placed in the hold. Everyone disappeared and they were left alone as they floated out into the sea.

Chapter 17

LAST STAND

As they had predicted the Cladhach army had started their attack as soon as the sun had begun to creep over the horizon. Isabel stood atop the west wall, hoping and praying that they would be able to make it through the day, and also hoping that Temperance would arrive with aid.

The Taruks were contentedly in their cove down by the water and they seemed to understand the battle that was going on in Nain was not a battle they were supposed to be in. At least for the time being.

As the day wore on, they fought through the onslaught of war, which started with the catapults throwing fiery projectiles into the wall and the city. By the time midday came, much of the city was burning out of control as everyone fought to keep the walls secure.

By now, all three walls were breached in some way, a great amount of Cladhach soldiers had made it to the top and now controlled portions of the wall. Isabel and her men fought back fiercely, but they were still losing ground and she already knew what the Cladhach army was planning to do.

Both sides of the west gate were held by the Cladhach army and already the enemy was pressing their way down to the winches and levers that would unlock the gates so they could send their troops in.

Around Morgrin and Rade's part of the wall, they had maintained control of the gated sections. Battering rams were ravaging the gates and it was questioned how long any of them would hold. Isabel quickly dispensed of her opponent and looked out to the west for any sign of Temperance.

The horizon was empty as far as she could see and just outside bow range Halar and his men, some on horseback and some on chariots waited to rush into the city.

"Tero!" Isabel yelled. He turned to face her.

"I need twenty men, now!" Tero ran off and quickly came back with twenty men.

"We can't hold this much longer!" Tero yelled above the clash of the battle.

"I know. But we need to try!" Isabel urged.

"What are we supposed to do?" Tero asked.

"They are going to try to open the gates from the inside," Isabel pointed out. "Let's disable it so they can't do that!"

"Destroy our own winches?" Tero asked. Isabel nodded. The men all gave their approval and they rushed into the fray, fighting their way to the small room built within the wall.

Once inside they were looking at an impressive amount of winches and counterweights that would unlock and raise the gates so they could be opened.

Using whatever they could find, they worked as fast as they could to break or dismantle the winches and counterweights. They entered back into the main path leading up to the gate.

They were immediately attacked by Cladhach troops rushing down the stairs towards them. They blocked the best they could but eventually were pushed down towards the gate once again. More and more soldiers began appearing at the top of the walls and before long they were going to be overrun.

The relentless pounding of the battering ram shook the gates behind them. They were now starting to crack and splinter and as the moments passed it became evident that they wouldn't be able to repair it. To their surprise, the soldiers blocking them stopped attacking.

Isabel and the others slowly let their swords fall as they looked on the strange sight. Moments later a great horn rang out beyond the walls and with it, the thundering of hooves came rushing to their ears. In an instant, the gates cracked and fell apart and the Cladhach army poured in.

***

Morgrin blocked the blow and kicked the soldier off the broken and battered wall. He stood to his feet and took a moment to catch his breath, knowing that

224

their time was running out. It was nearly nightfall and still, there was no sign of Temperance.

The assault on this side of the city had started much like the others, with catapults, but most of them had been aimed at the wall. The wall was now cracked and splintered and in some places was ten feet shorter than it had been previously.

Despite their best efforts to thwart them, Giants had been firing large ballistae into the wall, attaching ropes to them, and then pulling with all their might. Throughout the afternoon large sections of the wall had been pulled apart and more troops came rushing over the top. For now, they were keeping the Cladhach army from getting any further over the walls than they already were.

Morgrin peered into the enemy's camp far beyond, vaguely seeing a big black shape moving here and there. Chills came up and down his spine and his breath was momentarily taken away.

"The Mage!" Morgrin exclaimed to himself. "Gregthan!" He came running. "Tell Rade we found the Mage!" Gregthan nodded and disappeared into the frenzied battle.

The minutes passed and then Morgrin's fear took the best of him as the Mage faced the city and began walking directly up through the ranks.

"Take him out!" Morgrin yelled. Anyone who was able fired arrows, but they disappeared in a flash as soon as they reached him. Proudly and confidently he walked up through the ranks, his troops moved to the side and bowed to him as he passed. Morgrin shuddered when the Mage came into full view.

He was a Gog.

Without flinching he strode towards the city gate and touched it. The gates exploded in a brilliant flash of light and color. Rock and dust were thrown a hundred feet into the air and Morgrin and his men were scattered all over the ground. Morgrin grabbed his horn, blowing several frantic notes through the air.

As quickly as they could they jumped to stop the onslaught of soldiers pouring into the city. The entire procession was brought to a halt as they reached the new second wall that they had built during the early morning hours. It was plenty high and sufficiently stopped the invading army.

The men who had been posted along the top of the new wall let their arrows fly, skewering hundreds of them within seconds. Morgrin felt like cheering but stopped short as the Mage began casually walking up through the ranks once again.

Morgrin picked up his sword and let out a yell, running headlong towards the Gog. In an instant, his sword became too hot to handle and Morgrin was forced to drop it or else injure himself.

Gregthan ran up from the side but quickly moved out of sight. The men up above continued shooting arrows into enemy soldiers and except for the crowd all around, the rest of his troops were doing quite valiantly.

The Gog gave an amused look and stood as though he was a street fighter and was egging Morgrin on. Morgrin stepped out, acknowledging the challenge imposed on him. The Gog laughed and threw off his sword. Morgrin drew a deep breath, trying to calm his nerves.

"Sorry you won't be able to go running to your mommy little girl!" the Gog taunted. "I'm afraid she'll be dead by supper!" Everyone assembled laughed and jeered. A couple of soldiers came forward and offered him a club.

"Not if I have anything to say about it!" Morgrin said. The Mage rushed him and swung the club. Morgrin narrowly darted out of the path and it struck the corner of a building. To Morgrin's horror, half the building was reduced to a pile of rubble, and in a blinding flash of light, the new wall that was holding the enemy at bay was destroyed.

In his shock, he paused longer than he should've because in an instant he had been picked up and thrown down the street. Morgrin got to his feet as quickly as he could, but even as he got to his feet he was knocked backward again.

The sound of hooves coming towards them grabbed their attention. A dozen men of Nain rode in and trampled the Cladhach soldiers. Morgrin looked towards the Mage only to realize that the Mage had vanished.

A horse stopped next to him and offered a hand. Relief flooded through him as he looked up at Isabel. A nasty gash was on her head and blood was dried onto the side of her face, but she still offered a smile and a nod as he jumped on the back of the horse.

"Fall back!" Morgrin yelled, blowing his horn in the manner that would signal that. "Fall Back! Retreat!" At once the soldiers of Nain began fleeing towards the east wall where hopefully they would be able to make a stand and hold out a little longer. Isabel and Morgrin let everyone else pass in front of them, guarding and blocking from behind in whatever way they could.

They made it to the east wall and felt a great burden lift off them as soldiers hastily closed the new gate that had been made in conjunction with the wall. There was a great clamor and crashing noise as the Cladhach army tried at once to break the gate down, but were unable to do so. Rade rushed up through the soldiers and came to them.

"The Mage is a Gog!" Morgrin exclaimed.

Rade nodded. "So I've heard."

Night came, but the battle did not stop as it had previous nights. Large portions of the city still burned and if there were any survivors outside of the small section they were in, then it would be a miracle. Isabel, Morgrin, Terro, and Rade sat in a circle in an empty house trying to figure out what to do next.

"They keep getting more troops and supplies in," Rade said. "I've been watching all day. A horn blows and then another five hundred soldiers come out of nowhere to help Cladhach. I'm not sure what to advise next."

"We are surrounded," Tero said. "There's only one way out and that is to run out and take out as many as we can on the way. Maybe we'll make it to the other side and escape."

"No," Rade said. He looked at all of them knowingly. "We will not run like cowards and give these demons what they want!"

"But we-"

"Yes we could die and we very well might!" Rade declared. "But at some point, you have to ask yourself what you believe in and then stand for it. I believe in the words of Lathon, and the way these thugs rule their lands does line up with Lathon's ideals in the least."

"Well said," Isabel agreed. Tero was speechless but looked at Rade as though he was doing it in a way that he hadn't before.

"Do you think any help will come?" Tero asked. The three of them exchanged glances.

"No. I don't think any help is coming," Rade said sadly. "I do not know what happened to Temperance, but even if she did show up, I doubt she would be able to effectively break the masses of troops between us."

"Still there's the Mage to consider," Isabel said.

"It's beyond my comprehension why he hasn't shown up to shatter the walls like he did to the gates earlier in the evening," Morgrin said.

"I haven't figured this out either," Rade admitted. "I could seek him out, but I'm not sure that I could do it."

"Maybe not by yourself," Isabel said.

"I know Lathon is with me."

"That's not what I'm talking about either," Isabel said. All of them looked to her. She reached into her pocket and pulled out the ganaske ring with the purple stone that Rade had worn for almost as long as he could remember. Isabel turned the ring over in her hand and then tossed it to Rade. It was the same ring that Rade had given her after he had defeated Gravv just a few days earlier.

"A ring?" Tero asked. Rade and Morgrin both stared at it. "How is the ring supposed to help us?"

"It's just Lore," Rade said, anticipating the thoughts of Morgrin and Isabel. "I've lived for thousands of years and I'm not even sure of the entirety of the rings power. How do you know what it does?"

"I don't," Isabel said plainly. "At least, I don't know for sure, but this has been on my mind since you gave this ring to me. It might just work."

"I'm confused," Tero admitted. Rade stepped forward and stared at the ring.

"Okay," Rade agreed. "We'll hold out as long as we can. Then we will ride out and take our chances."

"So this is how it's going to end?" Tero asked.

"No," Rade said. "This is only the beginning. We will stand. We will fight alongside our brothers, and Lathon willing we will see the dawn of a new day!"

IDOLS & TRINKETS

The night grew old and the morning came without the slightest hint of sunshine in the sky. Grey overcast clouds blocked out all the sun. Fires still burned in the cities and the streets of the city were completely trashed or filled with their enemies.

Eventually, the sun broke out, illuminating the land and offering them a sliver of hope. The three of them stood near the base of the eastern wall, which against all odds was still standing and fully intact. Isabel, Morgrin, and Rade didn't speak, but each knew what the other was thinking.

"Gregthan!" Rade called out. He came running. "Ready horses for us and for anyone who wishes to ride with us."

The orders were carried out and everyone present mounted their horses. Rade pulled the ganaske ring out of his pocket and slipped it onto his index finger. He looked to Isabel and Morgrin.

"Are you with me?" he asked.

"Yes."

"Are we agreed?" Rade asked. "Is everything ready?" They both nodded. Rade nodded too looking nervous but still holding his head up high. He turned to face the soldiers behind them. Several still fought on the walls.

"This is the moment of truth people of Nain! We have been hurt, we've been smeared, and right now we're being hunted. But in the name of Lathon, I urge this...Throw aside the hurts, the struggles, the things that you have no control over. Those things that have been holding you hostage for so long. They will not serve you, but instead bring you to destruction as you focus only on yourself and less and less about others and the greater picture. I do not know if we will live. It is likely that we won't. But remember we serve a God greater than any war. There is a bigger picture that we cannot see, and therefore we do not know the effect of what's about to happen. Perhaps an enemy soldier will be moved by our love and devotion, and on some future day inquire about Lathon and the soldiers they fought on this day. Fear, shame, disgrace...they have no place now. Instead stand strong, for freedom, for love, for Lathon!" Rade let out a cry and the soldiers within earshot of him cried out.

229

They let another battle cry out and everyone blew on their horns. For a moment all the fighting in the city stopped at the sound. Their resolve grew as Aspen, Ezzion, and Destan all flew overhead and in a flurry of motion, destroyed the city walls and gates with their feet.

Rade let out another cry and everyone followed, charging out of the broken gates and into the fields beyond. The sea of uniforms ran in a wild and frenzied panic as the Taruks chased, hunted, and ravaged the soldiers of Cladhach on the east side.

As planned the men stayed with Isabel and Morgrin who led them towards the battle on the east fields of Nain, while Rade went straight south getting behind the enemies that were now distracted by the Taruks and the coming horsemen.

Isabel and Morgrin led everyone in a charge on the eastern flank of the Cladhach army. Some of the army ran, but most stood their ground, even if they didn't want to. A few times Isabel and Morgrin glanced to the south, watching as Rade who was now riding at breakneck speed through the masses and supply tents, set them on fire. Leaving a trail of devastation behind.

Within minutes there was a great commotion as explosions rang out all around the battlefield, the ammunition blowing up. Then Isabel and Morgrin were unable to see him.

***

Rade urged his horse faster, throwing balls of fire anywhere he wanted and doing as much damage as possible until he knew he would be caught. The people he passed hardly got a glance in his direction before something of theirs was on fire.

The panic and the confusion associated with balls of fire 'appearing' out of nowhere threw everyone over the edge. Soldiers ran wild, the Cladhach army began killing each other as each of them thought the gods were angry at them.

Rade formed another large fireball and hurled it at the weapons carts. They went up in flames, but unintentionally threw dozens of swords and other weapons flying through the air. He swerved to the side but was still caught in the arm by a long knife that had been sent flying.

IDOLS & TRINKETS

He pulled the knife out of his arm and defended himself against a cavalryman who had rushed to attack him. Rade blocked the man's assault but was thrown off his horse where he tumbled to the ground.

Not wasting any time, he leapt to his feet, as he was being approached by twenty horsemen and soldiers. Rade dropped the knife and held both hands in front of him, forming another ball of fire. The men slowed and stopped, their horses shifting and stamping around anxiously.

"Think about what you're doing men!" Rade yelled above the noise of the battle. "I do not seek to harm you, but I will if you insist on harming me."

Several of the men acknowledged what he said and put their weapons on the ground, but several of them rushed forward, swords drawn.

Rade threw the fireball to the ground. The fire spread out and consumed the men who had been attacking him. The ones who had laid down their weapons were fine, even if they were in shock at what had just happened.

"Truly your God is more powerful than ours," one man said.

Rade smiled. "After the battle is done, I'd be glad to tell you about him."

The men turned and picked up their weapons joining a group of Nain soldiers after Rade explained what had happened.

Rade pulled his sword, fighting and taking down as many Cladhach soldiers as he could. The time passed and the contest became harder and longer. The sun was just beginning to set in the west and everyone knew there would be no rest until the battle was done.

Rade swung at the next soldier confronting him but never got a chance to take another swing, as his sword was wrenched from his hand and crumpled as though it was tissue paper. Rade looked up to see the Mage standing before him.

The Gog stood nearly ten feet tall, but Rade still stood as tall as he could. The Gog breathed heavily and his eyes were filled with a malice and a hatred that Rade had only seen one other time in his life.

That was the last time he had seen a Mage.

Without warning the Mage swung and backhanded him. Rade stumbled but didn't fall. Forming a fireball and hurtling it in his direction. The fire dissipated.

"Nice feeble effort," the Gog said. His voice was deep and rich and with it came a power to tempt the soul, desire, and will of a person. Rade didn't speak and instead locked eyes with the Mage. "I hope you realize just how much of a mistake you've made. I will lay waste to every single soldier. And then I will seek out, the woman and children and do the same."

"Who died and made you king?" Rade asked.

"I am the king fool!" the Mage answered. Rade was momentarily filled with fear as he realized the weight of what had been revealed. This was the king of Cladhach.

"Not for long," Rade said. Though he said the words his feelings were anything but. Despite the show the king was making Rade could see that the Mage was tired and starting to weaken.

"I am King Arioch!' the king said. "Bow before royalty you insolent fraud!" The king grabbed him with one hand and cut him with the spikes on his knuckles. Rade doubled over in pain, already feeling the flow of blood from his abdomen.

"Control the Taruks!" Rade said. Arioch stepped backward.

"You challenge my authority?"

"No, I challenge your power!" Rade said. The king hardened his eyes on Rade. "Go on, control the Taruks!"

Arioch kicked Rade and let him fall backward.

"I will never bow to the whims of a ragtag king!" Arioch roared.

"You can't do it can you?" Arioch was silent. "You don't have the power. Your god can't do it."

"Control the Taruks or not, I will still slay everyone in this valley! Your friends will be dead and you get to watch them die."

"I don't think that will be happening today."

"You talk like a fool!"

"I talk because I have faith."

"Well then, let your faith try to save you now!" Arioch grabbed him by the collar and threw him through the air, where he crashed onto the hard ground.

IDOLS & TRINKETS

Rade's head throbbed and he struggled to remain conscious. The Ganaske ring which was on his finger began to glow lightly. A purple light seemed to shine behind it. As Rade lost the battle to remain conscious strange horns were heard in the distance.

***

Morgrin and Isabel turned towards the sound of the strange horns. They came from the west and against the setting sun, a wall of dark horses emerged on the horizon. For a moment it seemed as if all time stopped and everyone was fixated on the coming army. Amidst all the shadows they could see a person out in front, a helm by her side and bright red hair glowing in the fading rays of sun.

"Temperance!" Isabel exclaimed. As soon as Isabel had said her name, everyone within earshot felt their resolve grow and word quickly spread through the army.

"Why don't we send her a proper greeting!?" Morgrin said. He pulled his horn from his belt and let a long note ring out. Again the strange horns, the horns of Dengar rolled over the plain.

***

Temperance felt her heart soar as she heard the answering notes of familiar horns coming to her. She looked at Nain, burning and broken, but amidst it all she was filled with relief knowing that the people of Nain had hung on.

With her, nearly eleven hundred horsemen rode. Half of them were members of the Dengar Military, while the other half were volunteers. Citizens who had come to do their part in the defense of Nain. She pulled her mount to a stop and the five soldiers that had been assigned to come with her in the first place brought their horses over towards her.

"Only one strategy," Temperance started. "Run them through!"

The soldiers took their places at the head of their companies and then in unison, they blew on their horns long and hard. The entire company let a great cry escape as they began their final approach to the enemy lines.

Arrows were fired and some of them went down, but still, the tidal wave of horses rushed towards the enemy ranks.

233

***

Rade woke after some time, but how much time had passed he didn't know. He still heard a great panic and confusion among the army of Cladhach as he was chained in the middle of their camp. The soldiers ran here and there, not paying any attention to him.

He quickly glanced at the Ganaske ring, seeing that it now appeared normal, and wasn't glowing like it had been earlier. Rade formed a small fireball, holding it to the chains. They were heated and then easily snapped.

He spotted an empty horse and made for it, but was grabbed from behind before he could get there. The iron grip of King Arioch threw him to the ground where he was repeatedly kicked and beaten by Arioch.

The ring on Rade's hand began to glow again.

A shout came from a horsemen on the left. Rade turned to look and caught a glimpse of Temperance's red hair as she flew at Arioch, sword extended. The stunned Arioch was helpless to defend and was knocked clear off his feet. Temperance swung her sword but found it to be much like it had been when Rade had tried that. Her sword was crumpled up and useless and she was yanked off her horse and thrown next to Rade.

Temperance pulled a dagger from her belt and let it fly. Arioch caught it in one hand and threw it back at them. It struck Temperance in the side.

Rade jumped to his feet, the stone inside the Ganaske ring now glowing brighter by the second. Arioch rushed at the both of them and struck Rade across the face with the spikes on his hand.

The ring glowed brighter. He was kicked to the ground again and in one swift motion, Arioch had picked both of them up and threw them into the ground.

"I am king!" Arioch boomed. Rade said nothing, but instead stood to his feet, helping Temperance do the same. Arioch looked at them confused but then hollered to some men. Twenty of them came each with a bow.

"Finish them!" Arioch yelled. Rade held Temperance by the hand and held up his other hand with the glowing ring. Arrows were fired at them, but each one was destroyed as an invisible arch was created over the two of them.

Time after time it happened, and all the while the ring glowed brighter and brighter. Even they thought from within the ring they could hear voices crying out and cursing Arioch.

A moment later a deafening explosion of purple light filled the camp, spreading from them and continuing through the army. The shockwave rolled on like thunder shaking everything and frightening the army of Cladhach.

There was a great commotion as everyone panicked and began running into the desert, but as the shockwave reached them the soldiers of Cladhach fell over dead. Within ten seconds the thunder had ceased and the only people standing were citizens of Nain and Dengar.

***

Isabel and Morgrin looked on the battlefield with awe as every Cladhach soldier had been defeated. Chills ran up and down her spine as she realized that against all odds Lathon had delivered them from certain death.

The following morning the citizens who had been hidden in the caves were permitted to come out and immediately everyone began cleaning up and clearing everything in the city and fields beyond.

It wasn't until the evening that they found Rade and Temperance among a sea of Cladhach soldiers. Despite all odds, they had found them to be unconscious but alive. Isabel curiously looked at the Ganaske ring which was still on Rade's finger. The gem was split in the middle. To her surprise, the inside of the gem was empty and hollow.

Quickly, they took them inside the city and did whatever they could to keep them well until they woke from the coma that had overtaken them.

That evening food was brought from the cave and they shared as great a feast as they could manage seeing the circumstances. The next morning they found Rade and Temperance to be awake and well, surprisingly not injured in the slightest from everything that had happened.

"Thanks for looking for us," Rade said. Isabel and Morgrin smiled. "And...thanks for giving me the ring back."

"What happened with the ring, exactly?" Temperance asked.

"It was a Ganaske ring," Rade answered. "The was ring created by dark hands of an ancient time. It 'trapped' shapeshifters and held them within the ring." Temperance's face drew a blank, but she nodded as if she was trying to understand. "I don't know how old it is or how many souls were trapped inside, but according to what little lore surrounds rings like this, the 'Spirits' inside can at any point choose to help the one wearing the ring."

"So the 'Spirits' in the ring *chose* to help you?" Temperance asked.

"In a matter of speaking," Rade said. "I know weird right?"

"Yes," Temperance said, her eyes lighting up. "But I think I'm getting used to it."

"What happens to the Spirits now?" Morgrin asked. Rade and Isabel both shrugged.

"Hard to say," Rade said.

"I feel a leading that the souls are both redeemed and at peace," Isabel said. They nodded and were lost in their thoughts for a moment.

"I'm glad to see you returned from Dengar," Isabel said. Temperance smiled proudly.

"What took you so long?" Morgrin teased.

"It took a while to fully convince them," Temperance started. "Turns out most of the people of Dengar had wanted to reach out to us for some time, but they were too afraid of their king and his agents. Only a month ago the king died in his sleep.

"They were in the middle of a memorial for the king when I arrived...so that was interesting. But after that, they read Rade's letter and agreed to help, but it took longer to assemble everyone than I had hoped."

"You arrived just in the knick of time," Isabel complimented.

"Anyway dear," Temperance turned to Rade. "You, no doubt, have many people who will probably want to meet with you to discuss trade and other boring monotonous things."

Rade smiled. "Looking forward to it."

The next three days were spent cleaning and fixing the city to the best of their ability. The bodies of the enemy were piled and burned, while the bodies of their fallen were laid to rest in the ground. Overall only two hundred of their own had fallen in battle.

As Temperance had warned Rade was pulled into many negotiations and meetings that all went very well. Temperance joined him as often as she was able. She would often take over whatever task Rade had to leave in order to go to the meeting in the first place.

Isabel and Morgrin smiled at the two of them, who they could tell were still very much in love with each other even if they were still adjusting to everything that had happened to them.

***

Morgrin awoke on the fourth morning wishing he could sleep for another several hours. He grew anxious as he felt tremors coming through the ground. Some of them were strong and powerful, others were short and brief, while others still were a constant rolling thunder. He quickly stood, but nobody else was anywhere to be found.

Fear began to creep over him as he grabbed his sword. He stood fifty paces off of the west gate of the city and looked into the distance. Large clouds of dust billowed through the desert away to the east. He sprinted towards the city, adrenaline taking hold of him.

He paused and then was overcome with confusion as he noticed the gates of the city were wide open. He scanned the wall directly in front of him, seeing nobody, not even a guard. He listened, hearing a sound he had not heard previously...laughter.

Morgrin hesitantly put away his sword and walked through the ungarded gate. He climbed a flight of stairs and then ran towards the people, who had gathered on what was left of the south wall. By the number of people on the wall, Morgrin guessed at least half the town was present.

His confusion and anxiety grew until he started laughing just like everyone else. In the distance, Destan, Ezzion, and Aspen all dashed around tackling each other like kittens. Morgrin looked at all the people and then out at the Taruks, unexpectedly amused by the show. The Taruks were relentless, tackling and diving and rolling each other. Never in all his life had he ever seen Taruks acting like this.

He searched the area by the Taruks finally seeing three small figures frantically running around and yelling at each other. Morgrin turned and hurried down the wall grabbing a horse and riding out to them.

"Don't come any closer!" Isabel frantically yelled as she ran towards him. He nodded and stifled a laugh as she herself must have been caught in a dust storm created by the Taruks. She was covered in brown desert dust from head to toe and her frizzy grey hair was a tangled mess.

"Do you need any help?" Morgrin asked.

"Don't worry! We'll have this under control in a minute," Isabel exclaimed. She turned and ran back towards the Taruks. "You idiots! Act like Taruks for once!" She was swallowed up in a dust storm as Aspen bolted after Ezzion, only to be tackled to the ground by Destan. Rade and Temperance could be seen frantically darting this way and that, as they were somehow trying to help Isabel. Finally, all three Taruks tumbled together, roaring and rumbling in pleasure. Morgrin readied his horse as Isabel, Rade, and Temperance were swallowed by an enormous cloud of dust.

For several moments the cloud of dust continued and everything was lost from sight. Then a flash of brilliant light illuminated everything. The rumbling of the Taruks subsided and after a few moments, everyone could see again. Rade held a great ball of fire in one hand and the Taruk's stared at it mezmerised. Isabel jumped to her feet, planting herself right in front of Aspen.

"Hey, you Taruk!" Isabel yelled. Aspen looked at her and seemed to chuckle. "Yeah, I'm talking to you! What has gotten into you?" There was a pause and then Isabel's face softened. "I see." Isabel paused seeming to be thinking. "Well then, when you're back to yourself come back and then we can talk." Aspen turned away. "I'm not done talking!" Aspen turned and laid her head on the ground like a dog who knew she was doing something wrong. "Stay at least ten miles from anything important. We don't want anyone getting squashed as a result of this." Aspen nodded her agreement and jumped to her feet, wagging her long tail and staring at the ball of fire that Rade held.

"You want to play with that?" Isabel asked. All three Taruks jumped excitedly. "You guys are ridiculous! Go ahead Rade, throw it for them."

Rade threw the fireball into the air, it changed to a large bolder, but still, it went on and on. The three Taruks sprinted across the desert, fading from view as they raced after the rock. The crowd cheered and slowly began to disperse as the trio began walking back. Morgrin greeted them with smiles and laughs as each of them looked like they had been through a hundred deserts and battles.

"Good morning darling. So what exactly was going on?" Morgrin asked.

"You know the Lumaflor that we came across that is said to have the effect of eating too much sugar?" Morgrin nodded. "It is reported that they cleared an entire field of it before they showed up here."

***

It wasn't until early evening that the Taruks, sluggish and tired, met them outside the walls of the city. Morgrin and Isabel laughed at the sight, having never seen Taruks so tired in all their life.

"You will sleep good tonight won't you?" Isabel asked. Ezzion seemed to nod her head in agreement before resting her head on the ground. Rade and Temperance sat around their fire with Morgrin cooking some stew for the four of them. The waves gently lapped at the shore.

"I think we'd better spend another day or two here, let our crazy Taruks recoup their strength before we set out across the ocean."

"I can't thank you enough for all you've done," Rade said.

"We wouldn't have gotten very far without a good leader," Isabel said. "Luma is under good leadership and hopefully you'll all have many many happy days to come."

"Thanks," Rade said. Temperance took his hand and gave him a knowing glance. "I'm glad you'll be here tomorrow because Temperance and I are getting married at sundown."

Isabel and Morgrin smiled at them both.

"We could wait longer," Temperance admitted. "But what's the point? Like Morgrin told me. The heart is what matters, and Rade has a heart I want to grow old with."

"You do realize you're marrying a thousand-year-old man right?" Morgrin asked.

Rade made a funny face. "Do I look a thousand years old?"

"On occasion," Temperance flirted.

"Bah!" Rade replied. "Anyway, we hope you can join us."

"We'd be honored."

"Thank you again for everything you've done for us and Luma," Temperance said. "Is there anything we can do to help you on your quest?"

"I do have a favor to ask," Isabel said. She reached into a small sack and pulled out a Maurivan cube. "Have you ever seen something like this?"

"Heard of them, but never seen one," Rade said, inspecting it with wonder in his eyes. "Certainly never seen one that glows."

"If you travel east along the coast you'll find a whole boatload of them buried in the sand. I was hoping you could retrieve them for me and store them for safekeeping. I sense that I have some future with these boxes, but right now I can't stop and study them as I would like."

"Consider it done!" Temperance agreed.

"And Rade, I have one more thing to ask of you if you don't mind?" Isabel said. She pulled the map out of Morgrin's coat and handed it to Rade. Rade looked at it intently for a moment. Finally, he looked up with a blank expression.

"How did you come by this?"

"Kind of a long story," Isabel said. Rade nodded and looked at it carefully. "I believe it is a map that has multiple layers to it. Each race seems to see something different, I was wondering what you see."

"I can confirm the kind of map that you think it is," Rade started. "It's a Spirit map. I can see everything. Right now I see Elvish, Dwarvish, Gog script, and Hunir. There must be a dozen languages."

"What is a Spirit map?" Temperance asked.

"It's a map made by...people like me," Rade said, looking again at the map. "I knew most of these languages at one point. What do you want to know?"

"Ellizar noted some strange wind and water currents, where it would seem that an island should be there, but wasn't," Morgrin explained.

"Just tell us if there's anything unusual about it," Isabel said.

"I have a hard time knowing what would be unusual when I don't know what you saw, but I do not see any strange things on the map. I'll be glad to mark down everything that I see."

"That would be great," Morgrin replied. They sat and talked for nearly an hour as Rade immediately set to scribbling down everything he saw. When finally he was done he handed the map to Isabel who looked like she had been given the best news ever.

"Keep a close eye on that map," Rade warned. Isabel and Morgrin both noted the concern in his voice.

"Is there something wrong with it?"

"That map appears to be a Spirit map, but I can assure you no Spirit created it. I'm not sure how the maker of the map managed to pull it off, but the map is a forgery. When I look closely at the map, the crest of the Spirits is visible in the background. That being said we would always put our seal in black ink, whereas this one is in blue."

"Anything else?"

"There are about fifty islands between here and the next landmass. Most of them are covered in crests and insignia some of which I don't recognize. Then, there's a line of Islands that wind their way through the sea that have no markings on them. Whether they are uninhabited or the names are left off for a reason I do not know."

"So everywhere we see the air and water currents, there is actually an island?" Morgrin asked. Rade nodded.

"What course would you suggest?" Isabel asked.

"Stick to the islands without any markings on them. Keep high in the sky unless you need to, that way you're not spotted by any ships."

"Where are you two headed?" Temperance asked.

"North is all we were told. So north we will go," Morgrin answered.

"That's a bit vague isn't it?" Temperance asked. "Who wants you to go north anyway?"

"Aiden asked them," Rade answered. Temperance's reaction showed surprise.

"Is Aiden really the heir of Lathon?" Temperance asked. "I've only recently learned of all this, but how can you know it's the truth?"

"I've been many places and seen many things. With Isabel and Morgrin as my witnesses, I can say with utter certainty that Aiden is the heir of Lathon! The one spoken of by the ancient scrolls and prophets of old. I have met him many times and only because of him am I able to tell you of this today. I'm sure we'd be happy to fill in all the blanks for you as the night wears on."

The wedding came the next day with all the ceremony that could be managed in a city that was still rebuilding itself. The soldiers who had come from Dengar happily stayed and witnessed the wedding, before heading back to their nation the following morning. Though everyone knew the two nations would now interact often.

Morgrin took Isabel by the hand walking out under the stars. The city was still bustling with life as the light of many bonfires in the various city streets drifted up over the walls.

"Tomorrow we finally travel further north than either of us have previously," Isabel said.

"Nervous?" Morgrin asked.

"A little. The way Agram talked has rattled me," Isabel admitted. "The hatred in his voice. The anger in his soul. I guess for the first time in my life I want to stay in one place."

"We have to keep going though," Morgrin said. Isabel nodded.

"I know. I guess a part of me enjoys this," Isabel motioned towards the town. "I'm not sure I want to see this part of it end." Morgrin wrapped his arm around her.

"How about this? Whenever we get to where Aiden wants us to go we'll come back and see Rade and Temperance."

"Sounds like an agreeable plan," Isabel acknowledged falling into silence for a moment. "I think what I fear the most is that the Sorcerer seems to be deceiving more and more people. It's as if people aren't even questioning what they're being asked to do, they're just doing it because everyone else is. How fast has everything seemingly become this way?"

"One thing I'm sure of is that this is not 'just' happening. On the greater timeline, the Sorcerer has carefully considered everything, looked for weaknesses, and formulated his plan. Even he knows in the end he cannot stand against the power of Lathon!"

They fell silent for several minutes enjoying both the silence of the night and the music coming from the city. They looked out into the sea, wondering what lay ahead.

Chapter 18

TRIALS & FIRE

The waves pounded the ship for the first day of their voyage. From up above they often heard frantic shouts and orders being given. The sailors came and went without so much as even a glance in their direction. The only one who ever looked their way was Rodum and his eyes were only filled with a sinister malice.

It was long into the night before the storm died down and men were given rest, leaving the three of them in their cell virtually alone. While Drake and Rachal had spoken much during the day and tried to talk to crew members who went by, Barnabas had been uncomfortably silent.

He sat in the corner hugging his knees, looking into the empty space in front of him. At first Drake and Rachal had said nothing but as the time wore on, their spirits began to falter as they watched him.

"Cat got your tongue, Barnabas?" Drake asked. Barnabas flinched and looked up.

"Sorry," Barnabas said, remaining silent for a while longer. "I suppose I'm just not myself."

"So we gathered. What's your story?"

"What do you mean?"

"It's quite clear that you're from Bazarran in some respect. Do tell. It's good to talk about hard things," Drake said. Barnabas looked up and in that moment Drake realized he had never felt the sorrow and pain that Barnabas was feeling.

"I was born in Bazarran, the city of Eim. About half a day's walk from the place we just left. My mother was of the noble house and had a high standing with the king. I had three other siblings, but as you likely know, or will know soon enough, pagan gods require detestable practices. I lost all three of my siblings to these practices.

"With my mother being of high nobility it only made sense that I enter the king's service. I was a man of fifteen and all was looking good for me. I started working for Rodum, and he immediately took me under his wing and taught me everything he knew.

"The next year I was in port at Meo, when I laid my eyes on a beautiful woman, not a day over fourteen. I struck up a conversation with her and within a year we were wed. The next year was the best days of our life. I built a house on a nice piece of countryside and we were going to raise our children there. Then it all went bad.

"There are many rules that govern everyone who is in the king's service. For one who is nobility, there are special rules. The one that started my misery was the tribute clause. Every third year the king can ask you for something. It could be a possession, money, a job he needs done, etc. In return, there are usually very generous rewards, promotions, gems, gold, and things of that sort.

"I presented myself before the king. It's rare for the king to ask someone who's paying their tribute for anything other than money, but alas he didn't ask me for money. He asked for something far more precious to me."

"Your wife," Rachal said. Anger and remorse filled Barnabas's eyes.

"Yes. My wife." For a moment he sat silent. "He didn't want to marry her, he just wanted to see her once a week if you take my meaning. I agreed to the terms but had no intention of letting it happen. We both plotted our escape. The night before we were to leave, Rodum and his men showed up by order of the king to seize my property. We fled on horseback but we couldn't outrun them. When we were caught I was faced with death. Either I would be killed and they would take my wife or I could save my life and still lose my wife.

"I suppose I'm a bit of a coward because I chose to live. They dragged her from my arms and I never saw her again. If I had known then the turmoil and trauma that decision would bring upon me I would have chosen death. It would have been better than all of this pathetic excuse of existence that I call a life."

"What happened after that?" Drake asked.

"I worked for Rodum for another year or two, when it came time for my next tribute I deserted."

"Did you look for your wife?" Rachal asked.

"I came close several times, but I was never able to find the courage. Several years later I finally burned all the maps, charts, and anything I possessed from Bazarran, and vowed never to return."

"Looks like Lathon had something else in mind," Rachal said.

"If tormenting me is what Lathon wishes to do then he's doing a rather good job of it," Barnabas said with a sigh. "The only thing I've ever done worth anything is starting a shipping business."

"I'm not sure I'd say that," Rachal replied.

"Why not? What good, honorable things have I done?"

"That's not the point," Rachal replied. "What matters is what you do with your life from this moment on. The past is, what the past is. It doesn't control you, it doesn't shape you, it doesn't guide you unless you allow it to do so. There is much you don't know."

"Thanks for reminding me," Barnabas sneered. Rachal ignored the bitterness but stared long and hard at Barnabas. Uncomfortable silence followed, until Rachal spoke again

"Your wife's name is Evawyn isn't it?" Rachal asked. Barnabas grew as white as a ghost, staring at Rachal in disbelief.

"It was," Barnabas finally answered. "How do you know that?"

"I met her when I was a guest in Rodum's home." Rage filled Barnabas's eyes. "She too is considered a guest in their home. An unwilling guest."

"Tell me more please!" Barnabas begged. Rachal nodded.

"I fooled everyone aboard the ship that I was Enya so when we made port they made sure to take good care of me. The king didn't have a place to put me up for the night so I was taken to Rodum's house. I met his wife. They have five kids together. After the meal, his wife showed me to the guest house a short walk from Rodum's main house. I was told that I didn't have to talk to the people inside because they too were guests and were no one of real importance."

IDOLS & TRINKETS

"I was greeted by three children and their mother. The children were ages six, four, and two. Nice kids. Their mother seemed scared and remained silent until Rodum's wife left.

"Of course, I talked to them extensively. The kids were so charming and polite, I wished I could take them home for myself. Once the kids went to bed their mother and I got to talking she said her name was Evawyn. Something about her seemed familiar to me so I kept prying and asking my questions, trying to learn something about her.

"She intrigued me because she kept using the term 'husband' but it never seemed to be used in the way that would imply Rodum. I suddenly felt a great spirit come over me and with it an overwhelming sense that she would know your name if it was spoken.

"When I spoke your name and that I was here with you, well, I've never seen a face grow so excited. Giddy as a school girl. She told me all of her story and then some. After you left she was taken to the *Burnaks Heights* for a while. When the king was done with her he sold her. Rodum bought her and kept her as a mistress in their guest home. They have five children together two older ones that are grown and then the three younger ones I met, but he refuses to see any of them. He only comes to see her late at night.

"I know some of this must hurt to hear, but her heart is and has always been loyal to you. She was more than excited when I mentioned that I was going to try to get you released. I'm only sorry that I failed to accomplish that."

"You did the best you could, far better than I thought possible," Barnabas said. "Just now you've done more for me than I can even begin to tell you. To be away from someone for so long and then to even hear the notion that she hasn't forgotten about me is like a dream come true. I wish I could see her face again."

"Maybe you will get to see her face again, you never know," Drake encouraged. Barnabas scoffed.

"Face the facts, Drake, we're in chains, again. We're on our way to Nargaroth, a place that once you're in you don't come out, not alive anyway."

"I know a person who escaped from there."

"Well good for him," Barnabas snapped. "Do you even know where he is right now? I thought not." He paused, lost in his anger for a moment. "I'm sorry, I'm just frustrated. Right now I wish I was free of these chains. I wish I could run back, give Rodum a piece of my sword, and then whisk Evawyn and her kids to a better life…but I can't."

Silence lingered for several minutes, soon becoming uneasy and awkward. Rachal and Drake sat together on one side of the cell while Barnabas stared into the space in front of them, living through whatever he was imagining inside his head. Anger filled his eyes as the time passed on. Finally, Drake looked to Rachal.

"What happened to all the men in your room?" Drake asked. "Were they dead?"

"Very dead I'm afraid," Rachal started. "It's hard to explain and only now can I suppose that I understand what happened. They closed the door and left me alone. I had a few attendants who tried to press some fancy garments and jewelry on me as I was going to be tested in a couple of hours. I refused and they left.

"A while later I heard steps coming down the hall. I began to grow afraid when a person appeared in the corner. I have no idea how to describe him, but he was terrifying to look at. More weapons than I could comprehend. I thought for a moment he was going to kill me.

"He must have sensed my thoughts because he immediately said to me *'do not be afraid. I have been sent to protect you and ensure that no one touches you.'*

When I asked how it was that I was to be saved he said *'Lathon always comes through for the people who call on his name.'*

"The rest is kind of blurry. Men would enter and as soon as they touched me the man in the corner would jump from his spot and ruthlessly attack the men until they were dead.

"Afterwards he would take up his post in the corner without speaking a word. Kind of freaked me out at first. But enough about me. It was interesting to hear a little more about your past during the court. Did you remember any of it?"

"Not before that moment," Drake said. "Now I can recall the moment as clear as day. Iratha was a giant, ten feet tall at least. I couldn't even begin to guess how much he weighed. His sword was massive, his helmet was made of bronze. He was intimidating to look at, even from a distance."

"How'd you kill him?" Barnabas asked.

"I'd call it an accident, but now I see that it was providence. The eldest of each family was called to battle. We were trained for fighting, although I was not very good. We were assigned to assist the men along the northern borders. Long story short, we got there, and no one was doing anything but taking council inside their tents. I asked around and it seemed that for nearly a month Iratha had been challenging the Rinevah army to a one-on-one contest, winner takes all, but no one would do it.

"King Zebethar happened to be there that day, so I requested an audience and said I'd do it. They were hesitant to let me, but I insisted. Not long after Iratha was on the ground and the army was in retreat. Afterward, I was brought to the palace to work for King Zebethar, which is where I met James. Worked in the military until I ended up fleeing for my life."

"Which is when you met me?" Rachal asked. Drake nodded. "I can't say I've ever heard of siblings before."

"I was on the run, it was better to leave my family out of it, and then I lost my memory. I have five siblings, all brothers. A set of twins, and the other three are a few years behind. I can see the house I grew up in as clear as day in my mind, but I don't know where it is."

"When we get out of Nargaroth we'll have to find it," Rachal said.

Barnabas scoffed.

"You're fools to think we'll get out of Nargaroth."

"You're the fool, Barnabas," Rachal retorted. "Even if the odds are stacked against us there's always a chance."

"A fool's chance."

"Then I'll take it."

They spoke no more for several hours, the night passing into day. Finally,

249

the sound of horns came from the deck above. Answering horns came from somewhere in the distance. A while passed before the ship came to a standstill and a great commotion was heard on deck.

After a while, Rodum came down from the main deck, several Dwarves with him. They scowled and frowned at them from under their big bushy eyebrows, their eyes pierced right through each of them. Rodum and the Dwarf next to him spoke in another language for a few moments before the Dwarves returned to the deck above. Rodum turned to the three of them.

"They have accepted the terms and will joyfully exchange money for all three of you. After that, you'll be taken through the Imahirian gate and I'll never see your faces again,..I think this is rather a good start to the day."

Rodum motioned to some Dwarvish warriors standing at the foot of the stairs. They came forward and promptly secured their wrists and their feet with chains. They were then led to the upper deck and placed at the bow where a dozen more Dwarvish warriors stood waiting. Six large ships flanked them on either side.

"What are you thinking about?" Rachal asked.

"Wondering what Ellizar would think of all this. This is something I've never experienced, the last time I passed over these mountains they were desolate, now they're filled with Dwarves. From the way everyone talks they're not the friendly sort."

"I wouldn't worry yourselves about it too much," Rodum said, coming next to them. "Soon I'll be rich and you'll be dead. The world will be better this way."

The time passed slowly as the ship turned to the east and followed the coast for some time. The mountains towered over everything, dampening their spirits. The base of the mountains was desolate with no sign of life, while the tops were covered in snow. A large wall bordered the sea.

The air grew heavy and silent, shattered moments later by strange horns that echoed low and deep, shaking the mountains at the core. Drake shuddered, feeling a presence that both calmed him and strengthened his resolve as he stood taller and more proud.

IDOLS & TRINKETS

At last, the ships turned hard to the left, sending them through a large gate in the wall of the cliff. Statues of strange and deformed creatures bordered the gate and above the great arch they now sailed under, a stone Taruk, carved from red stone, loomed over them.

Cold and dread filled each of them as they passed under the shadow of the Taruk.

They passed through the arch and left the Taruk behind them. Slowly their thoughts of dread and cold left them until they once again stood firm and resolute.

They were now in the midst of a large bay, which spanned nearly a half mile across. Around the entire perimeter, a large stone wall loomed over them. Fifty feet at the highest point and easily twenty feet at the lowest. The ships sailed straight ahead and came to rest next to the wall. The wall was steep with no clear indication of where they should make port. After a few moments, they were greeted by soldiers who opened up a door in the side of the wall, which had been completely unnoticed up until that point.

Drake, Rachal, and Barnabas were moved off the ship and into the opening, which was large and expansive inside. Still, as impressive as it was, the space was only filled with a wide staircase that led to the top.

They climbed the stairs and soon stood on top of the wall. Ahead of them, a long bridge, made of black stone stretched a great distance until it joined up to a large ominous gate in the side of the mountain. The entire company halted. A minute of uneasy silence passed before the gate in the mountain was opened. Out of it came a company of Dwarves.

"Allow me to translate the words over the Imrahirian Gate, through which you shall soon enter," Rodum started. "Although many things are said in strange languages it is best summed up by the large writing directly over-top the gate, in the common tongue it reads 'To enter is to die'; Something to look forward to."

The company of Dwarves reached them and stopped, an important-looking Dwarf stepped forward. He spoke first in his strange language. Rodum seethed.

"In the common tongue you mongrel rat!"

"We have your money," the Dwarf said. "But we have questions about the woman. What good is she to us?"

"She is currently pregnant with the child of Drake Thomas," Rodum lied. "I'm sure something like that would be worth a bit of money."

The Dwarf grunted and thought hard for a moment. "Worthwhile or not you won't be getting the full price for her! Half the price or we pass."

"It's a deal," Rodum said, shaking the Dwarves hand.

"Load their ship and see them out of the harbor so he does not get killed by the sentinels!" the Dwarf replied. Immediately people began running to and fro. They were forced to move, leaving Rodum and the ship to fade out of sight as they traversed the bridge.

The bridge was longer than they had first thought, nearly two miles long, and built over a massive gorge, of which they could not see the bottom. Smoke rose from the gorge, and no vegetation grew anywhere that they could see. The bridge steadily grew in height until they reached the dreaded gate that Rodum had mentioned.

The gate itself was ordinary but the brickwork that formed the gateway was anything but. Large black bricks formed the entrance while small red bricks formed the shape of a Taruk. From inside they could hear a commotion as if a large assembly was ready to give them a warm welcome.

The company stopped and released the chains and shackles from the three of them. A large key was handed to the lead Dwarf who slid it into the gate and turned it. The gate creaked open and the roar of a great assembly reached their ears. The guards took their belongings and then shoved them through the gate and slammed it shut.

They found themselves locked in a large pit. Far above them walkways and railings were carved into the mountains and they were filled with people. The people shouted and yelled and cursed them in their own tongue which Drake couldn't hope to understand. He had only learned a little dwarvish in all the years he had known Ellizar and they weren't using anything that Drake might recognize.

Rachal cried out and grabbed at her side as a rock struck her and then tumbled onto the ground. Drake and Barnabas rushed to Rachal's aid, getting struck multiple times as the people above began throwing things at them. Some were rocks and some were old tools and sticks. As they were trying to avoid getting stuck, they became aware of skeletal remains scattered over the floor, or limbs of past victims being thrown into the pit. Time faded from them and slowly one at a time they each lost consciousness.

Drake was the first to wake from the uneasy sleep that had come over them. The room was dark, save for a few torches that burned on the higher levels. He sat up, his head throbbing with pain. He gently shook Rachal's motionless body and she stirred. Soon they had awoken Barnabas who was in no better shape than the two of them were.

"I was hopeful when I woke up that this was all just a bad dream," Barnabas said. "Should've known better."

"At least we're alive," Drake said. "I don't think we were supposed to live to see the light of day."

"Indeed you weren't," a voice said. They looked ahead and a Dwarf with a light brown beard and a head full of hair came walking towards them. "As sure as I stand before you now you must believe me when I say never in all my years have I seen anyone come out of it alive."

"We're okay with that," Rachal said, as the three of them struggled to their feet. The Dwarf instinctively reached for his sword but pulled back his hand a moment later. "What happens to us now?"

"I don't rightly know," the Dwarf said. "I was just on my normal patrol when I heard you stirring. I suppose I'm obligated to turn you in and present you to the king's guards."

"Sounds comforting," Barnabas replied.

The Dwarf shrugged.

"Either they'll take you to the king or they'll kill you, I wouldn't have much of a say in a matter like that."

"What's your name?" Drake asked. The Dwarf stood a little taller.

"My name is Corvil son of Corvall," the Dwarf answered.

"Pleasure to meet you Corvil," Rachal said, shaking his hand. Corvil stared at the three of them.

"Pleasure to meet you as well," Corvil managed after a moment. "I sure wish I didn't have to do this to you, but if I don't it'll be my head that is sent rolling."

"We understand," Drake replied. "We won't resist. Take us to your king and we'll see what happens from there." Corvil shrugged his shoulders and then pulled a large horn from his belt and let a short note ring through the mountainside.

Dwarves came from all around and soon they were led out of the pit, upstairs to the upper halls. For a while, they didn't go anywhere as there seemed to be some confusion about who was supposed to take them to the king, and how many Dwarves could be sparred in order to do so. Drake listened intently to the conversation, wishing he understood the language better.

At long last, it seemed to be sorted and close to fifty armed Dwarves came alongside. They walked at first and occasionally would come to an abrupt stop for several minutes as the Dwarf leaders would partake in some ritual. Drake and Rachal studied the surroundings, trying to see what it was they were paying homage to.

They continued on their journey through the dark silent halls of the Dwarves, the torchlight flickering off the dark black rock that made up the mountain. They passed over great bridges with no barrier keeping them from what they expected was a very long fall. Every now and again they would enter into dark chasms that went on as far as the eye could see.

They would join the tunnel for a little while and then turn off into a side alley, which would lead them back into the open. Drake marveled at the complexity and skill of the tunnels and bridges that spanned in every direction. Several hours passed and the first hint of light began to creep through openings in the side of the mountain.

All at once the company stopped and fell silent. A deep rumble came through the floor, if there was a sound associated with it, they couldn't hear it. The Dwarves were thrown into a panic and began running. The Dwarf masters whipped anyone who was falling behind. It was a couple of hours before they slowed to a walk and after that, none of the Dwarves said a word.

It was difficult to tell how long they were traveling in the dark tunnels of the mountains. Depending on what part of the tunnels they were in it could be bright as day, or dark as night. The only thing that gave them any concept of time was that the Dwarves stopped for a meal. It was usually a very quick light meal and then they would be off again, usually running.

Despite the Dwarves eating, Drake, Rachal and Barnabas were given nothing and were never allowed to sit or speak, even when they did stop for one of their 'meals'. Most of the time they were forced to run and whipped if they ran too slow. The Dwarves seemed to be particularly conditioned to running and seemed to do it effortlessly no matter how long they went without a break. Rachal had the hardest time keeping their pace, often being struck by the whip of the guards' who ran behind.

Eventually, time seemed to become a blur to all of them, but Drake guessed it was about two days that they had been running when finally they reached their destination. They were led down narrow winding stairs, and all natural light was lost. Torches were the only light now. They were led through many winding tunnels and corridors. Every now and then a heavy wood or steel door would be to their left or their right. Finally, they were stopped and a large steel door on the right was opened.

They were shoved inside a small cell, lit by a single torch. The room had nothing in it, just a hard rock floor and walls. A loaf of stale bread was thrown on the floor. The door was quickly shut and the Dwarves hurried off.

"Looks like home sweet home," Barnabas bitterly remarked.

"We'll make the best of it and see what happens tomorrow," Rachal said. Even sorrow tainted her voice. They all lay down on the hard cold floor, finding it easier than ever to fall asleep. As Drake fell asleep he imagined far off the noise of hammers and tapping from somewhere below them.

The sounds of shouting and armed Dwarves startled them out of their sleep. They were pulled to their feet by their hair and then shoved out of their cell. They began running again as they had the past two days, whips licking all of them as they failed to keep pace.

After close to an hour they were brought into a great hall, with so many torches and candles that they all thought the entire hall was on fire. The floor was black with a white strip going up the middle. Armed guards filled the entire hall, and stood at attention while they were paraded up the middle.

At the head of the room was a great throne. The base of the throne itself as well as many of the furnishing were made of gold. While the curtains and hangings throughout the hall were a deep burgundy. On the throne, at the front, a large dwarf sat, with a crown upon his head. His beard was a mix of black and silver, and if he had been standing it would have likely reached down to his waist.

Every dwarf in the room bowed when they reached the front, leaving only the three of them standing. The Dwarf at the front of the room closed his eyes and muttered unintelligibly for several seconds. Finally, his cold hard eyes focused in on the three of them. An uncomfortable silence came over them, but to their surprise, the feeling of dread that had plagued them since they had entered the mountain, vanished.

"Names and Business of the Outsiders," the Dwarf said. Corvil stepped forward and bowed. "Drake Thomas, Rachal Thomas and Barnabas of Bazzaran. "They are here because they have survived the Imrahian stoning my Lord Grenish. My name is Corvil; I was the one to find them and therefore have presented them to his royal majesty for judgment." The king motioned a person to the left forward.

"Please give this man a handsome reward for bringing these prisoners here and then send him away," Lord Grenish ordered. Corvil was led aside by three others. Drake and Corvil exchanged glances as he left. Sorrow was written in Corvil's eyes as he turned from them. The king's glance turned back to them. "It is said that you have survived the stoning, but I know this cannot be! The stoning was demanded for prisoners over five hundred years ago by the great god Imrahiria himself, and no one has ever lived through it. How did you do it?"

"I wish I could tell you a fantastic tale of how we dodged every rock that was thrown in our direction and defied all the odds until your people got bored and left," Drake started. "But the truth of the matter is that we fell unconscious and did not wake until late during the night. Corvil will vouch for that."

"Of course, he would," Grenish snapped. "If you were working with him, he would say anything, and make it appear as it if he found you."

"Indeed he would," Drake agreed. Even the notion that a prisoner was agreeing with him, made Grenish sit back for a second. "If you do not believe us you should try asking the citizens. They were participating and they would be able to tell you better what happened. Am I wrong?" Grenish thought long and hard for a moment.

"I cannot say that you are," Grenish replied. "Still the fact of the matter is that you were sent to this nation so you could be killed for the many crimes that you have been found guilty of. You shall be killed, we have many gods and if Imrahiria is not angry enough at you perhaps there can be a different explanation."

"Maybe Imrahiria was sleeping," Rachal replied. The entire room gasped. Drake tried not to laugh.

"I'm sure Imrahiria would be angry enough at your blasphemy to kill you now."

"And yet we still live?" Rachal retorted.

"Stop it, Rachal!" Barnabas whispered. "Don't make it worse." Several moments of silence passed as the king was lost in his thoughts, muttering the entire time.

"I have a proposition, one that could spare your lives if you so choose." Lord Grenish paused as if pondering some great decision. "We have many gods under this mountain but it is no secret there is one god that is greater than any other." He snapped his fingers and Dwarves came forward, grabbing hold of long ropes and pulling on them. Slowly, but steadily a great curtain behind the king's throne was pulled aside revealing a massive statue.

It stood nearly twenty feet tall and was cast in solid gold. The arms of the great statue were stretched out wide, while the bald head and face of the statue looked down on all of them. The statue's eyes seemed to glimmer in the dim lighting, peering into their souls, threatening to conquer them. Dread once again consumed their souls.

"Hail the great god '*Meurduricke*'." Everyone bowed to the statue except for Drake and Rachal. The king looked at them knowingly. "You know that it is against the law to disobey the order of the king, don't you? This law has been in effect for near three hundred years and it will not waiver now."

"We're well aware," Rachal started. "But we're not going to bow to this imposter!" The room gasped again, the king's rage evident in his eyes.

"You most certainly deserve the death you will be given," Grenish replied, seething. "The god '*Meurd-*'"

"It's pronounced Merderick," Rachal corrected.

"Silence or I shall run you through with my sword!" the king yelled. The king glared at Drake. "Do you refuse to bow to this statue?"

"Yes, we do. Merderick has no power over us, and we do not need to defend ourselves before you," Drake started. "You may do with us as you wish, the God whom we serve is able to save us. He will rescue us from your power, your majesty. But even if he doesn't we want to make it clear to you, that we will never serve your gods or statues, no matter what the threat. If it be death, then so be it. Our souls are secure."

A deep rumble filled the mountain and at that moment the statue behind the king cracked. The king jumped and people scattered away. They looked to find that the statue's head had split open.

"Guards!" the king boomed. The Dwarves came forward and surrounded Drake, Rachal, and Barnabas. "Take these prisoners to a holding cell, they are to have no visitors! Tomorrow we will see if your God can rescue you. You will be thrown into the *Rioblu Trenkvs*. May you die slowly and painfully?"

A great commotion erupted as the king yelled out orders at everybody. Drake, Rachal, and Barnabas were once again forced to run ahead of a whip as they were led back to the cell they had been in the night before. They were shoved inside, and after the footsteps had vanished from their ears, they rose to their feet. They were surprised to see a Dwarf step out of the shadows and help them up.

"There is certainly a great God looking out over you!" Corvil said, his eyes full of wonder. "The things you have said and done in such a short amount of time? And yet you still live to see tomorrow?"

"For what good that will do us!" Barnabas vented. "Live through the day so we can be thrown into some god-awful torture. We should have just bowed and been done with it."

"He wouldn't have set us free Barnabas and you know it!" Rachal exclaimed. "Besides, I would never do it."

"Good for you," Barnabas snapped. Corvil watched with interest.

"You do not have the faith your friends have," Corvil noted.

"Do you?" Barnabas asked. Corvil thought hard.

"My faith it seems is growing by what I'm seeing," Corvil said, studying them carefully. "There is great intrigue in my heart about you, though I know not why. Perhaps it is because our culture would never show love or kind words where hate is evident. Certainly, you must have perceived the hatred?"

"Indeed we did, but an eye for an eye leaves the whole world blind. There is a time for battle and a time for a step of faith. We chose the latter and we have lived to see another day," Drake said.

"May you see many more," Corvil said. "How did you know about '*Meurduricke*'? All my life I have been told he is a god of peace and love and protects this mountain from many foes."

"Then I'm sorry to say that you have been deceived all these years," Drake said. "We have traveled much and seen even more. We've seen enough to know that Merderick as we call him, is in many places of the world turning many hearts away from the true God Lathon."

"I hope you live through tomorrow, so I may ask you more about this Lathon," Corvil said. "I must return to my room for the night so as to not raise suspicion. I will be watching tomorrow."

"Can you tell us anything about what's going to happen?" Rachal asked.

Corvil thought long and hard.

"I'm afraid to say," he finally replied. "You must understand. If it is evident that I have given you some kind of advantage, my life would most certainly be in danger. All I can say is that no one has ever come out alive."

"Something to look forward to," Barnabas said bitterly.

"May your God protect you tomorrow! Goodnight." Corvil exited the cell quickly and was lost from sight.

The hours passed and silence came over them. Hunger gnawed at all of them as each one replayed the events of the day in their heads. Outside their cell, nothing was heard, no guards, no people. For the moment it seemed like they were alone.

Drake woke to the sensation of a pounding against his head. A moment later he jumped and quickly aroused the others. They pressed themselves into the shadows and held their breath as the pounding continued. A wooden shaft broke through the floor. They watched in amazement and fear as a man's hand appeared.

Slowly the man worked, pounding with the shaft to break up more of the floor until finally the man could stand and sit on the edge of the hole he had just made. He looked around in confusion and muttered to himself, holding a piece of parchment up to the failing torchlight. The light, faint as it was, provided enough light to verify that the man was an elf and clearly a prisoner of Nargaroth.

Drake used the darkness to his advantage, quickly grasping the torch on the wall and knocking the elf onto the ground. Rachal rushed forward and put her foot on the elf's neck.

"Name yourself or we'll set you afire!" Drake cried.

"Thank goodness," the man exclaimed. Drake's will wavered for a second. "I had thought I had gone the wrong direction."

"I said name yourself!" Drake exclaimed.

"I need not to answer that question, I would think by now you have put two and two together. Drake." A sense of relief swept over everyone and Rachal allowed the man to sit up. James rubbed his neck from the pain. "You sure know how to welcome a friend."

"Well, in our defense, people usually don't come through the floor," Rachal said. Drake helped him up and he dusted himself off. He embraced the two of them.

"I have missed you guys more than you know," James said.

"I'm getting the impression that you never made it back home?" Drake asked. James shook his head.

"Try as hard as I did, I was unsuccessful. I made it as far as Lanarka. I thought I had found a captain to take me the rest of the way, but he betrayed me. Somehow he discovered who I was. I guess it was to be expected that I should be a wanted man in Nargaroth, but I was still less than pleased to be brought back here again. So now it's been back to my old tricks as you see." He motioned towards the whole in the floor.

"You've been busy," Barnabas said.

"I'd like to take credit for digging the entire tunnel, but I cannot. It's been a long tradition for Nargaroth prisoners to spend their days tunneling. That's how I escaped the first time. Though admittedly I spent a long time after that looking for a way out of the mountain."

"How far do the tunnels run?" Barnabas asked.

"I'm not sure I could answer that," James replied. "There are so many tunnels connecting different places, it can get a little confusing unless you have a map, and those are not common."

"At least you have one," Drake said. James smiled weakly.

"I do have one, but I did not have it before this morning," James told them. Confusion was written on all their faces. "There's more than one peculiar happening that brought me here tonight."

"Do tell?" Drake said. James nodded and they all sat down on the floor.

"They don't feed the prisoners here. Maybe on special occasions, you'll get a few scraps that the dogs didn't eat, but for the most part, you're on your own. Prisoners usually die within two weeks, either by natural causes or via sacrifices."

"How did you survive so long without food?" Drake asked.

"Mystery number one," James said. He turned and leaned down into the hole in the floor, grasping a large burlap bag. He reached inside and pulled out four smaller bags and distributed one to each of them. The three of them opened the bags as he watched. Their faces clearly showing their confusion.

"Almonds?" Barnabas asked.

"Yes indeed. For whatever reason every day I was in these mountains a bag of almonds would be waiting for me when I woke. It didn't matter what time I fell asleep, or how hard I tried to see who was giving them to me. Go ahead and try one." They all tried one.

"That tastes good!" Rachal exclaimed.

"That hardly tastes like an almond," Drake said. James nodded. "It tastes amazing."

"You're telling me," James said, they laughed and quickly ate the almonds. "For nearly ten years a bag of almonds has always been waiting for me. It naturally infuriated the Nargothians at first, that I didn't seem to die. After a while, they seemed to forget about me. Or else maybe they thought I was a ghost."

"How did you end up with four bags this morning?" Rachal asked. James shrugged his shoulders.

"They were just there, along with the map to your cell and this note." James handed them a piece of parchment which read,

Please deliver these bags to Drake and his companions as they are in the cell marked on the map. Thanks!

"Unusual note," Drake said, a sense of familiarity coming over him.

"Could be a trap," Barnabas said.

"If it was a trap then I'm sure I wouldn't have escaped the first time."

"Can we get out of here?" Barnabas asked. James shook his head.

"Not anytime soon," James answered. "The map I have doesn't have anything else on it but the tunnel I came through. We could try and dig through the walls of the tunnel, but it might get us nothing more than a headache as we would be without a map again."

"Great," Barnabas said bitterly. "What are we supposed to do?"

"Wait," Drake replied. "The note said for James to deliver the bags, it said nothing about getting back to his cell and escaping." After a heated debate, Barnabas finally conceded and they sat down in the darkness, each lost in their own thoughts.

The sounds of keys fidgeting in a lock woke Drake. He quickly woke the rest of them and they stood just as the door was flung open. The four of them pressed back against the wall as the Dwarves came barging in. Within seconds the three of them were chained and shackled.

Only when they were about to be pushed out of the door, did the Dwarves notice James. A heated debate followed as they noticed both James and the hole in the floor. Within a few minutes, they had finished their quarrel and chained him as well, shoving all four of them out of the cell.

Their chains were hooked to a cart, pulled by something similar to a donkey. They were forced to keep pace or else be dragged the entire way. Rachal tripped once and was dragged for some time before they came to a momentary stop, allowing her to get on her feet again.

They walked for nearly an hour until in the distance they could hear the great thunderous roar of a stadium. The four of them exchanged looks, different emotions ran through them as they were led towards a large granite door. There a large dwarf with a big black beard stood. He was dressed like a warrior.

"What's going to happen?" Barnabas asked.

"Like I know?" Drake asked. "You were there with the rest of us. No one said what would happen once we reached the *Rioblu Trenkvs* ."

"I've been sent to translate as none of the soldiers know your tongue." They turned to see that Corvil was standing next to them. Looking as nervous as they felt.

"You certainly get around," Drake said.

"A friend of yours I assume?" James asked. Drake nodded.

"It was discovered that I spoke with you last night. In a retaliatory move, they told me that I could translate for you, and die alongside of you."

"Nice to know we're not alone," Barnabas remarked.

"Shut up Barnabas," James snapped. "Regardless of what's on the other side we need all the optimism we can get and you're not exactly an encouraging voice at the moment." Barnabas fell silent, muttering unintelligibly to himself.

"What happens in this place?" Rachal asked.

"Death happens in this place. They throw you into a large pit and release wild beasts on you, sometimes they send in warriors to slaughter you. Other times they strip you naked, beat you till you can't get up, but are still alive, and then leave you to be picked apart by vultures. Sometimes they starve and torture you until you're mad. Everything is viewed publicly. It's not a pretty sight."

"Can't we just kill ourselves and be done with this hell we're in!" Barnabas yelled, frustration in his voice.

"Whether we die or not, I'm glad to be here with all of you," James said. The others nodded their agreement except for Barnabas who looked more conflicted than ever before. Silence came over them. The doors in front were opened and they were shoved out onto a balcony.

The balcony encircled a large deep pit, with a steep slope leading down to the bottom. Large rocks and trenches were scattered throughout. Remains of former victims could be seen lying on the bottom. Above them for three or four levels were more balconies, filled with people. They chanted and roared as prisoners were brought out of their holding cells and slowly marched toward small gates at various places along the balcony.

"They're going to make us fight! There are weapons on the floor of the pit," Corvil explained. "Probably Borags. Those are the usual warriors they put in. Do you guys have any experience with them?"

"Enough to know they're ugly and dangerous," Drake said.

"I've never heard of Borags, but I have skills with a blade, lets hope I'm up for the challenge," James said. They were shoved closer to the gate as the group in front of them were shoved down the slope.

"How's your skill with a blade Barnabas?" Rachal asked. Barnabas appeared lost in thought for a moment.

"Not that great."

"Stick as close to each other as we can and we'll get through this!" Drake exclaimed. "Barnabas, if we get separated stick close to Rachal."

"The lady is good with a blade?" Corvil asked. Drake nodded.

"She's very good and that's not my bias that says so," Drake answered. They were shoved to the gate but not pushed over the edge. The king who was seated at the head of the great pit held a hand up. The crowd became silent.

"If you want to see some sport, you'll certainly see it today!" the king said. The crowd cheered. "Drake Thomas, Rachal Thomas, James of Rinevah, their captain Barnabas, and a traitor of our own kind Corvil of Retimes!" The crowd cheered and then quieted down again. "Nice knowing you!" The king taunted. Everyone laughed.

All of the prisoners, nearly thirty in all, were shoved off the balcony and onto the steep slope. They fell onto the hard rock, rolling uncontrollably down the slope until they came to rest on the stadium floor. Horns echoed and the sounds of foul screeches came to their ears. They scrambled to their feet, frantically moving about the pit, searching for weapons.

Dozens of Borags streamed into the pit, their claws helping them scale the great slopes with ease and stability. Some of the prisoners ran trying to climb back up the slope. Only a couple made it and once they grasped the railing they were struck with rocks. Others hopelessly begged for mercy and were hewed down in an instant. Others still grabbed whatever weapon they could find and took their own life.

The five of them hid behind a large rock and waited for their moment. The Borags moved off, leaving their victims to die in the pit. Drake jumped out from their hiding spot and grabbed the sword of one of the dying victims. The others followed suit as they stepped into plain sight and stood with their weapons drawn.

The Borags turned but were soon running in fear as the five of them rushed towards their enemies. After a moment the Borags turned to fight but were quickly disarmed and killed. Gasps and cries of both amazement and anger filled the area above them as one after another was slain by their weapons.

Finally, after several minutes, the last Borag fell onto the ground and died. The crowd watching was silent and Drake felt that even the beating of his heart was too loud of a noise, for fear of breaking the silence. Great discussion could be seen happening on the king's balcony. After several minutes of awkward silence, the king stood to speak.

"Everyone! Please congratulate Mr. Thomas and his friends, for proving how good they are at fighting! It seems that they have forgotten that this is the reason their blood was wanted in this country!" The crowd cheered in approval. "Clearly, they are skilled with swords, let's see how they do without swords, or as I like to say…how about something that doesn't fight with a sword!" The crowd cheered. The king stood smiling, seemingly congratulating himself. Great commotion was heard from the wall below the king. Already the sound of great muffled cries of all kinds echoed from below.

The crowds quickly quieted as the five of them stood facing the great gate in anticipation. Drake looked at all of them one at a time, trying his best to instill confidence and hope in them. The great gates were thrust open and the long dark chasm within was revealed.

Out of the chasm large beasts came. One of them sent nightmares into Drake as it was the same kind that they had fought in the Dead Mountains years ago. The one behind was larger still. Six heads came from one large body that looked as deadly as the rest of it.

More and more came until they were surrounded by the large gigantic beasts. The crowds became quiet and it seemed as if time stopped altogether. A whisper rode on the wind and with it, their confidence was strengthened. Drake turned to face them.

"For Lathon!" Drake exclaimed. The five of them brandished their swords and let out a cry. To the bewilderment of the crowd, they rushed towards the great beasts in front of them. Time became a blur as they continued to fight and the beasts began to fall one by one.

Drake pulled his sword out from one of the beasts and looked at the next. For a moment Drake looked to the right barely catching the glimpse of a person carefully sneaking around the floor of the pit. Drake felt his limbs burning and his sword suddenly became too heavy to lift.

Rachal felt the same and fell to her knees, turning white and trembling. James and Corvil stood with their mouths open, their weapons also on the ground. Barnabas cowered under an outcrop of rock. Drake turned his attention to the six-headed beast in front of him. Its eyes burned with rage and the smell of smoke radiated from each of the heads.

In an instant fire was spewed from the mouth of the six-headed beast. Drake imagined pain and death, but in the end, it was only his imagination. He looked up seeing that the fire had stopped. A great wall of fire was in front of them, but it wasn't consuming them. Instead, it was stopped at a single point as it struck the top of a great staff.

The wind struck them, forcing them to shield their eyes from the light which grew greater. A great figure could be seen holding the fire at bay with his staff. After what felt like an hour the flames subsided and Drake and his company let out a sigh of relief.

Drake studied the area with interest, quickly noting that not even a second had passed since the vision started. The six-headed beast still glared at him, but now seemed powerless. The creatures all around them retreated until they could go no further and then they lowered their faces to the ground.

"What's happening Drake?" Barnabas asked.

"It looks like Lathon came to our rescue and closed the mouths of the beasts," Drake answered. "And if I'm right, the people didn't see a thing."

"Corvil, did you witness the things that we saw happen?" James asked. Corvil sat on his knees, his face washed white.

"If the people saw even half of what I saw, they would not be standing on their feet in disapproval of our living. As sure as I sit on my knees, I indeed saw a miracle before my very eyes and your God has saved us!"

"How do we know for sure?" Barnabas asked. "Maybe some Sorcerers have tricked us?"

"There was no trick," Rachal said sternly.

"How do we know?" Barnabas countered. Drake pointed in front of them.

"Look," They looked to the spot that Drake was pointing to. The ground smoldered but quickly grew green. Within seconds a sprout appeared and then grew a couple of inches. Within another few seconds, it became a strong sapling about two feet high.

"What kind of a tree is it?"

Their question was answered a moment later as the tree shook and three or four almonds fell onto the ground. Their attention was brought back to the pit and the crowds watching which were completely silent and staring at them.

"This is good," Rachal said. With the silence, everyone heard her voice. The king looked as if he tried to speak but was unable to get any words out. Awkward silence continued. Rachal looked around at the crowds. "Maybe this god was relieving himself!"

Chapter 19

THE GRIM ISLANDS

Thunder rolled through the sky and lightning flashed almost endlessly. This was the third night on the island and they sat hunkered in a cave, hoping to wait out the rain before departing. The rain came down in sheets and wind gusts blew harder than any that Isabel had ever experienced.

When they had landed on this island for a rest from flying, it had been sunny and warm. An hour after they had landed the sky had turned black and the rain had started. They had thankfully found shelter rather quickly, as there was a large system of caves on a seaside cliff.

The caves were big enough for all three Taruks to get in and still move around comfortably. They had explored much for the past three days and had found other tunnels and shafts that bore through the rocks and led to other places. One led to the coast, the other led to a lush forest where they had briefly scoured for some food. Their efforts had been in vain though as the rain was so heavy and so thick they couldn't keep their eyes open.

Isabel and Morgrin didn't speak, listening to the deafening rain all around them. They had just enough supplies to start a fire for one more night. Time passed and Morgrin felt uncomfortable while Isabel seemed to study everything with skepticism.

"This is a very strange island," Isabel commented.

"No kidding. In what way are you thinking?"

"This kind of a storm is familiar to me. Reminds me of the ones we used to have in Grimdor."

"That's comforting," Morgrin replied. Silence came over them. "We'll have to do something tomorrow, our supplies are almost used up." Isabel nodded.

"I suddenly feel as if time is slipping away from us too," Isabel said. "I'm not quite sure how to explain it."

"I too am feeling restless. A spirit of unease hangs over this island."

"I'm almost thinking we need to leave tonight," Isabel said. Morgrin gave her a look of surprise.

"We can hardly see anything to begin with how are the Taruks even supposed to fly in wind and rain like this?"

"Perhaps I can be of assistance," a voice said from the mouth of the cave. They turned to see a strange cloaked figure. His cloak was deep purple in color and plain in every other way. He stepped forward revealing a middle-aged man. He was tall and muscular and had a good demeanor so far.

"We thought we were alone," Morgrin said.

"You were until just a moment ago," the man said.

"What's your name and how did you come to be here?" Isabel asked.

"My family has lived on this island for many generations," the man started. "My name is Huta. Come!" They stood and followed him through the caves and tunnels, all of which were able to accommodate the Taruks with ease. They descended a flight of stairs which took nearly twenty minutes to reach the bottom. The air was cool and moist as they looked down a large tunnel that felt as though it stretched into the abyss. A small purple Taruk sat, tied up to the wall like a horse to a hitching post. Huta untied it and climbed on. Motioning that they should do the same.

"I will explain in greater detail once we are free of this island. There is much about this island that makes it not the best place for important conversations," Huta said. The Taruks all took flight and followed single file through the winding and twisting tunnel.

Aspen and Isabel followed directly behind Huta and his small Taruk. She felt a calmness and a feeling of peace come over her as they left the island behind them. She studied the tunnel as they passed through it, noting several strange things about it.

First was that the tunnel was filled with holes leading to other shafts of equal size. The second was that the tunnel was made out of black rock and had small flecks of gold and silver throughout. At times Isabel even thought that they glowed or let off some light.

Three hours later Huta put down on a large area of flat rock. Another large staircase awaited them and they climbed for nearly an hour before they reached the top. Their spirits soared as they felt warm dry wind and heard the sound of birds chirping. They stepped out into the sunshine and smiled uncontrollably. A large valley lay before them. On one end a tall narrow waterfall, and on the other a small menagerie of buildings and huts were sprawled out.

Huta led them down a small path that wound its way down to the sprawling valley below. The Taruks took to the sky, flying joyfully in the warm sunlight. They walked along the river until they reached the small town they had seen from above.

Isabel and Morgrin glanced at each other warily as they followed Huta through the completely empty town. All sound seemed to fade. Even the sound of the river was blocked out. Instead, a throbbing silence filled their heads as they heard faint but clear, part of the song or poem that they had heard before...

> *There was a land, I saw it once*
> *We were young and so was it.*
> *In the midst of all, there stood before thee*
> *A large and luscious Vemroliet tree.*

In an instant, the song faded and the sound returned to the world around them. Huta stared up at the sky, unmoving.

"Is everything alright?" Morgrin asked. Huta wiped his eyes.

"That song is sung frequently on this island. When I was young I cursed it, but now I treasure it. I'm not sure what the song means, but it does my heart good to hear it, even if it's just on the wind."

"What happened to everyone?"

Huta grew sad and seemed to sink in size and stature.

"Dark evil days have occurred," Huta started. "Worst of all, I am the one who brought them! It was by my hand and my clouded and war-torn mind that I destroyed the people of the town. My town." He wept. "Now, I live here to protect others who are trapped on the Grim Islands." He wept to himself for several minutes, taking them into a large and spacious dwelling.

"What are the Grim Islands?" Morgrin asked when finally he had composed himself.

"Six islands, connect to this one. All of them are connected by underground tunnels. They are as you saw them. They look like a beautiful paradise, but soon after you land the true nature of the island is revealed! They are cursed with some dark magic that I don't understand. My family has lived here for near fifty years. And now I am here with only myself for company or companionship."

"Where are we exactly?" Isabel asked. "We've gotten a bit lost and blown about by the strange winds that govern this ocean."

"There are a number of maelstroms that surround the islands, which make the ocean a very hard thing to navigate. But to answer your question you are here." He pointed to the island on the map. "Third island from the mass of land from the south. Its name is Mulvor, a province of Cordell. Several islands in the ocean are under their control. This is one of them. They choose not to inhabit these islands, but rather to use them as prisons for the ones they hate the most."

"That's horrible," Isabel said. Huta shrugged.

"I've come to make peace with it." Huta looked back at the map for a moment. "This is a strange map as it clearly shows Mulvor, but none of the other six islands are on it."

"This is why we're having a hard time."

"Where are you headed?" Huta asked.

"Wherever north is," Morgrin said. "We need to get to the next land mass on the map."

"Then you'll want to avoid these islands," Huta said, pointing to a large cluster of islands near the middle of the map. "There are some strange people on those shores. Cannibals. I don't think any of you wish to become a meal."

"That's definitely on my list of things not to do," Morgrin said.

"Many of these islands are dangerous places, but if you are headed towards Cordell I urge extra caution. They are not a people to be trifled with."

"What do you know of them?" Isabel asked.

Huta turned away. "Too much."

For the rest of the afternoon, he refused to speak and instead went about his business on the island by himself. Morgrin and Isabel walked through the quiet ghost town and then down by the river where the Taruks were resting.

"What are you thinking?" Morgrin asked.

"It's a curse to be a person like me sometimes."

"Why do you say that?"

"Because I see one thing and I'm like 'I need to stay and study that for the next five years' and then another thing pops up and I want to study that too, and I know I have to keep going north."

"One thing I've always loved about you is your curious mind," Morgrin said. "Though it is kind of different to see you so confused by things."

"I just hope someday I get to come back and study them all. Learn how this part of the world works. Just what did Lathon create for us to look at and admire? This trip so far has been a challenge, but I'm enjoying it at the same time."

At that moment Huta came up to them and bowed slightly.

"Supper is served and waiting for you."

The supper more than satisfied all three of them. No matter how much they ate, Huta would always go and bring in more food, as if he expected to have a host of people arrive. How he had prepared all the food by himself in the first place was beyond her understanding.

They talked by the fire long into the night and the Taruks happily hunted for their food and were rarely seen by any of them until just before they fell asleep. The Taruks rumbled in pleasure, each of them falling into dreams made of the things that Taruks dream about.

During the night Isabel was woken several times to hear different voices singing into the night. She strained her eyes, trying to see where the voices were coming from. Some of them seemed like they were just beyond the reach of the lights, while others seemed like they were miles away.

Huta also sat awake listening to the strangely beautiful music, seeming as though it was easing his fears and worries. Isabel tried and tried to place the language but in the end, she failed.

"The music is unique," Isabel commented after quite a while.

"Yes, many nights have I heard it. I can never find the source of it though. I think it is some song that our heart tells."

"Do you know what it is saying?" Isabel asked.

Huta shook his head. "I am not so educated in the language of God."

"Language of God?" Isabel asked. Huta nodded.

"I am convinced that there is a tongue known only to Lathon by which he created all that we see. And I do not think we can hope to understand such a tongue."

"I suppose you're right," Isabel agreed. "So you know of Lathon?"

"Many things reach my shores, but this one is the only one I've ever been able to believe without hesitation."

They talked for some time before drifting to sleep. When they woke they found that Huta was gone, but breakfast was prepared for them. They graciously ate some food, even though they were still considerably full from the feast the night before. When they were done with their food they gathered everything and secured it to the Taruks. They swiftly rose into the sky and the island disappeared from their sight. Isabel's heart was torn as they continued their journey to the north.

The day wore on and the warm sunshine lifted their spirits and almost made them forget that they were traveling into the unknown. The ocean below was empty of everything as far as they could tell. During the course of the day they passed by many whirlpools and maelstroms that churned the seas but otherwise, their day of traveling was rather uneventful.

As sunset approached they descended out of the sky to search for any piece of land that might serve as a place of rest for the night. They searched for nearly an hour, with all three of the Taruks separating and reporting back to Isabel and Aspen.

They climbed into the sky once again, Isabel's eyes observing a strange

274

shape on the horizon. They made towards it bringing into focus a plume of mist and ocean water that drifted into the air.

A large ring lay before them. The ring was nearly a half mile across at any point and fell sharply, creating an endless waterfall that encircled the entire opening. In the middle, a modestly sized tower of grey rock jutted up out of the churning water at the bottom.

"You don't see this every day," Morgrin yelled from atop Destan.

"Indeed not. But it looks like the best chance of rest that we've seen." They eventually landed on the island of rock, which had more than enough space for all of them. They slid off the Taruks, surprised when their footsteps echoed thunderously. Isabel tiptoed over to Morgrin who appeared to be too frightened to move.

"Interesting place," Morgrin said, as cheerfully as he could muster. They explored the slab of rock as much as they dared. The churning water around the isle of rock was filled with the wrecks of the great ship who clearly had sailed down the falls by accident. As they explored they found several caverns and tunnels that bore down into the rock. It didn't take long to determine that although the caves had been inhabited or used in the past, they hadn't been used in recent years.

They explored further, noticing spherical shaped rocks two feet in diameter They were smooth and glossy in appearance as though they had been meticulously polished and cared for throughout history. Isabel stooped to try and move one but failed. No matter how hard they tried they were unsuccessful in their efforts.

They eventually found their way into one of the caves and ate a few morsels that they had rationed for themselves. They spoke little, enjoying the sound of the water rushing into the strange surroundings.

"I can't help but wonder where all this water goes?" This hole hasn't gotten any more filled with water than it was when we arrived.

"Mystery of the world I think," Morgrin said. "I'm sure Aiden could tell us."

"Either that or he would say that he knows but he wouldn't want to spoil the fun for me." They both chuckled.

The light faded from the sky and soon they were amerced in total darkness but still Isabel couldn't sleep. She rolled over several times, but instead of sleeping found herself staring out the opening of the cave and up above to the falls that surrounded them.

She stared for several minutes, a strange feeling of curiosity coming over her. From where she was looking she could see faint light growing and then fading a second later. She stood and moved towards the opening of the cave, peering out into the darkness.

She walked over to Aspen who was curled up next to one of the polished stones. She looked on in wonder as it flickered bright orange for a moment before fading again. She watched for several minutes, concluding that the stones only flickered when Aspen exhaled in her sleep. She quickly went back down and woke up Morgrin.

"Looks like the same thing is happening where all the Taruks are breathing," Morgrin pointed out. Isabel looked to see similar things happening with the stones near Destan and Ezzion as well. "What do you think it means?"

"I'm not sure," Isabel said. "But I have an idea if I can get Aspen to wake up."

"Waking up a sleeping Taruk?" Morgrin asked. "I'm not sure that's a good idea. I'm just going to take a few big steps backward." Isabel tried not to laugh as Morgrin took large exaggerated steps away from the Taruks.

"Aspen," Isabel whispered in her ear. Aspen just flicked her tail sleepily and didn't stir.

"Aspen!" Isabel said, this time with a little more force. Still, the Taruk didn't stir. Finally, Isabel went back to their supplies and grabbed a frying pan and a large spoon. She quickly crept back to Aspen's ear and held the frying pan over it.

"Say a prayer for me Morgrin."

"I already have," Morgrin replied. Isabel frantically began smacking the frying pan with the spoon. Aspen jumped to her feet and let out a roar. Isabel ran to get clear of her feet and massive tail as Aspen and the other Taruks searched for the threat that had awoken them. Morgrin laughed in the background.

"That could've been worse," Isabel said. "Sorry Aspen, but I need you awake now." Aspen understood her thoughts and settled down and let Isabel get on her back, but not before putting the frying pan and spoon away. She motioned for Morgrin to join her and he quickly climbed on. "Destan and Ezzion, when we're clear, breathe all the fire that you can muster on these rocks!" The Taruks rumbled in pleasure moving up to higher ground, one of them on each side.

Aspen launched the three of them into the air, above the roaring waterfalls. All at once Destan and Ezzion spewed an endless stream of fire from their powerful mouths. The night sky was lit up in vibrant orange, yellows, and reds. When the fire ceased they could see clearly that every spherical rock on the island glowed and burned brightly. The polished stones were laid out in a formation, creating a shape that sent chills up and down their spines.

"Isabel," Morgrin said, nearly speechless. Isabel didn't bother to respond. Below them her family crest lit up the sky, burning brighter and clearer than anything she had ever seen before. For several minutes they flew in tight but slow circles, looking down in disbelief. "Why is your family crest on this island?"

"I have no idea," Isabel said. "Take us down, Aspen." Aspen gently landed on the rock. Isabel slid off, walking through the rows of now glowing rocks, hardly believing what she was seeing.

"Whatever the mystery of these rocks is, I think it's safe to say that they were not put here on accident," Morgrin said. Isabel stared ahead only half hearing what he was saying. She turned to face him a moment later.

"I agree," Isabel said. "The only question is why are they here, and who put them here?"

"Maybe they were put here for the right person to find them?" Morgrin suggested.

"This is getting confusing, even to me," Isabel admitted. "In the morning let's search the island again. Maybe there's some clue we overlooked that might give us some answers."

At the first light of day, Isabel and Morgrin ate their breakfast and then began searching the island for clues of any kind. After searching the caves again and again Isabel and Morgrin both sat down on the spherical rocks feeling defeated.

"There has to be something we're missing," Isabel said. Morgrin nodded his agreement and stared at the ground.

"There is something we've missed," Morgrin said with enough certainty that Isabel sat up straighter. "Look." He pointed to her feet.

She moved her left foot and looked down at her family's crest, carved into the rock. It was small, only the size of a coin, but it now glowed like the rocks had the night before. She moved aside as they looked at the small crest and then at the one-foot by one-foot slab of rock that it was engraved on. Some kind of grout or mortar had been put over the seams of rock, sealing it.

They both reached for their knives, chiseling out the layer of mortar. An hour passed until finally, they were able to get their fingers beneath the edge. They heaved up the heavy slab of rock and moved it to the side, finding a dark hole waiting for them. Isabel stuck her head into the hole. Small incisions were carved into the rock wall and descended about fifteen feet.

"Looks like there's a ladder of sorts," Isabel said. "Do we have anything we can use as a light?"

"We have Taruks," Morgrin said, grabbing a stick which was promptly lit by Destan. Isabel carefully placed her feet and hands in the incisions in the rock and lowered herself down. She put her feet on the bottom and breathed a sigh of relief.

"Drop the torch!" Isabel yelled back. Morgrin dropped the torch and then joined her. They stood now in a vast open cave, which was completely dry and dark of all light except that of their torch. They quickly did a sweep around the outside of the vast area and found only one opening.

They moved through the doorway, coming into a smaller room that was much the same as the first one. The only difference was the large number of tunnels that connected to the room they were in. A single stone table sat at one end of the room with a large chest underneath.

Morgrin pulled out the large trunk, which appeared to be various shades of purple and deep red and made out of metal. An intricate pattern was painted on the top. A large lock held the chest shut.

"Any ideas on how to get it open?" Morgrin asked. "Even if you had all of your special items with you, I don't believe you have one that will break metal. Without blowing up the whole cave."

"I can't think of any. It's too heavy to carry. I'm not even sure how someone could have gotten it in here in the first place," Isabel said. "Maybe there's a back door that we don't know about."

Morgrin moved about the room looking for any sign that might indicate a different way out. Isabel turned her eyes to the stone table, searching first under it and then on top of it for anything that might be helpful to them. She moved her torch closely over the table and wiped away the layers and layers of dust. A sealed envelope bore the same insignia above the wax seal.

"Morgrin come here," Isabel said. Morgrin rushed to her side and showed him the envelope. As if it had been designed to do so, a faint flash of light formed on the outside of the envelope. It wove this way and that eventually spelled out Isabel and Morgrin's names."

"This is creepy," Morgrin said.

Without hesitation, she broke the wax seal and unfolded the paper. She looked at the words, struggling to make out all the letters and symbols.

"I'm not familiar with the script," Morgrin admitted.

"I've seen it before but not in many many years. I'll read it to you."

To whom it may concern:

If you have made it this far, I commend you. In the chest below are many things. The things in the chest consist of my life's work. As it is such, it turns out that many adversaries seek to keep me from completing it. Regretfully they have nearly succeeded.

Nonetheless, the placement of this chest is my last final attempt to hide my work and keep it from its destruction. Many oppose me and everything I stand for. They think they have won and that all my work has been destroyed. Well, we shall see.

I leave the chest and its location in your care, I shall also ask that if you are reading this letter, you deliver it to the Count of Durio Helmar who resides in the small town of Per-Vom in the nation of Cordell. There you may learn the location of Prater. Further details will be found on the backside of the flagstone that covered this cave from detection.

Once you deliver this letter to the Count of Durio Helmar or his descendants in the case that the Count has died, you will be considered. If you are thought a wise, truthful, and honest person the key to the chest shall be handed to you and you will likely be doomed to finish the work that I was not able. For I am getting old and things are not as they once were.

I wish you all the luck that I have to offer and hope that this letter is presented to the Count of Durio Helmar in a timely fashion.

Also, when you begin asking for the Count you may find you become the interest of many in Cordell. Reveal nothing about this letter to them or else it may bring you to ruin.

Sincerely,
Your Friend

"It's dated four years ago," Isabel read. She and Morgrin sat in thought for several minutes.

"What should we do?" Morgrin asked. "I hardly think it was for this reason we were sent to the north."

"What if it was?" Isabel asked. "Could we really stand by and do nothing? The letter was only four years ago. It's likely that this Count is still alive. I think we should check it out as it appears we are headed to Cordell."

"I suppose," Morgrin agreed. "Still there is a great danger."

"I'm not arguing that," Isabel replied. "Perhaps we can take the letter with us and with extreme caution seek out this Count."

"As long as we're careful, I'm in." Isabel smiled and kissed him before they both returned to the opening. They crawled out of the hole and flipped the flagstone over, seeing a map etched into the rock. They pulled out their map and carefully added all the towns and places that were marked on the stone, before putting the flagstone back in its place.

The stones, which had glowed so brightly when they had entered the caves were now dim and cold. They shivered in the fading light, confused that it already seemed to be sunset. They made camp and curled up together to fight the bitter cold that plagued that sea. When the dawn came so did the warmth, much to their enjoyment.

Chapter 20

PROPHETS OF NAROTH

"This is not what I signed up for!" Barnabas yelled above the noise. The guards that were assigned to them had been doubled for their return trip to their prison cell. They forced them to move. all the while furiously debating in their own tongue.

"At least we're still alive!" Corvil yelled back. "I call that an improvement over our former situation."

"Yeah sure," Barnabas jeered. "For how long? That wife of Drake's is going to get us all killed."

"First off Barnabas, her name is Rachal!" James exclaimed. "Say something against her and Drake again and I'll drag you out and throw you back in that pit myself!"

"Bring it on!" Barnabas yelled. They were shoved into their cell and the door was quickly locked. The Dwarves outside continued their arguing and it didn't seem to be winding down at all.

"I don't think arguing is helping us at all," Corvil said. Everyone fell silent. "It's certainly not helping Drake and Rachal."

"You would say that," Barnabas snapped.

Corvil's eyes sharpened on him. "Yes, I would say that. I hardly know anything about Lathon, but after what I've seen today I do not doubt that there is some special protection over all of us. Even if I don't understand it. I'm siding with James in this matter."

"Figures," Barnabas retorted. "I shoul-"

"Shut up Barnabas!" Corvil warned. Weapons were drawn outside their cell and within moments the hallway was silent.

"Corvil is right," James said. "We can argue all we want and it won't help us figure out our next move. I understand you're upset about being here, but none of us chose it either."

"Sorry if I yelled at you guys more than I should have," Barnabas said. "The simple truth is I'm scared. All my life, I've heard horrible things about this nation. My nerves are starting to get to me."

"I'm sure we will get out of here," James replied. "Right now I'm more worried about Drake and Rachal. Any insight as to what might be happening Corvil?"

Corvil shrugged his shoulders. "Hard to say, with the level of insult that you have brought, I'm surprised that you've lived this long. They'll be interrogated for sure, and in my experience, I wouldn't expect them to be walking back through the door. Most likely they'll be executed for their crimes."

"What crimes?" Barnabas asked.

"Were you even there?" Corvil asked. "Those two talk with authority that I've never seen, and it's going to rub the king and everyone else the wrong way. Have they always been this certain of things?"

Barnabas shrugged.

"It's hard for me to say as I was a prisoner here for many many years, and I only recently found Drake just before he got married," James started. "Despite that, I feel there is very much different about him, I just don't know what it is. When we were growing up he was a good friend to me, but perhaps a little timid and withdrawn. He seems to have lost those traits and a fair amount of other things, which I would no doubt see if I gave the matter serious study. Whatever happened during the past ten years or so, it's done him good and I trust his judgment now far more than I did then. Perhaps the last ten years were what he needed for Lathon to really work in him.

"What do you mean by 'work in him.'?" Corvil asked. "My culture for the most part gives the sacrifices, and pray we don't get smote in their fury."

"Strange culture, but I'm not surprised," James said. "To answer the question about 'work in him' I'm not sure that I completely understand the answer myself. One of the things that I've never fully understood is that Lathon will place something on your heart. It might be something he wants you to do, but more often than not, before that, it's something that he's asking you to change or let go of. It is hard, but if you follow the leading of Lathon you will gain something, even if it's not worldly fame."

"What happens if you don't follow the leading?" Corvil asked. James thought for a moment.

"You end up wandering more and more; despair and jealousy begin to take hold of your heart. If they are unchecked and allowed to run rampant in you, eventually they destroy you. I've seen this first hand as my father has become more selfish and angry over the years especially since Drake was appointed."

"What do you mean appointed?" Barnabas asked. "I was always led to believe that he was some kind of royalty."

"Hardly the case my friend," James replied. "He's been my good friend and loyal companion for many years but he is not what people would consider to be noble blood. My father was first appointed by the prophet Sarule, to become the king of Rinevah. When it was time he was anointed and my father has been king ever since. However, the prophet Sarule, as well as a few others over the years, have come to warn my father that he was on the edge of losing the favor of Lathon. There are several things that my father was supposed to do, and instead, he failed to do or attempt them. That list is longer than I would like to admit and I won't bore you with it now.

"In fact, when Drake threw down the giant Iratha it was a sign of my father's weakness. My father and the entire army had been stagnant for thirty days, too afraid to confront the giant. Known to few, Sarule under the guidance of Lathon had anointed Drake to replace my father as king."

"Why aren't you going to be the king?" Barnabas asked. "That would make far more sense. Just get your dad to step down, or arrange an accident. It happens all the time."

"You would so lightly throw your family aside? And for what?" James asked. "For the power and the prestige that would come with being the king? If I was to follow that path I would be haunted in the night and in the day by the things that I had done. Many may have done similar deeds before. But that does not make them right, and rarely will you hear the honest regrets and feelings on the matter from those people. Certainly, all of us here have regrets that haunt us and I will not have the death of my father on my watch, be any part of those regrets."

"Say what you want, but I think you're getting gypped," Barnabas said. "After all these years it seems I still don't understand the Elven culture. You're the prince! Anywhere else in the world, it's common practice that the prince takes over when the father is dead or unable to rule. How are you okay with stepping aside?"

"I trust Drake with my life, and his heart is pure, this I am sure of. We swore an oath of friendship long ago and I will serve him in whatever capacity I am allowed. For I can see now more than ever, that the spirit of Lathon is with him." Silence followed for several minutes.

"So what of his family?" Barnabas asked. "Last I checked he's not Elvish, doesn't that make him an outcast in your society."

"In the days of old, it most certainly would. But the fact of the matter is that the prophet Sarule appointed him, a man, to become the king of a nation primarily of Elves. Even though I am confused by this, I have learned that it is futile to argue with the will of Lathon. No matter how right you are, or how much you think you know. Lathon knows best."

The night passed slowly and uneasily for all of them. Much of the night was filled with unpleasant dreams that woke them and left them to wonder and ponder whether the dreams were true. Sounds of torture surrounded them as the prisoners were interrogated or punished in some form or fashion.

The next day came with nothing much changed from the first. A few new prisoners were brought to the prisons, but otherwise, the entire prison was left untouched. James spent a large part of the day sitting near the door and listening for anything helpful that might be said either by a prisoner or by the passing guards. The day faded and wore into the night as hunger began to take its toll on the prisoners.

As expected three bags of almonds were found in the corner confusing both

Corvil and Barnabas who spent much of the evening arguing about how they hadn't noticed the person come in to drop off the bags in the first place.

The second day James was woken from his dreams by the sound of the cell door being opened. James sat up, while Corvil and Barnabas remained asleep. James started to shake them awake but was stopped as a hand grasped his wrist.

James looked and saw a man holding his fingers to his lips. James nodded in reply, remaining silent. A few moments passed before the two guards came near to their cell. To James's surprise, he could hear them in his language, though they were speaking dwarvish.

"I'm sure I heard someone come down here," the first Dwarf said.

"I think you need to go have a drink," the second Dwarf said. "There's nothing down here but a bunch of deadbeat prisoners."

"Didn't you hear a door close, just a minute ago?" the first Dwarf asked again.

"No, I didn't! You're imagining things, and if you keep us down here much longer there will be trouble waiting for us. I don't want to be accused of leaving our posts to chase shadows that don't exist."

"Would you shut up!" the first Dwarf retorted. "I'm not interested in listening to your opinion. We're going back, we'll find someone, to watch the gate for us, then we'll come back, search all the cells and I'll prove to you that I'm not going crazy!" They began moving back the way they had come and eventually, all sound of their argument was lost to the silence. James looked to the man, who had now made himself quite comfortable and was sitting cross-legged on the floor.

"Hello?" James said uncomfortably. The light from the torch seemed to flicker a little brighter illuminating the man's face for only a moment, in that moment James recalled the man's face, though he couldn't recall his name. "Can I help you?"

"Sorry. I was making sure no one else is listening, you never know in a place like this," the man said. "I was coming to give you these." He pulled from a small pouch at his side three bags of almonds.

"You're the one who's been leaving them for us?" James asked.

"For tonight I'm the one dropping them off. You'll be taken first thing in the morning, so make sure and eat those before you go."

"We will," James said, feeling both at ease and unnerved about how comfortable the man seemed to be. "Where are we going to be taken in the morning and how is it that you know about it?"

"You're going to the *Karem-Luvi*. It's the highest peak in this forsaken mountain nation. I spoke with Drake earlier and everything is all set."

"You spoke with Drake?" James said. The man nodded. "How do I know you're telling the truth and that this isn't some sort of trick?"

"You know enough about Nargaroth to know that they wouldn't have the patience for an elaborate trick such as this. The only thing they use prisoners for is entertainment as they're ripped to shreds in contests like the one you took part in a couple of days ago. If I was an agent of Nargaroth I would not have let you live this long if you suspected anything about me. I would more likely have been mascaraed like a prisoner so that you would trust me."

"So you're dressed not like a prisoner so that I will trust you?" James asked. The man laughed.

"Sounds reasonable, but it just so happens this is how I was dressed when I came. Besides I couldn't even remotely pass as a Dwarf could I?" James and the man both chuckled.

"I suppose you're right," James said. "You sure don't look like a Dwarf. May I ask for your name?"

"You don't remember?" the man asked. James thought deeply, finally shaking his head. "My name is Aiden. A close friend of Drake's for many years."

"I remember meeting you, though I'm sorry to say I only vaguely remember. I thought you were headed West? What are you doing out here?"

"Questions for another time. I need to get going before the guards get back." Aiden stood up and went to leave.

"Wait!" James said, standing and moving to the door where Aiden now stood. "What's going to happen tomorrow? I know you said it was on top of some mountain, but what happens there?"

Aiden thought for a moment. "We'll have to wait and see."

Before James could say another word Aiden had slipped out the door and was lost to the darkness. A few minutes later as predicted more guards came down the hallway, searching every cell without warning. They spoke only in the Dwarvish tongue. James pondered the meaning of this.

The only indication that morning had come was that the guards had entered their cell and quickly bound and gagged all three of them. They were carried and then thrown into the back of a large cart, which was hastily driven away from the prisons. James tried his best to figure out which direction they were headed, but before long he gave up.

The cart was driven swiftly through the streets and seemed to not stop for anything. Occasionally they would all be shoved together as they went over a large object that was in the way. Judging by the size of the jolt and the amount of yelling and cursing that came before and after, it seemed likely that the driver had run over the people who stood in his way.

Besides the occasional slowdown, the cart and company rolled along at a brisk pace, covering an unknown amount of distance under the great mountains. James paid close attention, noticing that it felt like they were slowly rising higher and higher within the mountain.

Another hour passed and finally, great shafts of light could be seen breaking through the canopy of rock overhead. Warm dry wind swept through the mountain. The three of them grew hot and tired. The heat seemed to get greater and the wind dried out their skin faster than would have normally happened, leaving them thirsty and achy.

After a while, the cart slowed to a stop as great gates waited before them. The gates were made of metal, though what other qualities it had they could not tell. James thought they were a deep red color, but when the gates opened they appeared to be silver or white.

The cart rolled ahead and they moved through the gate into the outside world. The sunlight blinded them and it took several minutes before their eyes adjusted to seeing natural light again.

"This is unexpected," Barnabas said. They looked around seeing that they were nearing the peak of a great mountain and although on every other mountain peak there was snow, there was none to be found on this one. The ground was various shades of brown with dark lines that ran through it. Only a sparse clump of greenery grew on the entire peak and even those looked sickly. Weather-torn rocks and remnants of old fortresses and battlements could be seen scattered here and there over the top of the mountain. Away off in the distance, they could see large statues standing atop the mountains.

"What do you know about this place Corvil?" James asked.

"It's called *Karem-Luvi,"* Corvil answered. "And if ever there was a reason to despair this would be it. In the common tongue, this peak is called the temple of the god Naroth, for which our nation is named. He is the greatest of all the gods. Naroth is the Dwarvish word, but the real name comes from Elvish, it's pronounced Merderick.

"If you noticed all the statues on the surrounding peaks you might notice they are all facing towards this mountain. This is because as Nargothians are told, all gods bow to Naroth."

"They'd like to think that," James said. "But I know someone who is greater."

"I hope you are right," Corvil said. "My heart gives me reason to hope, while my fear threatens to consume me."

Silence fell over them again as they climbed closer and closer to the peak. Every inch they traveled the heat became more uncomfortable. Sweat rolled off of them and even the Dwarves leading the way seemed to be struggling in the intense heat.

Low humming began to reach their ears, followed closely by an occasional rumbling that would shake the mountain for a moment. Along the way they saw Dwarves dressed lavishly, with their hands raised, facing the summit of the mountain.

They reached the top and were promptly dragged out of the cart and set up on their feet. They were forced to walk forward, the hard rocks unbearably hot.

They were taken to a bench and a large entourage of Dwarves marched up the path they had just traveled.

In the middle of the summit was a large courtyard of black stone. In the middle of the courtyard, there were two stone alters that looked as if they had never been used before. The entourage continued their march until finally Drake and Rachal were seated on the bench next to them.

"Fancy seeing you here," James said. "I'm glad to see you though."

"That makes two of us," Drake said. "It was a bit tough to get them to agree to you being present, but finally they gave in."

"What are we doing here?" James asked.

"It seems, they didn't like that all their gods were being defeated. We survived the stoning at the Imrahirian gate and the contest at the pit. Both of which made their '*gods*' look foolish. It was quite easy to get them to agree to one final contest to see whose god was the better."

"So what's the game?" James asked. "What are we asked to be a witness to?"

"They have built two alters and they have prepared their offerings to be laid upon it. We'll both call out to our God and we'll see whose God accepts the sacrifice," Rachal said. James was taken aback; for a moment his own faith wavered.

"You are a bold one as I've been told," James said. "What's in it for the winners?"

"If they win, we die. If we win, they set us free tomorrow morning," Drake replied.

"They're not going to set you free," Corvil stated. "They would never do that, you've seen too much."

"We know," Rachal said.

"I just want this to be over," Barnabas lamented, looking more nervous than any of them.

"Then start praying," Drake said. "The contest is soon to begin."

Loud trumpets rang through the air as a great host of people began coming up the mountain road.

"Goodness!" James exclaimed. "How many of these noble people are coming to this contest?"

"Hard to say, but these…these are four hundred of their *holiest* priests, which I insisted come and perform their rituals so that their god 'Naroth' would be most pleased."

"It seems the stakes keep getting higher and higher," Corvil said, clearly unsure of what to say. The entire assembly paraded up the mountain with a thousand more joining, forming a circle around the large group. The priests stood and began to move before their altar; laying the sacrificial meat on it. The king stood to speak.

"Here we go," Drake said. The king stood tall and proud.

"High and most noble priests! Citizens of our great and glorious nation Nargaroth. You are here today to be a witness to all that is happening, so you can be sure of the truth! Many of you are aware of the great heresy that has happened and of the blasphemous talk of the Thomas family. Now here we are to prove once and for all that our gods are not sleeping, nor are they relieving themselves! It is clear to me that our gods allowed them to live this long, only so the great Naroth could unveil his power and majesty in a manner that would prove the superiority of our god.

"For this contest to work you must know the rules agreed to beforehand. Both alters have been prepared with sacrificial meat. Both groups will call out to their gods in the customs required by their gods. The god who is the true god, will send forth fire from the sky and devour the meat on the altar. Have I left anything out Mr. & Mrs. Thomas?"

"No you have not," Drake said, standing for a moment. "And I would like to announce that I will surrender the summit to you, Your Excellency. This is your mountain and I do not doubt that your god will answer your call swiftly. You may begin the contest and go first." Cheers went up all around. The king smiled and motioned everyone to be quiet.

The four hundred priests stood on the outside of the blackened stone, facing the altar. Slowly there came a deep rumbling from under the alter. The earth shook and the rocks trembled as the priests began humming a strange low tone.

Slowly the tone began to change, turning into music that was strange and dark and hard to listen to. The Dwarves began chanting songs that they couldn't understand.

"What are they saying and singing Corvil?" James asked. They turned to see Corvil standing white as stone, as though he was seeing something they weren't. "How are you doing Barnabas?" But Barnabas was lost in his thoughts and paid them no mind. "I wonder what's going on in their heads."

"I don't think we want to know," Rachal said.

They watched the scene around them play out as the minutes faded into nearly an hour. The priests, immersed in their trance-like state, began to dance to their music. Their eyes were closed as they sang and hummed. Strange instruments were brought forth and added to strange eerie sounding music. The skies darkened as deep grey clouds rolled in.

Before long the views of the distant peaks were swallowed by the sea of grey and the wind stopped. The priests seemed to not notice and continued in their rituals. The ground had stopped shaking but still, the people persisted.

Three hours passed with little change. The music, humming, and prayers of the priests echoed through the mountainside, all the time getting louder and louder, though nothing visibly changed. The ground shook every now and then, but it had become so infrequent they seldom paid attention to it. The thousands surrounding them, stood vigil, while the king looked annoyed.

"What do you make of this Corvil?" James asked. Corvil came forward, his face full of color and life once again. Barnabas still made no sound.

"The wind will soon change and not in their favor!" Corvil answered. Almost immediately a strong south wind swept up the mountain, offering warmth and assurance to all of them. Faint as it was a distant roar echoed through the high winds.

"Is this all you can muster?" Drake asked. "We've been here over four hours and what do we have to show for it? Clouds?"

"You guys might want to step up your game, I'm getting bored," Rachal challenged.

"Is this god asleep too?" Drake asked.

"Maybe this one's off somewhere else?" James said.

"It must be tiring to be demanded of so much," Drake retorted. "You guys seem to be having a hard time getting his attention. Does he not listen to you?" The king fumed from his seat but didn't speak.

The priests however weren't going to be belittled and without speaking a word to each other, began to draw swords and knives. They danced and cut themselves, sending blood down their robes. For twenty more minutes this went on, with several of the priests collapsing on the ground from loss of blood.

"Enough of this!" Drake yelled above the noise. The entire assembly fell silent. The priests cursed him for a moment but then fell silent, too weak to do anything but listen. "I think it's safe to say that you have lost. Or would you rather have more of your precious priests wither on the mountaintop?"

No one spoke a word in reply.

"My turn now and I hope to make this quick!" Drake exclaimed. He looked to the king. "Send for twelve canisters of water to be brought and poured over the sacrifice." Every eye turned towards the king who looked as dumbfounded as they did.

"But my Lord," the king started. "If you pour out all that water on the offering, it will never be lit."

"Why should that bother you?" Rachal asked. The king was lost in bewildered thought for a moment as he tried to say something that made sense.

"It will be impossible for-"

"Am I flinching?" Drake asked. The king looked at Drake for a moment and then looked away. "Send for the water and do it as I have said, for I serve the God of the impossible."

The king gave word and servants were sent to fetch the water which they were told might take up to an hour before the servants were back. During all that time the crowd didn't disperse, they didn't leave their spots. They talked and mumbled to themselves but mostly in hushed tones, for fear that someone might hear.

Finally, the servants arrived with twelve large canisters of water. The priests carefully poured the water over the offering and stepped aside, motioning that

Drake should come forward. Drake, Rachal, James, and Corvil all stood. Barnabas watched with a blank expression on his face.

"What now Drake?" James asked. Drake looked to the distant peaks which were now visible again. Drake smiled. James looked in the same direction, searching for what Drake had spotted.

Finally, James's eyes rested on the person and chills ran up his spine. A man in a robe stood atop one of the other mountains. He was small and hard to see from a distance, but James sensed there was something different about him. Drake stepped forward, and his foot sunk into the mud.

"Now you will see with your own eyes that there is a greater power in this world than the Sorcerer Merderick. He is nothing but a pathetic pretender, an imposter! He cares not that your priests have been lost to your pagan rituals. He cannot care. His heart is full of hate and destruction so that's all he can do. It's all he's capable of. Now people of Nargaroth; witness the power of Lathon, who is not merely stories and myth as some people would like to believe!"

James jumped when he saw a man standing next to Drake. He wore a beautiful robe and bore a large staff with sprouts growing off the end of it. His back was turned so James could not see his face. The man looked at Drake and then tapped his staff on the ground. The ground became dry and in an instant an explosion of light split through the sky striking the altar where it lay.

The light faded within a few seconds and when the smoke cleared they looked at everything that had happened. Everything on the altar had been consumed by the fire and the mud had disappeared. The entire mountain was covered in vegetation, lush and beautiful. The priests and prophets of Naroth lay dead on the ground.

Gasps of wonder and astonishment spread through the crowd as they surveyed the change, but no one spoke. James looked around looking for the robed man but he was nowhere to be found. Finally, the king struggled to his feet.

"Take them to their cell," the king ordered. Protests broke out among everyone atop the mountain. Some called for the king to set them free as he had promised and others wished for immediate execution. The king held up a hand

and everyone silenced themselves. "This matter will be discussed with advisors, for it is a circumstance we have not foreseen. Mr. Thomas and his entourage will be kept overnight until these questions are answered." Guards moved in and ceased the five of them, dragging them to the cart they had been brought in.

"I'm not sure our position has improved any Drake. What do we do now?" Barnabas asked. The cart bounced along uncomfortably.

"Wait."

Chapter 21

MELCHIZEDEK

The familiar flicker of torchlight was the only thing Drake could see when he woke. He faced the cell door, offering an empty hallway beyond. Chains bound his wrists and his ankles and held him to the wall. Drake looked at the others who were also chained to the wall as he was.

"Welcome back to the land of the living," James greeted.

"How can you call this living?" Barnabas asked.

Rachal rolled her eyes.

"Don't mind him," James said. "They gave us a pretty bad beating when we got back, you bumped your head on the wall and you've been out for…well… time doesn't seem to exist in here, so I'm not sure how long you've been out. I'd say at least three hours."

"Corvil here?" Drake asked.

"Yes, I'm here. After what I saw today, I have no doubt in my mind about the truth of things. I'm with you to whatever end."

"The only end we'll be having is mangled up in a pit!" Barnabas exclaimed.

"Can we leave him here?" Rachal asked. Barnabas narrowed his cold icy eyes on her. "He can get kind of depressing."

"Like we're going to get out?" Barnabas asked. They were silent for several minutes until footsteps echoed through the dim hallways beyond their cell doors. The footsteps stopped and the sound of a key turning in a lock came to their ears.

"And now, another level of Hell," Barnabas scoffed. The door opened and only one person entered.

"I can assure you one thing Barnabas," a familiar voice said. "I am not from

Hell." The person stepped into the light, and their hearts leapt for joy as the light fell across Aiden's face.

"Boy, are we glad to see you!" Drake exclaimed.

"Who is this?" Corvil asked as Aiden began releasing their chains.

"Someone who is here to set your chains free and deliver you from this horrible place." Aiden undid Corvil's chains and dropped them to the ground. "How does it feel being on this end of things?"

"Like a great burden's been lifted," Corvil answered. Aiden motioned for them to be quiet and follow behind. They moved into the hall, moving through passages and corridors that Drake and James alike hadn't noticed before. Three hours later they came to a stop as a group of men appeared in front of them. Drake grew tense until he realized that Aiden wasn't alarmed. Each of them held a bag in their hands. Aiden quickly handed them to everybody. When Drake looked up again the men had vanished. They opened the bags, finding all of their belongings that had been taken from them along their journey.

"Never thought I'd see this again," James said, drawing his sword. The blade flickered in the torchlight. "I'm not sure how you managed to find this, or how you managed to get it. But from the bottom of my heart I thank you."

"Glad to help," Aiden said. "We are about five minutes from the gate out of the mountains. Hopefully we can make it there undetected."

"And then what?" Barnabas asked. "Get chased across the land. Probably by the entire Nargaroth army, no thanks to the fact that we are escaping."

"Take it or leave it my friend," Aiden said. "The choice is yours." They started down the halls and tunnels once again, coming to a large open cavern with one single stone bridge spanning a large chasm. Aiden stopped.

"The door to the outside world is on the other side of that bridge. There appears to be only a few guards at the gate. Although I've learned it's never as easy as it looks."

"They have bowmen overhead ready to shoot anyone who isn't escorted by a *Juinha*," Corvil said.

"What's a *Juinha*?" Rachal asked.

"In the common tongue I suppose it would mean commander, and they have to have the papers to back it up or else they're killed and thrown over the edge."

"The world is really a dark place," Rachal said.

Aiden nodded. "People search for the meaning to life, not realizing their maker has put signs of his glory all around." Aiden studied the surroundings. "The way I see it, we have only one choice. Run as fast as we can, get to the landing and open the gate before we get captured or killed."

Aiden looked out at the bridge and then to everyone else. Without speaking they sprinted from their hiding spot and out into the open. Their footsteps, echoed through the great hall. Moments later, a great clamor was heard all around as the alarm was raised. Warriors poured out into the open from both sides, blocking their way off the bridge and blocking the way they had come.

Aiden stopped and the others followed suit. Archers appeared on the balconies overhead.

"My men wait for my command," a large dwarf near the gate said. He strode forward his long dark beard flowing. "I know who all of you are, and you certainly didn't escape by chance. Renounce your vile god and save your lives."

"We would sooner be killed for standing firm," Rachal said.

"That can be arranged," the dwarf replied. An arrow streaked through the air and struck Rachal in the side. She staggered and toppled over the edge of the bridge, her cries lost to the darkness. "Anyone want to reconsider your choices?"

"Jump," Corvil whispered to them. They hesitated, fear over taking them for a moment.

"Anyone wish to save your lives?" the dwarf asked. "Or shall I give the command to fill the rest of you with arrows."

"Go ahead and try!" Aiden said. All at once they jumped off the bridge, falling into darkness. Arrows whizzed overhead. Drake floundered in the air and then braced for impact as a pale light began to grow beneath them. They struck the bottom, being thrust into icy water. They gasped for breath and desperately tried to get their bearings, spotting the shore to their left.

They frantically pulled themselves onto the shore. They collapsed, shivering uncontrollably. Drake stood too his feet, searching the darkness.

"Where's Rachal?" Drake stammered. After a moment they spotted her body laying on the shore a couple hundred feet from them. An arrow protruded from her side and blood flowed freely from the wound. Drake broke the arrow shaft and felt for a pulse. "She's alive, but weak."

"She won't last long," Corvil managed. "Prisoners like us, they likely used poison tipped arrows. She'll die within a few minutes. And so will we unless we get dry fast."

"What is this?" Aiden asked. He pointed to a flask tied around Rachal's waist.

"Something Isabel gave us. She said not to take it unless we were in dire need. She cautioned against taking too much of it." Aiden sniffed it and gagged.

"I have no idea what it is," Aiden said. "However, I think we are in dire need." He put the flask to his lip taking a sip. He flinched and then grabbed at his stomach. "I know what this is now! No more than a small sip." Each of them passed it around and then they forced a sip onto Rachal's lips.

Drake flinched as it burned all the way down and then seemed to consume his stomach in fire. Drake held his stomach on the ground wincing and trying not to cry out in pain. A couple of minutes later the pain had passed and they felt as if though fire was flowing through their veins. Aiden was the first to fully recover, standing to his feet and shaking his head.

"You said Isabel gave that to you?" Aiden asked. Drake nodded. "Where does she find this stuff?"

"Question of the ages that's for sure," Drake said.

Rachal stirred and then sat up. To their amazement the arrowhead had fallen out and the wound had sealed itself. They looked down at their clothes, noticing that they weren't wet at all. Also the serum had solved their physical injuries, but still left them with the pain. Drake helped Rachal to her feet. She grabbed where the arrow had struck her.

"You alright?" Drake asked. Rachal nodded.

"A little disoriented. Where are we?"

"Any idea Corvil?" Aiden asked. Everyone stared ahead to see the wall of an abandoned fortress standing overhead. The top was jagged and the entire structure looked as if it had been long deserted by anyone living. The wall went as far as the eye could see, wrapping all around the underground lake they had been submerged in. Far above they could vaguely see the bridge where they had been standing.

"I've got one, but I'm not sure if it can be the correct one. It was said many generations ago that our ancestors lived much deeper in the mountains. This must be proof of that claim."

"Why's there no one living here now?" Barnabas asked. "Seems it a shame to waste such hard work and leave it to itself."

"I only know rumors. As legend tells great enchantresses dwelt in the deep places of the earth and brought life and hope to them. As such they became worshiped as deities. Eventually the enchantresses became displeased with the Dwarves for whatever reason and their anger could not be abated. They promised to kill everyone in the mountains unless one chose to stay for them to torture for eternity.

"As far as I know that is all that happened and there are many songs and stories about that day that have been crafted and written, and many of them are far too dark for me to utter."

"This was the great fortress of *Biryuk*. Quite powerful back in the days," Aiden said.

"It was once beautiful, now it sits desolate."

"As do many things that *chose* to do so," Aiden replied. Immediately great terrifying screeches echoed through the mountains. Their hearts quailed in fear though Aiden stood and faced the city wall, drawing his sword. "Hiding behind the wall like a coward? I should have expected as much. Come out of there and show yourself!" Again another terrifying screech was heard and still Aiden didn't flinch. "Come out!"

"*Why does it call us out?*" A voice asked. Raspy and deep. "We know who it is! *We're not going out!* Stop talking fool. *Maybe it will leave. It won't leave us alone you know that.* Shut up or I'll kill you all. *If we go out we will be killed.* He never said that."

Finally after what seemed like an eternity the person stopped arguing and appeared at the gates. He was dressed in tattered rags that hardly counted as clothes, and a great grey beard reached down to his knees. His hair was overgrown and shaggy and his fingernails and toenails were long as claws. As he came near they could see the Dwarf was skinny as a rail, his bones nearly visible in the dim lighting.

"You shall not interfere with us!" the dwarf screamed in their faces. All of them exchanged confused looks.

Aiden looked undeterred.

"You came out to meet me!" Aiden said sternly. "I will most certainly interfere with you."

"We didn't want to!" the man snapped. "*Yes we did!* I thought he was told not to speak?"

"What's going on here?" Barnabas whispered to Drake. Drake paid him no mind, watching the scene that was playing out in front of them. The man argued with himself until finally Aiden grew tired of listening.

"What is your name?" Aiden asked. The Dwarf recoiled momentarily.

"Legion," the man replied.

"Odd name," Barnabas remarked. The man's gaze instantly narrowed in on Barnabas. He turned to face Aiden again.

"Why do you come before it's your time?" the Dwarf screamed.

"If I have come then it is my time!" Aiden exclaimed. "Now come out of this man; all of you!"

"What man?" the Dwarf asked.

"Either you doubt who I am or you think I'm stupid. I'm calling you *Legion* out of this man that you've tormented for far too long with no just cause!" Aiden said forcefully.

"He offered himself," the Dwarf said, a couple of other voices said the same thing all coming from the same person.

"He has done honorably and in the name of Lathon, I demand that you come out of this man immediately!" Drake and everyone else jumped back as the man groveled and floundered on the floor seeming to see things that weren't there.

"How could it be?" the Dwarf asked himself. "We haven't heard that name in thousands of years. *We're afraid of it after all this time?* He's going to kill us! *No he wouldn't do that.* Yes he would." A moment of silence passed before the Dwarf began to speak in a more normal voice. "Don't kill us, please! Let us instead drown in the water." The pleading and begging continued for several minutes as Aiden seemed to be considering all possibilities. At length, Aiden spoke,

"You fear being killed by me, but by your deserting this man and drowning yourself in the water you will no sooner escape your destiny. For you *know* at the end of the ages you will be dealt your punishment. Your price for your deceit and sedition. If it is drowning in water that you seek then go do so and trouble this realm no longer. But hear me now! If you should come out of that water for any reason than you will be killed immediately. And you certainly know who will do that!" The voice inside the man groaned and wined pathetically. "In the name of Lathon go and trouble this man no longer!"

The Dwarf fell to the ground, limp as a fish caught from the water. The sound of a great commotion reached them, as though a great race was happening. Screaming pierced the air and soon they could see hundreds of footprints dotting the shoreline. Drake thought for a moment he could even see shadows making the footprints.

In a thunderous roar the invisible Spirits reached the underground lake. The water splashed violently as they went further and further into the lake. Finally the Spirits had become submerged and within a few seconds the lake was silent; though now the lake was boiling.

"Don't see that every day," Barnabas said. They turned their attention to the Dwarf who was still motionless on the ground. Aiden rolled him over and Corvil quickly felt for a pulse. After a moment he let the hand gently drop to the ground.

"He's dead," Corvil said. They all fell silent, while Aiden seemed to look on with interest.

"What now?" Barnabas asked. "We're hopelessly lost in the dark with no escape and now we have a dead body."

"I'm sure there's a way out of this place," James said. "We'll just have to try and find it. I have no doubt that our almond supply will continue to be sent."

"You are all mistaken. He is most certainly not dead. Just sleeping," Aiden said. Even as he spoke new life seemed to be breathed into the man and he again started breathing and his pulse became easily detectable. They looked in wonder as the Dwarf sat up, having lost his overgrown beard and hair. He now appeared put together and composed and fully dressed. The Dwarf opened his mouth to speak but for a moment nothing came.

"I am Melchizedek. Leader of the Third Order of the Elivon descendants of the great Travelers of Timith Ur." He paused and looked at all of them with interest and fascination. "I know not where your faces are from or when in the great tale of time I now awaken. My thoughts were stolen from me and though done so by my own fruition, I never thought I would awake. This is a great joy." He stood to his feet.

"Drake and Rachal Thomas of Merisyll. At your service." They all introduced themselves, though when it came time for Aiden's introduction. The Dwarf turned white and nearly fell over. Aiden steadied him and for several moments the Dwarf struggled to speak.

"I know your face!" Melchizedek exclaimed. "For it appeared to me in a dream before my greatest day. Though my thoughts have been stolen from me for all this time, your face and your name have remained in my heart. You are Adonai, son of Elivon-"

"And your day of restoration has come!" Aiden cried with authority. "This Melchizedek, is your greatest day. You did what was asked and now you have been set free." Melchizedek wept, though everyone understood they were tears of joy. "We will stay here the night, and in the morning we will escape these infernal mountains."

***

Barnabas shifted uncomfortably, unable to sleep. He sat upright, seeing only Corvil awake, staring up at the rock. Corvil took notice but said nothing for several more minutes.

"What's keeping you awake?" Barnabas asked.

"Just replaying everything that's happened. It's been quite a busy couple of days for me. For all of us really."

"Tell me about it. This has been my life for the past month. I've had just about enough of it."

"You've made it this far alive and yet you frown upon it?" Corvil asked. "How does that make any sense?"

"I've lost everything, my ship, my crew, my life. What do I have to show for it? And now after all of that we're still stuck in the dark places of the world."

"It could be worse," Corvil reminded. Barnabas scoffed. "What are your opinions of what has transpired?"

"I don't believe them. It all seems like a great trick to me. I have a hard time believing this Melchizedek has actually been alive down here for three thousand years, or whatever number he came up with. It doesn't make sense! I'm beginning to think this Aiden character is no good. Casting out demons; Ha! There's the deception. He is the demon."

"Your skills in logic are not that great Barnabas," Corvil replied. "He could not possibly be a demon otherwise he would be fighting himself! A house divided against itself cannot stand. Aiden is no demon, but he does have a power and authority beyond the reach of Merderick and his demons."

"So you've bought into their thinking?"

"It's the only thinking that makes sense!" Corvil exclaimed. "All I know in my brief time with Drake and his companions is that they've lived through things that no one else should have. They have been delivered through every circumstance. The gods of our nation have been defeated in stunning fashion; then at the end of all of it a man, who has been legend and myth in Nargaroth for a very long time gets restored to perfect sanity? That doesn't just happen Barnabas! Aiden is the heir of Lathon, and I've seen more than enough to make me believe."

"So I'm by myself in this matter?"

"Only because you want to be." Silence lingered and Corvil rolled over and went to sleep. Barnabas remained awake, pondering everything.

The dawn came, but they could hardly tell. The only indicator was a small opening in the roof of the mountain, which let in fresh air and sunshine. Melchizedek and Aiden woke them and motioned to get ready but not to talk. Soon they were all up and set out at a slight run. They moved in silence, delving deeper and deeper into the darkness. The day wore on and it was many hours until they took a rest.

"Where are we exactly?" Drake asked, in as quiet of a voice as he could.

"We've made good time and are now one hour from the exit from the mountains," Aiden said. "Though it is vital that we keep as quiet as possible. There are not friendly things ahead of us."

"What's up ahead?" James asked.

"The priestesses that possessed Melchizedek until recently, all dwelt in the mountains, many years before Dwarves inhabited them. There are many shrines and or places of their worship where dark things still happen."

After that, nobody spoke a word. Soon they started again with a sense of urgency growing on them. Their dampened spirits began to rise and even the air began to feel a little better to them. Suddenly the tunnel they had spent the last two hours in, came to an abrupt end. In front of them a single wooden door separated them from the outside.

"Hard to believe we're here," James said. "Are you sure this is the door to the outside?"

"As sure as I'm standing here before you!" Melchizedek cried. "But we must wait until morning to go any further."

"Why morning?" Barnabas asked. "Why not go out and make a run for it?"

"This door may lead to the outside world, but it will be night soon and there are things worse than the guards we'll have to contend with if we leave now. The mountains have many strange creatures in them."

"If we wait until morning we'll have just the guards," Aiden explained. "I've made arrangements for getting away, because I'm sure we'll be spotted and it won't take them long to put two and two together and give chase. Get some rest and when the dawn comes we will try our hand against the strength and might of Nargaroth!"

Barnabas was woken in the night by a whisper that came too his ears. He looked around the darkness unable to find any source of light. The whisper continued, growing and then lessening, almost as if he was listening to someone breathing. Aiden appeared, torch in hand.

"Don't you ever sleep?" Barnabas asked.

"Sleep when there's foul things about? Life lesson, don't do it."

"What's out there? I keep thinking I hear something resembling breathing."

"I told you there were strange things in the dark places of the mountains and I have not misled you. Any skeletal remains that are in this place breathe in the dark night air."

"Impossible!" Barnabas exclaimed as quietly as he could manage. "They're dead. Aren't they?"

"Somethings take too much time to explain," Aiden answered. "I would love to answer your question, but sleep will be the better remedy at the moment." After that Aiden didn't speak again and instead starred down the long hall behind them until the dawn came.

When Barnabas woke again his head pounded and throbbed unlike anything he had ever experienced. The others were already up, eating their portion of the almonds that had shown up in the dead of night. He sat up, each limb feeling as though moving was a great burden. He struggled to his feet and walked over to the door where everyone was waiting.

"There is about ten minutes of tree cover and then we'll enter into many leagues of desolate wasteland before we will reach the border of Rinevah," Aiden explained.

Melchizedek pulled open the wood door before them. Where they had expected warm clear sunshine to come pouring in, instead only dim grey light came. They stepped out into a forgotten and strange world. The trees towered nearly fifty feet above them.

Barnabas studied the trees with distrust and despair. They were a dark grey color, almost black and their trunks from the base all the way up to the highest branch were covered in long, sharp thorns. As high as Barnabas could see the branches were cruelly twisted together and blocked out all light.

The ground was soft and moist and a small clear cold spring trickled down a couple hundred yards away. To the left and the right they could see they were now standing at the base of a large wall.

The wall had been cut into the mountains and ran the entire length of the mountain range. It stood fifty feet tall and was without flaw or blemish. The rock was black and strange, feeling rough to the point where Barnabas's hand bled after running his fingers along them for a moment.

The time passed and soon they had come to the edge of the strange twisted trees. They stepped into warm sunshine, which made their spirits soar higher than they had been up to that point. A gentle breeze comforted their souls. The others moved on, leaving Barnabas standing at the forests edge.

"Come on Barnabas or you'll be left behind," Drake said. Barnabas stood, unsure of what he should do.

"No," he answered. Drake and everyone looked behind wondering if they had heard it right. Even Barnabas questioned whether he had said the words, even if it had crossed his mind more than once. Barnabas hesitated, seeing the questions in all their eyes. "I can't do it Drake!"

"Do what?" Drake asked. Barnabas thought hard.

"Live this life you guys live," Barnabas replied. "All my life I've been working like a dog to have a good shipping business, and I've lost it."

"There's more to life than a good business," James said.

"I've lost it all! I have no life. This is not what I signed up for."

"So what's your plan?" Aiden asked. Barnabas looked at the ground.

"I don't need a plan to know that I have to leave you guys and find… something."

"I think you should stay with us, at least till we get through this wasteland," Rachal said.

"I can't stay with you any longer!" Barnabas cried, anger welling up inside. He turned to leave but stopped when Aiden spoke.

"Don't do this Barnabas. Despair and hopelessness have clouded your vision, but I warn that you shouldn't let a feeling such as that make your decisions."

"I know," Barnabas snapped. "But I have to do it." Barnabas didn't wait for a reply. He turned from all of them and walked away.

Chapter 22

JIKE

They were in the air before the break of dawn, settling in for another long day of traveling over the seas. They kept high, coming down now and again just so they could get a bearing on where they might be. Isabel and Morgrin both poured over the map, charting the best course that they could seeing the circumstances.

The second day proved to be more interesting as they began turning to the northwest ever so slightly. As the day faded the sea below was filled with nearly a hundred rock pillars that jutted up out of the water. Each of them was identical, but other than that they could not make out any other interesting details about them.

When it was nearly evening they came to a large vast expanse of uninterrupted ocean. The sunlight danced off the gentle waves and the wind seemed to cease altogether. Far in the distance, a small black speck hovered above the water.

"I think that's the island we're looking for if my map reckoning is correct," Isabel yelled to Morgrin who once again rode upon Destan.

"I hope so because I do not see any other land for us to stay on," Morgrin replied with a laugh.

"What, you afraid of the water or something?" Isabel jested.

"Seeing that all we have under us is a big ocean...yes!"

Several more hours passed until the island came into greater focus. Lush green trees were cast in dark shadows as the sun was now dipping behind the mountain that jutted up in the middle of the island. They flew low and slowly began to circle the island, trying to figure out just how big it was. Twenty minutes later it didn't appear they were any closer to getting back to their starting point.

"Where do you want to stop for the night? Morgrin asked. He stared at the coastline intently.

"Right here looks good!" Isabel exclaimed. She jumped off Aspen's back and let out a yell as she landed in the water. She resurfaced and sputtered only momentarily. Destan and Morgrin circled above her. She could see Morgrin both smiling and shaking his head at her. "Why don't you join me?"

"I'm not that much a fan of water," Morgrin yelled back.

"Just give it a try."

"No thanks."

"Destan would you help him into the water?" Isabel asked. Morgrin started to object but not fast enough as Destan did a flip and sent Morgrin flailing through the air. She swam over to him trying not to laugh as he resurfaced. "Glad you could join me." They both swam to the sandy shore. Large clumps of rocks and pieces of stone lay piled in various places on the beach.

"Nice place," Isabel commented.

"Nice castle," Morgrin added. Looming before them a large empty castle lay waiting. The rocks were blackened as though a fire had consumed the city at some point in history.

The castle sat atop a cliff that ran for several hundred feet in both directions. To the left, the forest grew wild and free, while to the right the forest now grew through the ruins and pieces of the castle that had fallen when the cliff deteriorated over the centuries.

"Iminy," Isabel said. Morgrin gave her an amused look. "It's the name of the castle."

"Of course it is," Morgrin replied. "We've been traveling for weeks, through places that you have admitted that you have never seen before and now you somehow know the name of this strange ruined castle?"

"It's on the map dear," Isabel replied, handing it to him. He took it and then shook his head.

"There's nothing written on here!"

"Sorry, it's in ancient Elvish."

"Well, how am I supposed to read it?" Morgrin asked, amused. "This map only shows you the language that you belong to."

"True."

"Okay, hold on woman!" Morgrin cried. "You're not elvish."

"My mother was." Morgrin thought for a moment.

"Okay...so this map shows you the writing even if you belong to half that race?"

"Seems so," Isabel said. "Ellizar's notes say that this island in particular is a hot spot of some kind, though there was no mention of what it was people wanted."

"Shall we explore now or in the morning?" Morgrin asked.

"No time like the present, besides I have a feeling when the tide is in this area is flooded," Isabel answered. They searched for a way up the cliff for twenty minutes, only to find that the natural cliff that the castle was built atop, went far further than they had realized at first glance.

The Taruks met them on the shore and helped them traverse the one-hundred-foot cliff. They were set in a great stone courtyard, which was overgrown with brush and ivy.

"So..into the spooky ancient abandoned castle?" Morgrin asked.

Isabel led the way, entering through the gates which were crumbled and twisted. Inside the stones were covered with a thin layer of water, which reflected the enormous hall.

In a few places where the roof or walls had been broken, trees or other plants had started to creep in and wind their way through the structure.

"I wonder what the story of this place is?" Isabel said, sitting on a piece of broken statue.

"I'm glad it's still standing," Morgrin said. "I am grateful that you have an insatiable curiosity. People often pass by things like this and forget they have a story and a life. I wonder what will be said of us?"

"Only Lathon knows," Isabel said. "All of time is held in his hands."

"What do you think we'll find when we get to Cordell? If that's where we're actually heading."

"I'm not sure. I'm curious and feel led to get this letter to the right person, then we'll see what happens from there."

The next three hours of fading light were spent exploring the ancient castle and imagining how beautiful the castle must have looked when it was new. They traversed a large bridge that led to a tower that climbed sharply into the sky. The door was broken off its' hinges, but still, they entered and climbed the stairs to the top.

At the top, they came to a large room covered from top to bottom in stones made of gold. Windows brought in the fading sunlight from outside illuminating the gold and revealing a shallow pool in the center of the room. The water flickered like fire as it sat completely still and void of life.

A raised edge made with black-tinted rocks rose two feet above the floor, holding the water at bay. Despite how long the castle had likely been deserted the water was crystal clear.

"Explanation?" Morgrin asked.

"It's a Sorcerer's pool," Isabel stated. "Enya had one in her house. Rumor is there were seven of them."

"Seven pools like this?"

"Don't quote me on that. It's been a few years. Don't touch the water!" They looked around the room, admiring the beauty and intricacy of the trim and woodwork. Finally, they came to the last darkened corner of the room finding a staircase. "Up we go!"

They both climbed until they came out into a large open area with a marble floor. They admired the view enjoying the almost faded daylight. From the growing darkness somewhere they could hear indistinct shouts and conversations. They looked to the sea, seeing lights bobbing up and down on the waves.

"I guess this island isn't deserted after all," Morgrin said.

"Hopefully we can go undetected, but at any rate, they might all be here to use this pool. We can't stay in this castle tonight or we might be discovered. They quickly left the top of the castle and exited the way they came.

They returned to the vast courtyard they had started in and moved further away from the shore, climbing into the hills, only enough to avoid detection. The Taruks flew in silently and lay around the two of them, keeping them from harm.

They both lay down and fell asleep together, but several different times during the night Isabel woke with bad dreams. She got up and crept as far up the hill as she dared, looking out at the sea and noticing that nearly twenty ships had arrived.

Morning came, bringing with it the sounds of birds chirping peacefully. Isabel opened her groggy eyes and breathed deeply the smell of the dew on the plants. She sat up, becoming alarmed when she heard voices in the woods near them. She quickly woke Morgrin and scanned the area for the Taruks, none of which were to be found. They ran further inland, moving away from the voices.

"Where do you think the Taruks are?" Morgrin asked.

"Don't know, but they can take care of themselves."

"I'd love to know what everyone wants on this island!" Morgrin exclaimed.

"I thought it was the pool in the castle, but it appears I was wrong." Isabel stopped in her tracks, nearly knocked over by Morgrin. They both dropped to the ground, ducking behind a fallen log. A large open space lay before them. Lush green grass filled the natural valley.

Flowing down the middle of the great valley was a river of sparkling clear water that was fed by four waterfalls at the far end. They both noticed strange clumps of brown scattered everywhere on the floor of the valley.

"What are they doing?" Morgrin asked.

"There they are! Grab them!" voices cried out from behind. Isabel and Morgrin tried to run but were held to the ground, their hands tied, and large sacks were promptly put over their heads. They were tied onto the back of horses and taken away from the valley.

Isabel calmed herself and tried as much as possible to figure out which way they were headed. Roughly ten minutes passed until the path that they were traveling became level and smooth. The sound of water falling reached her ears.

Isabel and Morgrin were untied from the horses and lowered to the ground, the sacks pulled off their head. Isabel scowled at the man who looked increasingly afraid.

"Sorry," the man said.

"You messed up my hair!" Isabel yelled. Morgrin tried not to laugh as the man was speechless and backed up further.

"I'm just the messenger," the man defended.

"Who in their right mind ordered us to be captured?" Isabel asked.

"Me." They turned to see a tall man with hard dark eyes. His beard was short and well-trimmed and his clothes were made of fine silks and fabrics, unlike the rest of the men. "For I have the authority to do so! Now who in their right mind permitted you to be on this island?"

"There was no one here when we arrived," Isabel said.

The man laughed. "This is the island of Jike. No one comes to these shores without permission. Whoever gave you permission is more guilty than yourselves and should be dealt with as such."

"So you agree we've done nothing wrong? Thank you! Release us and we'll be on our way."

"You're bold," the man said. "You may, in your eyes, be 'less guilty' but I'm sure the king will order your execution just the same."

"What king would that be oh exalted one?" the crew snickered at the sarcasm that dripped from Isabel's words. Isabel was struck across the face.

"Careful," the man said. "You're on the edge of heresy and serious crimes in addition to all the ones you've already committed by coming to this island without permission."

"We are travelers who were looking for a place to stay for the night!" Isabel argued. "What's got you so out of joint?"

"Perhaps I'll talk to the guy instead." The man moved over to Morgrin who gave him an amused look.

"It is as she said. Tell us some basics that we don't know and I'm sure we can answer your questions," Morgrin said.

"Very well," the man agreed, turning to face Isabel. "You see he's much more reasonable than you." He turned back to Morgrin unable to see the mocking expression Isabel was making behind his back. Several of the men held back their chuckles.

"I am Captain Borea. I take the helm of the ship *Trinin*. The finest supply ship in Cordell's fleet. I am under the authority of King Drayvin to do as I see fit, regarding complications with the supply of food to his royal majesty! You have interfered with me and my operations and now it is my job to ascertain the truth and decide how to deal with you. I may choose to present the matter to the king, but at this point, I do not believe it to be necessary. Do we understand each other better?"

"I do not doubt your authority or your power," Morgrin replied. "I sense you to be a just and kind ruler and not a rash and harsh dictator. Please present your case now. Unless there are specific allegations of crimes, besides the one of *accidentally* coming to your shores without any knowledge of this place; there can be no reason to restrain us."

Borea's expression softened a bit, slipping into his thoughts. "Indeed I am not a rash and harsh dictator. I have worked for many people like that through my service to Cordell. Very well, here is my charge against you. This morning my crew and I came ashore for the harvest as we do every morning. When we reached our spot we were surprised and frightened to find three Taruks sleeping in the fields.

"Every precaution was taken, but we were able to secure the Taruks without them waking. We returned to the fields, alarmed when it came to our attention, that a third of the field was taken. I am sent by King Drayvin to harvest Dail, the brown things you saw a few minutes ago. It tastes like bread with butter on it. Very sweet and very satisfying to both body and soul. It will keep for only twenty-four hours, give or take. If it is not processed the Dail will rot overnight. It is a precious commodity known only to this island. If I let you live you will have to explain to King Drayvin why part of the shipment is missing. Can you think of another way for me to get all of this out of the mess? I may be forced to kill you right here."

"Well perhaps there can be another way," Isabel started. "Instead of carrying out justice that you seem hesitant to take, in which case we would likely die, perhaps you can show us mercy for things we did not know about. You have three Taruks that you've held captive. I assure you that when they wake up they will lay waste to you. We do not wish to see you die, and we do not want innocent deaths to be on either of our consciences.

"If you let us all go now, I can assure you that no harm will befall any of your ships or men. Tell the king whatever you wish or tell him nothing. Perhaps we got away through some well-conceived plan. Perhaps we fought you valiantly and were killed or otherwise injured too badly to pose a threat. Tell whatever story you wish, but no matter what I'm sure you can make it work to your advantage."

Borea stroked his chin in thought for a moment, his eyes looking to his crew.

"What do you say, gents? I cannot deny that this course of action will benefit all of us, provided all of you say only what I say. Is this agreed?"

"Aye!" the men quickly replied. Borea nodded his head.

"Very well. I declare you are free people," Borea said. " Darrison!" The man Isabel had scolded for her hair came forward hesitantly. "Untie them and lead them to their Taruks. I'm sure you understand that if any harm comes to any of my men between now and when you have left this island my oath of safety and mercy will be thrown away and I will strike at you in whatever way I can."

"We understand," Isabel and Morgrin both said in unison.

They were helped to their feet, untied, and escorted almost a half mile to the north side of the clearing where their Taruks were tied and chained to the ground. The men started the process of untying and unchaining the Taruks but cried out and jumped back as ropes and chains alike turned to a fiery glow before snapping. The Taruks stood to their feet, their eyes threatening to scorch everyone in sight. Isabel caught Aspen's gaze, her thoughts known to the Taruk.

The Taruks stretched and they climbed aboard and the Taruks pushed off the ground and sent them sailing straight into the sky. Isabel and Morgrin breathed in the cool crisp air as they circled above the island for a moment. They looked out to the sea, both of them speechless.

"Isabel?"

"I see it," Isabel said, nearly in a whisper. Nearly one hundred ships lined the coast and waters along the shore. Their sails were drawn up and anchors were down, but their eyes were drawn towards the flags that flew atop the ships. The flags, bearing the crest of her family, were in full display as they blew in the wind.

"I think perhaps the symbol of your family crest...isn't just your family crest." They flew in silence over the ships. They flew for nearly an hour without speaking. "You okay Isabel?" She nodded.

"Heading to Cordell might prove to be more interesting than we bargained for."

Two hours later, they still flew over the empty ocean. Isabel and Morgrin were both lost in their thoughts, as they searched the horizon for any sign of land. They both stirred when a small island of green appeared below.

"It's a small enough island, it's probably uninhabited," Morgrin called out. Isabel nodded.

"I hope so. I need some time to think."

They came in closer to the island and circled it, finding it to be almost a complete circle that was no more than a mile across. When they were satisfied that the island was uninhabited they descended and landed on the soft sandy shores. Isabel slid off Aspen's back and went and sat down on the shore without speaking. Morgrin soon joined her.

"What are you thinking?" Morgrin asked.

"I can't help but wonder what my father's backstory actually is. I thought it had just been our family crest all these years. Now it appears it belongs to an entire nation? It's hard to catch up with."

"I agree," Morgrin said. "We had planned to fly right to the shores of Cordell. Do you want to play things differently?"

"I think they need to be played differently," Isabel said. "I'm just not sure how the cards should be played yet."

"As much as you might not want to do it, it might be time to use your disguises again," Morgrin suggested. Isabel nodded.

"We can't be far from Cordell," Isabel stated. "Captain Borea said the bread would only last twenty-four hours."

"If it wasn't processed or changed in any way," Morgrin pointed out.

"So Cordell is out there on the ocean somewhere nearby," Isabel said. "Ezzion and Destan!" the two Taruks stirred and came close to her.

"Fly the ocean and report back what you see, make sure you stay high enough in the sky to be undetected," Isabel ordered. The Taruks seemed to nod their heads and then jumped into the sky and took flight. "Now we wait." A rustling of leaves came from behind them, they turned and looked but saw nothing.

"Do you think Aiden knew what we would find this far north?" Morgrin asked.

"It's Aiden. I have no doubt he knew what was up here and there's also a specific reason that we were brought here. I'm sure when the time is right we will know what it is." They fell silent for a moment, each of them thinking they had heard something in the trees beyond. Morgrin motioned to Isabel, wondering if they should investigate. Isabel motioned him to stay. "We're not alone."

The Taruks returned at sundown and thoroughly reported everything that they had observed. Isabel patted them on the back and they disappeared down the coastline somewhere. Morgrin came out of the trees with some wood for a fire. He put it down on the ground in a neat pile and then called for Aspen. Aspen, looking half amused, opened her powerful jaws and spit out a small ball of fire.

"That's a good Taruk," Isabel said, stroking her hard skin. Aspen sat up straighter, taking it all in. Morgrin walked towards the two of them.

"What did we learn from the scouting mission?"

"The large landmass we now know as Cordell is no more than six miles northwest of here. It's a major shipping hub and is extremely large. The shipping route for the boats we saw today comes within two miles of this place, but for whatever reason none ever land here. They also said that Captain Borea's ship made landfall in Cordell in the early evening."

"What do you think we should do?"

"I was going to ask you," Isabel said.

Morgrin thought hard for a moment. "I think we need to get to the shore without being spotted with Taruks."

"If we time it right, we could do something bold and stupid, like dropping onto Captain Borea's ship."

"That was my best thought," Morgrin said. "It's rather risky. General maritime laws say that stowaways get thrown overboard."

"We had an agreement the first time I don't see why we couldn't figure something out," Isabel said. Morgrin nodded and started laughing.

"You'll have to be a little nicer to him this time around. Otherwise, he'll only talk to me again."

"Ha, ha, ha," Isabel mocked, smacking him in the side. "Don't worry I'd be totally civil this time. Half the time when I am as bold as I was with him it's on purpose. In a situation where you know nothing... you can often make them forget everything they knew by your audacity."

"Explains a lot of your conversing tactics on this trip."

"It's been a fun card to play," Isabel admitted.

"You've done it very well," Morgrin complimented.

"Thank you, kind sir."

"Just so you know, it does scare the crap out of me when you do that." She kissed him and they prepared a small meal with things they found nearby. Then as the sun slipped below the horizon they lay down together and fell asleep.

Isabel woke with a hand over her mouth.

Morgrin lay facing her motioning her to remain silent. Isabel listened intently to their surroundings, finally hearing what Morgrin was hearing. Footsteps approached in the dark. Isabel reached for her sword which lay next to her, while Morgrin grasped a knife.

The footsteps were heavy and uneven and filled with the sound of armor. The footsteps approached and they both heard a sword being pulled out of it's sheath. They both jumped from their place. Morgrin spun in a half circle, knocking the person off their feet. Morgrin swiftly pulled his dagger and held it to the person's throat.

"This is no soldier!" Morgrin exclaimed. Isabel came forward. Morgrin eased up as the girl beneath him began crying. Morgrin let her sit up. She was Elvish and dressed in armor that was far too large for her. "Name yourself!"

The girl sobbed uncontrollably but melted into Isabel who took the girl by the hand and helped her up, embracing her.

"Give her some time and space. There's a story here we don't know."

They started another fire and made some tea for the three of them. The girl didn't say anything as she stared into the flames.

"Feeling a little better?" Isabel asked. The Elvish girl nodded. She hastily removed her armor and let it clatter to the ground. She was young, with mid-length red hair that appeared to be naturally curled. She was barefoot, with a plain dark blue dress covering her.

"As good as I'm going to be," the girl finally replied. Her voice was soft and conveyed a deep pain. "I'm sorry."

"It's alright," Isabel said. "We are strangers to your shores, no doubt about that. I'm sure you had a perfectly good reason for attacking us. We beg your forgiveness, when we made camp here we thought that there was no one on the island."

"At least I've done something right," the girl remarked. Isabel and Morgrin exchanged a look. Morgrin watched, while Isabel pondered.

"I think we got off on the wrong foot. My name is Isabel, and this is my husband Morgrin. "What's your name dear?" Isabel asked. The girl looked at them with confusion written all over her face.

"Iyla," the girl answered.

"Pretty name. From your mom's side of the family no doubt." Iyla looked at them warily.

"Yes. How did you know?"

"Isabel was my great-grandmother's name, at least so I'm told. Never met her, but still, it's a good history."

"I suppose," Iyla agreed, a slight smile on her lips. "Though I wouldn't be surprised if no one remembers me."

"Seems a bit drastic," Isabel replied.

"You really don't know where you are do you?" Iyla asked. Isabel and Morgrin both shook their heads.

"As we said, we are just travelers who were looking for rest," Morgrin said. "What is this island?"

"It's called Shalong," Iyla told them. Isabel flinched. "It means-"

"Shame," Isabel said. Iyla's expression showed her surprise. "Ancient Elvish?"

"Yes. How did you know?"

"We are both well-learned of the Elvish ways and customs," Isabel said. Silence fell over them for a few moments.

"That's very unusual. Neither of you look Elvish," Iyla finally replied.

"I learned a long time ago that you can't always judge a book by its cover," Isabel replied. "What's the story of this island? Why's it named shame?"

"Because Cordell only puts here the ones they are ashamed of. The disgraces, the cheats, the impure."

"And which title do you fit under?" Morgrin asked. Iyla stared at the ground.

"The impure. I'm Elvish." She was silent for several moments. "Long and short of it is when they put you on this island it's because you are deplorable. From that moment on you are left by yourself. No ships are allowed to touch the island or else they too must be killed. When I heard your voices earlier I was very afraid, for no people have been on these shores in three years."

"You've been here three years?" Morgrin asked. Iyla nodded. "By yourself?" Iyla nodded. "Where did you get the armor? When a nation expels anyone, they never give out armor." Iyla looked away.

"It's okay to tell us," Isabel said. "If we were here to kill you we would've done it."

"My husband got it for me."

"Husband?" Isabel asked. Iyla let a weak smile escape. "You hardly look old enough for that. How old are you?"

"Fourteen," Iyla replied. "We have promised each other, but there are many complications that have gotten in the way. He got me the weapons for self-defense if it was ever needed."

"He didn't teach you how to use them very well," Morgrin said.

"He doesn't know how himself. He's a sailor on a merchant ship, not a warrior," Iyla said.

"Tell us about him," Isabel said. "I always love a good story. What's your story together?"

"His name is Darrison, he's a sailor on the ship *Trinin.* I believe the Captain of the vessel is Borea. I grew afraid when you were talking about him earlier," Iyla started. "All through our childhood he and I were good friends, we did much together even though he was two years older than I was. When I ended up here, I never thought I would see him again, but a week after my imprisonment on this island started he found me. He had secured a small boat and came to visit me. There's a small inland river that he can sail into so no one sees him. I didn't love him then, but he kept coming back. We built a house and he taught me how to survive and...gave me a reason to look out to the horizon with hope. Somewhere during all of that I fell in love with him. It was scandalous we knew, because no one would ever marry us, but we didn't care."

"Why would no one marry you?"

"Marriages to Elves are forbidden in Cordell. The government puts bounties on Elves. These days, even to associate with one could mean you have to be put to death." Isabel pondered everything.

"How often does he visit?" Morgrin asked.

"Every other weekend. He is at sea for the rest of the time. He will be here in two days and my heart is more than ready to see him again."

"So do you and Darrison have further plans, other than living here?" Isabel asked. Iyla smiled.

"He's saving his money and when we can afford a life. We'll head south as far as we can. From other sailors, he's heard of a land named Goshen, which allows for marriages of Elves and Humans. Our plan is we would go there and start our life together, free from all of our current plight."

"Sounds like a wonderful dream, and I hope you get to see it come to fruition," Isabel said.

"Thank you," Iyla replied. "I think those are the kindest words anyone has ever said to me."

"If you can't try for your dreams then why have them?" Isabel asked. Iyla studied them curiously for a moment or two, a sparkle now in her eye.

"So what's your story?" Iyla asked. "Where are you from? How is it that you seem to know nothing about this area?"

"Like we said, we are weary travelers," Morgrin chuckled. "We've had a full life of adventures, trials, danger, mishaps. I suppose some of it might make a very interesting book someday, but for now, we're still living out our part of the story."

"I'm from a region near Goshen," Isabel started. "In between the Dead Mountains and Cavil is a truly wonderful paradise that I still call my home, even though I have not lived in it for a great long while."

"So Goshen is a real place!" Iyla exclaimed.

"Yes, it is. We have many friends there. As for us, we've been to a lot of different places but a friend of ours has asked us to travel north. So that's what we're doing."

"What are you supposed to do up here?" Iyla asked.

"We're not actually sure," Morgrin answered. "But we always seem to stumble upon interesting things. You for one."

"Actually since you're from this area, you might be able to help us," Isabel started. "On a previous island, we found a rather cryptic riddle and instructions to deliver it to the Count of Durio Helmar at Prater. Do any of those names sound familiar to you? We'd be grateful for any help."

"The Count of Durio Helmar?" Iyla looked to be both surprised and confused.

"Yes, that's right. Do you know of him?" Morgrin asked.

"Yes," came the reply. "The Count of Durio Helmar is my father." Isabel and Morgrin gave each other a look.

"Your father?"

"Yes."

"I'm a bit confused," Isabel admitted. "If you have been banished just for being Elvish how would your father be a Count? If I am reading the political scene correctly that wouldn't be possible."

"You are right, but I'm only half Elvish. My father is human and has lived in these parts all his life. It's where he grew up."

"Half Elvish?" Isabel asked. "We must be some kind of kindred spirits then because I am half Elvish too."

"Really? Your mother or your father?"

"My mother. Her name was Avalee. They both died a long time ago, but now I think I understand your situation a little better," Isabel said. "What was your mother's name?"

"Lydia," Iyla answered, beaming.

"So am I to understand that the Count married an elf and you are their offspring?"

"Yes, that's correct. They both got married late in life and I was, as most people put it, a *surprise*."

"That's the kind of surprise that everyone could enjoy," Morgrin said.

"Did you have children?"

"No. I had been married before we met and had two children in that marriage, but the two of us were not blessed as such the second time around."

"I'm sorry to hear that," Iyla said.

"It is what it is," Morgrin said. "It's been our calling to help and fight for Lathon in a world that has in some respect, forgotten him."

"Very true," Iyla agreed.

"Do you know what happened to the Count?" Isabel asked.

"I believe both my parents to be dead, though I cannot know for sure."

"And what do you know of Prater?"

"I have never heard of it. If such a place exists I have not been there. But if this note you have mentioned my father and this place, then it must be real. He had many secrets and I was not aware of all that he did."

"What do you know of his work or what he did?"

"Only that it was dangerous and highly sought after. He was constantly being talked to by royalty of all kinds, and high government officials. As I understand though, he kept a large amount of his work off the books."

"So he didn't trust everyone in Cordell?"

"Hardly," Iyla replied. "My Uncle, King Oshland, was hardly trustworthy with great secrets, at least when it came to family. But as bad as he was his descendants are even worse."

"What's your experience with them?"

"For the most part I've been spared from their torments, but only because of who my father is. They are spoiled, selfish, and prejudiced against the Elven ways and beliefs. Often they would go out at night and invade the houses on the outlying farmers and peasants, and of course, they were only the Elven places that got attacked. They would assault, abuse, and then kill everyone.

"In the days leading up to my banishment, my uncle and his heir to the throne were both found dead in their chambers. My father said it *appeared* to be vigilantes from the bordering kingdom of Irn."

"'*Appeared*'?" Isabel asked. Iyla nodded.

"My father didn't believe the reports and began immediately making arrangements for us to leave. With both the king and his heir dead, the throne moved to my Uncle's grandson. His name is Drayvin and he is far worse than the two of them. I know there had been several animated discussions in the past about the very fact that the Count had married an Elvish woman. Drayvin had always said it was preposterous that my father was allowed to keep his marriage and image together, while the laws of the country were being blatantly broken."

"So Drayvin cracks down on such things, banishes you, and most likely kills your father and mother?" Morgrin asked. Iyla nodded sadly.

"Your letter gives me hope that father may have lived, but I cannot be sure of anything. What do you think?"

"I think everything we're doing here just got more complicated," Isabel replied. She sat down in the sand and let herself be immersed in her thoughts for several minutes. "We were hoping to make our way to Cordell tomorrow, but if it's learned that we've stepped onto this island in any way, all three of us could be in trouble." They fell silent, each of them lost in their thoughts.

"This is getting to be far more of a trip than we had expected it to be," Morgrin said when finally they were alone.

"I know," Isabel replied. "There's an aching in my gut that says we need to help this girl somehow."

"You want to take her with us?"

"Yes," Isabel admitted. "However, we can't take her with us because someone could recognize her. Still, I feel as though we will condemn her to death if we leave the island and never keep any kind of watch on her."

"I agree with you there. She can't fight worth beans."

"I don't think Darrison can either. I wonder what role he plays on the *Trinin*?"

Isabel sat down on the porch of the small cabin that Iyla and Darrison called their home. It was small with only one room inside, but it was plain to see by Iyla's face when she had shown it to them that they were both proud of it. Iyla had kindly offered some of the little food she had, which mostly consisted of fish she had caught from the river.

They had accepted a little but otherwise left the rest to her. They had talked for several more hours until Iyla, not used to having other people around, had fallen asleep mid-conversation. The house was built on top of a small hill in the middle of the island, providing what would've been a beautiful view if it had been daylight.

A cliff descended sharply until it met a small river that led out to the sea. A warm breeze blew through the trees, bringing with it the sound of people talking in hushed tones. Morgrin quickly darted around the corner and grabbed his sword. Isabel followed suit. She listened intently, unable to distinguish any of the conversation clearly.

A voice quickly called out but was silent a few moments later. The sound of a person running up the path reached their ears now. Isabel and Morgrin peered into the darkness, able to make out the shape of the man. He was tall and moved swiftly. Isabel and Morgrin both jumped out and swung their swords. The man, who was stunned by their appearance, hastily blocked away the attack with his own.

"Once again I say do not fear, for I come to you in peace!" the man exclaimed. Isabel was taken aback by recognizing Michael's voice.

"What are you doing here?"

"I come with a warning," Michael said, looking over his shoulders.

"I'm sorry who are you?" Morgrin asked.

"This is Michael, Captain of the White Ships," Isabel explained. Morgrin's face showed his shock.

"*The* White Ships!"

"We need to get off this island."

"Now?" Morgrin asked.

"Yes, now. There are four ships anchored in the surrounding waters. They already have soldiers headed towards the shore. It's now or never."

"Go wake Iyla," Isabel said. Morgrin hurried back to the small house. "Where do we go? I don't like the idea of fleeing in the night."

"I don't either, but you don't have a choice," Michael said. He opened his mouth to speak, but never got the words out as fire flew through the air and crashed into the surrounding forest. The trees were consumed by flames. Another plume of fire came through the air and struck the front porch of the house. Isabel cried out, running towards the house. The fire recoiled and formed a doorway for her to run through, Michael came right behind.

Inside they found the heat nearly unbearable as the cabin was engulfed in flames. Iyla and Morgrin both lay on the floor. Iyla was unconscious while Morgrin stirred. Michael rushed ahead and scooped Iyla up in his arms, while Isabel pulled Morgrin to his feet. They rushed towards the doorway of flames escaping the burning house.

Voices cried out all around them as they descended the steep valley to the river. They collapsed by the river and steadied their breathing, keeping quiet as men and torches appeared at the top of the cliff. A few minutes later the voices passed while more plumes of fire landed all around them. The entire island was being burned.

"What next?" Isabel asked.

"Morgrin and Iyla escape on Ezzion and Destan," Michael answered. "We fight off everyone and then you have to get to Cordell!" As if on command all three of the Taruks came crawling down the hillside, unconcerned by the fire. Isabel and Morgrin knew better than to argue and immediately began fitting the unconscious Iyla with ropes so she wouldn't fall off if Morgrin had to let go. Morgrin came and kissed Isabel before jumping atop Destan.

"Don't leave for five minutes and then only with Ezzion in the lead!" Michael exclaimed. Morgrin nodded as Michael and Isabel jumped on Aspen. The Taruk pushed effortlessly into the air and then turned and headed down the river at incredible speeds. They finally rose above the trees, seeing nearly ninety percent of the island engulfed in flames. The beaches in front of them were lined with a hundred soldiers, who stood watching.

Aspen landed in front of the men. The soldiers backed up and yelled for help. Isabel and Michael drew their swords and charged the men. Aspen took to the sky, heading towards the north side of the island.

Michael and Isabel swung at the first soldiers and easily defeated both of them. Man after man, challenged them but Michael and Isabel were stronger and within twenty minutes had defeated everyone who had been standing on the beach. The rest of the night was spent circling the island looking for any other men who stood watching the island burn.

Isabel swung her sword one last time, taking out the last man. Isabel and Michael looked at the men remorsefully as they slid their swords into their sheaths.

"Did Morgrin and Iyla make it?"

"Yes," Michael answered. "They made it." A calmness came over both of them as they looked out to the dark water. Relief flooded over her and she collapsed onto the ground. The only sounds on the island were that of burning vegetation.

"You did good Isabel," Michael congratulated. Isabel smiled at the compliment.

"It's harder without my disguises on."

The dawn came earlier than Isabel would have liked as she slowly peeled herself off the sandy beach. Her limbs burned and her head throbbed as she moved over next to Michael who stood looking out to the horizon. The ruins of four great ships were smoldering in the water.

"Good morning Isabel!"

"Good morning Michael."

"You doing alright this morning?" Michael asked. Isabel nodded.

"Trying to make sense of what happened yesterday. What, ah-happened to the ships?"

"I heard the White Ships were in these waters last night." They both chuckled.

"If you had shown up any later we would've been dead," Isabel stated.

"I'm glad I showed up right when I was supposed to," Michael said. Aspen lazily walked across the sandy beach.

"Are you coming to Cordell with me?"

"I wish I could, but I have other business to attend to," Michael said. "I'm here to encourage you and point you in the right direction."

"Thanks," Isabel said. "Where are Morgrin and Iyla?"

"Headed back to Nain," Michael answered. "Don't worry about them, the White Ships will keep them plenty safe. I promise."

"I miss them already, but I know I must keep going north!" Isabel said.

"To Cordell!"

"Anything I should know before we part?"

"When you get to Cordell, you'll want to find Iyla's young man named Darrison. Tell him what happened here and give him this envelope." Michael pulled from his pocket a sealed envelope. Isabel took it.

"What's in it?"

"It's from Aiden to Darrison."

"Anything else?" Isabel asked.

Michael smiled. "Aiden is proud of the faith that you and Morgrin are showing. It is certainly not going unnoticed. Keep on pressing forward and everything will become clear."

Chapter 23

THE ROAD HOME

Drake looked to the barren wasteland stretching out before them before taking one last look over his shoulders. The mountains, though distant, still loomed far above them and horns now echoed through the desolate land as they were learning of the prisoners that were now walking from the great city.

"Will he be alright?" Drake asked. The company stopped and looked at him. "Barnabas I mean."

"That is up to him," Aiden said. "As a friend to him, you have done well, but his heart is troubled. He has made his choice and we will see to what end it brings him."

"I just wish it was different," Drake said. "If they marshal their forces he's going to be the first to be spotted."

"Every choice has a consequence," Melchizedek warned. "To tarry here any longer, or to go back and try and find him would prove disastrous for us."

"He's right," Aiden said. "We have to keep going."

Rachal held Drake's hand as they started walking. More horns echoed through the deep parts of the mountains. The first tones were low and menacing, while the second tones seemed shrill and desolate, instilling fear into their souls.

"That's a sound I've never heard in all my life," Corvil said, his face washing white. Melchizedek seemed to shrink back for a moment as well.

"What does it mean?" Rachal asked.

"It means the army is ready to attack, and it means that they have legions of Soldiers belonging to the Order of Merderick going in front of them," Corvil answered. More horns echoed through the air followed by a creaking and grinding as the great gates of Nargaroth were opened. Company after Company poured out of the city gates and also at two other gates along the mountain range. They began running as the great army was released from the mountains and proceeded across the plain in front of them.

"Hate to be a naysayer but we have nearly twenty miles before we reach the forest," James pointed out. "The chances of us making it there alive are shrinking."

"Ah, but you forget who you serve," Aiden said. "He pointed to the horizon in front of them. Drake and everyone else strained their eyes unable to see what Aiden was pointing to.

Finally, after a moment a dark line appeared. Drake and everyone looked to the ground as bones began to sift themselves out of the ground and rise to the surface. The bones clattered and slid across the ground and connected themselves until skeletons covered the horizon as far as the eye could see.

Melchizedek smiled and then began laughing. "You forget who you serve!"

All eyes turned to the horizon as the thin line of black had now become thicker and more pronounced. A man in a shining white robe sat atop a magnificent white horse, leading the new army closer.

The air was filled with strange speech. Though it was strange it brought peace and comfort to their hearts. They watched in amazement as the skeletons stood to their feet. Within seconds ligaments formed, then skin, and finally full armor and weapons formed. They moved into formation and began marching towards the great Dwarf army that was still coming through the gates of Nargaroth.

"Who are these people?" Corvil asked. Drake and James smiled, recognizing the crest they bore on their armor.

"Warriors of Rinevah. Who've been killed in battle in front of the mountains of Nargaroth for what looks like a very long time," James explained.

"Yes, indeed some of these men are from the very first days of Ariamore," Aiden said. The man in the shining white robe passed them by. War horns sounded all around them as the army now moved by them.

A group of seven broke off from the main group and approached them. They were Elvish, but different in a way that none of them could explain. Drake now understood why Rachal had never been able to describe the one who had kept her safe while she had been in *Burnaks Heights*. He stood tall and proud and had they not sensed that he was a friend and not a foe they would have been terrified. They bowed to him and he bowed in return.

"Welcome my Lords and Lady," the man said. "You have all done well in the eyes of Lathon. As you have fought so boldly for him, now he will fight for you!" He motioned to another who brought forth horses. "These horses are for you to keep, may they serve you well and speed you along your way!"

A great cry went up as the two armies now rushed at each other and collided in a wave of fury.

"Thank you very much," James said. The man nodded again.

"Also I have this message," the man said. "James, make haste towards your home. Your father must Marshal a force and bring forth the army by the seventh day from now. This great army around us will devastate the army of Nargaroth, but it will not cure their wrath. They will march upon Rinevah soon. Though it will look hopeless, if you do as you have been told, Lathon will be with you on the day of battle.

"To Drake and Rachal, take rest and solace in the home of your family." As if it had suddenly been commanded Drake's mind filled with light and sound, after a moment Drake could remember much of his childhood.

"Corvil and Melchizedek, go with James and confirm the truth of the matter to Lord Zebethar, though do not expect a warm welcome." With that the men bowed and turned, heading towards the battle that was raging. They mounted their horses and rode away.

"These are strange horses," James said after they had been riding for a while. The battle was now far behind them, only visible by the great cloud of dust that was drifting through the sky.

"Strange how?" Melchizedek asked. "Dwarves rarely use horses, but they are exactly like I remember them. Have horses changed since I've been gone?"

"I'm sure they look the same, but these horses seem to feel different to me," James replied. "I'm not quite sure how to explain it, their stride is smooth, and their temperament is perfect. I feel as though they walk with purpose and certainty, no matter what would be put in front of them.

"They are quite like Queman's horses," Drake observed. Rachal nodded her agreement.

"Well you know Queman, he wouldn't have just any horses now would he?" Aiden asked. "In all things, Lathon puts signs that point to his glory and power. To have an animal such as this is to remind you that Lathon's ways are perfect and his wisdom infinite."

"I've been around these horses for years and still I'm amazed by them," Drake said. "I can only imagine what the world was like before it was corrupted by the Sorcerer."

"Yes, I'm afraid that's all you can do," Aiden said remorsefully. "Take heart though, soon things will happen to allow followers of Lathon to experience the perfect creation that was intended when this world began."

"I've heard of this Sorcerer since being reunited with you. Who is he?" James asked.

"Deceiver of many," Aiden answered. "Despite signs of wonder and the truth of the matter being displayed for all to see, many will follow his dark ways. He has taken many forms over the years and he will take many more in the years to come. Evil never rests; it is always thirsty, always looking for new ways to devour innocent people and forever enslave them. When the Sorcerer, Merderick, is defeated in one form, he vanishes for a while and then he strikes again, looking different than he did the first time. This is why every follower of Lathon needs to be strong, vigilant, and see his next move before he strikes."

"Will he ever be destroyed for good?" Corvil asked. "If one is so corrupt and evil why is he allowed to live?"

"There is still much to be done in the wide world before he shall fall as he should," Aiden said. "There is a greater timeline of which this part of the story is but a small part. The date and time for the Sorcerer's judgment is set, but it is known to Lathon only. Any who predict such things are fooled by what they think is wisdom."

They rode until the sun dipped below the horizon, leaving everything in deep shadows. They tied their horses up and were allowed to start a fire for the night. Aiden took the first watch while the rest of them slept. Rachal was the first to wake and walked over and sat down next to him.

"How are you doing Rachal?" Aiden asked.

Rachal shrugged. "Glad to be free of Nargaroth that's for sure. Strangely nervous for tomorrow."

"Nervous how?" Aiden asked, watching the horizon intently. "We shall arrive safely at the house of your husband's family tomorrow."

"Nervous to meet his family," Rachal replied.

"Worry not. Everything will be just fine, you'll see. I'm sure Drake's family will be more than delighted to see him and you."

"You sure?" Rachal asked. Aiden chuckled.

"If they recognize him." Aiden laughed. Rustling came from the darkness in front of them. Aiden sat taller, staring ahead unblinking as though he could see better in the darkness than she could.

"What's out there?" Rachal asked. Aiden's lips parted into a smile.

"Friends," Aiden said. "We can sleep the rest of the night in peace."

The night passed without incident and soon they found that the morning sun was gently beginning to lighten the sky. They rose and mounted their horses, grabbing one of the six bags of almonds that had been by their fire when they had woken. They rode in silence for several hours as the sun continued to wake the sleeping land.

The morning progressed and grass, covered in dew began to dot the hard ground in clumps. Within an hour the ground had become completely grass covered though it was still short and coarse. A while later, they stopped for a short rest and sat among the tall grass which flowed peacefully in the warm breeze that came out of the south.

"I should probably know this, but where are we?" James asked. Drake laughed.

"You don't know?" Drake asked. "And I thought I was the one with memory problems."

"We are near the southern border of Rinevah," Aiden said. "If I'm right, we should reach our first destination by late afternoon. From there the next morning we can make the final stage of our journey to the city of Merisyll."

"I didn't remember Drake's family having lived so far south?" James said, looking at Drake funny.

Drake shot back a humored look. "Like I remember?"

"There was a great drought and famine after Drake fled to the west," Aiden explained. "They now live just a short while from here, and have a great number of flocks and farmland."

"I can see why you ended up working for Queman," Rachal said. "This is a beautiful country."

"Yes it most certainly is," Aiden said. "It has seen its fair share of wars and mischances though, and will see many more in the years that remain."

"I've never seen anything outside of the mountains," Corvil lamented. "But seeing how beautiful this place is, it's a mystery to me why Dwarves like to hide in the mountains so much."

Melchizedek chuckled. "We're so small, we need a great mountain to feel important!"

"Probably more true than we know," Corvil agreed. They all shared a laugh.

They talked for a while longer before setting out again, anticipation filling the air around them. The grass grew thicker and eventually, a well-worn path appeared, winding through the rolling hills.

To their south, a great forest stood, mostly pine with a few fir trees scattered here and there. To the north and in front of them the rolling hills continued. One great mountain stood far in the distance.

Soon the path came along a winding river, which sparkled in the sun. They walked alongside for only a short time until a large wooden bridge gave them passage over the river. On the other side, the rolling hills became filled with wildflowers; daisies, rosebushes, and lilacs all in bloom. Rachal smiled.

"I like this place. We should put a house right in that clearing!" Rachal pointed ahead to an empty hilltop.

"Sounds like a fine idea," Drake replied.

IDOLS & TRINKETS

Their path continued to wind through the hills but gradually began to get nearer to the forest. In the distance on the hilltops, clumps of white could be seen dotting the horizon.

"What are those?" Corvil asked.

"Sheep," Drake answered.

"Those are some of your family's flocks if I'm right," Aiden said. "I believe we are getting close to the house of your family."

"Hard to believe," Rachal said. Drake nodded his agreement.

"What's even harder to believe is, with all the wars and battles I've been in, I don't think I've ever been so nervous in my life," Drake replied. "They probably all think I'm dead."

"We could freak them out really good and pretend you're a ghost coming to haunt them!" Corvil suggested.

"Funny idea, but I think I understand what Drake is feeling right now," James replied. "It's been long since I've seen familiar lands too, and for that matter, it must have changed a good deal because I have no idea where we are right now."

"I've been out of this for three thousand years. Imagine my confusion!" Melchizedek asked. "Do any of us know where we're going?"

"I'm sure Aiden has some idea," Rachal said. Aiden remained silent, studying the path in front of them intently. "You do know where we're going don't you?" Aiden was pulled out of his thoughts.

"Kind of," Aiden finally replied. "I've never actually been here before."

"He's never been here- you've never been here before?" Corvil asked.

"I learned the location of Drake's family from some mutual friends of ours, but I have never seen the house with my own eyes," Aiden said. "I think if we take the next road into the forest, we'll find what we're looking for!" They rode in silence for another moment before Drake and everyone else started laughing.

"Something amusing?"

"Just the fact that you, the heir of Lathon, seems to be lost," Drake stated. They laughed again and Aiden chuckled. "If you can't find it…who can?"

337

"Good one Drake Thomas. Good one. You go ahead and have your laugh, we'll see who's laughing when we get there."

The forest grew deep and thick and within a couple of minutes, they were in the midst of trees as large and round as they had ever seen. The branches covered them from high above, offering them relief from the hot sun. The path continued for a couple of miles without any sign of a house or dwelling belonging to anything but animals.

Slowly the path became wider and soon had a stone border along the edges and finally a few footprints could be seen in the dirt.

"See!" Aiden exclaimed, pointing them out. "Told you we were on the right track."

"Well, you've proved that there's life in this forest, but how sure are you that this is actually where Drake's family is?" Corvil asked.

"I'm sure of it!" Aiden exclaimed.

"How sure?" James asked.

Aiden smiled. "Sure enough."

"That doesn't sound very sure," Drake jested. Aiden looked back at him with a cheerful light in his eye.

"Let me ask you this Mr. *Drake* Thomas! Did you calm that terrible storm we were in once upon a time? And was it you who split the Sea of Mar so a great nation could pass through unharmed?"

"No. Definitely not," Drake answered, trying not to smile.

"There then. Sit back, enjoy the ride, and have a little faith. We'll get to where we're supposed to be," Aiden said. "Eventually." They laughed and then quieted as an enormous house appeared through the trees on their left. "I believe our destination is at hand. Let me do the talking and if it's the wrong house you can tease me for eternity."

The path wound to the left and then came into a clearing where several large brick and stone buildings stood, each of them two or three stories tall. The pathway turned to stone, where the echoing of the horse hooves announced their presence.

Several servants took notice of them, looking up from their work in the various garden spaces that filled the great courtyard. Kids of varying ages played and ran in the vast and lush yard. They continued riding to a large house that was at the head of the enormous complex.

"I'm curious about this place," James said. Studying everything intently. "It seems familiar to me."

"There will be plenty of time for discussion later," Aiden said. They rode in silence the rest of the way, bringing their horses to a stop. Aiden dismounted and bowed as a pregnant woman came out of the house, another child tagging along behind. The lady bowed back.

"Welcome my Lords, of what service can I be?" the woman asked.

"We are looking for the descendants of Sedric and Bethany of Venti."

"Sedric and Bethany of Venti have vanished some years ago."

"And what of their descendants? Is this not where they reside?"

"It is. I can send for them if you wish."

"Please do. Inform the master of the house that I have need for me and my companions to stay here for the night and that I bring him a mighty gift in exchange for whatever hospitality he wishes to show us."

"I will do as you have said," the woman said. She motioned for one of the servants to come, and at once he was given a horse and sent out into the pasturelands. "Is there anything I can do for you, my Lords? We have many fields and I cannot say how long it will be until my husband is located."

"No thank you. We will be content to enjoy the beautiful day out here in the great outdoors that Lathon has created for us to enjoy!" Aiden said. The woman smiled.

"As you wish. I will wait with you and keep the kids from bothering you too much. They do love it when visitors stop by."

"Don't worry about it, after all that we've been through some kids sound like a nice change. Right everyone?" Aiden asked. The others nodded and tied up their horses. The kids soon came and proved to be good company and soon they were all playing together in the vast courtyard. When finally the kids got tired they all sat down on benches on the front terrace of the house.

"Do you recognize anyone, Drake?" James asked.

"Afraid not. Some of them look familiar, but I can't say that I *know* any of them. Truth be told I'm a little nervous to meet the master of the house."

"Why's that?" Corvil asked. "If these are your kin, then wouldn't they be happy to see you?"

"Remains to be seen," Drake answered. "I've been gone a long time and they don't know where or why."

"Don't think on it too hard Drake. Everything will be alright," Rachal reassured. The minutes faded and it was nearly an hour before the sound of a galloping horse reached their ears. They looked to see a man with short dark brown hair riding up to them. He stopped and dismounted, Aiden stood and bowed. The man followed suit.

"Sorry for the delay my Lords," the man said. "I have just received word and will gladly assist you in any way I can."

"We are very grateful," Aiden started. "My name is Aiden of Masada and I need to stay here for the night."

"Certainly," the man replied. "I have many guest rooms for you. If you would join us for supper perhaps you could educate me on where Masada is. I've never heard of it."

"I think there's a lot you haven't heard of Daniel!" Drake exclaimed. Unable to keep quiet any longer. Daniel looked at him and froze, his face white. Drake stood up and walked down off the porch.

"It can't be!" Daniel exclaimed and then kept repeating it. Finally, Drake stood next to Aiden. Drake held back a laugh as Daniel's look of shock didn't change.

"You look ridiculous!" Drake exclaimed. Daniel's thoughts were shaken and he came out of his dumbfounded expression.

"Who you calling ridiculous you big-footed cyclops?" Daniel asked. Humor tainting his voice.

"You, standing there with that *ridiculous* expression on your face," Drake jested. "You look like you've seen a ghost." They laughed.

"Well, what do you expect when you've been gone for a hundred years?" They embraced and the others came down off the porch. "I can see tonight and perhaps the next several nights will have to be spent telling whatever great tales have happened to us. How long has it been anyway?"

"Eleven years or something like that," Drake replied.

"Is that all?" Daniel jested. "Welcome home brother! Now I might like to pick on you for just a moment. I know when you fled for your life you were on the run…where did you end up?"

"A town called Laheer in the nation of Goshen," Drake answered. Daniel once again looked dumbfounded.

"I have no idea where that is! My point is, don't you think you went just a little too far?"

"That's what I told him," James said.

"It matters little now," Aiden said. "He was meant to be gone for the time that he was, but now he has returned. We indeed have many tales to tell."

"Judith!" the woman they had first spoken to approached. "Everyone, I would like you to meet my wife Judith."

"Pleasure to meet you."

Drake and Rachal shook her hand.

"Is this man your brother?" She asked.

"Yes. Yes, he is. Please call the servants, and tell them to prepare a great feast for tonight. For a long lost brother has come home!" They were silent for a moment until the sound of dogs barking reached their ears.

"*Drake!*" Two voices exclaimed. They jumped back when two wolves came bounding out of the trees. Daniel and Judith rushed out of the way. Corvil and Melchizedek drew their weapons. Aiden held a hand to stay them. The two wolves jumped right up on Drake and Rachal who had been expecting that.

"Willard and Miles!" Drake exclaimed. The two wolves stood as Drake and Rachal petted them. "It has been a long time my friends."

"*Too long. We've been very impatient for you to get here!*" Willard said.

"*Did you have a hard time finding this place Aiden?*" Miles asked. Aiden gave a humorous expression.

"He knew right where to find it," Rachal answered with a smile. "I'm assuming these are your sources for finding Drake's family?" Aiden nodded.

"Aiden asked us to go east, so east we went," Willard answered. *"Your brothers are pretty nice I must say. We've been posing as guard dogs until you got here."*

"I see," Drake said. Daniel looked at all of them in disbelief. Drake looked at Willard and Miles. "So, have you spoken to my family before now?"

"Are you kidding? Talking wolves tends to freak people out," Miles said, looking at Daniel and Judith who were speechless. *"Nice to meet you."*

Daniel stammered and finally fell back onto the grass, unconscious. Miles looked at all of them. *"Was it something I said?"*

***

The day turned to evening as the entire household had gathered in honor of their guests. Rachal watched everyone and tried to keep track of all the names as people were introduced. Drake had five brothers and three of them were married with at least three kids.

Mostly during the meal Rachal's eyes were fixated on Drake. She smiled for him, trying to imagine what it must feel like to have lived for so long without remembering any of the joy that his life had held with his family. She kept mostly quiet just watching everyone enjoy themselves.

"So Rachal, you have to tell us and don't hold anything back," Elijah started. Elijah was the third of the brothers and one of the two who were unmarried. "How on earth did you ever meet this guy and get him to marry you?"

"I met him on a horse farm near where I lived," Rachal answered. "But really, it was him who made the first effort. I was far too shy to approach him."

"Really?" Elijah asked. "That almost doesn't sound right, I don't remember Drake ever being bold when it comes to talking to women anyway." The brothers all agreed. Drake held up a hand, quieting everyone.

"It was totally and completely the will of Lathon that gave me that confidence," Drake said. "I had seen her several times and felt rather intrigued. It became my goal to get her to talk to me every day."

"I'd say it worked!" Daniel exclaimed. They all laughed.

"That it did," Rachal pipped in.

"How long have you two been married?" Judith asked.

"A couple of months." Surprise and questions were evident in everyone's faces.

"There is much more to the story and it is better told on another day," Aiden said. "For that tale could go on for two hundred nights, if we had the patience to sit and listen."

"We must ask a few more questions, the night is still quite young," Elijah said.

"Ask away, and then I have a few of my own to ask," Drake said.

"Me first," Kaleb announced, (the fourth of the brothers) "Where on earth did you get those magnificent horses? In all my life I've never seen horses like those!"

"We were given them," James said. "Made our trip from the mountains of Nargaroth much easier."

"What kind of horse are they?" Kaleb asked. Drake looked at Aiden.

"They are *Fee-Yord*. It's a mostly forgotten breed, save in a few places in the world," Aiden started. "They lived mostly in the Mountains of Timner in the first age of the world. Though their greatness comes actually from farther back, for they were there when Timner was first settled. They have rarely been touched save by a few since their creation. Many historians over the ages have concluded that their descendants could be traced back to Erathos."

"Erathos?" Daniel asked. "You speak the name with authority, though it is in these parts legend and myth."

"He speaks with authority because he can," Melchizedek stated.

"Wherever they come from they're magnificent to look at," Kaleb said. "I wish I could have one just so I could study the great beast and learn more about it."

"If I can borrow a horse for our journey tomorrow I will gladly gift the horse to you Kaleb."

"No, Drake I wouldn't think of it."

"I insist," Drake said. "It is a great horse and I would be glad to release it into the permanent care of one who I know has always had a great love for animals."

"Can I give you another horse in exchange?" Kaleb asked.

"I'll be just fine, I'm sure I can get a horse from Merisyll. Besides that, I do have a Taruk if it's ever safe for him to come." The room fell silent.

"A Taruk?" Elijah asked. "You have a Taruk?"

"I have one too," Rachal stated. They stared unbelieving.

"In the world beyond Nargaroth, they're quite common. Perhaps too common," Drake said. "Many people have them and we have great races; I've won a couple of them."

"I don't know what to say," Elijah said. Drake sat up straighter.

"That means it's my turn to ask questions," Drake stated. "Question number one, what is this place and how did you come here? This place is far bigger than anything we could have dreamed up when we were kids."

"We had to leave our home in the north, due to drought and famine. It was a hard time, and it pained us all to leave," Daniel said. "There was no choice in the matter. If we had stayed our flocks would've starved and we would've died as well.

"This was the third year after you vanished. We wandered aimlessly through the countryside for some time until Lord Zebethar found us and offered us this place for basically no money. There were no strings attached. We accepted and came here. Zebethar's motives behind selling this place so hastily have always been a mystery to us. The leading theory is that he had a guilty conscience from trying to kill you, and therefore was very generous."

"I thought this looked vaguely familiar," James exclaimed. "What is this place called?"

"Eshunna. It means *Silver River*. Named so because it sits on-"

"An old silver mine," James interjected. "Explains why I recognize it. I used to accompany my father here. I'm surprised that the mine is closed though, it used to be the most lucrative mine we had."

"Things change when you're gone so long," Rachal said. Silence fell over them for a moment, Daniel shifted uncomfortably.

"Drake I have to ask you a question. Did Mom and Dad find you? Were you able to see them before they died?"

"Yes, I saw them. We kept in touch, best we could but I'm afraid that the last I knew was that they had tried to return here."

"They never made it," Aiden replied.

"How do you know?" Kaleb asked.

"Because they haven't shown up here; however Willard and Miles have traveled many leagues and might provide insight." The two wolves stood from their spots in the corner and sat down next to the table.

"What happened to mom and dad?" Daniel asked. "Do you know?"

"Yes we know," Willard started. *"Aiden sent us to look for them and told us to go east. We traveled across the plains of Megara, which in those days didn't look so bad. About three days from the mountains of Nargaroth we finally picked up their scent. There was a pass that had been used to traverse the mountains. It was relatively easy traveling and it only took a couple of days to get through if you kept a good pace.*

"We were following the scent and about halfway it disappeared. There was no trace of them to be found. We must have looked all over that mountainside for them but to no avail."

"Our only conclusion was that they must have been captured and taken in the mountains," Miles continued. *"We looked for one of the doors into the mountain and waited for those horrible creatures to open it. We fought our way into the mountain, taking out a great number of people. Long story short, when our pursuers' gave up the chase. We picked up their scent again and eventually found and gained access to their cell. They had been beaten and tortured beyond any hope of leaving alive.*

"We spoke with them as much as they could and then stayed with them until they had both faded into forever sleep. We escaped the mountains and sought your family out. We may not have ever been able to bring them back, but we could be your friends. We just didn't talk until today for obvious reasons."

"I completely understand," Daniel replied. Silence lingered for several moments. "Thank you for everything that you did and have done. You are extraordinary creatures."

"You're not bad yourself," Willard responded.

"I gather you knew Drake beforehand?"

"*Over ten years. We've had many adventures together.*"

"Incredible."

"*After almost fifteen years of adventuring and exploring we've enjoyed taking some rest as guard dogs for your family. Much more relaxing.*"

"I'm starting to gather how unique of a species you are. You are welcome to stay with us as long as your hearts are content, but if you are needed somewhere else feel free to go," Kaleb replied.

"*I like this guy,*" Miles said. Both wolves slowly walked back to the corner and lay down.

"How long can you stay?" Judith asked. "Your company must certainly be headed somewhere, but when one who has been lost so long returns you must understand our excitement."

"We are headed to Merisyll," James replied. "We must return to the home of my father and present ourselves to him. There is much to discuss and let's pray that it all goes well. War will be upon us soon if we cannot convince him to act. We must leave at dawn."

"So soon?" Elijah asked.

"Afraid so," Rachal said. "I do hope afterward that we will stay here for many years to come. Put down some roots, so to speak."

"Excellent!" Judith exclaimed. "I would love to have another woman here. You should stay with us tomorrow while the men go to speak with the king."

"That sounds lovely," Rachal replied. "We've had quite a journey and a day to relax would be wonderful."

They talked for several more hours until the candles had burned low and they were nearly falling asleep at the table. They were all given accommodations and were left by themselves for the night. Willard and Miles lay in the corner sleeping, while Drake and Rachal crawled into a small bed.

"I've almost forgotten what a bed feels like," Drake said.

"Me too. Are you going to be alright tomorrow if I stay here?"

"I'll be fine. I'm nervous as ever, but perhaps the very fact that James and I are alive will be enough to make Zebethar forget everything that's happened. At any rate, I think you'll have a good time with Judith and the kids."

"I imagine so," Rachal said. They lay down together and Drake fell asleep instantly. Rachal lay awake enjoying the sound of the wind outside their window and the peaceful look upon Drake's face.

Rachal was awakened in the night by a horse neighing. She moved to the window and saw Aiden standing in the courtyard, with Willard and Miles on either side. She slipped a cloak on and made her way outside into the cool chilly air. Aiden and the wolves didn't move or motion at all as she approached.

"Good morning Rachal," Aiden greeted, almost in a whisper.

"What's going on?" Rachal asked.

"I must leave at once."

"I thought you were going to the city with everyone else?" Rachal asked.

"I came to make sure you found Drake's family, and now we must part ways. I have business in other places that demand my attention."

"What places? What's happening?" Rachal asked. Aiden mounted his horse and circled around.

"Spies of Nargaroth. We have a long morning of hunting if we hope to stop all of them. In the morning make sure and remind Drake and James that they must convince Zebethar to act swiftly. If Nargaroth already has spies abroad it will not take them long to find their way here."

"But didn't that army that passed us when we were leaving Nargaroth to eliminate the Dwarf army?"

"There are many gates to Nargaroth," Aiden replied. "These likely come from the southern gate."

"Be safe. All of you."

"We will," Aiden said. In an instant he spurred his horse into the night, swallowed by the trees moments later. Willard and Miles sprinted after him, appearing to keep up effortlessly. A great winged shadow passed over the moon for a moment and from somewhere high up in the sky a great roar of a Taruk echoed through the night.

Chapter 24

DURIO HELMAR

Isabel dropped onto the deck of the *Trinin*. Isabel stumbled and fell to her knees. She brushed herself off and stood straight and tall, seeing a menagerie of stunned and speechless faces.

"Hello everyone!" Isabel cried out. None of them moved or made a sound.

"I thought I said I didn't want to see you again," Borea greeted starkly as he came up the stairs towards her.

"I don't recall you saying that," Isabel said. "I recall you saying if I did anything to any of your ships or people mercy would be taken aback, I am not here to harm you."

"You just boarded a ship of the Cordell navy. Do you expect mercy?"

"No," Isabel answered. Borea wrinkled his brow with confusion. "I know that stowaways are generally thrown into the ocean to drown. But I am not a stowaway. As you pointed out I willingly climbed on a vessel of Cordell. That has to be a capital offense of some kind."

"It is most certainly a capital offense," Borea agreed. "However...I cannot yet agree to these terms without knowing *why* you are here, and why you are so eager to hand yourselves over to the mercies of the King."

"Could we perhaps talk somewhere privately?"

"No," Borea answered. "If there is to be any deals made then the men need to know about it. You strike me as a strange person and I am not yet sure what to think."

"Very well," Isabel started. "I have need of getting to shore. Due to certain complications, landing in Cordell aboard my Taruks would not be advisable. There are many reasons why boarding this vessel was a good choice though."

348

"Do tell?" Borea asked, seeming amused.

"Because *you* are not all that you say that you are. A hundred ships were surrounding that island, and all of them proudly flew the flag of Cordell. However, the men on those ships were members of the King's Navy and were dressed in uniform. Your men are not. You set me and the Taruks free, when you should have turned us over to the King. By not doing your royal duty, you could be in trouble yourself. If I should arrive on the shore of Cordell as I am now, it would take away from the credibility of your story." Borea shifted but didn't look away as he stared into Isabel's eyes as if trying to read her thoughts. "I take you to be some sort of pirate or unofficial crew. Do I read things correctly?"

"What is your business in Cordell?"

"I need to find the Count of Durio Helmar!" Isabel exclaimed. Everyone gasped and even the Captain seemed taken aback by the name.

"Darrison!" the young man from the day before came forward. "Put her in the cabin. I'll finish with her in a little while."

Isabel thought of resisting but thought better of it as Darrison and another man took her down a flight of stairs and through a set of doors at the stern of the ship. The doors were shut and locked, leaving Isabel to her own company for several minutes.

The cabin was modestly decorated and otherwise sparse with a large window that looked out over the ocean behind them. Distantly, she could still make out the small almost invisible speck of Aspen, watching from high in the sky.

The cabin doors were thrust open and Borea walked through. He casually walked around to the chair and the desk. He motioned for her to sit down.

"What's this all about Captain?" Isabel asked. Borea didn't speak for a moment.

"You have a great intellect," Borea complimented. "You are right to suspect that I may have other loyalties beyond the crown because I most certainly do. However, that information needs to stay between us."

"So which are you? A thief or a pirate?"

"Are those the only two options?" Borea asked. Isabel pondered carefully.

"Unless I'm mistaken."

"Perhaps you can help me figure out who I am. I don't steal for the pleasure or joy of stealing," Borea explained. "For I do not find such pleasure in it and I keep nothing for myself. When we dock, everything that is harvested off Jike is taken to King Drayvin's storehouses, where it is processed. After they've been processed one crate, is taken by an associate of mine to a different location three hours away, where it is distributed to those in need of food."

"King Drayvin takes much from the people and cares little for their plight. It has been a calling on my heart for many years to help in whatever little way I can. I started working on one of the king's ships so I would be able to eat food every day without wondering where I would get it from. As the years went by though, I often felt guilty about being so well cared for, when the people of the land, my own family among them, were struggling and starving. I do what I can, even though it's not much. In our short conversation, I could see that you had not committed crimes intentionally. That is why I let you go and didn't tell anyone about you. I couldn't bring myself to take innocent people to the king. So tell me, Isabel. What does this make me?"

Isabel pondered for a moment.

"Compassionate and loving. Two admirable traits. Traits that might make the beginning of a good friendship between us."

"Aye," Borea said. "People need good friends." Silence fell between them for a moment. "On the deck of the ship to most of the men, I am a captain of the Cordellian Navy. But now I sit here as a friend. How do you know of Durio Helmar? What do you know about him?"

"Nothing. The night before we met, on a different island my husband and I found this letter." She pulled the letter out of a pocket and handed it to him. He carefully read it. "I have no idea what any of it means. It was only written four years ago, so I figured it was likely The Count of Durio Helmar was still alive. I have conflicting thoughts on whether I think he's alive or not....what do you know of this man?"

"I know him by reputation. I have never met the Count personally. Nor have I met Durio Helmar in the flesh, for he was dead before I was alive."

"I'm grateful to learn anything I can."

"As you might have noticed from on deck, the name Durio Helmar can get people rather animated. If you must speak the name, be ready for all different reactions."

"Who was he?"

"He was an interesting sort as far as the tales go," Borea started. "He's been dead nearly fifty years but still the myths and legends surrounding him are real enough. He came from the nation of Ritil. It's an Elvish nation nearly a week sailing from the farthest of Cordell's cities."

"Durio Helmar is Elvish?" Isabel asked. Borea nodded.

"According to the legends and tales. He was nearly six feet tall and never cut his hair. Lathon's power was certainly with him. His fame and influence were legendary and with each battle, he seemed to only get stronger. He killed thousands of soldiers by his own might. He pulled the gates of Gyni right off, carried them up the mountain, and threw them at the summit. He fought with weapons of all kinds but his favorite choice weapon was that of a donkey's jawbone." Borea caught Isabels's surprised face. "It's strange but everyone swears by it. They even say there's a great hill called Jawbone Hill. Everywhere he led them he was victorious. It seemed none could stand the power of Durio Helmar."

"What became of Durio Helmar? You said he had died before you were born?"

"I am forty, he died fifty years ago. Give or take," Borea said. "He had married a woman, Delani, who ironically was from Cordell. They certainly loved each other at first, but when you're the daughter of Cordell, a sworn enemy of Ritil things can get complicated. The King of Cordell at the time was Oshland. He sent men to coerce his wife to betray Durio to them. I've seen the financial records in the royal books. They paid nearly eleven hundred coins for her to figure out what his secret was and destroy him with it.

"She nagged him endlessly. Finally, he did admit that Lathon had blessed his hair and that was how he got his strength. So one night she lulled him to sleep and had his hair cut off. When she woke him he didn't realize what had happened and was easily captured and carried off to a Cordellian prison where he became forced labor. Mostly assigned to grinding grain.

"When his hair began to grow again, his strength began to return. Out of fear they gouged out his eyes and paraded him throughout the streets of Harbrigge. They beat him and tortured him endlessly. Then in a moment of sheer stupidity, they stopped and asked him if he had any last words. He cried out to Lathon for strength one last time. He put his hands against the great pillar in the temple of Eshtoal and the entire thing collapsed and killed all of them. They've never rebuilt the temple. There are still ruins you can go see for yourself.

"I know much of this to be true, for Durio Helmar's wife Delani is in my lineage. What I have just told you has been passed down to me as I have told it to you."

"How did he have two names?" Isabel asked. "I'm not aware that was a custom."

"It's not. It's not known to me how he came to have two names. I'm not even sure what his real name was. He had a large following of people that liked him, and just as many, if not more that wanted to kill him. It could be that his own family gave him two names because they didn't want to claim him as their own. I simply don't know."

"Am I to understand that the Count, then, is his son?"

"Natural assumption would say that, but reality says he is not. How the Count and Durio became acquainted in the first place is beyond anyone's knowledge. But there was a strong bond and friendship between the two of them. The Count is not Elvish in any way, though he did marry an Elvish woman. Before Durio was taken away he named the Count his soul heir inheritor of his estate."

"Do you know this Count to be alive?" Isabel asked.

"I believe he is, and with a few well-placed favors I can figure it out better once we're in Harbrigge, perhaps even arrange a meeting. The Count was better at playing the political game than Durio had been, and between you and me I always thought that the Count must have some dirt on the higher-ups in Cordell, because they never touched him, despite some obvious disgraces on his part, like a marriage to an elvish woman for example."

"That's very interesting," Isabel said, sinking back into her seat for a moment. "Back to the letter...have you heard of a place named Prater?" Borea smiled.

"Rumors and tales are rampant when it comes to *The Prater*."

"The *Prater* was a ship?" Isabel asked. Borea nodded.

"Said to be of great size. Some say it was the largest ship they had ever seen. It's not clear where it came from, but supposedly it was a tribute offering to Durio Helmar. For all the fame of the ship, it's never been found."

"Any guesses as to where it is? This letter says it's real."

"I have no idea where the ship might be. If it exists at all!" Borea exclaimed. "The thing with Durio Helmar and the Count is that they went lots of places, did lots of things. They were both known for collecting strange things and hiding them away. If you believe the legends they had storehouses of things hidden all around the world. I do not know if the rumors have any basis in reality." Isabel and Borea were both silent for a while.

"Let me ask you this," Isabel said, breaking the silence. "You mentioned something about a few well-placed favors. What would it take to convince you to use a couple of them to get me into the palace? Perhaps even an audience with King Drayvin?"

"I'd say that's a tall order. However, I know people who can do this and I will try my hand. I have questioned events in my head and heart for a long time. I would love to put them to rest one way or another for good. As soon as we are in port I will do what I can. Can you write?"

"Yes sir," Isabel answered. Borea smiled.

"Very good. Let us get working. We have three hours until we reach Harbrigge.

.

The port of Harbrigge was larger than Isabel had expected and proved to be more challenging to gain entrance to. Nearly a half mile from the shore they were greeted by a large grey wall of rock that rose out of the water. Six gates with archways were built within the wall and there they stopped every ship, checking their cargo and crew until they would open the gates and let them pass.

Once inside, ships filed into long lines and would wait until it was their turn to dock at one of two dozen long docks that dotted the coast Borea shifted anxiously and the minutes passed into nearly an hour as they waited.

"I have business to attend to on shore. Lower a long boat!" Borea said. The orders were executed and one of the boats was lowered into the water. He looked to Isabel "I'll get this letter delivered and return it. Darrison!" A young man, with black hair came forward. "Take charge of the ship in my absence."

"Yes sir," Darrison replied. Captain Borea climbed down into the longboat and was rowed to shore by another crewmember. The crew went about their business. Isabel lent a hand where she could, knowing a few of the tasks for sailors. Overall though she hadn't done any true sailing in her life. Two hours later their ship was given permission to dock and Darrison took charge of the ship. Skillfully performing his duties and bringing the ship to port.

Immediately fifty men came aboard and began the process of unloading the ship. To Isabel's surprise with everyone working on it, they were done in a little under two hours. The crates of Dail were unloaded into numerous carts that were waiting to take their supplies to the king's palace.

Captain Borea returned before the unloading was done and joined the crew in the labor. When they were empty they were ordered to sail to the sixth gate, where they would be able to dock the ship as long as they needed to.

"Well done Darrison," Captain Borea complimented. He turned to face the entire crew. "Here we are at our two-day break. Spend it how you wish. Go home to your families if you have any. Find pleasurable company if you wish. Stay aboard the ship...the choice is yours. I expect you all back Monday morning at dawn!" The crew slowly filed to the dock and left the ship, leaving only Isabel and Borea on the deck.

"Were we successful?" Isabel asked. Borea beamed as he pulled out a sealed envelope and handed it to her. Isabel took it and opened it, reading it aloud to Borea

By order of King Drayvin, it is hereby ordered that Captain Borea and his

guest Ms. Avalee join the king at his table for tomorrow's feast. In this matter,
we are more than willing to hear news from Ms. Avalee and assist her in
whatever way we can.

"What did you tell them to get permission so swiftly?" Isabel asked.

"I told them that you were a distant relative of the Count of Durio Helmar. Needless to say, they wished to meet you almost immediately."

"I thought they didn't like this guy," Isabel replied.

"They don't, hence the intrigue. As an amazing coincidence, I heard from several people that the Count himself is going to be in attendance. If we play our cards right we may be able to speak to him ourselves." Borea looked around as if he suspected someone might be listening. "To say all of this is going to be dangerous is an understatement. If they find out the letter I gave them today was fabricated and paid for, or if they suspect we're more than we are, they may kill us before the dinner is served."

"I understand. I've been in many situations of high stress over my lifetime, I'll be able to hold myself tall," Isabel replied.

"Very good," Borea said looking towards the shore. "Supper is at dark tomorrow, but we can arrive as early as three o'clock."

"Then let's arrive early. If we can get an audience with either the king or the Count before supper I'd rest easier."

"Very well. Do you have money? you'll need some fine clothes if we're dining with the king."

"I have money and will take care of that," Isabel replied. "And now though it does mean I must leave you by yourself for a while, I have other business that needs my attention."

"Yes of course," Borea said. "Do whatever you need to. Just meet me here tomorrow and we'll tempt our fates and head to the palace."

"Thank you for all you've done," Isabel said. Borea nodded.

"I'm eager to learn the truth, I'll gladly do whatever I can." Isabel thanked him once again and stepped onto the dock and then onto the shore. Buildings that looked as if they hadn't changed in a hundred years greeted Isabel. The cobblestone streets which at one time must have been beautiful were now grey and dingy, covered with dirt and grim.

The buildings themselves appeared to be made out of a bluish-colored brick, which now appeared grey. The entire coastline was filled with people, carts, commotion, and everything that one would expect from a bustling harbor. Isabel turned to her left and began walking, mentally taking notes of all the soldiers that were posted on nearly every corner or top of buildings. Unease began to come over Isabel.

She scanned the large crowd, looking for any sign of Darrison who had vanished as soon as he had been given permission. She walked for several minutes and finally spotted him speaking with one of the vendors at the market. She went past him without drawing his attention and left the busy area.

A half hour later she escaped the busy harbor and the sea wall that bordered the main harbor. Only open ocean could be seen and a few seagulls called back and forth to each other. Unable to resist, she slipped off her shoes and walked ankle-deep in the water for another half hour until she found Aspen curled up in the underbrush of the forest. Past Aspen, a little way was a small river that wound its way inland.

"Good to see you, my friend," Isabel said. Aspen seemed to smile at her. "Did you find what we were looking for?" Aspen rumbled her answer and carefully stood and walked through the trees. A minute later Isabel spotted a fair-sized boat, anchored at a small dock. "Might want to stay hidden, if you know what I mean." Aspen carefully crept into the forest and once again hid herself in the vegetation that was the same color as she was. Isabel also crept into the ferns and sat down waiting.

It was nearly an hour before the sound of a small cart and horse pulled Isabel from her thoughts. She looked to see Darrison at the shore, carefully looking over his shoulders before turning the horse and cart onto the path that wound its way along the river.

Isabel stayed where she was and watched him as he pulled up to the small dock and began loading the boat with food and other supplies. She stood and carefully sat down on the dock and nearly laughed at his expression when he turned around and saw her. As hard as she tried she couldn't hide an amused smile.

"You again?" Darrison asked. "As if dropping onto one ship wasn't enough, you decided to drop on mine too?"

"I guess so," Isabel replied. Darrison appeared to be flustered for words as he stammered but didn't say anything intelligible. "Don't worry I come in peace."

"You mentioned the name Durio Helmar earlier today. Sorry, but it's a hard thing to believe that you come in peace when you speak that name so boldly."

"Maybe you should get out more?" Isabel suggested. Darrison once again was silent.

"I'm working on it," Darrison said, moving around her with a box. Isabel stayed where she was.

"It's a nice ship," Isabel complimented. Darrison eyed her warily.

"Thank you."

"I bet Iyla likes it," Isabel said. Darrison stared at her, fear in his eyes. "She told me she did."

"How do you know of Iyla?" Darrison asked.

"It's from that island that I've come. Landed there quite by accident not long after I met you at Jike." Silence fell over them. "Don't worry, I'm your friend and ally and that's why I'm here. I have both good and bad news for you. Which would you like first?"

"Good?" Darrison asked hesitation plaguing his voice.

"Good news is that Iyla is safe and well. She's on her way to Nain, with my husband. The reason she is not on the island is the bad news. The entire island was burned and is now a desolate wasteland. We barely escaped."

"The whole place burned?" Darrison asked. "That's not possible."

"The island was surrounded by four Cordellian ships. Enough men were on shore to ensure that if anyone came out of the flames...they wouldn't be alive for long. We fought them off and lived to tell the tale. I know you have no reason to believe anything I say. After all, we just met. So I have this for you." She reached into the pocket of her coat and pulled out the sealed envelope Michael had given her. His hand trembled as he broke the seal.

He read the words and then a new expression came over his face. One of gratitude. He sat down on the shore, head in his hand for a moment.

"It seems you're telling the truth," Darrison said. "For I can see this envelope was sealed with the mark of Lathon. I do not believe you could fabricate such a thing on a whim. Where did you get this?"

"The letter is from Aiden right?" Isabel asked. Darrison nodded.

"How do you know him?"

"Aiden is a friend of mine. Has been for many years. He's the reason I'm traveling in these parts in the first place. How do you know him?"

"He's also been a friend and our counselor for these three years. It was he who told me where to find Shalong. What am I supposed to do now?"

"For reasons that must remain secret for the moment, I may be forced to flee the country at a moment's notice. I also need this way I escape to be by ship as we'll have to pick up some cargo along the way. Your ship looks like a fine ship and with two at the ropes I have no doubt we'll make good time. We'll be small and fast and should easily out maneuver larger ships that may pursue us."

"I'm not sure I understand," Darrison said. "Why will you need to leave the country so fast when we've only just arrived?"

"I have some suspicions, and if they turn out to be true then running will be the only option. If anyone figures out that I was on Shalong then it'll only be worse. I can't promise you that we'll get out of it alive or unscathed, but I can promise you that if we succeed, we'll be looking on the fine shores of Lumar and you can finally have Iyla as your bride. What do you say?"

Darrison was quiet for several moments, looking first at the letter, then at Isabel. It was as if he was thinking things through to see if there was any loophole in her story. Finally, he looked up, clarity in his eyes.

"We have an accord!" Darrison cried, shaking her hand. They prepared a small fire, enjoying a meal with the things he had brought. They talked much as the night wore on. Isabel took in everything, enjoying the life and vibrancy of every memory of Iyla that he shared with her. As she listened to him she could see how deeply he loved her.

When finally the fire burned down they both went to sleep, but Isabel slept unrestfully. She woke up several times with dreams and strange visions and when she rolled over to sleep again, she was unable to forget the images.

Her heart longed to know if Morgrin and Iyla had made it to Nain safe and sound. She whispered a prayer to Lathon as she waited for sleep to take her. Her spirits were lifted and the vision faded from her thoughts allowing her to fall to a restful sleep.

Chapter 25

HOMECOMING

The company once again found themselves on horses. Drake and James led the way, while Corvil and Melchizedek followed a few paces behind. Rachal had awoken them immediately after Aiden and the wolves had left. Unable to rest, they had set out immediately, leaving Rachal with Drake's family for the time being.

They rode in silence until mid-morning when they stopped to share some of the bread that they had taken on their way out of the house. They had ridden through the forest and now found themselves among a strange mixture of rock and grass. Drake looked at it and remembered vividly having passed through this area countless times when he had served Lord Zebethar on errands and such.

"How far is it to this city of yours?" Melchizedek asked.

"We've still got far to go, but these horses of ours do speed things up," James answered. "If we keep the pace, we should arrive by sundown, if not a little sooner."

"Will we be welcome?" Corvil asked. "Nargaroth doesn't treat visitors well, as you know."

"I will not let a single hair on your head be harmed."

"Nor I," Drake agreed. "You are our friends, but also guests of honor, and allies in a coming battle. It would be foolish for Lord Zebethar to do anything rash." They fell into silence for a moment.

"I can hardly remember what the city looks like," James lamented. "So long in the dark, yet there was always hope that I would see my home again."

"We'll see it soon enough," Drake reassured. They mounted their horses and started again, soon finding a river and riding alongside it for a while. A large white bridge spanned the river at the narrowest part and they passed over into another forest.

This forest was dense and the air was heavy. In between the trees was overgrown with bramble and thickets. Only occasionally would they come to a large clearing where the forest floor was bare and the riding was easy. An hour later they broke free of the forest, their spirits rising. Plains stretched out before them as far the eye could see.

The road became more traveled and wound between dozens and dozens of farms that covered this part of the countryside. The people stared as the four of them went by.

"They're not used to seeing Dwarves," Corvil noted.

"No. They're not." James replied.

The afternoon faded quickly and the sign that they were nearing supper time became evident. Music could be heard echoing through the countryside, and in every town and village they passed through the smell of good food, came to them. The travelers tried to ignore the good smells, for it made them realize how hungry they were.

Singing and dancing soon filled the streets, pulling each of them from their thoughts and allowing them to watch the people enjoy the end of their day. They led their horses out of the city, following the road.

"Almost there," James cried. Excitement was evident in his face. An hour later with the sun beginning to set, a great mound of rock and stone appeared on the horizon. They turned towards it and pushed their horses into a gallop, excitement flowing in their veins. They rode further and the mound grew in size until they could see lights and beacons shining brightly on the peaks of the towers.

"Well James, there it is! Even from five miles out it looks like the best thing I've seen in many a long year," Drake exclaimed, having to choke back a few tears. James looked on in disbelief but looked happier than Drake had seen him in a while.

"It's been so long for both of us," James said.

"How about you use your horn and give us a well-announced arrival?"

"Yes. They would not easily forget the sound of this horn!" James exclaimed.

"Is there something different about it?" Corvil asked.

"It's the Horn of Zebedee," Drake answered. "Its very name means 'thunder'."

"It has been passed down by my family for generations and it's sound lives up to its name.

The hills will rattle.
The waters will roll.
Thunder will come, as the righteous return home!

"Never has it seemed more fitting!" James declared. He pressed the horn to his lips and let a mighty note ring forth. The sound was low, growing from a distant sound to that of a great rolling thunder that shook the area. They rode a little further and they blew the horn again, this time horns and bells within the city echoed back to them.

"They welcome us," James said, relief flooding over all of them. They slowed their horses as they strolled toward the massive city.

"What city did you say this was?" Melchizedek asked.

"Merisyll," James replied. They watched the Dwarf carefully as he intently stared at the city.

"Dun-Vatar!" Melchizedek exclaimed. "This is Dun-Vatar. I thought something looked familiar about it!"

"Dun-Vatar?" James asked. "I've never heard of that name."

"Three thousand years ago it was called Dun-Vatar. I can tell you for sure once we get closer to the city, but I'm nearly sure of it now. What is the history of this place?"

"Not much to tell of. I know it was nearly two thousand years ago when my ancestors' found this place. It was completely overgrown and abandoned. Do you know more about it?"

"Oh yes, a great deal!" Melchizedek exclaimed. "There were many stories and songs about the great joys and evils that lurked. Yet despite everything that happened, the people remained and filled the city with life. Built by the Elves of ages long past, with knowledge that is now forgotten. Then darkness came and crept in through the cracks in the wall, or so they say.

"There were many tales and songs spun and created in the corners of the earth, about the events that transpired here and produced the downfall of the Elves. When finally I was locked in the great below to be tormented for what I now know to be three thousand years. The city had been besieged by Gongor. Strange nation from the north. Deadly beyond comprehension. We called them Gongori, which later was adopted into the Dwarvish language to mean grey stones. For that is what they looked like to us. Tall as mountains, as strong as a thousand horses working together. To be pursued by the Gongori was to meet the bitterness of death."

"What became of them?" James asked. "Do you know?"

"I've been in a cave for three thousand years. I have no idea how the Elves came to inhabit it again, but I am glad the Gongori are gone. They were a vile sort."

"If Gongori are what I know to be Gogs, then they are not all as vile as you might think," Drake replied.

"Forgive me, my Lord, I am going on limited knowledge of them," Melchizedek said.

"What were the ancient Gongori like?" Corvil asked.

"With them came great sorceress, promises of wealth but empty hands, and they are in my opinion the same dark beings that came to the mountains of Nargaroth so long ago."

"The ones who cursed you?" James asked. Melchizedek nodded.

"I am cured now, though. Praise be to Lathon!"

Silence overtook them as they drew nearer to the city, each of them silently thanking Lathon for everything he had blessed them with.

Horns filled the air again and a great host of horsemen filed out of the city at great speed. James stopped his horse and the great host drew near and circled around. The captain of the company moved his horse to the center of the circle.

"Dismount your horses at once!" the elf yelled. They did as he said and they were shoved forward until they were standing directly in front of him. "Name yourselves and your business, and also how you acquired the horn of Zebedee! Speak quickly for I have no time for pointless banter!"

"My name is James, son of Zebethar Lord of Rinevah! Ten years ago I left in search of this man Drake Thomas. Having now found him, I am returning. I am not dead as some have likely thought! These two fine Dwarves are friends and allies of mine and will be treated with honor as you would treat me! As proof of my claim, I have the signet ring given to me by my father!" James pulled it from his pocket and displayed it in the air. Gasps went through the host, but they didn't budge.

"A lovely ring that is no doubt," the captain said. "Who's to say you didn't kill the king's son and bring the ring as proof?"

"If I had killed the king's son I would bring his head. Parade it around in the streets. Most likely I would also have a large army with me, ready to destroy everyone who stood in my way. I have neither."

"Who else can vouch for you?"

"I assure you if you put me before the king and the princess they will confirm that I am telling you the truth, but this I can offer. Your name is Jero son of Darun, Captain of the guard. I worked with your father on many occasions and he will certainly vouch for me!"

"Indeed I will!" A booming voice exclaimed, pushing his horse to the center. He smiled when he reached the center. "Jero this man certainly speaks the truth. I was in disbelief when I heard the horn of Zebedee sounding from far places, but it would not be like an enemy to bear a horn so noble and to let forth such a note.

"Give the prince and his companions an introduction like none seen before! Alert the king and the princess. Sound off every horn you can muster in celebration when they come through the gates, and let the heralds announce their presence as they are paraded through the city to the palace."

"Yes sir," Jero said yelling out the orders in the Elvish tongue. The larger group waited while ten of the horsemen hurried back to the city.

"It is good to see you again my prince," Darun said.

"It's good to be back. It's been quite a long trip, but I did not come back empty-handed," James said, motioning towards Drake.

"It's good to see you as well Mr. Thomas. The men of the guard will be greatly encouraged to have both of you back. I'm sure there must be much to tell of your journey, but I feel as though your father and sister should hear it before I do."

"I will be more than happy to tell of everything that's happened as soon as I'm able," James started. "But you are quite right, there is much to tell. Is my mother not well? Why is no one sending for her?"

"I regret to inform you my prince that she died five years ago on this day."

"The very day that I return? Ironic isn't it?"

"Ironic indeed, but perhaps this will lighten your father's heart. He has been consumed in sorrow all week."

"Sorrow is understandable, but right now it will be a hindrance," James replied. "May we enter the city now?" Immediately afterward a magnificent noise of different horns filled the air. Without speaking they started riding towards the city. Darun rode first, with James, Drake, and the others immediately behind. Behind them, the host rode in formation.

The outer wall of Merisyll stood far above the plains, standing nearly forty feet high. Behind the edge of the wall, the ground rose steeply another thirty feet until it reached a second wall, also forty feet high. After that, a sloped path brought you down into the vastness of the city that was beyond. In the center, a palace towered even further into the sky, a lone beacon in the empty and flat plains.

"It's never been known how this city was built," James told Corvil and Melchizedek. They both nodded.

"History of it I know, but still the actual beginning is not known to me," Melchizedek replied.

"Unusual stone this wall's made out of. What kind of rock is it?" Corvil asked, noting the walls' deep red color.

"It must be something new because when Drake and I left they were grey like the mountains."

They rode up to two large steel gates in the outer wall. They creaked and groaned as they were opened, each pushed by ten men. Beyond that, they entered into a dark tunnel which steadily declined as it took them through the wall.

Torches burned and several passageways branched off to the left and right. In the tunnel were five draw gates that were opened by winches. Along the ceiling, holes about two feet wide were cut throughout, letting small dots of sunlight into the dark place.

They emerged on the other side of the tunnel, both overcome with joy as an enthusiastic crowd lined the path to the palace gates. The palace gates were opened without hesitation. The people were forced to stay on the other side as the iron gates were shut.

The palace was built atop a large slab of rock that could only be reached by a large drawbridge that spanned a natural sixty-foot-wide chasm between the two. Beyond the draw bridge, there was another long tunnel, with another gate. Once inside, the tunnel continued for several minutes going further and further up.

They soon reached the top and were greeted by a host of armed guards who were lined up in formation as though it was a great parade. They rode their horses until they reached the large courtyard before the palace.

The courtyard was built with a rare pale blue stone that contained flecks of another mineral, which made it look smooth and shiny. The palace in front of them was white with a dark brown trim that went all the way around the massive structure. Beautiful gardens and lush trees filled the rest of the courtyard and beyond. A small bridge over a bubbling stream that came from within the rock brought them to the palace doors.

IDOLS & TRINKETS

They dismounted their horses and followed Darun into a well-lit chamber. James and Drake both smiled seeing everything as though it was new and yet remembering all the good times that had been shared in these halls. Their fears of Zebethar retreated, allowing them to enjoy their homecoming for the moment.

They rounded a last corner entering into a large room, which was not as lavish as the throne room, but still very nicely decorated. Zebethar and his advisors sat staring in disbelief and confusion as they were brought forward. They stopped at Duran's command.

Zebethar's dark brown eyes studied them from under his greying hair. A long beard came down to the middle of his chest. Although he was dressed lavishly, it was evident that time had taken its toll on the king since they had been gone. An uncomfortable silence filled the room as the king continued to stare at both him and James, unblinking and expressionless.

The scar on Drake's hand began to go icy and his thoughts faded for a moment. Drake silenced the thoughts of fear and doubt and life quickly returned to him. As if in reaction to this, Zebethar blinked hard and his eyes softened. He slowly stood to his feet and came forward. His eyes were fixed on James who stood tall and proud.

"My Lord Zebethar," Duran started. "This is the man who claims to be your son James. He bears both the signet ring and the Horn of Zebedee. I believe him to be true my Lord, but a father's eyes are far sharper than a Captains'. It is my-"

"Speak no longer Duran," Zebethar interrupted, his voice was deep and powerful and contained a malice that could be matched by no one if the situation was serious enough. "I can see with my eyes that this is indeed my son. Lost and thought dead he was, but now he is alive. It is beyond my imagination to think of the misadventure that has kept you away so long.

"How I wept for you; and for Drake. How I regret my decisions! My choices of the past. They brought me to ruin, but now I see the greatness of Lathon. For I repented of my great evils three years ago and then I received in my sleep a dream that you would come back. And at last, it has come true!

367

"I am filled with so many emotions at the moment that I cannot hardly think. I must know everything that has happened and then I must promise you both in front of witnesses that I will never again do the horrible things to you Drake that I have done. For when I chased you away, so my son the heir of Rinevah went too."

The guards were dismissed and for the next hour, they sat with Zebethar in seats drawn up for them on a great balcony overlooking the city. They spoke as briefly as they could, while still providing enough detail to satisfy Zebethar who seemed to be listening intently and with some other intention that they couldn't guess.

When Zebethar was satisfied he called in the servants and Duran who had been waiting in the other room.

"Duran, please make sure our guests tonight receive the finest of everything in the kingdom. Give them whatever they ask for! Also please send out a proclamation that the next two nights will be nights of festive celebration. A night to honor first my son James and the next to honor a man who is like to a son to me, Drake."

Duran left to do as the king had said, while the five of them remained. Zebethar took a drink from his cup and stared out at the city for several minutes without speaking. Drake and James exchanged glances.

"I'm sorry if I'm quiet," Zebethar replied. "I have known you to be dead so long, I hardly know how to act with you both alive. Please leave me and let me process all that this day has brought."

"I understand your majesty," Drake started. "But if I may be so bold, I would say that there is a time for both grief and reflection, but this is not that time." Zebethar looked at him knowingly.

"What time would it be?" Zebethar asked. "Is there some great calamity that is following in your wake?"

"That could be truer than you know," Melchizedek said, standing. Zebethar's eyes shifted to him, boring into his soul. Melchizedek was unbothered and stood tall and proud. "Our escape from Nargaroth was anything but ordinary and we believe they have lost many thousands of warriors, my kin, in a great battle that followed. We are all wanted men. They will no doubt hunt us and do anything to get revenge for what has happened."

"So this is what you have brought to my halls?" Zebethar asked James. "A spy? If you escaped as I am led to believe, what else is to be concluded but that you were meant to escape so that you could bring one of their kind through the grand doors of our nation and spy on us all?"

"Don't be a fool father. What they say is true, and the threat is real. We must marshal the army and be ready to march on Nargaroth within nine days."

"I will do no such thing," Zebethar said firmly. "If there was indeed a great battle, then much of Nargaroth's military was likely destroyed. They are defenseless perhaps, but of no threat to us. I will not risk war."

"There are many things in that mountain that are far worse than any army," Corvil stated.

"Then let them stay there!" Zebethar cried. "Nargaroth has not attacked us in years so why should I rush to attack our peaceful border? Exposing other borders that need protecting. No, we will not marshal the army. Now leave me alone for a while so an old man can consult the only one around here with some sense."

When it became clear that Zebethar would not budge on the matter they left him alone, walking through the grand halls of the fortress as people quickly scurried from here to there, preparing for the feasts and celebrations that had been decreed by the King. They walked for a long while in silence.

"Your father's reaction was less than I had hoped for," Melchizedek lamented.

"I have no control over what my father does, but in his defense, there have been many other things to pay attention to over the years and Nargaroth has not been one of them."

"He doesn't seem to like change too much," Drake said.

"Indeed not," James agreed. "Less with each year that passes. After nine years away it becomes even clearer."

"I am only vaguely familiar with your history," Corvil started. "And by vaguely I mean only rumors have reached within the walls of Nargaroth. How is it that your family came to power? In the Dwarvish custom, we have many families of high prestige that can trace back their lineage to ages long past. Mostly our clans gain power by taking it by force. Is that not how it works here? Surely you as prince could marshal the army and do as you know should be done."

"I could do that," James said. "If I wanted a divided nation. It would be like overthrowing the king. I could do it, but it would have disastrous consequences that none but Lathon could foretell. My father is the King and I never will be, because Drake was appointed by the prophet Sarule to be the next king of Rinevah.

"As for my father, he never sought to be king. He was humble in that regard. He was entrusted to the Farsees as a young boy, as part of an oath sworn by his mother to Lathon. He was raised in the great temple and grew very wise and smart. Sarule came and officially anointed my father to become the king. However, when it came time for my father's coronation, he was nowhere to be found."

"Where was he?" Corvil asked.

"Hiding," James admitted. "Tucked away where he thought no one would look for him. Eventually of course he did become king, but it's a strange beginning. I love my father dearly, but he has faltered and missed the mark in several areas, which is why under the guidance of Lathon, Sarule came and anointed Drake to be the king."

"Your father did not mention that," Melchizedek noted. "But I suppose it can be expected for a father to only want his son, his heir, to follow in his footsteps."

"In any other kingdom on the face of the earth, it would indeed be that way. But this nation is different as you well know. All of us, even the king, have to answer to Lathon in the end. In the end, I suspect that when we die we will see Lathon face to face and we will have to give an account of our actions and decisions." They fell silent.

"What are we going to do if we can't get your father to marshal the army in time?" Covil asked. Silence plagued them for several minutes.

"We make a stand," Drake stated. "We take the four of us and as many of our close friends as are willing to go."

"Lathon said he would be with us in the battle and we must trust that," James said.

"James!" A woman yelled from behind. They turned to see a curly brown-haired woman jump into his arms and embrace him.

"It is good to see you, Lucille!" James said. "Corvil and Melchizedek, I would like you to meet my sister, the princess of Rinevah, Lucille!"

"It's a pleasure, Your Majesty," Melchizedek replied with a bow.

"Duran came and told me you were here, but I didn't believe him! And now you're standing here in front of me, and so is Drake. It's the best gift ever!" She embraced Drake who was trying not to laugh. "Is there something funny Mr. Thomas?"

"Kind of," Drake replied. "It seems that when I had to leave, you were stuck in some orchard tree, with your hair all a mess and your dress looking like you had worn it for a year; and now ten years later here you are, with your hair all a mess and your dress looking like you've been in an apple orchard, and no shoes. Somethings never change."

"True enough," Lucille replied. "I was helping with the apple harvest."

"Helping, or *helping*?"

"It doesn't really matter, all that matters is that I was there," Lucille answered, breaking into laughter. "Anyway, what have you been up to *Mr. I'm going to vanish for a long, long time*?"

"Long story," Drake replied. "Quick version. I ran away, got married-"

"Oh my goodness you're married!"

"Yes, we-"

"Where is she? What's her name?"

"Her name is Rachal, and she's with my family," Drake answered. Uncontrollable joy lit up in Lucille's eyes.

"This is awesome! Drake is married. I have to go meet her." She turned and ran down the hall.

"Lucille!" James yelled. "Aren't you forgetting something?" Lucille thought hard for a second.

"I need my boots and my horse!"

"If you leave now, you'll be arriving at midnight or –"

"Don't care! Gotta go! Bye!"

Lucille ran off faster than they could think of a reply other than to say *good luck* and *goodbye*. The four of them stared down the hallway in disbelief for a moment before Drake broke into uncontrollable laughter.

"She hasn't changed a bit."

"Somethings never do."

The night passed uneasily for Drake and James. The feast and celebration in James's honor had taken place and though they had both enjoyed it, a feeling of discontent threatened to overwhelm them. They said nothing while the party was going and enjoyed it as much as they could.

The second day brought no relief to them. Aiden's words lingered in their hearts. Despite another effort to persuade Zebethar to mobilize the army, nothing happened. Even Corvil and Melchizedek were growing restless although they all said nothing unless they were behind closed doors.

The second night passed slowly with both Drake and James lying awake in their chamber. A fire burned in the corner and cast the light in its warm golden colors. They had talked at great length about their options but were still undecided on any clear action that they should take. But they all knew that their time was running short.

Suddenly a distant roar shook the sleeping land. Drake and James both sat up straight and moved towards the window, seeing a great shadow block out the moon for a moment.

"Taruks?" James asked, backing away from the window. "My grandfather told me tales of Taruks, but there hasn't been Taruks in these parts for a hundred years. What can it mean?"

"Don't worry," Drake reassured. The sound of the Taruk landing on the roof reached their ears.

"Don't worry?" James asked. Corvil and Melchizedek were also aroused. "A Taruk just landed on our roof! If my father finds out we're going to be in even more trouble."

"It's Elohim. I think Aiden is with him." Even as Drake finished speaking a man dropped down to the roof next to the window. Drake immediately opened it for Aiden who climbed inside.

"Glad to see you," Drake greeted. "Though they do usually like it if you use the doors."

"Ah, what are you kidding?" Aiden asked. "I'd probably freak them out." They laughed as he sat down among them.

"What news of the outside world?" James asked.

"Nargaroth is on the move. They cannot be seen, but there is movement beneath the mountain. Willard and Miles have been running errands for me and have verified a large number of spies lurking on the outskirts of the borders."

"Is my family in danger?" Drake asked.

"Nothing is certain, but your family is likely to be the first to take any damage if they should attack first. An abandoned silver mine with all the housing that it has would make a great place to stage an army for other attacks."

"What am I to do?" Drake asked. "I feel like I'm sitting here with my hands tied."

"Ride back to your wife and make the best defense you can. Still, ride to the gates of Nargaroth at the time I said. Hopefully, Zebethar will not be late."

"Perhaps you can talk to him and make more progress than I have," James suggested. "As of yet, he won't do it. Unless I overthrow him I don't see what will make him change his mind."

"I've taken care of that, there is something that will happen tomorrow that will change his mind. Though when you see it happen, urge him with all tact and care that haste is more important than numbers. At this point, you have no time to waste. It's a two-day ride to the mountains."

"Very well," James replied.

"Is there anything for us to do?" Melchizedek asked. "Zebethar has not called on us to learn more."

"There will be much to do and explain when he finally makes a move," Aiden said. "There are many things about the mountains he does not know. You of all people should know that."

"Sometimes I wish I knew less, but I know it was for this moment that I was meant to know it."

"Lathon can use any bad experiences to show his glory and this is a perfect example," Aiden said. "I have other things to attend to, so I must go. Drake, ride hard and fast to your family. James, Corvil, and Melchizedek remain here until you cannot wait any longer." They nodded and said goodbye as Aiden climbed back out the window and disappeared into the night. Drake stood.

"You're going to need help."

"What did you have in mind?"

James pulled out an envelope closed with the royal seal and handed it to him.

"I had this prepared for you. I had a feeling that you would have to leave in haste. These are orders to give to Duran who you will find in the main hall. Take him aside and have him open it. He and fifty of the best warriors in the city are ordered to ride with you to the defense of your family. I may not be able to marshal the entire army, but I can send a small regiment if it is needed." Drake took the envelope and they embraced.

"It seems like we must part yet again my friend," Drake said.

"Hopefully we don't meet each other in prison this time," James teased. They smiled and said their goodbyes.

Drake found Duran and gave him the letter and without question, the orders were sent out. In a matter of minutes, fifty of the best and most well-armed warriors were mounted on their steeds. Drake led the way out of the city, leaving it behind them. Drake stole a glance back at the city, watching the lights fade into the horizon.

Chapter 26

A MATTER OF CONSCIENCE

Afador fell on the rough uneven floor of his cell. The door was shut and locked. Afador struggled to turn himself over, his body bruised and nearly broken from the torture he had been put through. His left arm burned like fire with excruciating pain and the rest of him wasn't in any better condition.

He managed to scoot himself over to the far wall of the cell and lean against it. The cell was small and square, twelve feet wide. The top of the cell was open, leaving the person inside exposed to the outside elements. A cold rain had fallen for the past two nights and Afador's spirits had sunken lower than he wanted to admit.

An hour passed and food was thrown in through a small hatch above the door. It was too high for prisoners to reach, but designed that way on purpose to keep prisoners from rushing the door. A lump of stale, half-moldy bread fell to the floor, and after that a canteen of water. Afador was thankful for the food and quickly ate it, for fear that someone would come in and take it away.

He curled up in the driest corner he could find and wished for sleep though it evaded him. Instead, he was haunted by memories of the past few days, and by the unknown. It hadn't surprised Afador at all that his father had grown furious when he had seen all the changes that had been made while he was gone. But even in his anger, Afador could not have predicted everything turning out this way.

Within minutes of his father's homecoming, his father had him taken away and ordered him tortured and beaten. He hadn't heard from his father since. Even the guards had been ordered to remain silent or else dire consequences would follow.

Time ceased to exist as minutes faded into hours and hours into days. Afador barely kept any sense of morning and night. Storm clouds had blanketed the great mountains ever since his father had returned. Almost as if the weather was in league with his father.

Without warning the cell door was thrust open. Afador scrambled against the wall as soldiers rushed into the cell, grabbed him by his hair, and pulled him to his knees. Several of them drew their swords and held them to his neck. Afador watched the scene unfold as a dark shadow filled the doorway.

His father, King Sador, walked into the cell. His heavy footsteps, increased Afador's anxiety. Sador stopped when he was directly in front of Afador. He stood tall and menacing, his beard and hair were grey but neatly groomed. He walked with his chin high and a smug demeanor. He looked down on Afador who stood six inches shorter.

"Glad to see me?" Sador asked, pacing. "I have examined many things and find that your treachery is far greater than I could have ever fathomed. Not only have you done unthinkable, and unspeakable things to the citizens of this city, but you have taken me to be a fool!" He stooped low and grabbed Afador's hair holding his eyes level with his own. "I am no one's fool!" He shoved him on the ground. Afador tried to stand but was swiftly met by Sador's boot.

"What is it you hoped to gain from this great deception of yours? If you wish to be king, then be a man and we'll see who's the better swordsman! But instead, you manipulate and deceive me? Send me away while you do whatever you want? I see now your loyalties.

"If you had hoped to gain the trust and the hearts of the people, then save your breath and your effort. They are like blind beggars ready to follow the next fool that comes along. Bring him."

Afador was dragged from his cell, his feet were tied to a horse that his father rode. Afador was dragged through the tunnels and corridors of the prisons, his father keeping the horse at near a full gallop.

Afador struggled to remain conscious. Afador's senses awoke as his hearing seemed to be improved and he could easily hear a Taruk roaring from somewhere far beyond. His body came alive with energy that he had never felt before.

Finally, his father stopped the horse. Afador was untied and forced up a large set of stairs, when they reached the top Afador became aware they were at the highest point in the city, which was now spread out before them.

"Take a good look, my son," Sador taunted. "I have told the people nothing about where you have been. Only that you are gone for a while. They already are falling back into the traditions I have set in place years before this moment. As you are now learning, they easily lose interest in the fool when he's taken from their view. The people have betrayed you, my son."

"They do as you bid out of fear!"

"As they should. If a ruler does not invoke fear into his men, then what kind of a leader is he!? He's a coward and unworthy of life."

"To rule with the iron fist as we have done is to leave people no choice at all!"

"To allow commoners to have any kind of say in matters that are none of their business...I can't imagine what ruin would come to the world. They are too stupid to handle such issues," Sador boomed. "They need a shepherd who will lead them as I have done! As your ancestors have done! What can be said of you?"

"If that is the standard by which you judge, then I am doomed to fall short of your mark. Though I did at one time, I can no longer agree with you Father. I have had an awakening of my mind and soul and a new voice that speaks much louder than all your *precious gods* that do nothing!"

"They have condemned you to death and I am liable to follow their leading! Why they have not smote you yet, I cannot guess."

"They smote not, because they cannot. Against the Unknown God, none can stand."

"Even now you call this *'unknown'* god, an unknown god. You do not know this god any better. You have never had a conversation with this *god*, you can't even give me his name!"

"I have learned the name of the Unknown God," Afador declared. His father though he didn't show it was taken aback and remained silent for a moment. "It is you who does not know his name and I sense that you do not care to learn it either."

"I do not wish to be a spineless sap like you," Sador remarked. "I'm a man of vision and a man of force. Neither of which you have."

"I must be quite a disappointment father."

"Mark my words," Sador declared. "I wish I had never allowed you to live in the first place. From now on anyone associated with you shall be publicly shamed, starved, and executed in the square."

"Anger and malice eat at your heart like a hungry wolf. If you do not change your ways now, you will be destroyed!"

"We'll see who's laughing in a couple of days. You'll be tied to the Great Wall bordering the Great Falls. Your hunger will gnaw at you, the birds of the mountains will love to come and get a piece of you. Fear will take hold of you and you will once again see that fear is how a person should be handled. Three days ought to be enough time for you to rethink your life choices as of late. Then we will speak again."

"You are lost and perhaps you always will be. Regardless of your stance, I will always remain your son and you, my father. I will never stop praying for you. You speak of fear, but I am not afraid. You do with me what you want but at least my conscience is clear."

"Good for you," Sador mocked. "So good that you have your precious conscious intact. Fear will find you. You may deny it but I will see it in your eyes. As of right now, my men are searching the nation for one thing. Might you guess what that is?" He paused and Afador came to understand. "Your precious wife and children will soon join you on that wall, and when they do....then you will have to choose to follow...my lead, or this *unknown* god that put you there."

"I am sorry it has come to this father," Afador said. "But I am not sorry for the choices that I made. You choose to not see it, but love is behind all of it, with no other motive."

"From this moment on I refuse to see you as a son. In fact, I refuse to see you as anything greater than a slave who is about to be slaughtered! I know you not!" Sador said, refusing to look at Afador.

Afador was led away by the men, this time thrown onto the back of a large cart and accompanied by five soldiers. They hastily made their way through the city, until they reached the spot that his father had spoken of. He was pulled off the cart and led over to the wall. There was soon a great crowd that watched in silence and disbelief as Afador was chained and then lifted into the air. One of the soldiers stood atop the wagon and unrolled a scroll and read in a loud voice.

"Citizens of Jermin! Nation of Tuthar! Here ye, here ye, the message from your king. Prince Afador is hereby convicted of high treason against his imperial majesty. Charges include, but are not limited to, destruction of sacred property. Manipulation and coercing private citizens. Bestowing gifts on people who were never invited to come to this island in the first place. And also failing to fulfill his duties as a prince!

"None may speak to this wretched soul and any who show signs of loyalty to Afador shall be immediately humiliated to the highest degree and banished. Furthermore, it is demanded of your king to inform immediately on the location of the princess Hadassar and her two children. They too must suffer the same fate as the disgraced prince."

The man got down and the guards took up their post. The people slowly dispersed, without saying a word. Afador was able to see from their expressions that they did not approve or believe the king's message was real, but they carried on with their life as they were supposed to. To be afraid to do anything else.

The second day was the longest Afador remembered. For the first time since his father had come home, the sun appeared in the sky. Afador welcomed the sight but soon wished for it to go away. The heat and humidity grew unnaturally hot in the city, considering the time of year.

Hunger, Fatigue, and dehydration all began to take a toll on Afador, testing his resolve and threatening to push him over the edge. Still, Afador kept his head up, looking to the mountains and hoping that Remus had succeeded in getting Hadassar and his kids to safety.

The day ended with nothing changing. Even though the sun went down the heat seemed to grow, alarming Afador. Two guards were stationed next to him for the night and they stared straight ahead and didn't speak to him or each other.

Afador woke to the sound of water, rhythmically flowing toward him. A thud on his left caught his attention. He looked to the source of the sound seeing a man in a small rowboat pulled up against the bank of the river that fed the falls. The man looked his way but didn't speak and instead spent the next few minutes glancing around at the city, as though he was waiting for some signal.

Afador's senses became much more alert as he noticed that the two guards who had been stationed to him for the night were both gone. The man by the river walked over to Afador, finally stepping into the moonlight for his identity to be revealed. Afador's heart soared.

Remus came before him, with a large set of keys in his hand. Without hesitation, he lowered Afador from his spot on the wall and undid the locks around his hands and feet.

"What are you doing here?" Afador asked.

"Good to see you too," Remus said with a smile. "Thought you could use some company and some time out of chains."

"Indeed I could," Afador said, carefully sitting down on the empty street. "How are you able to be here and let me down without being killed? Won't someone see us?"

"You have many friends in this city. The only ones who agree with your father are his own personal security. Everyone else was more than eager to help me, though keeping their distance as in I wasn't to approach until both guards were gone and that sort of thing."

"There is certainly some protection among you!" Afador exclaimed as quietly as he could. "I hope you are not planning on breaking me down from here though, because I would have to refuse."

"And why would you refuse?" Remus asked.

"Because to take me away would be to sentence the two guards to their death as well as many other people that my father might kill in a rage. I cannot stand to see innocent blood spilled any longer."

"Good answer," Remus complimented. "I merely came to bring you some food and drink to help you stay strong."

"You're a good friend Remus." Afador took a small bag of food from Remus, which consisted of bread and a small canteen of water. Afador took a bite of the bread and felt his senses come alive with wonder.

"What kind of food is this?" Afador asked. He quickly took a drink of the water, feeling the same strange sensation rippling through his body.

"The food of the Makkara," Remus replied. "It's something special isn't it?"

"I've never tasted anything so good," Afador replied, puzzled and amazed at the same time.

"How are you holding up?" Remus asked. Afador shrugged.

"Better now. What happened to Hadassar and the kids? I take it you found the Makkara?"

"They're safe. That map you gave me was the strangest map I've ever used. Down hills, up hills, climbing ravines so steep we didn't think we would ever make it to the top. For several days I wondered if we were going to find the spot or not. Then lone-behold it was the dead of night and we had begun to despair when a great light appeared on the horizon.

"A man came forward, though I don't feel as though the term man should be applied to him. I understand now what you mean when you say you cannot accurately describe your first meeting with the Makkara when you were a boy. He was different. He appeared to be elvish, but somehow he did not seem elvish. It was strange and my own heart is confused on the matter.

"He looked at me strangely. I do not know whether he expected me to be there or was surprised by my presence. He walked down the ravine without saying a word. Nothing! Not even a simple crack in his stoic expression. My fear grew as he approached and I drew my sword. He drew his own but didn't attack. Instead, he stared at me and something in me said that I could trust him.

"After what felt like an eternity he asked me who I was and when I told him a smile finally appeared on his face. They led us to their camp, which was even more difficult and all of us had to be blindfolded in order to go any further. They offered us food, beds, drinks, anything you can imagine."

"I understand perfectly," Afador said. "I can remember when I was in their camp like it was yesterday."

"We all fell asleep to the wonderful music and singing they were making. When we woke up in the morning I found that it was only me and one other person in the forest all by ourselves. I grew afraid, but he calmly told me that Hadassar and the children would be okay and that I was to come back and help you."

"How about you can join him!" A loud voice boomed. They looked to the source of the sound seeing King Sador standing in the shadows. He stepped closer and soon a great number of torches filled the empty street with light. Sador stepped closer. Remus seemed to shrink, while Afador remained unmoved where he was.

"This is a very interesting turn of events," Sador said. "So you've hidden your wife and children with warriors who hide in the mountains like cowards? Here me now! As surely as I live both of you will be chained to that wall and you will not come down until we have found your family. For then they can die right next to you and you can talk about many things." Sador laughed sadistically.

"You won't find them," Afador said. Sador studied him long and hard, anger brewing beneath his bushy brows. "You can look as hard and long as you want and still it will be useless. Search the woods if you like, the mountains, the deepest cave in the most remote place on earth. If you search that long you will only discover you're not meant to find them. You may think that you are the master of your fate, but that is not the case.

"Perhaps not," Sador replied, reaching for his belt. "But I am the master of yours." Even as he said the words a whip flew from his belt and stung Afador's arm. The guards rushed forward and hastily chained both of them to the wall as Afador had been. The sounds of soldiers marching resonated through the silent night. Sador looked at them with keen interest. "This street is now closed until the day that I return. You will have no food, no water, you know the drill." He turned and began walking away leaving Afador and Remus chained to the wall.

Three days passed without anything of great importance happening. The street was now totally closed off and in the way of anyone who would try to aid them were nearly one thousand soldiers armed and given orders to kill anyone they thought was here to harm them. The soldier's reactions were mixed, some refusing to look at their prince, while others looked and conveyed sorrow and apologies with their eyes.

Every day the sun grew hot with fury and vengeance. Every night the sun would set and leave the two prisoners in a cold clear night. Despite their predicament, Afador and Remus both remained in good spirits and often talked to each other about things that were of no importance, but still lightened their spirits a bit.

Much to everyone's confusion, their bodies seemed to be holding up far better than they could have expected seeing the torture they had both received. Every day at dawn they were publicly flogged and beaten in the town square while citizens were forced to watch. But by the end of the day, Afador and Remus hardly felt like anything had happened to them. Their hunger didn't grow and their bodies hardly lost any weight, despite not being given any food or water for the time they were chained to the wall. Afador could only assume there had been something in the food of the Makkura that was giving them the boost they so desperately needed.

The fourth day began much like the first. As expected they were publicly flogged and then chained up to the wall. Now in an attempt to get the birds to come and cause them harm, they doused the two men in water and dumped leftover food on them. But still, no birds would come near them. Instead, Afador noted that all the birds were sitting on the large inner wall surrounding the entrance to the king's living quarters. If he attempted to come out they all swarmed to him as though it was a great battlefield and he was a piece of carrion.

Later that afternoon they were surprised to hear the sound of a horse approaching from the east. They strained their necks, able to see a single man on a black horse. He sat tall in the saddle, his head without hair. He wore a great sword at his side and a flowing black robe. The soldiers gave him room and he was allowed to approach them along the front edge of the falls.

"Good morning my fair prince!" the man greeted. "I am pleased to finally meet you, though it is unfortunate that we must meet in conditions such as these. That being said I have a considerable amount of clout and influence on your dear father, our beloved King Sador."

"What is your name?" Afador asked. "I would have sworn I have met all my father's advisors and important officials a dozen times."

"My name is Merderoc. For reasons that do not matter, for the sake of this conversation I have need to live on the northern shores of Tuthar. I often send messages to your father with my own opinion on the nature of things as he demands by his right as a king. I am usually only here in person for a day or two every year or so."

"You're story sounds reasonable. What do you want? As you can see we have nothing to offer you at this time."

"You misunderstand why I'm here," the man said. "I am a person of power, but it seems as if your father has become rather angry at your current situation and is beginning to throw around the idea of publicly executing whoever might be loyal to you. It seems to be in the best interest of many people if I was to bring you back to the king and say 'here is your son' and he has confessed and abandoned all of his foolish actions." Remus and Afador exchanged glances. "If these things were carried out, I think I might be able to cure the situation. Won't you confess your silly crimes and come with me? I'm sure rewards will be in abundance."

"You sound convincing," Afador replied. "But my resolve is stronger. I cannot lie and say that I regret doing the things that I have done. I do not have interest in such ideals."

"So you are turning away from your father and into the hands of this *unknown god*?" Afador and Remus both nodded and a look of concern came over Merderoc's face. "So what am I to do when I go up to your father? He will no doubt ask what council I have in this dark and disturbing matter. For it is currently my position that a prince who refuses to bow to the king should be worthy of death. Am I wrong in my council?"

"You are right in your council," Afador said. "I know very well that our choice may be the end of the two of us. However, I'm willing to take my chances. We are in very good shape despite everything we've been put through and we will stand strong until the end if that be necessary. Nonetheless, I do have a proposition for you. I know what the laws say and there is a particular law that may be appealing to my father."

"I would be most curious to learn of this law which I might have overlooked," Merderoc said, seeming to hang on every word.

"It is written that if disputes among members of the royal family cannot be settled by diplomatic means then both parties can request a duel be arranged. Fight to the death, winner takes all. In this case, whoever lives from our duel would take the throne and with it the hearts and minds of the people. My father is a brilliant swordsman and I've been through interesting circumstances the past few days, which would by chance give my father an even greater advantage."

"So you wish to challenge your father to a duel?"

"Yes," Afador replied.

"Are you prepared to kill your father?" Merderoc asked. "To kill anyone that you know requires a great amount of courage."

"You worry about presenting this to him and let me do the rest!" Afador said. Merderoc thought long and hard before speaking again.

"Very well," came the reply. "I shall do as you have suggested. I worry about what your father will think or do, but so I always do. I will present this to him and be back with you at first convenience."

Without speaking another word he mounted his horse and started his way up to the palace. As much as possible Afador and Remus watched him disappear, the soldiers shifted nervously.

"Do you really think he's going to speak with your father?" Remus asked.

"Hard to say," Afador answered. "My father has many contacts and associates, some of which I've intentionally kept at arm's length."

"I understand. What do you think we should do?"

"Wait."

Night had fallen before the flickering of torches aroused them from their uneasy sleep. A group of soldiers, numbering twenty, had gathered around. Afador and Remus were lowered to the ground and set on their feet, their chains taken off. Afador and Remus both felt considerably lighter without the heavy chains to weigh them down.

"What's going on?" Afador asked. The soldiers didn't speak. "In the name of the King answer me!"

"I have proposed your request to the king," Merderoc cried, coming up through the group to stand with them. "He has refused your offer and plans to have you shot full of arrows and thrown over the falls with great weights strung about your neck. I'm giving you the only chance of living that I can and that is to set you free and pray that your *new god* will save you."

"You are setting me free?" Afador asked.

"Yes," Merderoc said. Afador and Remus exchanged looks.

"So my father will not fight?"

"That's right, he said it was a waste of time. Now let's go before anyone figures out what has happened." All the men started to walk except Afador and Remus. They stood like statues, watching in unbelief.

"I can't go with you," Afador said.

"If you stay you will die!"

"No, I won't. I have a different plan," Afador replied. "Since my father is too much of a coward to take on a fight as I've requested. We will have to force his hand."

"I'm sorry but I'm not sure that I can allow that to happen. Right now for all our sakes, you need to get yourself out of this city, and fast. You can plan a little revolution later."

"This is not a revolution. I guess you could say it comes down to a legal matter. I requested a duel, and I need to make sure it can happen. If I leave this city now I will surely never get in again."

"Seeing the situation how is that a bad thing?" Merderoc asked.

"It is not for myself that I choose to stay in a city and defy my father yet again," Afador started. "It is for the people of the city, whom I love, that I stay."

"The people of the city-"

"You will not talk me out of this Merderoc!" Afador said. "My mind is made up, it's now your choice if you want to continue to aid me or stand in my way!"

"I can't let you go down this course of action," Merderoc said carefully. He nodded to the guards. They strung their bows and leveled them at Afador and Remus's heads. "I wish you had accepted my help." Merderoc turned and vanished somewhere in the darkness, while the soldiers released the arrows.

By the time the arrows were loosed, both Afador and Remus were on their knees, then stood to their feet. They looked at the soldiers, who had completely encircled the two of them. All twenty of the men that had been assigned to them lay dead on the ground, arrows protruding from them. Afador and Remus grabbed the swords from the two men.

"Are we really going to do this?" Remus asked.

"Yes we are," Afador said. "

Their attention was captured by the sounds of hooves echoing on the hard stone in the night. Afador held a hand to Remus, who jumped to defend him. Horses appeared at a casual walk. They bore great riders. Both Afador and Remus knew immediately that they were the Makkura. Afador and Remus bowed low as they approached.

The horsemen kept approaching and stopped a few feet from them. The entire line stopped in unison and dismounted in the same fashion, their movements perfectly in sync with each other. The man in front of them was tall and muscular, his ear pointed like that of an elf, his long flowing hair escaping his helmet. His armor sparkled in the dim lighting, making it difficult to know what kind of material it was made out of. Sometimes it appeared black, other times it seemed to glow or shimmer.

"Afador and Remus," the Makkura spoke. His voice was heavy with authority and they could barely keep themselves from looking away. Afador trembled as he recognized the voice from his childhood so many years ago.

"Yes my lord it is us," Afador finally replied.

"The Unknown God, Lathon is greatly pleased with your character and your audacious faith. Do not be afraid, for we have been sent to help you. My name is very different from your own, but you may call me Michael, for my true name is too long and complicated for you to speak on this earth."

"We are indebted to you," Afador said. "How have we achieved this great honor?"

"Your heart is true and has remained true, despite your circumstances these past few days. Now, time is short so we cannot tarry. You are to take no more than twenty men and go to your father's house and demand your challenge as before. He will be so frightened by the fact that you're there that he will agree immediately. Then leave your men with him and come back to us. We will protect both you and Remus tonight beyond the city gates."

"What about tomorrow?"

"Tomorrow you will enter the city by yourself and have your contest, your twenty men will bring your father to the city square and you can have your challenge. We will be with you but understand that we are not permitted at this time to go beyond this point in the city. This could always change in an instant, but as of yet that is our orders."

"I'm not sure I understand," Afador replied.

"It's complicated for people of the earth to understand or even to imagine. Rarely are we ever seen by people of the earth. It is not because Lathon does not care that we are not seen by people of the earth often; rather there is much work to be done that we alone were designed for. We are but willing servants.

"The people of the earth have a far greater opportunity. You not only get to work with Lathon and learn from Lathon as we do...you get to *lead* with Lathon! It is a great wonder that you perhaps right now cannot fathom, but you soon will. Lathon made everything you see, but he did not make people of the earth to dictate and achieve for their own personal satisfaction.

"He made you to learn, work, and lead those in your life around you. For you, you are a prince of a nation that is tired of the empty ways of the lifeless gods of the Sorcerer Merderick. Their hearts are open and there is great opportunity.

"For you Remus. You may not be a prince, but because of Lathon's goodness, he does not make this gift of leadership for only a prince, but also for everyone. There is great work for you to do if you're heart is willing."

"I am, but I'm not sure how," Remus said admittedly. "I'm just an attendant to the prince."

"Do not look at yourself from your point of view. The biggest piece of advice that I can give you is to look at yourself from Lathon's point of view. Do you know what he sees? He sees your character, your heart, and your desires. In addition, he above all, sees the potential of who you could be in him. Partnered with him. That is where Lathon's heart lies. That is why he sent the heir of Lathon in the first place! For if he did not come to live among us then why would we want to know him?"

Afador and Remus were lost in wonder, pondering the words and letting them go right to their hearts.

"The night is short," Michael said. "Go and do as we have said and we will see you soon!" Afador and Remus left him and were swallowed by the darkness of the night.

Chapter 27

GAMES OF DECEPTION

The bells of ships rang through the air as Isabel stepped back onto the deck of the Trinin. The ship was empty save the Captain who stood at the bow, staring at the city with great concern on his face. Isabel walked up to him.

"Something wrong?" Isabel asked. Borea shrugged his shoulders.

"I'm not sure. Normally though the crew disappears for a while, they return the next morning. Most of them are back by nightfall, save one or two. As you can see no one is here right now."

"What's your thoughts?"

"That we're playing with fire," Borea said. "Maybe I played too many cards on the table yesterday and someone's onto us."

"Lathon will be with us," Isabel said. Borea half scoffed. "You doubt the name of Lathon?"

"Only because I was raised that way. Though if either stories of Durio Helmar or the Count turn out to be true then a curse shall be placed upon me if I ever scoff the name of Lathon again."

"Well said," Isabel said. Borea laughed.

"Nice ally I have agreeing that I should be cursed."

"I know Lathon." Borea seemed to pause when she had said it, but he didn't reply. Instead, he finally looked at her.

"You look quite fine today."

"My husband would think so too," Isabel reminded.

"I wasn't saying anything like that."

"Just checking," Isabel said. "I figured these look a little better than my very travel-worn clothes."

"Indeed. These are the best I have," Borea said. He was dressed in his fine garments which proudly bore the crests of Cordell on them. "Shall we?"

They left the ship and walked for a while until they reached a large street filled with horses and carriages. They wound their way through the confusing maze until they found one with a driver standing alongside.

"Greetings sir," the driver said. Captain Borea pulled a large lavishly decorated envelope out of his pocket and handed it to the man. The man quickly glanced over it and then placed it in his pocket. "Captain Borea, Ms. Avalee. It will be my pleasure to escort you to the palace of King Drayvin."

The chauffeur helped them into the coach and they started through the congested streets. Many people cleared out of their way as their coach bore the flag atop it. They passed through many streets of the people who in Isabel's opinion were the nation of Cordell.

A few minutes later they passed into a district of the city that was clearly for those who had more money. The streets were all made of stones and the houses were grand and lavish. Each street they turned down seemed to be more magnificent than the last.

"Wouldn't it be nice to live in a place like this?" Borea asked.

"I might like it for a while, but I'm afraid my heart is far too wild for a life like this. I would sooner sell everything and give the money to those who need it."

Borea didn't respond but instead looked as if he didn't understand her.

They continued the tours of the wealthy districts until finally, they climbed one last steep hill to a large gate. The gate in the wall was nearly fifty feet wide, and twenty feet tall, while the actual wall was nearly twice the height of the gate. Isabel and Borea both felt their spirits shrink as they approached.

Their invitation was given to the guards and they were immediately allowed to pass to the inner courtyards. They pulled up to a stone path that was lined to either side with great gardens fountains and lanterns. Guards came alongside and escorted them up the path, guiding them closer to the main doors.

A set of steps led up to a large and grand archway and the main entrance. They were stopped at the bottom, and each company was escorted up the stairs by a different set of guards. While the guards that had led them up the path were nicely dressed, these guards clearly were dressed to serve a king. Their fabrics and colors were of dark blue and crimson red, while gold laced trim finished their uniforms. Isabel looked over to Borea who seemed uncomfortable.

"You've never been here before have you?" Isabel asked.

"No, my Lady," he answered.

"There's nothing to it. Compliment their wealth, their family, and their mind and heart for justice. In that order."

"So that's the secret to these parties? Brown-nosing?"

"Sadly yes. It's one of the reasons I hate them so much," Isabel said. They were met by two of the palace guards and escorted up the stairs to the door. When they reached the top they were met by a nicely dressed gentlemen who stood straight and stiff.

"What names shall I give the great assembly?"

"Borea of Harrbigge and Ms. Avalee of-"

"Epirus," Isabel cut in. The man nodded, turned on his heel, and began walking down the lavishly decorated hall. The tiles were dark blue and shone brightly in the light from the windows. They reached another set of doors and were walked through. A great staircase led down to a large open floor. A second-story balcony circled the entire space.

"Introducing to his majesties court, Borea of Harrbigge and Ms. Avalee of Epirus!" The people who were watching clapped politely as they were allowed to go down the stairs. Isabel and Borea took their place in the ever-growing line of people. The introductions kept on coming as more and more people were added. When finally the last person had been introduced. The people were divided down the middle of the room, creating a walkway that led to a great throne at the head of the room.

A man walked down from the stairs, entering onto the walkway that had been created. He stood tall and proud but was riddled with signs of aging. His hair was long and his beard was longer and fitted with various colors of jewels and gems.

IDOLS & TRINKETS

"Lord and Ladies, Counts and Countesses, distinguished guests; King Drayvin of this fine nation of Cordell is on his way here. My name is Maru. Since I know there are some who have never been in the presence of a king before, I am obligated to lay down the rules and laws of this palace. These rules will be strictly enforced!

"When the bell tolls and your king enters into this great hall. Each person, man or woman is to bow facedown on the floor. If one looks up at the king as he passes they will forfeit their life. Once the king is seated on his throne the bell will toll again and food and music will begin. The feast will last until the stroke of midnight, at which time you will be escorted out of the palace the way you came.

"And know this. Unless you are called on by the king you are forbidden to speak with him in any way. When you were invited here you were all given a chance to present your intrigues to the king. He has selected several to converse with and shall entertain no one else. Is this understood?"

"Aye!" the great assembly said.

"In that case, prepare to meet your king! Enjoy the party. We're watching." the man turned and walked up the stairs. The crowd murmured in excitement.

"Never thought I would say this, but I would give an awful lot to be anywhere else right now!" Borea exclaimed in a whisper.

"Just relax. Our only reason for being here in the first place is to find the Count. Or find someone who knows of his whereabouts. You said he would be here right?"

"In theory yes," Borea said. "My source is never wrong but now I'm not so sure."

"That's your fear talking, and it will not help you now!"

The bell tolled and immediately everyone ceased what they were doing and as ordered, dropped facefirst to the ground. Isabel steadied her breathing, hearing the heavy doors grind open. Footsteps of guards entered and lined the path to the throne. Each guard could be heard drawing his sword and raising it into the sky.

Silence passed for a moment before heavy, important footsteps trembled through the floor. Heavy boots struck the tile floor and with it struck fear into every soul. No one moved as the king slowly and steadily walked down the prepared path. Once he had passed, Isabel let her breath out and waited for the bell toll.

The guards put their swords back into their sheaths and the bell toll followed immediately. Orchestral music began playing from the second-story balcony and the crowd quickly rose to their feet and anxiously awaited as the food was paraded down the stairs and to the side where countless large tables waited.

The tables were covered in richly covered tablecloths and the food was presented on silver and gold plates and serving dishes. The line formed and several people took to the open floor to dance.

"Sorry I freaked out earlier," Borea said. "I think though, the smell of the food is going to cure the rest of my fear." As he finished speaking they were greeted by Mura who stood over them.

"Mr. Borea and Ms. Avalee. The king invites you to dine with him and discuss any matters that you feel would intrigue him."

"Thank you very much. We would be honored," Isabel said. "Please just give us one moment."

"Yes of course. You may present yourself and this invitation to the guard over there," Mura said. He pointed to a single guard dressed all in black. He turned and walked away. Borea looked dumbfounded.

"I didn't think this would work," he whispered.

"Good work Captain Borea. Now let's go meet the king," Isabel said. "What specifically did you put on the form about what we would like to talk about?"

"The only thing I thought would get us in," Borea said.

"The Count of Durio Helmar?"

"Aye. The Count of Durio Helmar.

They presented themselves and their invitation to the guard and they were led away to another more private chamber inside the castle. The sound of the music and the party faded away, and a feeling of dread momentarily came over them. Isabel stood tall and walked proudly despite the apprehension she had about meeting with the king.

They entered into a lavishly decorated room with a table nearly twenty feet long. At the end, three chairs and dinnerware were laid out. They were shown to their seats and left alone. A couple of minutes passed without any sounds besides their breathing.

The door they had come through opened and a great robed figure stepped in. Isabel and Borea immediately stood to their feet as the king entered and strode to his place at the head of the table. His long flowing black cape whirled behind him as he stood before his seat. The king waited for an attendant who took his cape away.

"My apologies for making you wait," King Drayvin said. "The problem I find with parties is that you always have to go here and do this, and go there and do that. Rarely do you get to have a good conversation with anyone. Nor get to enjoy the spoils of your own kingdom. But now we shall eat a meal unlike any you will eat in this kingdom!" He clapped his hands and immediately doors opened on the sides and a great spread of food and wine was brought for them. King Drayvin motioned that they should help themselves.

"Certainly the rumors of your wealth are proven to be true," Isabel said. "There is no food as fair as this in my Epirus. It was always said by my grandfather, who once lived in this region that fine men make fine food. He swore on his father's grave that the ruling class of this nation were fine men indeed and therefore would have the best food. I can see now that he is right." Drayvin smiled at the comment.

"I am honored to get such compliments from a guest when the meal has only just begun."

"A woman can tell a good thing when they see it, your majesty."

"Indeed and that is my point. I dine with many men and often they want something or have some person they wish for me to kill or something of the sort. In this way their compliments, even if they mean them with good intentions, are tainted by snobbery."

"Certainly you do not take my comments for snobbery?" Isabel asked. Drayvin gave an apologetic look.

"No, no my lady, on the contrary. When a woman pays me a compliment I normally ignore it. But when a fine lady like yourself speaks in approval how can I not take that seriously?"

"I see wisdom is also a trait that is in abundance in the men of Cordell." They shared a laugh. Borea remained silent, too scared at the moment to say anything.

"Does your dog talk?" Drayvin said, referring to Borea.

"Sometimes. He seems to be rather tongue-tied in the presence of nobility. Nonetheless, he has been a good traveling companion and was instrumental in the construction of the letter that we submitted to your secretaries yesterday. Wisdom is seldom where I'm from."

"And is that why you've traveled so far Ms. Avalee? For wisdom?"

"No your Highness, although if I had, I would see no shame in such a trip," Isabel said. "Rather I came to your shores as more of a sentimental favor to my ailing father. You see, long has my family planned to return to the home of my grandfather, and long has it been delayed by the events of life as you might say."

"I understand perfectly, the wish of an ailing father is not one you can turn aside. Is your father present tonight?"

"No, my lord. He is far too ill to make such a journey. His family has long had a feud with a person called Durio Helmar. He was supposed to have lived in these parts. According to my father, he even controlled this city at one point." Drayvin laughed.

"I'm afraid that your father must be mistaken in his illness. Durio Helmar plagued my grandfather's rule, that is not secret. However, I can assure you that Durio Helmar never conquered any part of this city. In fact one of the greatest things my grandfather ever accomplished was delivering Durio Helmar to his death!"

"I am glad to hear that such a devious snake is dead," Isabel said. "But to come all this way and have little to take my revenge on seems like such a waste."

"Forgive me my lady, but you are holding out on me. I can see in your eyes and hear it in your words, you came for more than revenge. I do not think that revenge is even a part of the equation. Am I wrong?"

"You are wrong in the sense that revenge can look very different to different people. My father had in his possession a letter to Durio Helmar from someone named the Count of Durio Helmar. The letter spoke very clearly of great wealth stashed somewhere on Prater. Forgive me but I do not know any more than that. Unfortunately, my father was not willing to part with the letter, instead, he decided to burn it on an altar to his god so that his god would smite him."

"I think your father and I would have been good friends," Drayvin said, putting his fork next to his plate. "There is a Count of Durio Helmar who is still alive in these parts. He's supposed to be in attendance this very night. It's in some ways ironic as Durio Helmar plagued my grandfather's rule, and the Count plagued my father's rule.

"Though I've spoken little of the plan to other people I have recently arranged for the Count and any surviving family members to be exterminated as soon as can be arranged. They are a deplorable people and deserve to be made into carrion. However if what you say is true and there is indeed great wealth or treasure to be had, it would almost seem like a tribute that he's paying after he's dead. I would be willing to stay my plans of killing him and allow you to find him and discuss certain matters.

"He's an old man, and his memory and body are in decline. If you told him a lie well enough, he'd believe it. And if you were to tell him lies that he believed, he may lead you right to this treasure of his. I have heard rumors of this treasure as well, but in all my years it has never been found."

"I would be happy to assist in whatever way I can!"

"Very good," Drayvin said. "In that case, I will give you orders that give you full authority to carry them out with all haste. Find the Count of Durio Helmar and find out what you can. Once you've done that we can move ahead with the rest of our plan."

Isabel nodded.

"And once he's dead we shall split the treasure?" Isabel asked.

"I would take only a small percentage. I simply want his head on a platter."

"You said he was here? Do you know where he might be found?"

"That I do not know. At some times he seems to be a ghost even to me. It's uncanny. Even in old age, he can melt into shadows. He often likes to sit out on the coast and watch the waves. Sentimental old fool!" Drayvin sat back in his chair, seeming to collect his thoughts. "I will make sure that you have a room for the night. Search the entire castle and all the guests for the Count of Durio Helmar."

"Yes, my lord."

"His kind cannot be allowed to do any more damage."

"What kind is that? Is the Count Elvish?"

"He might as well be. He is actually Cordellian royalty. Or he was, till he was stripped of his title. There's a long complicated history that I won't bother you with right now. To give you the short version, it is long known that he has taken hold of the Elvish beliefs and adopted them as his own. They follow a guy named Lathon and are eagerly waiting for his heir. I cannot let that happen. I know the Elvish pigs in nearby kingdoms only wish for this so that he can kill me and take the throne. I'm not going to let it happen. It won't be long until Elvish kind is exterminated if I have anything to say about it, and I'm the king so I do!" They all chuckled.

"Furthermore my great uncle as it were, married several Elves during his lifetime, had a daughter who was nearly as hideous as her parents. To think of the two races breeding like such? It's revolting and a clear violation of our own country's laws."

"I understand now why you're so eager to kill them. I would be too if I was you," Isabel said, thinking for a moment. "I'll do my best to locate the Count quickly and then let you know what I find out."

"Very well," Drayvin said. "One warning. You are a visitor to my shores, yes. But when someone says they will do something they better do it or else I will have my vengeance. I don't care if you're a visitor or my own brother. Do we understand each other?"

"Yes, my lord."

The conversation continued throughout the rest of the meal, which much to their surprise lasted for nearly an hour and a half. Isabel and Borea both took their turns talking and through it all Isabel felt as if a spirit of dread was settling on the room. As far as she could tell there was no one else present, but as time went on she was beginning to think otherwise.

At length the king thanked them for the stimulating conversation and took his leave, making a few suggestions of where they might be able to spot the Count if they were so lucky. Isabel led the way, briskly walking down the halls until they entered into an outside garden that the king had suggested. Unlike the others, this one was deserted and strangely appeared not kept up as well as the others.

"I know I haven't been in this kind of a setting before but I didn't understand half of what was being said back there!" Borea said, in as hushed a voice as possible. "Who are you anyway? Are you really from Epirus?"

"No."

"Is that even a real place?"

"Yes."

"How do you know that?"

"Would you stop!" Isabel exclaimed. Borea fell silent. "I've been in many conversations like this one and I've gotten pretty good at reading their thoughts and knowing what I need to say. That's what I was doing in there."

"Sorry, freaked me out a little bit," Borea said, thinking. "So we're not trying to kill the Count as you said in the meeting?"

"No, we're not. As far as his disdain for Elvish people I don't agree with it at all. I can't. My mother was Elvish."

"I see."

"Look, we need to find this Count quickly. I have no doubt we're likely being followed. If we can get him to tell us where the Prater is then we can make a run for it."

"What's on this ship that's so important?"

"I don't know, but a whisper in the air is telling me that I need to find that ship. At any rate, we need to find the ship so Drayvin can't have it."

"I wish I knew what was on it."

"I guess we'd better find it then," Isabel said. They fell silent, thinking and slowly walking through the dark overgrown garden. The sounds of the waves crashing on the shore reached them, as well as the refreshing smell of salt water. Isabel sat down on a bench, putting her head in her hands. For a moment Isabel heard nothing, then she sat up hearing a voice ringing out faint but clear. She stood and headed towards the noise, with Borea following close behind. The voice was singing and the words to her were both familiar and haunting.

"Lost and Found
Day and Night
All that is hidden shall see the light.
Though stars have fallen, all shall see
The origin of the things that be

There was a land, I saw it once
We were young and so was it.
In the midst of all, there stood before thee
A large and luscious Vemroliet tree.

In the darkness, it would shine,
Alive and well in the darkest time.
Great were its limbs, long was its reach
Frightful and strong did it seem."

Isabel quickened her pace, her heart beating faster. The other voice was strong, yet reserved as though he didn't want anyone to hear. Controlled by a spirit she could only conclude was one of joy, she let her own voice join in the song.

IDOLS & TRINKETS

A spirit of strength, but also humility
Did this tree stand ever so diligently?
It watched the land, it made its mind
It would be here until the end of time.

Oh Vemroliet tree, how I wish I had known
Of the great sorrow that came upon that morn.
When the world, made as it should be,
Was destroyed by greed. Oh, Vemroliet tree!

Cursed is the land in which now it lives.
Whispers echo in the hillsides faintly.
They speak of life and death and pain
And even hope, though it seems little remains.

Its secrets are lost, and forgotten by time.
The Vemroliet tree still stands by and by.
The whispers are fading, they are barely heard.
Will they survive the dark?

Isabel stopped singing now, unfamiliar with the words that were being sung.
She listened carefully as she slowed to a tentative walk.

Oh Vemroliet tree untouched by time
Its beauty veiled and cast aside.
Still, whispers speak to the hearts of men,
Hope returns only then.

A mysterious force moves in the earth.
And then comes the painful birth.
But afterward there is a sigh.
'Well done' the whispers say.

DRAKE THOMAS

They're stronger now, I hear them clearly.
Hope renewed, will come quite quickly.
In the dark of night, hope will return
And take the faithful to what they've earned.

Our hope renewed, was short, and then shattered.
They left you in tatters.
But then I see, it is not so!
My eyes deceive me, at first I think,

But from the pain, from the hurt and anger
From the hatred and the earth.
Hope comes again, and our spirits soar!
We can stand tall through the storm.

When this day passes, none can tell
But one thing we know so very well
The whispers speak, they speak so loud
They strengthen us and send us out.

The darkness is left to its own desires,
The light unto the land of stars.
And in the garden, there shall be,
A large and luscious Vemroliet tree.

She turned the bend, coming out of a small grove of trees, able now to look at the shore and the ocean beyond. She looked now at an old man in expensive clothes, staring out at the sea. He had a beautifully carved cane in one hand that set upon his lap. Isabel stayed where she was, listening to him sing the rest of the song.

402

IDOLS & TRINKETS

Still as young as it was back then.
No aging has it done.
By wisdom unknown, the tree still stands,
It is held within the hands.

The hands of the three lookout for thee.
They see the pain and care for me.
They once reached down to a broken vessel
Repaired it new and set it there.

And on that day, when we finally see,
The three beneath the luscious Vemroliet tree.

Pain shall pass, death no more
As I walk through heaven's door.
And there I shall reside, beyond the farthest reach of time.
The three are one and I by their side.

"I've never heard the end of that song," Isabel said. The man jumped a little bit and turned to look toward her. He had a long silver beard and was dressed in fabrics of rich blues and reds.

"You must be the beautiful singer that joined me. Please, come sit." Isabel came and sat, Borea came and stood to the side. "Not many people remember that song anymore."

"I've heard it a time or two. On the wind, though much of what you have just sung I have never heard."

"And what do you think of the entire song?"

"I think it's beautiful, but ultimately I don't know what the song is talking about. I'm quite a studied person but I've never even heard of a Vermroliet tree."

"Few have. There are no known Vermroliet trees in existence today, but in history at one time...there were hundreds, perhaps even thousands."

"How do you know?"

403

"My research through the years has been devoted to *very* ancient texts, manuscripts, languages, things of that sort. Then one day after nearly a lifetime of trying to crack one of the languages that had evaded me my entire life...I did it! Once I had cracked it I started going through my findings and I found it was the story of creation. It spoke of a magnificent garden, filled with Vermroliet trees! It was the story of the Elves and of Lathon!

"Regardless of what you may think of those things yourself, one cannot deny it was a historic find and discovery. For centuries people have pondered the beginning of everything. Religions have sprung up, each of them trying to answer why we're here. What our great purpose is.

"In that moment it convicted my soul without a shadow of a doubt of the validity of the Elvish beliefs. I had never doubted them, but now it wasn't even a possibility."

"It's strange to hear one speak of Elves in a positive light," Isabel said. "I've gathered that they don't really do that up here."

"You can say that again!" the old man laughed joyfully. "I've had the great privilege of knowing a great number of Elves throughout my lifetime. In fact, I've even been married to two different Elvish women. It irritated many people, especially my brother, but I care not. Lathon has blessed me, even if the nation of Cordell despises the name of Lathon. In my house, I have never done that."

"I'll agree with that," Isabel said.

"So who are you and what's your story?" the man asked. Isabel hesitated.

"My name is Avalee, I'm from Epirus. Far from here."

"Avalee?" the old man asked. Isabel nodded. "That is a very beautiful name."

"Thank you."

"What brings you to Cordell?"

"I was asked to go north by a good friend of mine. Along the way, I found a strange island. On this island, I found a strange cave and a letter that I was supposed to give to the Count of Durio Helmar. On another island, I found a girl who claimed her father was the Count. Have you heard of him?"

"Aye, I've heard of this Count. He is well known around these parts."

"Where do I find him?" Isabel asked.

"You're speaking with him now," the old man said. A new light shone in his eyes and somehow he seemed to be not as old, sitting straighter and more proper.

"It's a pleasure to meet you," Isabel said, holding out her hand. He shook it and looked at her closely.

"How can I help you?" He held Isabel's gaze. Isabel found herself pulled into his gaze, unable to look away. For a moment she was speechless.

"I-uh-I have this letter," Isabel pulled it from her pocket. "It says I'm supposed to present it to either you or a descendant of yours. If you think me fit to continue your work then it says you'll give me a key." The man's eyes softened even more and a tear slipped down one of his cheeks and then laughter escaped from the Count. The sound was jovial and all of them began joining in the laughter.

"So many years have I dreamed of this moment, only now do I fear it is a dream. You shall certainly receive the key and all the work I've ever touched in my life, Isabel." Borea straitened at the mention of her name. Isabel looked at the old man and understood.

"Father?"

The Count smiled. "Yes, Isabel it is I. Though I do not understand how this moment has come to be. I can see now that Lathon's hand is working in all things. The great sorrows and mysteries of the past are becoming clearer."

"This is your father?" Borea asked.

"Yes. This is my father, Catterick," Isabel answered, hardly able to think straight. "How is this possible? You were killed!"

"Many years I wish I had been. For many years I've thought you were dead. However like an old sentimental fool. I hoped that one of you survived and we would be reunited someday."

"I've got so many questions-"

"We don't have time for that," A voice said. They turned to see Drayvin striding around the corner, cape flying up behind him. Soldiers flanked him on both sides. The three of them immediately tried to flee, only to find soldiers had surrounded them on both sides. The three of them were swiftly put in irons. "I'm placing all three of you under arrest."

"On what charges?" Isabel asked. Drayvin leveled his stare at her.

"Aiding and abetting enemies. If you remember in our conversation I intend to seek out and execute all the descendants of The Count of Durio Helmar, who is evidently your father. I thought at first the name Avalee was coming to my mind because of some woman I had met who may have had the same name, but then I remembered that the Count here, used to be married to a whore with a name very similar."

"You must feel very proud of yourself," Borea said.

"I can't begin to describe the immense joy I feel at this very moment. Iyla's already dead and the three of you will hang at dawn for your treachery and for your love of the Elvish people! Now I'm sorry I can't stay and chat, but I assure you I will come as soon as I get a spare moment." He looked to the guards. "Take them away." They cried out and fought the guards as much as they could.

"Calm yourselves, children!" Catterick called out. "There is a time for everything. and it is not the time for fighting, just yet!"

Isabel opened her swollen eyes, looking at the inside of a dungeon cell. Her head pounded and her body ached from the beating and whipping they had all received. She sat up and leaned against the damp stone wall.

"Is everyone okay?"

"All things considered, I'm still alive," Borea said, looking as horrible as the rest of them. "I finally know what happened to my crew members. They're here in the prison five cells down."

"All of them?" Isabel asked.

"No. It seems Darrison is not with them, but he usually disappears to everyone when we're in port." Isabel searched the cell, seeing the shape of her father huddled in the corner. She quickly moved over to him, looking into his beaten face.

"Are you okay father?" Silence followed for several seconds.

"I'll live. I'll live. Though my heart is unsure what to feel. I don't know whether I should mourn my daughter who is dead or celebrate the one who is alive."

"Iyla is alive," Isabel reassured. Catterick looked at her curiously.

"How would you know that?"

"Because I met her on my travels here. She said her father was the Count of Durio Helmar, and I had no idea that it was you. The island was attacked and set ablaze by the order of Drayvin I suspect. Apparently, he hasn't figured out that his men never returned."

"Where is Iyla now?" her father asked. "How did you get away?"

"I've come into the friendship of several Taruks. My husband took Iyla to safety. I felt I needed to help her. She thought you were dead." Catterick looked away, lost in his thoughts for a moment.

"Glory be to Lathon! He has been watching over everything."

"Yes." Isabel turned to Borea. "Darrison is Iyla's husband. That's where he sneaks off to every time you're in port."

"At least he's got a good reason," Borea said. "Though if she was on a forbidden island...that's some risky business."

"Indeed. He's waiting outside the city with a small boat. It's not much, but if we can get to it we can get away."

"Nice plan, but I advise against it," Catterick said. He looked at Isabel and motioned to Borea. "Who is he?"

"Sorry, I forgot all about introductions," Isabel said. "This is Captain Borea, he's been assisting me."

"Captain?"

"Yes sir," Borea replied. "I am the captain of the Trinin, a supply vessel of sorts."

"Pleasure to meet you," Catterick said. "Our time is short and there is much to say, please sit, so I don't have to speak as loud. They both sat next to him as he stared into space.

"Sixty-five years ago at the ripe old age of sixteen, I met the most amazing woman named Avalee. She was also my age, but she was of Elven kind. Such marriages are shunned and considered detestable. I went to my father Kurin to see if I would be able to marry her. Try to get the law changed. I was not able."

"Kurin?" Borea asked. "Kurin was your father? You're a prince!"

"I was," Catterick answered. "It was told to me very forcefully that I could not marry this woman or else I would forfeit everything and be condemned to death as the law dictates. It was with the guidance of my friend Durio Helmar, who actually introduced me to Avalee's family, that I forfeited my crown and title and left. Avalee and I were married the next day with the full blessing of her family. We lived in Ritil for the first year or two, but we knew it would not be possible to keep my identity a secret forever.

"We decided to move to Vonlouas, which we did and we lived very happily there for nearly eleven years. Durio and I were working together, mostly I would lend my knowledge and love for study to his cause. As such I started working on some strange artifacts, trying to figure out their meaning.

"I began working on strange boxes. I'm not quite sure how to describe them, but for years I had a couple of them-"

"Sitting on the mantle," Isabel said.

"Precisely. I've never been sure of how it happened but eventually, my brother Oshland, who became king after my father's death, learned of my location. In broad daylight, they captured me and forced me to watch as they caused an explosion that destroyed our entire house." He looked at Isabel. "How was it you didn't get killed?"

"I was at someone else house," Isabel said.

"I see. I was brought back to Cordell and thrown into this very prison and tortured and beaten. It appears word of the work I had been doing had reached his ears and for some reason, mostly due to his hatred of the Elves, he was determined to get me to give it up."

"The only reason I got out of prison was because of Durio Helmar. He gave Oshland a very hard time. Raided many towns, and killed many Cordellian soldiers. He said Lathon did not approve of many things that were going on in Cordell and would therefore it was Durio's job to teach him a lesson.

"At long last I was released, though I was never given the title of prince again. A week later Durio comes to me and makes me the inheritor of his estate. Four years later Durio died and with a very small part of the wealth I was able to purchase the title of 'Count'.

"Twenty years later my brother was seeking out a wife for his son. He sent men all through the nation and bordering nations to bring pure woman which would be considered. As they were paraded off the ship like cattle I noticed a woman I recognized."

"Iyla's mother?" Isabel asked. Her father nodded.

"Yes. Lydia was the youngest of your mother's sisters. Fifteen years younger. By what mistake she had been brought I cannot guess, but I knew if I did nothing she would be killed as soon as they got to the palace. I immediately spoke to Oshland and agreed to buy Lydia and marry her to save her disgrace. My brother must have had some goodness still in his soul because he let the marriage remain.

"To everyone's surprise, when I was the age of fifty-six, Lydia, who was forty-one conceived and gave birth to our daughter Iyla. The outrage on my family's part was great. We moved to a small village a few day's travel from here and lived very happily.

"Then three years ago. Drayvin became king, through suspicious events. He sought to destroy me, but could not because the people loved me so much. He killed Lydia and until now I thought Iyla was also dead." They were all silent, mulling over everything.

"What's the Prater?"

"The Prater is a ship. The biggest ship I've ever seen. It belonged to Durio and on it, he stashed most of his wealth and our research. It's stashed on the island Toinwer."

"Does Drayvin know of this?" Isabel asked. Catterick shook his head.

"The ship is a myth. Drayvin says he's not looking for it, but I know better. He hasn't set out to conquer all the islands between here and Luma for nothing. I suggested the island because it is one of the forbidden ones and he has not thought to look there. On this ship, you'll find the key to open the chest at

Sunkre, which is the name of the island where you found the letter."

"I hardly know what to say," Isabel said.

"Then say nothing. Durio and I stashed all of our work throughout the world we knew. I do not expect I shall be able to finish it...but you, my daughter can." He looked to Borea. "You said you were a Captain with a ship?"

"Yes."

"The time for action has come! Isabel." Isabel looked at him. "I need to you think with your head, not with your heart, and consider what I ask of you. You must leave me in this cell, but you must get yourself and anyone you trust to Toinwer to find the Prater. Drayvin has many dark ways to extract information from subjects and his methods will either kill us or give him what he wants. He wants the Prater and will stop at nothing to get it."

"But father-"

"Think Isabel. I am too old to be plotting an escape. I would never make it. I must take my chances and hope that I can withstand his torture. I suspect everyone will be making for Toinwer very soon. You must escape first and get the Prater as far away as you can." Isabel fell silent. "Do you understand?"

"Yes," Isabel said. "All these years apart and we must be parted again?"

"I know it hardly seems fair, but know that this father's prayers have been answered and if I should die, I have run a good race for Lathon's glory."

Chapter 28

QUESTIONABLE MOTIVES

James gently pushed open the door to the hall where breakfast had been prepared. He slipped in without saying a word and took his seat next to his father. The rest of the room was empty of people save one or two servants. They sat in awkward silence for several minutes as Zebethar stared blankly ahead.

Anyone else would've thought the king had nothing on his mind, but James knew him better than that. Beneath his father's beard and eyebrows, James could see that the silence wouldn't last much longer.

"What do you have to say for yourself, son?" Zebethar asked, still staring straight ahead.

"It's nice to be home," James answered.

"I have a company of soldiers that were on patrol last night and they never returned. Do you have any comment?"

"I sent them with Drake," James replied.

"Who gave you authority to give such a command?"

"Read the bi-laws father, as prince I can send a few troops somewhere else without notifying you."

"Why did you send them with Drake?"

"We received an autonomous tip that Eshunna was going to be under attack."

"No visitor came that I am aware of."

"He didn't come to see you father," James said. His father's glare turned icy. "He came to speak with Drake and those in his company, and them alone," Zebethar grunted in disgust.

"Ten years! Ten years my son! You've been gone and dead for that long, or so I thought. Now at last I see things clearly. You doubt my leadership. You seek the throne for yourself?"

"What would make you think so father?"

"The people love Drake. They always have. Perhaps more than they love you, but certainly more than they love me. Much thanks I've gotten for the years I devoted to the Elvish people; leading them as a king is supposed to. I see now you've gained great fame among the people though you've been gone for many years. You seek to overthrow me? Am I right my son, or am I seeing ghosts?"

"You are blinded by your jealousy," James answered. "In Drake's defense, the prophet Sarule did appoint Drake as he appointed you! The people respect that. I care not if I become king. I do not wish to stand in the way of the will of Lathon."

"So you would desert me? See me overthrown, and see Drake in my place?"

"If you would listen to yourself, you would see a man who is not who he used to be," James said.

"And so it seems my son is not who I remember."

"You are my father! I will not see you overthrown! But for the sake of others, I had to send men to assist Drake in protecting his family. What about that is hard to understand? There will be far more death and destruction if we do not ride with Drake to Nargaroth immediately."

"Spoken like a traitor who reveals his plan with intent. Hoping that I will take the bait, empty the fortress, and ride out to war. What then? Will your own force come and take over in my absence?"

"Drake's family lives in an old silver mine, which you know as well as I would make a great place to stage an army and attack other towns, and villages, and eventually arrive on your doorstep!"

"They would be hard-pressed to take this place. You've seen the color change to the stone?" James nodded. "It's a substance called Reph, we mine it from underneath this very city. We heat it till it boils. When it hardens it is nearly indestructible. An army trying to attack this place in any respect would only end with them breaking upon the wall as a wave crashes onto the shore."

"We need to march on Nargaroth immediately or we will be destroyed! For all we know Drake and his family could already be dead!"

"I will not send the army waltzing into a peaceful nation! As I told you last night!" Zebethar cried. He shoved his chair backward and stormed out of the room. James sat thinking and pondering, trying to clear his mind of the anger and frustration that clouded it. The servant in the corner timidly approached.

"Perhaps it isn't my place your highness," the man started. "But it seems in times of uncertainty, a clear head brings forth the best wisdom."

"Well spoken," James said. "But it brings me no comfort. I realize now more than ever that the king has not had a clear head in quite some time. I pity him. I really do. I know it must be hard to know that the same prophet that anointed him to be king has anointed another…but why resist the will of Lathon? The prophet, after all, only does as he is instructed by Lathon. What's your name?"

"My name is Remar, son of Terrahim."

"Yes, I recognize you. You've worked in the palace for some time yes?"

"Yes, Your Majesty. I have stood by your father and faithfully served since you were three."

"Was my father this stubborn when I was gone? Or did my coming back with Drake, bring up all of this?"

"He was always furious with you for pursuing Drake. He never said it to me, but I think he felt remorse for his actions that drove Drake, and ultimately you, away. After a while though, the remorse turned to bitterness, and bitterness if not dealt with carefully can destroy a person. I do not know what goes on in your father's head these days; I have been uncertain for some time. But I do know that there is one person in this instant who has a much clearer head. It is my belief that he should stand tall and proud, and with as much tact and thoughtfulness as can be managed, lead the way to Nargaroth."

"I'm conflicted, but I sense that you were led to say such words," James replied. James left and returned to his chamber where Melchizedek and Corvil were waiting.

"How did your father take things?" Corvil asked.

"He didn't. I leave for Nargaroth at once. I will gather as many people as I can from the villages between here and Nargaroth. We ride for Eshunna!" Corvil and Melchizedek were ready to ride as soon as James was and together the three of them rode out of the gate leaving the city behind them. James looked back, for a moment letting remorse and sorrow overtake him. Then he cleared his thoughts and looked ahead.

***

It was mid-morning when Drake and his men drew close to his family's house, Eshunna. The night had passed slowly and they rode in silence, anxious for what they would find.

"Looks like smoke," Duran said, pointing to the horizon. Drake looked and easily spotted grey smoke, drifting high into the air. Drake's heart grew uneasy.

"I see it," Drake replied. "Let us ride more swiftly now."

The horses thundered over the hill, the forest growing larger and more defined. Drake's uneasy feeling didn't relinquish any as vultures were spotted high above. They crested the top of the last hill and pulled their horses to an abrupt stop as the remains of a battle lay before them. Bodies were strewn everywhere and the stench of death greeted them harshly.

"Looks like more than a little skirmish happened here," Duran said. "I know this will be of no comfort, but if your family is all dead, they put up one great fight that will be remembered in tale and song for many a year after this."

"You are right Duran," Drake said. "That is of no comfort to me. Give a couple of notes on your horn and see what happens."

Duran blew his horn into the open air. For several long moments, they could hear nothing but the sounds of vultures circling over the tops of the trees. Finally, an answering horn rang out.

"That is no Dwarf horn!" Duran said. Drake left his horse and began navigating through the maze of twisted and mangled bodies. The dead were mostly Dwarves, but a few Borags, and other creatures Drake had never seen before were scattered throughout.

Enormous trees had been ripped out of the ground and now lay in pieces, others had been set ablaze and now smoldered trailing smoke into the sky. In addition to the trees that had been moved, there were also large rocks and old mine carts, pieces of railing, and other debris that bared their way. In some places the ground was soft, covered by thousands of tracks. Despite the carnage, catapults and siege machines lay off to the north undamaged.

Rachal and Lucille emerged from the edge of the forest, covered in dirt, mud, and grime. Rachal smiled warmly and Drake couldn't hold back a smile of his own.

"Greetings your majesty," Duran greeted. Lucille bowed.

"I'm glad to see all of you alive," Drake stated. "Here I was thinking I was going to be coming to your rescue and I find that you didn't need any rescuing after all."

"It's been an eventful night," Lucille said. "You should be proud of your wife Drake. She's got a sharp, clear mind. Rare to find these days."

"Lucille's being far too complimentary," Rachal argued. "Lucille was just as vital in our survival effort."

"How did you manage to hold off such a force? We must have passed some four hundred bodies on our approach."

"The explanation is more difficult than you might think, and for that reason, I ask that Drake and Drake only comes into the forest with us for the moment. Everyone else must wait here until Drake comes back."

"Very well," Drake said, nodding to Duran. He and the rest of the men turned around and headed for the clearing where their horses had been left.

Drake and Rachal turned and headed into the forest, Lucille followed behind seeming more timid than usual. Beneath the canopy of trees, they still found trees smoldering, twisted metal tracks, and other carnage all about them. The wall that ran around the entire mine, was charred and blackened. Parts of it were missing entirely, but still, the area was littered with fallen enemies.

They quickly glanced into the great courtyard, as they passed by the gate. Half of the house had been destroyed by fire, the remains still smoldered. In the middle of the great courtyard sat all the members of the household and all the servants and farmhands. A small breakfast had been prepared and everyone sat in silence eating.

"We all made it out alive," Rachal said.

"What happened here?" They continued walking around the perimeter of the wall.

"Willard and Miles were the first warning we had that something was going to happen. They said there was a large number of Dwarves coming here and to defend the best we could. We did everything we could think of. We fell trees and gathered anything that might gain us an advantage in the event of an attack. We held them off pretty well for a while, we set fire to a lot of things which kept them at bay for some time. Finally, in a move of desperation, we sent a herd of nearly a thousand sheep stampeding through the ranks."

"That must have been a sight to see," Drake commented.

"Yes, it was. Call it luck or call it providence, I would of course lean towards providence; not a single sheep was injured or hurt during the stampede."

"So what caused this damage?" Drake asked.

"This," Rachal said, leading him around to the backside of a hill. There lying in the undergrowth of the forest lay a great beast. His skin was colored like moss and if he had been standing he would've stood nearly twenty feet tall. Drake hesitated taking in the immense size and span of his arms.

"What is he?" Drake whispered.

"You don't need to whisper, he made it quite clear that he likes you," Rachal said.

"He did? I've never seen this creature before in my life! What is this?"

"Willard and Miles told us he is a Teller. A long-forgotten race of some kind. This one has had its tongue cut out, so it can't speak unless by thought. He's spoken with me and Lucille briefly, but only briefly. They have some dark history of being tortured by the Sorcerer and used for his purposes against their will."

"What made them so valuable to him besides sheer size?"

"According to Willard and Miles, a Teller can tell what your story is by your scent. They can tell everything, where you've been, who you've seen. The choices you've made when you're by yourself. We can't know for sure, but we think he's lived here for some time and maybe that's why King Zebethar abandoned the mine. He made it quite clear he does not approve of Zebethar." A moment of silence passed between them. Drake knelt next to the great creature, noticing large amounts of blood beneath it.

"He must have fought valiantly."

"That's an understatement," Rachal said. "He came in the middle of the night and sat down in front of the gate. Arrows bounced off him, and knives did little damage, but eventually, they began to fire catapults at him. He looked at us and then looked at them with fire in his eyes. He stood and crushed everyone in his path. Sometimes he would step on them, other times he would grab part of the wall and hurl it at them. Before long he bounded into the mines and brought out the old mine carts and picked up tracks as though they were nothing. It's only because of him that we outlasted the attack. We had done okay, but he was the turning point." Drake looked down at the Teller, his heart saddened as the sleeping giant lay in front of him.

"You've fought well my friend," Drake said. "If you shall die, you shall be remembered in songs, tales, and memory for many ages." The Teller groaned weakly and shifted uncomfortably.

"I wish we could heal him," Rachal said.

"So do I," Drake replied.

"Then why don't you?" a voice said from behind them. A man stepped out into the clearing. A long grey beard matched his grey hair. The man was dressed in well-worn clothes and bore a great staff with gold veins running through it. Drake and Rachal shared a glance at each other and then smiled, turning their attention back to the man.

"We're glad to see you again," Drake said.

"And I'm happy to see you," the man replied. "Now back to the situation at hand. Why don't you heal him?"

"I'm not sure how?" Drake answered. Rachal nodded her agreement.

"I don't believe that for a moment," the man said, kneeling and laying a hand on the great beast. "I tell you the truth! You could look over to the mountains of Nargaroth and tell them to move to the north and they would do it! If only you had the faith. Do you believe that you can heal this creature?"

"No," Rachal replied. "But we believe in someone who could. If he sees fit."

"You ask not and you get not," the man said, leaning on his great staff, looking gently into their souls. "It's time to ask yourself what you believe in!"

Drake and Rachal looked towards the Teller and laid a hand on him. A great sensation came over them and before their very eyes, the blood began moving back into the Teller's body and his numerous injuries began mending themselves. When finally he was healed in full, the sensation passed and he was without words.

"People are only held back by their unbelief," the man said. The Teller stood to his feet. He staggered for a moment and then sat down again, breathing heavily. He looked around at everything as if he had been awoken from a great dream. "Fresh air is good for the soul isn't it?"

"I've nearly forgotten what the smell of fresh air is," the Teller said. His voice was deep and strange but somehow less menacing than they had expected. "Is this a dream? Some cruel trick meant to torment me?" None of them moved or spoke a word but the Teller stared into the man's eyes for several moments. Finally, the Tellers' lips parted and he began to smile. "Far from the dungeon, I was once kept in. I have wandered far in my years, I remember none."

"Go forth and make new memories," the man spoke. "Your life of old was stolen from you, and now you may make a new life for yourself if you wish?"

"I do wish," the Teller said. Finally, he glanced at Drake and Rachal. "For many years I have been mute, but now at last I have my voice back. How can I repay you for such a thing?"

"Praise the one who made your healing possible in the first place," Rachal said.

"And if you ever feel like pummeling someone in a battle I'm sure I'll need a hand at some point," Drake added. The Teller chuckled.

"I'll keep that in mind. But now I feel like I must go on a journey, but to where I'm not sure."

"I hope our paths get to cross each other again in the future," Drake said.

"Me too," the Teller said. Without another word he stood and walked into the forest, humming a strange tune that to Drake seemed rather familiar. The three of them stood in silence for several moments.

"And now it is time for me to depart as well," the man said, glancing off into the west. "There are many things for me to attend to."

"I was hoping you'd stay and help us in the battle against Nargaroth," Rachal said. The man smiled and then turned and left.

Despite all the damage that had been caused the night before, everyone's spirit was in good condition. Drake's family had been more than overjoyed to see him and the extra help he had brought with him. By the time nightfall had come, much of the debris had been taken away, even if the restoration work was far from over. Drake and Rachal collapsed into their bed, eager to let sleep overtake them.

Drake's eyes fell shut, his thoughts beginning to grow fuzzy. Suddenly he was pulled back to the present as he heard horns ringing through the night. Drake jumped out of bed and looked out the window seeing a line of torches snaking its way across the forest floor.

Alarmed Drake shook Rachal awoke and ran downstairs. The rest of the household was quickly awakened as Drake and Rachal grabbed their swords. They ran out to stand with Lucille who was staring out the arch where the front gate would have been. The three of them drew their swords. Willard and Miles appeared on either flank of the gate and promptly laid down. Drake puzzled by their movements.

Horns rang out again, and this time relief flooded through everyone's veins as they recognized the tone. They waited patiently until two hundred horsemen appeared at the arch. James rode on a black horse at the head of the company. He quickly dismounted his horse and embraced his sister.

"It seems you didn't need any help after all," James exclaimed.

"That's what I said when I arrived," Drake said. "It seems your sister and my wife make a very good defensive team."

"I shouldn't be surprised," James replied. "In the little time I've known Rachal I've hardly known her to be anything but confident, and I know Lucille has fire in those veins of hers."

"I put it to good use this time!" Lucille cried. They all laughed.

"What now?" James asked. "Seeing my services are of no use."

"I'm not sure," Drake said. "We were thinking we would be heading to Nargaroth tomorrow morning, but if this is all the men we have, it may prove foolish."

"Foolish or not, we were told to make things ready and march tomorrow. Whatever we do, it must be at dawn," Rachal said. They nodded their agreement.

"What about your father?" Drake asked.

"It seems he is just as stubborn as ever. He will not come with us. If we go to the walls of Nargaroth. We will be alone. He doesn't even know that I have gathered these two hundred."

"I think it's too late at night for a decision like this," Daniel interjected.

"I'll agree with that," James said, dismounting his horse. "Men! Make camp, but light no fire. If Nargaroth intended to use this area to stage an army, there may be more troops on the way. Post a guard and get some rest!"

The men did as they were told, and within a couple of minutes, the entire camp was quiet leaving only the silence to comfort them. James came with them into the house and was given a place to sleep. They lay talking for a while longer, unease gnawing at them and weighing on their hearts.

The sun had only started to lighten the dark sky when they were aroused by another horn ringing through the forest. Everyone ran out to the gate and all the soldiers were already at arms as a rider on a horse came rushing in. They relaxed for only a moment as a rider bearing Zebethar's crest sat atop the horse.

"My prince! My prince! Lord Zebethar approaches from the east, bringing a great number of soldiers," the rider cried. James and Drake exchanged looks.

"A change of heart on your father's part?" Drake asked.

"Possible," Lucille answered. "Time will tell." They waited anxiously and the entire household made themselves ready to receive the king. The sun was fully visible in the sky when several horns rang out. Heralds rode forth, and

Zebethar and his entourage entered the forest.

"All hail, Lord Zebethar of Rinevah!"

They all bowed as Zebethar rode his horse up to the battered walls that surrounded the silver mine. He looked over everything with a stare that both penetrated the heart and filled them with fear.

"This place has looked better," Zebethar started. "Though I see now that it was indeed attacked as you told me. Please forgive my skeptical heart. I can see you are surprised that I am here, and I admit I would rather not be. It seems though that my scouts came across a small company of Nargorathian scouts. They left none alive, but it further gave credence to your story."

"We are glad to see you father," James said, bowing low.

"And I am glad to see you. All of you. That being said I am still *not* riding to Nargaroth. One small company of Dwarves is hardly a prelude to war. They could have had any number of reasons for going through our country and they should have been questioned instead of killed so rashly. I have severely dealt out judgment on the soldiers that killed them and then reported it to me."

"They might still have valuable information, we must question them at once!" Rachal exclaimed.

"Do not waste your breath. They are dead. And you woman should remain silent unless spoken to. I do not know who you are, for all I know you could be one of them." Rachal turned and stormed towards the house. Zebethar looked at Drake knowingly. "You'll probably say I spoke too harshly."

"I would only caution against making her truly angry. If you knew her family at all you would understand my reasons a little better," Drake replied. James chuckled, while Zebethar sat up straighter in his saddle.

"There are hosts of Nargothian soldiers approaching from the west. My spies think they are headed here to reinforce the first group that was wiped out. Little do they know? Our best estimates give us nearly two hours to make this place ready. I have been wrong on many levels today so now as humbly as I can, I ask your opinion on what we can do for defense."

Chapter 29

CONTENTION

"Take a deep breath, my prince. It'll all work out," Remus comforted. Afador heard his words but they felt like rocks on water to his soul.

"I'm not sure I can do this?" Afador asked. "Are you telling me that you would be okay with fighting, and if it came to it, killing your father?"

"I didn't say it was ideal," Remus defended. "If I may be so bold your highness, you are letting your head get in the way of your heart. Look at the facts my friend. By all rights, when we stormed into your father's sleeping quarters, made our demands, and then had him detained on top of that...we should have been dead. But not a single person raised their sword to challenge us. Why?

"Do you call that coincidence? Chance? Fate? No, my prince, it was but the hand of the once *Unknown God*, Lathon protecting you. Even now the Makkura are waiting outside the city walls, with your wife and children well protected. They are safe. Like you, I still don't know how this is all going to play out. But I feel that there is a bigger picture that we cannot see." Afador remained silent. A figure stepped out of the shadowed corner of the room they were in.

"Lathon is with you," Michael told him. Afador stepped back, surprised by his presence.

"You are in the city?" Afador asked.

"I have my orders," Michael replied. "If I may offer a piece of advice it would be to listen to your friend here. Wisdom is heavy on the words he has spoken. Stand tall, be strong."

"Will I win? Will I have to kill my father?" Afador asked, consumed by fear for the moment. Michael looked at him long and hard.

"You have will. You have determination. You have the wisdom to decide what course should be taken. There are many voices, but you need only listen to one." Afador thought for a moment and then a smile tugged at his lips. He understood what Michael meant. An attendant came and knocked on the door.

Remus stood. "It's time."

Afador stood and began moving towards the door. He stopped and took one last look back at Michael who nodded.

"May the glory of Lathon be your guard!" Michael said. In an instant, he walked back into the dark corner and disappeared. Afador felt his courage return as he put his armor on and followed Remus out of the room. Afador let himself slip into his thoughts as they were led through the familiar corridors. Finally, they entered a great arched hallway. The light could be seen on either side and the sounds of a large crowd were above them.

Finally, they reached a flight of stairs which they climbed. At the top was a gate with two guards showing their respect for the prince as he approached. Drums began beating rhythmically and the crowd, which had been murmuring to themselves fell deadly silent.

The silence deafened him and for a moment he could hear his heart beating nervously in his chest. The gate was opened. Afador gave Remus one final glance and Remus nodded, unable to go any further. The drums continued as Afador stepped out into the arena before him. Everyone else remained perfectly silent.

As part of the deal, they had given Sador his choice of where and when the battle should be. Much to everyone's surprise he had chosen to fight four days after they had taken him by surprise. He had also chosen to fight in the *Olem.* Afador had only been to the *Olem* a few times during his life and he had never liked it. Nonetheless, he knew this was his father's favorite arena.

The courtyard was sealed off by a ten-foot tall rock wall and after that nets. In addition, soldiers would soon be placed on the inside of the bordering wall, eliminating any chance of escape through those routes. The courtyard contained nothing else. Just a large open space.

Afador took his place in the middle, next to two soldiers. Drums started again, this time deeper drums and more of them. Still, the crowd made no sound as the gate on the other side was opened. His father walked out, his chin up high. He took his place twenty paces from Afador, also with soldiers to either side. King Sador snickered as he looked at Afador.

"Four days and this is the best you can look?" Sador taunted. "I wanted the people to see I wasn't going to be killing some innocent helpless whelp. But I guess if you insist on dying."

"I have no plans on dying," Afador said. Both of them put on their helmets. Sador laughed.

"Things never go as planned!" Immediately Sador pulled his sword and attacked Afador. Afador jumped back, surprised and caught off guard by his father's ferocity. His father swung again and struck Afador in the head. The sword bounced off his helm, but not without leaving a sizable dent. Afador was knocked off his feet by a blow aimed at his chest. Afador rolled to the side as his father brought down his sword again.

Afador blocked the next blow and then swung his leg at his father's feet. His father fell flat on his back but avoided being hit by Afador's blade. Sador quickly got to his feet, lunging forward with another fierce attack. Afador blocked them all but backed up eventually reaching the soldiers stationed along the wall. His father paused and let a heckling laugh.

"Is the big bad prince suddenly afraid?" Sador mocked. "I used to think you were a good fighter."

"I'm still standing," Afador reminded. "Perhaps one should not stop to talk because he needs a break." A few people in the crowd stirred at his remark as Afador launched into a vicious attack.

The match continued for almost an hour as the ringing of steel on steel filled the arena. Their armor was dented and uncomfortable as they repeatedly struck each other. Both of them had thrown off their helms which had been dented to the point they couldn't wear them any longer.

A fierce blow struck Afador in the leg and he yelled out in pain. The armor had stopped it, but damage had still been done. Sador paused for a moment, reveling in the injury he may have caused.

Afador launched himself in the air with his good leg and extended the other towards his father. His foot found its target, landing in the middle of Sador's chest guard. His sword and shield went flying as they both tumbled onto the ground. His father's head struck the ground. Still, Sador got up faster than Afador would've expected.

Afador scrambled to get up to his feet with a leg that was now throbbing and burning with fire. Sador grabbed his shield in one hand and swung his sword low with the other, Afador stooped low to block it and was swiftly struck in the face with the shield.

Afador ignored the blood coming from his face and stood. He was swiftly knocked to the ground again, kicked ruthlessly by his father. Afador swung his sword wildly, but his sword was easily knocked out of his hands. Sador brought his foot down on Afador's breastplate, pinning him to the ground. He stooped low, his foul breath chilling Afador to the bone.

"I think I call this defeat," Sador mocked through his heavy breathing.

"No!" Afador said. He grasped his shield and with both hands brought it against his father's shin. Sador cried out as the armor dented and split, each movement now causing it to cut into his skin.

Afador scrambled to his feet and with both hands holding his shield, attacked his father. Sador fumbled his weapons and was soon defenseless as Afador continued to strike, swing, and jab at his father with his shield. Sador finally fell to the ground and Afador stood over him. His father weakly held up a hand as he slowly got onto his knees.

"Five minutes!" Sador cried. His breathing was hard and labored, and sweat and blood covered both their faces.

"Three!" Afador exclaimed. He limped away from his father, back to the corner where the guards and Remus were watching.

"You've almost got him," Remus said. "You look terrible though." Afador chuckled lightly and then winced as pain filled his side.

"I hope this doesn't go much longer," Afador said. "I'm not sure how much more I can take."

"Just remember what you're fighting for," Remus said. Remus straitened and looked intently at the king. Afador followed his eyes and noticed his father speaking to a person in the shadows. "Not sure I like that."

"I don't expect my father to keep his word, even if I do defeat him," Afador said. Remus nodded grimly.

"Then there's only one thing to do."

Afador nodded.

"As your prince I command you to do the next things I say without question or comment," Afador started. Remus looked at him knowingly. "Leave this city now. Find Michael and urge him to come to my rescue if it's needed. If I am to die, then take my wife and kids, far from here to Rinevah, and seek the house of Drake Thomas. Marry my wife promptly and remain loyal to her for the rest of your days-"

"Afa-"

"This is an order, Remus!" Afador said as forcefully as he could while keeping quiet. "Spare her the shame and disgrace of being a widow in *this* nation. You know what my father will do if he finds her. Do not let that happen! Understand?"

Remus nodded.

"Good. Now go before your head is wanted like mine already is." Remus started to object but then nodded and was lost to the darkness beneath the stands. Afador picked up his sword and his battered shield in the other, making his way to the middle.

A few brave souls let their voices shout out in support of their prince. At the same time, Afador began to notice archers on the top of the buildings. Afador reached the center and thrust his sword in the air. The crowd came alive, defying the customs of the *Olem,* which were to remain completely silent. The soldiers in the arena shifted nervously. Afador's courage began to grow.

"Well, old man! Are we going to finish this or what!?" Afador taunted. Rage filled Sador's face as he grasped his sword and rushed to Afador. Afador blocked the blows, but with difficulty; his father's anger and hatred grew with every swing.

Sador's sword caught Afador in the hand, causing his sword to fall. Afador was numb to the pain as Sador swung again. He ducked the blow and grabbed his father's arm, twisting him around and throwing him to the ground.

A sickening snap reached his ears as his father's arm was broken. His sword dropped to the ground and Afador quickly snatched it up. His father immersed in pain, noticed the hesitation as Afador didn't swing to kill him like he expected.

"You will never be king!" Sador yelled. "You don't have it in you to kill a defenseless person do you?"

Afador cried out and swung the sword, letting it go right over his father's head. Afador released the sword and let it fly. He thrust his heel into his stunned father, knocking him back onto the hard rock. Afador walked over to him.

"I'm not a murderer like you," Afador cried. "This is your one chance at mercy! Turn and walk out and I'll give you a ship anywhere you please." Sador looked to the gate he had entered through and nodded. He signaled surrender and the crowds cheered. The soldiers at the gate started running out towards Sador.

Afador stood to walk back towards his own gate but hesitated when a great clattering was heard. Afador saw it too late, but Sador had pulled a knife from somewhere under his armor and thrust it into Afador's stomach. A searing pain filled his gut and a great light flashed.

Afador's sight cleared and silence greeted him. He stared at the scene in front of him unsure what was happening. Everything was still as if frozen in time. Afador could hear his own breathing. He glanced to the rooftops, noticing the bowmen were now ready to shoot into the arena. A bald-headed man, dressed in a long black robe strode out from the shadows. Afador instantly recognized him.

"Merderoc."

"I prefer Merderick." The man moved closer. "I must say I'm both surprised and disappointed in you. You have fought valiantly, but for what? Your new *god* Lathon, can't help you. *Isn't* helping you. With everything you've done, you've only succeeded in helping my cause and making yourselves so many enemies that you won't be able to make it out of here alive.

"And the worst part is, this whole thing could've been avoided. There didn't have to be a fight, and you'd still have your dignity. I could in one wave of my hand, reverse all the horrible things that have happened between you and your father.

"However, what I'm more interested in is knowing for myself what has caused you to so easily cast aside the beliefs and traditions that have been a part of your culture for longer than you've even been alive." He walked closer to Afador and paced. Afador tried to move but found that he couldn't. He was stuck in his place.

"Do us a favor Afador, try to think of everything as if you're a great puppet master behind the scenes. You have this fine nation of Tuthar, who has been at peace for generations. Never any real threats of war. You've been protected. The people who need something to believe in, *have* something to believe in. The rituals, sacrifices, and demands of the *gods,* have worked perfectly. Society is flourishing, the people are following the leadership. To me it all seems perfect and peaceful wouldn't you agree?"

Afador didn't respond.

"Your silence gives me joy, for that means you cannot think of an explanation. In short, it's because there is none. To speak the name of Lathon is to stir hatred in the hearts of men. To invite disaster upon yourself. As you can see my dear prince, you are now reaping what you've sown. Which is why I feel little remorse for you. You have brought this on yourself.

"Now for the big question!" Merderick exclaimed. "Since you've devoted yourself to Lathon, what have you gained that is worthwhile? Your friends are gone, your family is lost, and your own people have turned their backs on you. I suspect you will very soon lose your life! What has *Lathon* done for you?" Merderick struck Afador and he fell over. Afador stood to his feet, thinking deeply. Merderick relaxed, grinning like a schoolboy who had just accomplished a great feat. "Nothing?"

"I have gained many things," Afador said. The sorcerer made an expression, having not expected the conversation to take this turn. "I have gained compassion."

"Compassion is for the weak!" Merderick argued.

"Is it?" Afador asked. "Because last time I checked, it takes more courage to leave an enemy alive than to kill him in cold blood."

"If you believe that then you are a fool! You leave someone alive, they may come back and stick a knife in your back like Sador just did to you!"

"Conviction!" Afador exclaimed with more force. "I followed your ways and beliefs out of fear. Lathon does not cause a fear, the kind which would leave a person withering in the corner, unable to do anything. Instead, I am given courage in a desperate situation, the ability to think straight and clear though storms may come. There is truly a power as a result of following Lathon! For even now, this power gives me the words I am speaking and it is how I know that you are far from what you claim to be!" Merderick glared, but otherwise seemed undeterred.

"Anything else?" Merderick mocked. Afador held eye contact with him for several seconds.

"Something that I sense is so far beyond you, you cannot fathom it in any way."

"Do tell?"

"Love." Merderick blinked as if he was trying to hold his composure together but had failed in that one area. "You cannot give what you do not know, and I see in your eyes that you fail to see how love could possibly aid me in this situation. No doubt, you will probably tell me that it won't help me in my situation. Little do you know, that love is what gives me both compassion and conviction, and without the three of them you wind up with mindless, detestable rituals that leave you more empty than when you started. And what do you get for it? Nothing but a rotting corpse behind them!"

"Perhaps I can find a better way to convince you that you're making a wrong choice!" A blinding flash of light filled Afador's eyes and then he saw that everything was alive and moving again. His father breathed heavily, staring at the dagger in his hands, wondering why Afador was still alive. Soldiers grasped Afador tightly. Behind Sador, Merderick walked up.

"How are you still alive?" Sador cried. Afador didn't respond. Merderick pulled up alongside;' a sly grin across his face.

"How about a true test of his loyalties?" Merderick asked. Afador was unsure whether his father could see and hear the Sorcerer or not. Anger consumed his father's face, making it hard for Afador to look at him. Sador angrily threw the dagger on the ground and stomped to the gate in the shadows.

Afador watched in horror as his wife Hadassar was dragged by the hair, across the hard stone to the center of the arena. Sador threw her on the ground at Afador's feet. She was naked. Bruised and beaten. Afador hardly knew how to respond.

"I told you I would find the little wretch!" Sador boomed. "I have yet to find your children but they will soon join her in shame and disgrace. He stooped down and grabbed her by the hair, lifting her up. He stuck a knife to her throat. "Give up your ways and your wife will be spared!"

Afador hesitated for a moment, unsure of what he should do. He looked Hadassar in the eyes. She held eye contact for only a moment, before glancing back to the ground, lost in her shame. Time seemed to stop and the only sounds that Afador could hear were his wife's heavy labored breathing. She looked up to him again, trying to form words.

"What do you think he should do?" Sador mocked, throwing Hadassar on the ground. He picked up his sword and held it to her neck.

"Not do what you ask," Hadassar finally responded. Sador raised his sword and in an instant brought it down to Hadassar's neck. Afador's heart stopped and then came alive realizing another blade had stopped it from striking her. He looked to see Michael standing across from Sador.

Merderick who had been standing alongside Sador all this time, squirmed and tried to slip away. Hadassar breathed a sigh of relief, now dressed in a dark brown dress, saved from shame. Afador tried to move towards her but was still held by the soldiers. Sador looked at Michael's sword and then at him. Confusion and anger flooded his father's face.

IDOLS & TRINKETS

"I'm going to say this only once!" Michael stated, looking at Afador. "Run."

Afador violently spun, taking the soldiers off of their feet. Arrows were fired down from the rooftops. In dire need, Afador pulled one of the soldiers up and carried him, using him as a shield. Afador ran to the gate he had entered through and dropped the soldier on the ground. Five arrows protruded from his body.

The citizens watching cried out in one voice, many of them jumping the barricades, running to give their support in whatever way they could. The bowmen atop the rooftops fired down on anyone they wished. Afador rushed through the gate, which was hastily opened, and soon escaped the building to his horse which was saddled and waiting for him. The reigns were held by a Makkura.

Afador jumped on and urged his horse forward. He entered the streets, which were now filled with people who were hearing the great noise rising from the arena. Afador blew his horn, the sequence of different tones calling the people to arms. Many looked towards him as he stopped in the town square.

"Citizens! This is our fight! Stand for what you believe. May the blessing of Lathon be with us all!" The great crowd cheered and scrambled frantically as several soldiers on horses sped into the square, trampling and knocking over citizens. The soldiers on top of these horses were dressed differently. All in black, their armor bearing none of the markings of Tuthar.

Afador let out a cry and spurred his horse forward. Behind him, the black horses followed, whether he had lost them or not he couldn't be sure. For the moment they had all faded from his sight. Afador turned the last corner, seeing the gate before him. He sat up, startled as the gate was shut, and blocked by fifty men. Afador pulled his horse to a stop, but not before something struck him in the left side. Afador fell off his horse, which promptly ran off the way they had come.

"Afador. Really?" Merderick stepped into plain sight. Afador tried to make sense of how Merderick had beaten him to the gate and with so many men. "You didn't think I would let you get away that easily did you?" He paused for a moment. "I just was hoping to revisit that conversation that we started the other day, you know the one where you reconsider all of your actions, and I won't kill

431

your family."

"You didn't kill them the first time, why should I think that you will kill them this time?" Afador asked. "It seems you've revealed much and you're out of options. I'm not asking for your permission, I'm saying here and know that as for me and my house, we will serve Lathon. You have no foothold Merderick! Be gone and take your chaos with you!"

"Make me," Merderick taunted. Suddenly loud bells began ringing beyond the city gates. Afador's heart stirred for a moment. Merderick was seemingly unconcerned. "Go ahead, take your best shot."

"The bells of the watchtowers are ringing," Afador said, his mind racing to figure out what was happening.

"Of course they are," Merderick said. "What does it matter?"

"Those bells have not rung in all my life."

"You have had a peaceful life, thanks in part to me and the ways of your ancestors," Merderick explained. "Now either take your best shot at me or bow down and end this madness."

"You're not curious about why the bells are ringing?" Afador asked. Merderick was visibly starting to lose his patients, though he was trying to keep his composure.

"I do not care why the bells are ringing!" Merderick exclaimed. "I want one thing right now, and by the powers I have, I am going to get done!"

"You're trying to ignore them," Afador stated. "You know they will bring ill news."

"How could you possibly know that!?

"I can see it in your eyes," Afador said. He held Merderick's gaze for several seconds. Another watchtower joined in the ringing of bells. "Two towers? Most unusual." Finally, a horn was blown on the other side of the wall and Merderick's face washed white. He spun around, looking in disbelief as the gates to the city were shattered in a flurry of red and green sparks.

Panic came over Merderick and his men as they scrambled to get away. Hundreds of Makkura rode in on large brown horses, and Remus rode at the lead of the great host. Swords were drawn and a battle cry escaped them as they

432

quickly chased down Merderick's horsemen at the gate. Remus pulled up and let the others in the company go around him. Remus pulled his horse up alongside Afador. He snapped his fingers and another horse came bounding up alongside.

"Glad to see you, my prince," Remus greeted. Afador swung himself up into the saddle and drew the sword by his side. Together they rode into the battle, fighting alongside the Makkura. Within an hour the city was free of the noise of battle and they breathed a sigh of relief.

An hour passed as Afador and the city briefly celebrated their victory before turning their attention to cleaning and repairing everything from the battle that had taken place. Hadassar was brought to him and they wept in each other's arms, tears of joy staining their faces. A few minutes later his two children were brought. They sat together for some time and talked and shared things that they had been holding in for some time. For the first time Afador felt like they had finally become a real family.

"I'm sorry Your Majesty," Michael said as he approached them. They sat on the edge of a bridge, Remus alongside. "It seems I have to break this happy moment, with news."

"Please continue," Afador said.

"My men have chased the Sorcerer Merderick, from the city, he is nowhere to be found on this island. His men were caught and destroyed. However, there is still a king to contend with." Afador sighed heavily.

"I suppose I must?" Afador asked. Michael nodded.

"My orders say that you must do it. I am not allowed."

Afador rose and everyone else came with them. They made their way back towards the arena and in the center of it was his father. Chains were fastened to his arms and legs and he looked upon them with malice and hatred in his eyes.

"So the coward returns?" Sador cried. "How nice of you to come and see your lowly father."

"That's enough," Afador said sternly. "This city and the people have stood together and we reject your ways. Upon my word, if you give up your evil ways and change your heart you will be able to live. If you choose-"

"You're not going to kill me yourself?" Sador asked. "Just goes to prove what I said earlier about you is right....you are a coward and unworthy to be king. I regret your proposal. Kill me now and end this madness!"

"No," Afador replied. "I am not a murderer like you. I give you grace this one time. You will be marched out of the city and escorted to a place far from here by the Makkura. Return in peace and you shall be welcomed like a father should be. If you return and take action against any citizen or my family you will surely be killed. Do I make myself clear?" Sador seethed but finally nodded.

"Strip the king of everything he has, give him only the most tattered and worn tunic in the city. He is no longer a king and is no longer welcome. Remus, send word to everyone in the city about what has happened here."

The word was sent out and Sador was marched out the gates as Afador had said. They assembled at the main gate of the city as his father was marched out of the city and lost beyond sight. Afador stood atop the wall and addressed the crowd.

"My fine nation and people! This is a day that must be remembered forever. The day that we passed the test and our salvation was made possible, though it seemed like a lofty idea so far away that we could barely catch sight of it. Lathon has been with us and *that* is why we have come through the trials that the day has presented to us. I offer myself to be your king, but only if we should devote all our lives and being to serving and learning more about the great Lathon!" At that moment Michael stepped onto the wall, and Remus and another of the Makkura flanked him on either side.

"Such fine words, and truly the signs of a changed heart can be seen by all," Michael addressed the crowd. "Will you have this man as your king?" A great shout went up throughout the city. Remus stepped forward, bringing a crown that Afador had never seen before.

"Where did you find this?" Afador asked, inspecting it closely. Remus motioned towards Michael who smiled at him.

"The world is full of strange secrets," Michael replied. "I cannot reveal specifics about how or when this crown was given to me, but I can say that it is the crown of the tenth king of Tuthar. He was one of the finest of Tutharian kings. He stumbled across the ancient scrolls and for a while the nation followed in accordance with Lathon's will. Now that your heart is changed, I think it is only fair that you also bear the same crown."

Afador could hardly speak as Remus gently placed the crown on his head. Afador looked out at all the people and then down at Hadassar and their kids, smiling. Michael motioned for Afador to step forward. Afador did so, understanding everything in a new way.

"My Lords and Ladies, men and woman, all within this great nation. I give you your king. Afador! Hail the king!"

Two days passed and when everything was made right a great feast and celebration filled the city. Remus sat with Afador and Hadassar on the palace balcony looking out over the city, which seemed completely new. Music filled the air and the very air itself had a more pleasant aroma to it.

"So what now?" Remus asked. "The city and people are free. What should we do? I can't think we were meant to go through all of this and then sit back in our chairs and do nothing."

"I agree," Hadassar said. "There is much to work on here, but my heart feels like we need to look towards other nations. Where we may be able to also bring the same kind of peace and liberation that we have felt here." Afador thought long and hard for several moments.

"My heart is truly changed, and while I was hanging on the wall in the town square, I had much time to consider this scenario. I believe it is our calling to help other nations in some way, but I do not think it should be the way of giving food, drink, or bed to people. Any government can do that, and although those things are good; they do not address the problems.

"I feel like a better course of action is to share with them the good news of Lathon. Let him revitalize their souls, and then they may revitalize their own worlds. We must learn more about Lathon and the world around us. We have been an isolated nation for a long time. It needs to end.

"What I propose is we seek out the house of Drake Thomas and learn everything we can about Lathon and his ways. From there I wish to send for his friend, Ellizar the Dwarf. If he is willing I would very much like him to join us in Tuthar."

"Why?" Remus asked. "I'm not questioning it, I'm just wondering what your thinking is behind it. I would think he will be quite bitter and angry over what happened in the past."

"That may be the case, but still I need to see him and ask forgiveness and try to make right what my father did to them."

Chapter 30

ESCAPE FROM HARBRIGGE

Isabel and Borea remained in the corners of their cell. It was fairly dark in the prison so this part of the plan would be easy. They heard the unlocking of the dungeon door and the shuffle of guards entering. Two guards came to the door and stopped, Catterick was the only one who was visible and lay in the middle of the cell.

"I thought there were three of them?" one guard asked.

"I just heard bring the prisoners in cell number seven. This is cell number seven."

"But shouldn't we check again to see?"

"No."

A key was slid into the cell door and the iron door was pushed open. The guards walked in and Isabel sprung from the shadows. Borea did the same. They rushed the guards running into them, grabbing their swords as they fell to the ground. The guards scrambled to get back to their feet but stopped when Isabel held her sword across their throats.

"Don't scream and you won't die!" Isabel warned. The guards nodded. "Now get up and strip." Within a minute the guards had stripped of all their things and Isabel and Borea changed into the uniforms and armor. The guards were tied up in their undergarments which would make an interesting scene when their escape was discovered. Isabel gave Catterick one long hug and kissed him on the cheek. He smiled weakly as they both stepped out of the cell and closed the gate. Borea grabbed his newly acquired keys from his belt and walked to the cell where all the crew was held.

"Good to see you boys!" Borea exclaimed throwing the cell door.

437

"What's going on?" several of the men whispered.

"I'll explain on the way. We're going to have to make for the Trinin and make way in record time."

"It's not even stocked," one of the men said.

"It doesn't have to be. Like I said, I'll explain on the way." The crew happily walked out of the cell, joining Isabel at the dungeon door. She motioned for them to wait.

"Once Aspen starts making a scene the guards will leave this hall and then we can go."

"How is your Taruk even going to know where we are?" Borea asked.

"I can communicate with her through thoughts. She's on her way."

They waited anxiously. Without warning a rumble shook the floor. Bells frantically tolled from outside they heard many cries and calls for help. The guards outside the prison left their posts. Isabel motioned them forward and they stepped out of the dungeon. They followed behind the guards, but not close enough to be noticed. A minute later they stood looking out a large archway watching the carnage unfold.

The night sky was lit by fires that burned everywhere and amidst all the smoke and fire they could see the massive shape of Aspen charging around, occasionally taking flight. Arrows and spears were loosed but were easily blocked by her thick hard skin. A number of soldiers sat atop horses, their back to them."

"When we get out there, get a horse and a sword as quickly as you can," Isabel said. "Make for the Trinin and I'll meet you at Sunkre."

"Yes mam," Borea said. They walked out of the archway and rushed at the men who had their backs turned. They grabbed the men atop of the horses and threw them to the ground. They quickly scooped up the swords and mounted the horses, spurring them forward. Isabel and Borea led the way, hardly being noticed as they galloped past the chaos.

They rode out of the palace gates and through the crowds of party guests who were in a panic. A few minutes later they turned from the main road, starting on a path that Borea said would lead them to the coastline. They pushed their horses at breakneck speed through the forest and the trees.

They exited the woods and entered onto the street next to the harbor. To their surprise, the street was empty as everyone was focused on the fires and destruction that Aspen was causing. They rode hard to the docks, and Borea stopped them.

"We were suspected from the beginning. Our ship is missing!" Borea exclaimed.

"Get another one," Isabel replied. She turned her horse and galloped away riding down the coast away from the city. She galloped along the shore, dust trailing behind her. Ten minutes passed before she turned into the woods and pulled her horse to a stop at Darrison's camp. Darrison woke and cried out, reaching for his weapon. Isabel quickly withdrew her helmet, letting her grey frizzy hair fall down for him to see.

"Why on earth are you dressed like that?"

"Long story. We need to go now!" He sensed her urgency and quickly grabbed his few belongings and made for his ship. Isabel followed him aboard and within a minute they were starting down the river.

"What's the plan mam?" Darrison asked.

"We make way for Sunkre."

"Never heard of that island."

They exited the river and put down the sails, the small ship easily pushed through the water.

***

Borea searched the dock, unable to spot the Trinin anywhere. Panic overtook him for a moment as Isabel rode away as they had planned. The horses shuffled anxiously and the men mumbled to themselves.

"What now?" one of his men asked. Borea scanned the other ships.

"We take the Crooked Star!" Borea replied.

"The Crooked Star? It's a Cordellian navy vessel."

"And we're going to take it!" Borea said. "Anyone who objects stays behind now. Jones and Ciaphus ride the sea wall and open the gates for us when we get there."

"We're really doing this?" Ciaphus asked.

"Yes, now get moving or we'll all die. Everyone else ride with me and prepare to fight!" They spurred their horses further down the docks finding the Crooked Star, largely ungaurded. Borea pushed the horse up the gangway. The few crew members who were aboard stood to arms. Horns and bells echoed from the ship as the crew tried to raise an alarm. Within a minute all the crew members were tied up and Borea's men moved to their posts.

"Raise anchor. Sails at full. Ratori in the crow's nest."

"I won't see much at this time of night."

"I know where we're going and I'm not so much concerned about land as I am about the navy ships who will likely be in pursuit of us."

The ship soon pushed through the water, faster than was normal for in the port. The sounds of the Cordellian navy preparing to make way carried through the air. Horns and bells ran out everywhere. They sailed towards the opening in the sea wall. The gate was open, with Jones and Ciaphus standing to the side of the opening.

"Now or never boys!" Borea yelled as they passed through the archway. The two men got a running start and leapt onto the moving ship as they left the port behind them. "Snuff the lights!" All the lanterns were quickly snuffed or hidden below deck.

"Where are we headed?" the crew asked.

"One hour from here is an island known as Toinwer."

"Toinwer?" The crew exclaimed.

"Once there, we need to sail around to the southwest corner of the island. There we'll find a small bay. I have it on good authority once we're there we should be able to see what we're looking for."

"What are we looking for?" the men asked.

"A ship by the name of Prater." A few of the men stirred at the name.

"The ship doesn't exist," a crewman piped up, some others voiced their agreement.

"Don't worry, if what I've been told is true and there is a bay on the southwest corner then I will be able to find it without question."

"What if you're wrong?"

"We'll find out soon enough," Borea answered.

"Are you telling me we just escaped prison to send ourselves to a forbidden island where we may or may not find a mythical ship?"

"Yes."

"Why?"

Borea smiled. "Let me tell you a story."

***

Catterick listened to the chaos that was raging outside. The two guards were still tied up in his cell and as time passed it became clear that no one was going to be checking on the dungeons. He stood and hobbled over to the cell door, pushing it open as Isabel hadn't locked the gate afterward.

He smiled as he moved to the door of the dungeons and stepped out into the hall. He carefully crept through the halls until he reached the main courtyard. Fires burned uncontrollably and every soldier and guard lay dead. Sorrow overcame him as he looked at all the death and destruction.

He listened intently to the noise of the city, noting that it was free of fighting or panic. He carefully walked through the silent courtyard, unease overtaking him. With each second that passed the silence became thicker and heavier. It grew difficult to stand or even to move his feet.

With much effort, he made it to the gate which opened up to the city below. The gate was broken and charred by fire and the stone walls looked no better. The harbor was filled with activity as nearly thirty navy ships were being sent to sea.

"May Lathon's protection be on you my daughter," Catterick said. The ground shook as though a bell had tolled once. Vibrations rippled through the city and spread all the way to the coast. The rock walls that he stood beneath rattled and small pieces fell to the ground. The ships in the water seemed to bob up and down for a moment as the strange shock wave continued.

Catterick felt his strength return as he looked to the left and saw a massive green Taruk sitting in the empty street. The Taruk stood and faced him. Catterick trembled, slowly moving closer to the Taruk.

"I'm guessing your name is Aspen? At least that's why my daughter said." The Taruk seemed to sit up straighter as if to answer his question. "What I say to you next may not seem too strange to you, but it seems very weird to me, for I have never met a living Taruk before. Can I ride with you?"

Aspen lowered herself to the ground and Catterick with much effort pulled himself up. The Taruk started to move and Catterick called out to stop.

"I'm just an old man, I'd prefer to have a ride that won't give me a heart attack." The Taruk shook her head and lazily pushed off the ground. Catterick's fear melted away as he rode atop the great beast. They flew in silence, heading out over the open sea leaving the nation of Cordell behind.

***

Thick fog blocked the natural light from the sun. The ocean was relatively calm despite all the wind. Isabel sat up having let exhaustion overtake her for the past couple of hours. Darrison stood next to her as their small boat pushed through the water.

"I'm getting too old for this," Isabel said. Darrison chuckled.

"I have a lot to learn about all of this," Darrison said. "All things considered I think we managed to give everyone the slip. I haven't seen any Cordellian ships."

"Still we can't be too careful," Isabel said. "In this fog, anything could happen." Silence fell over them as Isabel moved to the front of the ship.

"What are you thinking about?" Isabel asked.

"Iyla."

"Good thing to think about. Don't worry we'll see her again."

"How can you be so sure of that?"

"Logically, it does a person little good to worry about things. And secondly, we serve Lathon, who can stand against him?"

"Good point," Darrison agreed. "It's just hard to imagine an entire island being burned. No matter how small it is."

"I was surprised too, but everyone got off okay. I understand that you miss her. I sent her with my husband and I miss him very much."

"If he could see the adventure we've been on!"

"He wouldn't be too surprised, he has been right alongside me for a very long time." Isabel stared to the east.

"What's on Sunkre and for that matter where is it? I've sailed for some time and have never heard of it."

"My father's work is on that island and he's charged me with the task of finishing what he started."

"What's your father's name?"

"Catterick. You know him as the Count of Durio Helmar." Darrison stood looking dumbfounded.

"Are you serious?"

"Very."

"That'll take me some time to get used to. This would mean you are Iyla's?"

"Half-sister," Isabel said. "We're just fifty or so years apart. It's interesting to be sure."

"So this further means once Iyla and I are married you're going to be my sister-in-law?"

"I guess it does," Isabel said. "I've never been a sister-in-law before. I hope I'm a good one."

"My mother used to always say, *'learn something new every day so you won't be stupid',* I certainly learned something new today!"

"Here to make your life interesting."

"You're succeeding."

"I'm about to succeed again," Isabel said pointing off the stern. He turned and they both looked at a single ship looming behind them.

"Well my sister-in-law, I'm not sure if you're a blessing or a curse," Darrison said. They both chuckled. "If that's a Cordellian navy vessel, then we're good as dead. This is just a small two-person boat. We don't stand a chance of outrunning them."

"True, but there are other alternatives." Darrison gave her a confused look. "We have two options. We can fight them, which would result in a very worthy, but memorable death. Or we can disappear."

"How are we going to do that?"

"You have storage compartments on the ship. I say we disappear into one of them" Nothing else had to be said. Darrison quickly opened one of the compartments and they laid inside it and closed it as best they could. Isabel lay her sword across her chest, while Darrison drew a knife. The little boat rocked unsteadily with no one steering it, but still, they lay still and quiet.

Before long the sound of a ship approaching reached their ears. Ropes, hooks, and the sound of feet hitting the deck reached their ears. Darrison and Isabel both grabbed the hilts of their weapons.

In an instant, the compartment was opened and Darrison and Isabel thrust their weapons up. They caught the first man off guard and he stumbled back in a fit of shock. Isabel jumped to her feet, fighting the next men as Darrison followed in her footsteps.

They quickly maneuvered around the small ship, blocking blow after blow. Darrison slashed at one man and then was overrun as three of them came running right towards him. Without much effort, they turned him to Isabel with a knife to his throat.

"Drop the sword, or we cut his neck!" the men growled. Isabel let her sword clatter to the deck of the ship. She was surrounded by soldiers who roughly tied her and marched her up the gangway to the ship that had the Vengeance written on the bow. Five other ships floated in the water nearby.

Isabel and Darrison were thrown to the ground and beaten before a commanding voice ordered them to stop. Isabel looked to see Drayvin coming down the stairs towards them.

"Tell me daughter of Catterick? Was your feeble escape attempt worth it? Your Captain Borea escaped to find that his ship had been detained, your father was left in prison, by you. And now at the end of it all, you find yourself once again at my mercy. You must forgive me, I was too polite last time."

"And you?" Drayvin said, turning his attention to Darrison. "I have no idea who you are. You are nothing and always will be, and today you shall die alongside this woman Isabel." He turned to one of his men. "Get some rope and hang them off the bow of the ship. If the sharks don't eat them before we get back to port the citizens will surely see what happens to those who cause problems in my kingdom!'"

Darrison and Isabel struggled to break free of the men, but their grip was iron and before they knew it, nooses had been strung around their necks. They were dragged to the front of the ship, where the ropes were attached to the railings. The men pulled them to their feet, one holding a knife to each of their throats.

"And now according to our laws, I must give you the chance to say a final last word," Drayvin mocked. "Go ahead! Try and change my mind."

"To Lathon be the glory!" Darrison called out. The men jeered and cursed him.

"If you had called out to me, I could save you...where is Lathon? I don't see him here," Drayvin mocked. "If you were trying to gain my sympathies, you failed miserably. " The crew laughed. Isabel meanwhile had her eyes closed, uttering a prayer they couldn't here."

"How about you half-breed?" Drayvin asked. "Any last words."

"If you throw us over the bow of this ship, the God we serve can save us from death. Know that. But even if Lathon does not save us, we want you, O great one, to know this. We will not serve you and we do not regret anything we have done. Our souls are secured and our debt has been paid. We will die in peace."

"Then enjoy dying half-breed!" Drayvin cried. The crew laughed and spit on them. "Force them to the rails, hang them when I say." Darrison and Isabel sat on the rails. Darrison looked to Isabel who was smiling. He gave her a confused look and she pointed to her ears.

Faint and distant voices echoed through the fog. Everyone aboard the ship was deaf to it as they were waiting for the king's orders.

"Hard to starboard!" voices frantically called out, from over the water. The Vengeance now grew quiet, crew members stared into the fog. Isabel carefully began to untie her hanging rope from the railing. Darrison quietly began doing the same.

"What?" came a confused voice.

"Hard to starboard!" the voices yelled out again.

"Why? I don't see anything!"

"A ship! A Cordellian navy ship!" voices cried out.

"Hard to starboard!" the voice who had been confused yelled. The curiosity of the men aboard the Vengeance turned to fear as the bow of an enormous ship larger than any Isabel had ever seen, was revealed from the fog. Isabel smiled, reading the name of the ship on the bow.

Prater.

The crew panicked and Isabel and Darrison grabbed onto the railing as the bow of the immense ship struck the back of the Vengeance. The Prater was pushed up out of the water as it rode up over the deck.

The ship was jarred and then split in two as the weight of the Prater was more than the Vengeance could withstand. Isabel and Darrison clung to the rail as the bow of the ship was lifted straight up. The men aboard the Prater yelled out.

"Captain! It's Isabel!"

"Get her and the boy!" Borea's voice boomed. Ropes were tossed out to Isabel and Darrison who were still clinging to the bow which was quickly being pulled underneath the water. They both grasped the ropes and let go of the ship, swinging freely until they struck the side of the Prater. They were pulled up onto the deck as the bells of the other ships rang fiercely.

"Nice to see you, Isabel!" Borea yelled from the helm. Isabel and Darrison quickly joined the crew as they carried out the orders that Borea commanded. Behind them the Vengeance had been sunk into the water, and a number of the men were clinging to the pieces of wood that floated in the water. "I have to say, I like this ship! It can take an impact."

"Captain, ship on Port side!"

"Ready the harpoons!" Borea yelled. Isabel joined them as they loaded large harpoons and put tension on them.

"These things are huge!" Isabel exclaimed admiring the two-foot diameter hook on the end.

"Everything on this ship is huge!"

"Hold tight!" Borea said. He wheeled the ship to the right, nearly cutting into the front of the ship running alongside them. "Fire!" the harpoons were released, and all of them easily pierced the ship below the water line. Borea wheeled the ship in the opposite direction jarring the lines and yanking the harpoons. The side of the ship buckled and gave way, ripping large holes in it.

"Cut the ropes and load again!" Borea cried. They did as ordered. Two more ships closed in on their stern, one intending to flank either side of them. Isabel left the crew, studying the ship carefully, a sense of familiarity coming to her. The two ships behind had now pulled alongside. They wheeled in towards the Prater, intending to ram it and come aboard.

The harpoons were fired and once again they pierced the ships on either side. Isabel stood staring at another mast on the bow of the ship. A single rope hung down and up above she could faintly see a folded-up sail. She pulled the rope hard and a large sail unfolded, soaring into the air twenty feet above the ship.

The Prater jerked forward throwing them all to the deck as the extra sail caught the wind. The two ships with the harpoons stuck in them were jarred and thrown off course.

"Cut the ropes!" Isabel yelled. Everyone did as she said and the two ships immediately fell behind the Prater. They watched over the stern as the two ships collided and crumbled into the water. They yelled out and celebrated as they made way.

"What in this good earth is that?" Borea asked, marveling at the large sail at the front of the ship.

"A unique feature I've seen on only one type of vessel. The Prater is a Gog ship!"

"What's a Gog?" Borea and the crew asked.

"Story for another time," Isabel said. "I see you found the Prater. Eventful?"

"You have no idea," Borea answered. "We finally got a ship and escaped the port. That was the easy part. About the time that Toinwer came into view, we noticed that three vessels were following us. We started going around the island and found the bay that Catterick had told us we would find, and sure enough at the top a lone clear crystal shone in the rising sun." Borea pointed to the crow's nest where a large crystal was secured in place.

"Much to our confusion the light was coming from the top of a large hill. We needed more time than we had, so we turned the ship slightly to hide the fact that we were letting down the long boats. We got in and cut ourselves free, carefully watching to make sure for a long while that we were hidden by our ship. We rowed into shore and the three ships kept on following our abandoned one and we haven't seen any of them since.

"After that, we made our way up to the hilltop where we had seen the light and found the Prater. We were at first in awe of the gigantic ship, only a few minutes later did we wonder how it was put there in the first place. It turns out the entire ship was sitting on carts of a sort and those were sitting on massive railings that led right down to the bay, much like you would see in a mine. Everyone climbed aboard.

"The ship was held in place by a tremendous bolder with ropes, thicker than any I've ever seen. The ropes were attached to the side railings so we were able to hack at them, though it still took nearly five minutes to get through one.

"When the ropes were cut, that ship hurtled down the rails so fast...just about gave us a heart attack. I thought the ship would crumble when it hit the water, but it's a strong ship and it's a deep harbor."

"And then you just happened to run into us?" Isabel said. Borea laughed.

"Literally. Truly though we had no idea where we were. Come this way." Borea led the way to a hatch that led to the lower deck. Isabel and Darrison both followed him down the stairs grabbing a lantern. They moved through the ship until they reached another hatch on the floor. They stepped down into the cargo hold. "Behold the great treasure of the Count of Durio Helmar!"

Isabel stood speechless as the entire hold was filled with boxes and crates from floor to ceiling. Isabel opened the first box, revealing gold and other trinkets. "I've kept the men from opening any of them. There is a large portion of the second deck that is devoted to the storage of such boxes. And if you can believe it there is a third deck below this one also filled to the brim. Also, we found this." Borea held up a large tarnished key. Isabel took it and studied it carefully before putting it in her pocket. She unlatched two more boxes. One was filled with gold and the second was filled with the same boxes that had set on her family's mantle so many years ago. Isabel held one in her hands wondering what secrets it held. She looked at several of them, noticing that no two of them were the same.

"Well done Captain Borea. When we reach Nain, take these two boxes of gold, and pay yourself and your men handsomely for your service. Until then make way for Sunkre."

"Small problem with that," Borea said, forcing a smile. "I'm a little confused by this map of yours. I quite literally have no idea where we are. If you and Darrison both could come up top and help us sort it out, we'd all be much better off." Isabel laughed.

"So it was literally an accident that you happened to run into the ship we were on?" Borea shrugged.

"Perhaps?"

"No," Isabel replied. "It's just further proof that Lathon can work things out far better than we can. I've planned a number of operations over the years and even I wouldn't have thought of that one!"

It was two peaceful days of sailing until they drew up some of their sails. They slowed their pace as they reached the great sinkhole that bore Isabel's family seal. They traveled around to the east side of the sinkhole for nearly a mile, where a small island no more than a half mile wide in any direction waited for them. They put down the anchor and several men went with Isabel to shore. Aspen stood on the shoreline to greet them.

"It's good to see you my old friend," Isabel said, stroking Aspen's neck. "Did you get father to safety?"

The Taruk hummed happily.

"We're here now what?" Borea asked. Isabel pulled out an old piece of parchment her father had crudely drawn a map on.

"According to the map ahead of us is a steep ravine and in the hillside there will be a door."

They ventured into the forest with Aspen snaking her way in and out of the trees. After several minutes they came to a steep downward slope which turned into sheer rock cliffs that encircled an area at least a thousand feet across. The hole below descended to an unknown depth.

They scoured the hillside for several hours unable to find any door as the map indicated. Aspen continued to walk with them, occasionally jumping into the air and circling the island from the sky. Isabel stood on the edge of the ravine and then noticed a strange narrow stair that descended along the ravine wall.

"Light a torch and let's go!" Isabel said. "I think we have to go down." Borea hastily grabbed a thick branch and looked at his men.

"Flint please?" Borea asked.

"We didn't figure we'd be here that long, we left it on the ship," one of the men replied. They winced as flames streamed through the air and consumed the end of the branch.

"Thank you, Aspen," Isabel said, grabbing another branch and lighting it.

"I think I need to get me a Taruk. Where can I buy one?" Borea asked.

They descended into the dark ravine, carefully descending the narrow stairs for nearly an hour. Finally, they reached the bottom, finding a dark shiny rock floor, covered in skulls.

"This is inviting," Darrison said.

"Must be people who fell in the ravine over the years," Isabel said. They spread out, searching the walls of the ravine. Finally, Darrison called out to them and they hurried towards his torch. Beneath an inch of ivy and overgrowth, a large wooden door lay. "Anyone have an ax?"

A man stepped forward and swung his ax with all his might. A flash of light blinded them and when they could see again they could see that the man was only holding the wooden handle of the ax. The ax head itself was shattered into hundreds of pieces. Isabel marveled at the door which didn't show a single scratch.

"Any other ideas?" Borea asked.

"Aspen!" The Taruk strode through the darkness. "See what you can do."

"They stepped back and Apsen let out a continuous stream of fire that lasted for nearly five minutes. When Aspen closed her powerful jaws they stepped forward.

"Impossible!" Borea exclaimed. "The door's not even hot! Any other ideas?" Isabel was puzzled as they sat staring at the door for nearly twenty minutes.

"The key!" Isabel exclaimed, pulling it out.

"There's no keyhole. How's the key supposed to work?"

"Durio wouldn't have had this key only open the chests would he?" Isabel said. Borea's eyes lit up. Isabel held the key in front of her and then tapped the door with it. A second passed before creaking came from the door. As though some unseen force was undoing a lock from the other side.

In an instant, the large door swung wide open, a wave of stale air hitting them in the face. The shaft was vacant and they started down the long dark tunnel until they entered into an area that Isabel recognized. They were now beneath the island with the sinkhole. In front of them was the same chest where she had found the note.

"One chest?" Borea said. "Seems a little disappointing after all the work it took to get here."

"Check all the side caves and rooms that we passed along the way," Isabel ordered.

An hour later everyone had reported that every cave and small room was filled to the brim with boxes and crates. Many of them were filled with gold and gems, but just as many were filled with parchments and the strange boxes that Isabel was eager to study further.

By midday the following day they had loaded the numerous boxes of cargo on the ship, courtesy of long ropes and Aspen who effortlessly lifted the crates to the deck of the Prater. When the boxes and crates were all loaded, there was hardly anywhere for them to walk. They made way and Isabel sent Aspen ahead to Nain to tell Morgrin they were coming.

***

The bell on the Prater rang loudly as the ship floated into the port at Nain. A great crowd had gathered almost as soon as the ship had appeared on the

451

horizon. Aspen flew happily in the sky, along with Destan and Ezzion. Isabel looked over the railing of the ship spotting Iyla standing alongside Morgrin. To his left, Rade and Temperance waited hand in hand, to greet them.

"Darrison! Tell me what you think of the view?" Isabel said. Darrison searched the people finally seeing Iyla. A tear came from his eyes.

"I like the view," he finally said. "Then again I think I'll like it better from shore." They laughed and waited as the ship was moored and they were allowed to step onto the dock. They felt their feet touch the solid ground and breathed a sigh of relief. They were quickly joined by Morgrin and Iyla who embraced them fiercely.

"My dear, I have never been so happy to see you alive!" Morgrin exclaimed.

"And I've never been so happy to be back on solid ground," Isabel said. "All the adventures I've been on and I've finally concluded that sailing is not the life for me."

"Perhaps not, but it sure has made for quite a tale," Temperance said. She and Isabel embraced.

"And how is Mrs. Rade doing?"

"Quite well thank you. But let's not talk business tonight. Morgrin and Rade have already worked out where to put all the cargo and we can talk more specifically about business later," Temperance said.

"I suppose I have to listen to you seeing you're now the governor's wife."

"I suppose you're right," Temperance said with a wink.

"Then in that case yes mam." Isabel turned to Morgrin. "Where is Catterick? Aspen was supposed to bring him here."

"She did. Come." Morgrin sent for Iyla to join them. Darrison came following after her. Morgrin stopped him.

"Sorry son, but let us have a few words with him first. He has heard you are coming, but there will be time for talking to him in a little bit. Darrison nodded and gave Iyla a kiss on the cheek as he rejoined the crew which had already started unloading the cargo. Morgrin led Isabel and Iyla down the coast to the caves where all the cargo was already being stored. They walked into the only cave with light emerging from it.

They walked through an endless maze of boxes and crates, the contents of which they could easily spend a year going through without giving any of them serious study. Eventually, there opened up a large space with long tables, chairs, and at the far end a roaring fireplace with bookshelves. Catterick sat in one of the chairs, reading a parchment and drinking a cup of tea. Isabel and Morgrin sat in chairs across from him.

"What are you doing?" Isabel asked.

Catterick shrugged. "Reading."

"Good book?" Isabel asked. He smiled.

"Aren't they all?" Catterick asked. "I was merely putting in time until my two daughters and my son-in-law could join me!" He chuckled and handed it to her. "This book, I must say, is one of my favorites." Isabel hastily flipped through the pages.

"Who wrote it?"

"I would love to say I did, but that would not be entirely true," Catterick said. "It took me many years, but finally I cracked the code and was able to translate the chronicle of time."

"Chronicle of time?" Morgrin asked.

"Yes. Isabel no doubt remembers the boxes I had on the mantel?" Isabel nodded. "They are a part of a much greater collection called the žodis."

"žodis?"

"It's the language that's written on the boxes."

"You might have to explain this better."

"The žodis is a language that stumped me for years. It was an interesting form of writing that involved the strange slashes and holes that covered the boxes. Translated into the common tongue žodis literally means 'word.' If you take these boxes and arrange them on a hilltop, when the wind passes through the boxes it will form sentences and words in this language. In one of the crates you no doubt retrieved from Sunkre are all my notes on how to translate it.

"It was difficult and the book nearly took me three years to translate in full. It was a compilation of nearly three thousand žodis blocks. This book tells of the beginning of the world. The beginning of us."

"The Elvish people?" Isabel asked.

"Yes, and everyone else. To say the boxes were created I fear would almost be heresy. I have suspicions on the matter, but this first translated book that I've worked on has only given me more hope and trust in my theory. In this book, in fact, in the opening chapter, you will find three names that would send chills up anyone's spine if they discovered them as I have. Lathon, Adonai, and Elohim."

"All three are spoken of?" Isabel asked. Her father nodded.

"By Lathon's power yes they are," Catterick said. "If you have a deeper knowledge of the ancient scrolls you too would recognize the magnitude of all three names appearing at once. It is my theory that these Zodic boxes...*are*...the ancient scrolls. It's where they were written from. Believe me when I say these boxes have power beyond all imagination...and not everyone will be happy about it, but the one who perseveres to the end will surely benefit in ways never imagined."

"So all of these crates are filled with these boxes?" Iyla asked.

"Most of them. Durio and I had multiple stashes over the countryside. Our work became devoted to the finding and translating of the žodis. Alas, I do not expect to live long enough to see the project to completion."

"That's what we're here for," Iyla pipped in. "I've seen you working on these, day and night, all my life. A powerful urge to help with this project is coming over me. I might be young, but I can still do my part."

"I'm in too," Isabel said. Catterick smiled as the two girls stood before him.

"In that case, I give up my title as the Count of Durio Helmar. I hereby bestow it to both of you. This is your inheritance." He motioned to all the boxes and crates. "I of course would gladly offer help and assistance."

"No time for leisure?"

"Should one rest when they're doing the work of Lathon? Besides I'm not going to sit back and be a boring old person."

"What do you plan to do with your time? Certainly, you're not going to work yourself into a grave," Morgrin said. Catterick thought for a moment.

"Well I'm not used to having lots of leisure time, so although I might take things a little easier than I have most of my life, I imagine I would like to spend it in the nice city of Nain, with my *two* daughters and if possible live in peace for the rest of my days."

"Sounds like a good plan father," Iyla said.

"I look forward to getting to know my half-sister," Isabel said. Iyla who had been filled in on the connection smiled and nodded.

"And perhaps I'll get to see some grandchildren in the future," Catterick said with a wink. "Aspen informed me there would be a young man named Darrison with you. Iyla was nearly overcome with joy when she heard his name." Iyla blushed. "Is he here?" Iyla nodded happily. "I shall sit with him at supper and unless he is very different from what you told me I suspect I shall be giving my blessing on a most happy and wonderful marriage."

"Thank you, father!" Iyla said. Catterick smiled.

"Go tell him I shall have supper with him tonight." Iyla happily left the cave, leaving the three of them by themselves. "And now my dear daughter. I will gladly sit and listen to any number of tales about you and your life for the last fifty-four years. How can I ever make up for the disasters that separated us for so long?

"The disasters were not your fault, nor were they necessarily intended. Let our story be proof that Lathon can take any bad situation and bring good out of it. He can make beautiful things out of things that were only dust and ancient memories."

"Praise be to Lathon!"

Chapter 31
THE WAGES OF WAR

Rachal sat atop her horse, adrenaline already coursing through her veins. Drake sat next to her, studying the terrain. They sat atop a great ravine, under the cover of trees. Altogether one hundred horsemen had been assigned to Drake's command, but all of them were staying well out of the line of sight.

She studied Drake intently, having never seen this side of him before. He studied each inch of the ground a hundred times over, as though there was some hidden message between the grains of soil. He sat poised and ready, seeming far more confident than she had ever known.

When they had met she hadn't known that he was a seasoned soldier, bore a mark, had been called. To say that she had been surprised by the difference between the man whom she had promised to marry and then the man he had become eleven years later was an understatement.

Overall she took comfort in all of this. She had changed too.

Drake sat up straighter as a black featherless bird landed in the tree far above them. Most of the men didn't take any notice of it, but at the sight of it, Rachal's heart came alive. Drake held eye contact with the bird and nodded in acknowledgment.

"The enemy approaches from the east, but in greater numbers than we expected," Drake said.

"How many?" Rachal asked.

"Nearly two thousand," Drake said, falling into thought for a moment. "We need to get a message to Zebethar before they enter the valley. That is more than we planned on and I don't want them to be ill-prepared." A messenger was sent for and within a minute the messenger rode away, sticking to trees for as long as he could.

They waited in silence as a great clamor of armor and feet began to reach their ears. The large army entered the valley and snaked out far behind. They waited impatiently, Drake and Rachal both took note that the black featherless bird had taken flight and was now descending to the valley.

To their surprise, the bird landed fifty feet from the oncoming army. The army stopped and looked around, fear and anxiety struck them and it was evident by the fact that they grew very restless. The Dwarves looked everywhere as though they heard something that scared them. The bird seemed unbothered by the army and casually pecked at the ground.

Finally, after a moment the Dwarf army gathered themselves again and began marching. The bird stood its ground, although by now Rachal wondered if they could see the bird at all. They watched in wonder as the first line of Dwarves fell to the ground as they passed the bird. The Dwarves jumped back in shock as the bodies decomposed in a matter of seconds until nothing but their clothes and armor remained.

The bird, unconcerned with the destruction, or the fact that the Dwarves were flustered, looked at Drake and Rachal. For a moment, all time stopped and they came to understand what was going to happen. The bird took flight and disappeared a moment later.

The army began marching again.

They continued to wait until the entire valley below was filled with the enemy. Drake and all his men began walking their horses out of the forest. They slowly proceeded down the great slope, unnoticed by the soldiers who were now a thousand yards ahead of them.

They continued the pace for another five minutes or so until the end of the valley was clearly visible. Drake let out a cry and spurred his horse forward everyone else doing the same.

Rachal drew her sword and let it swing as the horses crashed into the bewildered and stunned Dwarves. They were trampled beneath the horses as the Elves of Rinevah pressed into them.

As expected the Dwarves initially turned to run, but then were thrown into a manic panic as James and two hundred more horsemen flooded out of the trees and into the valley. They cut them off at the front, leaving no escape route as they slew enemy after enemy.

They pressed further and further into the ranks of warriors, and each time Rachal struggled more and more to kill the enemy attacking her. She grew weary and glanced over to Drake who was having no difficulty. She had never been in a battle before.

She lunged at the Dwarf who had attacked her and he fell to the ground dead. She paused for only a second and regretted it immediately as she was knocked off her horse.

She fell to the ground with a thud and tried to get to her feet as quickly as possible. A big burly Dwarf ran towards her, sword drawn. Instinct kicked in and she blocked the attack and sent her own in return. It was easily deflected and she was struck in the side by another Dwarf who had come barreling towards them. She crashed on the ground and struck her head on the helmet of a fallen soldier.

The world spun and faded, she fought the sensation of falling into unconsciousness and had enough energy left to roll to the right as a knife had been thrown directly at her. She stood to her feet and staggered as she tried to hold her sword. The Dwarf looked at her with a dark light in his eye. Slowly he raised his blade, intending to thrust it into her chest.

An arrow flicked past Rachal's head and buried itself in the dwarf's body. He fell backward and cursed before another arrow struck him. The body fell to the ground, joining the others. Hooves thundered behind her and Drake rode into sight, jumping off his horse and running to Rachal before his horse had even stopped.

"I really need more training before I do this again," Rachal said.

"I think you did just fine my dear." Drake helped Rachal onto the back of his horse and they began picking their way through the war-torn valley. "If it makes you feel any better my first battle was all but a total disaster."

IDOLS & TRINKETS

A shadow passed through the sky, quick and fleeting. Rachal looked but saw no clouds. Only a black featherless bird circled in the sky above as though it was waiting to swoop down and catch its prey. She pointed it out to Drake who held its eye contact for a moment.

"I think we had better get everyone out." Drake reached for his horn and let a great note rise. Other riders returned the call and began retreating. Drake's men pulled out to the rear of the army, while James and his men all rode to either side, leaving the enemy only one direction they could go.

Realizing their plight the Dwarf army began running, tramping many of their own as they fled the valley. The black bird swooped down out of the sky flying low in an unpredictable pattern. Every person that the bird passed over fell to the ground dead. Looking as though they had been through a hundred wars.

Drake and James watched in fear and then spurred their steads in pursuit of the fleeing army. For nearly an hour they chased and hewed down enemies who fell behind.

"This is what's annoying about Dwarves," James exclaimed as they rode together. "They may be short, but they can run like the wind."

"Hopefully they haven't figured out that they're running right into a trap," Rachal said. "As soon as we get to the forest they'll be –" Rachal was interrupted by horns blowing wildly in front of them. They eagerly searched the horizon, their hearts soaring when they spotted the flag of Rinevah shining in the sunlight. "What's your father doing here?"

"Beats me," James answered. "Either way, let's do this!" They drew their swords and the flustered Dwarf army, realizing that they were trapped, began to scatter. Some of them killing each other, eager to spare the other the humiliation of being defeated. Some of them ran, but in the end none escaped.

The sun was beginning to set before the last enemy had been slain. Drake and Rachal cleaned their swords by a roaring campfire. Most of the camp had fallen to sleep immediately, while still others were keeping watch while everyone slept.

"Long day," Rachal commented. Drake set his sword down.

"But we're all alive and well so we can rejoice about that."

"Tell me about that strange bird we saw," Rachal said "I've seen it before on a few random occasions, but from what I saw today I think you've seen it more. What do you know about it?"

"Not much more than you do," Drake answered. "I had until now thought it was just a spy for your mother because that seems to be how it's acted up until now. It clearly possesses some powers, but I did not know that before this afternoon. For all I know it's a different bird that isn't connected to your mother." They fell silent and were lost in their thoughts for several minutes before James approached the fire.

"My father wishes to speak with all of us immediately," James said. They stood and went with him. At the center of camp was a large tent, with purple coverings and lavish furnishings inside. They were announced and entered into the great tent. Large tables were everywhere as well as maps and other important papers.

"My Lord," Drake said. They all bowed before Zebethar who seemed to stand taller and more proud.

"I am glad we achieved victory today," James said.

"I received Drake's message and realized that time was more pressing than I had first thought. I set out at once and it appears we arrived only in time. I have summoned you first to ask for your forgiveness. All of you. I have treated you harshly and unfairly, and I see now that everything you have told me is the truth.

"In light of this, I would like to make it up to you. Drake, I will give you your job back as commander of my armies and I'll double the salary that you were receiving when you left. Also, I will restore Eshunna to perfect condition and give you any piece of land that you ask for as your own. Do you accept this and with it my forgiveness?"

"Yes my lord," Drake replied.

"And James I owe you an apology too, though I am less certain of how I am to repay you for the wrongs I have done. I have treated you like a little child who knows nothing about life or battle. But today you, Drake, and all your men have reminded me of how much I have to learn. Will you forgive your foolish father who is only ever trying to do the right thing?"

"Of course I will forgive you, father," James replied. "As far as how you can repay me, a changed and open heart will be plenty enough. I was most upset when you chased Drake away the last time and as a result, we were both lost for a long time. I do not wish for those events to repeat themselves."

"And they won't!" Zebethar declared. "As for other matters, it seems that a nation has sent forth a force in an attempt to overrun and control one of our towns. It is my belief that they planned to go further inland. Thankfully, they have been prevented from doing so. However, I will not stay idle and let this treachery go unpunished. Tomorrow at the crack of dawn we will ride to the mountains of Nargaroth and put an end to their heathen ways."

The dawn came swiftly and within a few minutes, they had moved out. To Drake's surprise, more soldiers had arrived during the night. Regardless of the motives, Drake was glad to have reinforcements in the event that they had to fight before they reached the mountains.

The sun rose high, shining down on the long trailing snake of soldiers. The procession was slow at first, with everyone trying to get out of the forest and assembled in an organized matter, but soon they were moving at a steady pace.

By midday, the mountains began to appear on the horizon. As they drew nearer to them they could see that grey clouds hung over the mountains. Many of the men, who had only heard stories of Nargaroth over the years, shifted uncomfortably in the saddle and nervously glanced back and forth.

Despite a few murmurs of displeasure from the soldiers, Zebethar pushed on, keeping his head held high. Drake too rode confidently. Despite the dark clouds looming over the horizon their spirits began to rise. James and Rachal also seemed to be lighthearted, a smile on their faces.

They reached the last crest that would reveal them to the walls of Nargaroth riding four abreast. They stopped almost immediately, everyone standing in awe of the sight in front of them.

Thousands and thousands of Dwarf warriors littered the ground that led up to the wall. The great wall of Nargaroth lay in ruins. In one spot it appeared as though a section of the wall and mountain had been blown away. Smoke drifted into the air and created the black clouds they had seen as they approached. Zebethar looked in silence for several moments.

"Heathens," Zebethar scoffed. "They put their trust in the wrong god. Serves them right!" He turned and began heading back the way they had come. Drake, James, and Rachal remained where they were. Finally, Zebethar pulled on the reigns and looked back at them warily. "You linger when we should leave? There is nothing here but carrion and vultures."

"We'll catch up with you and explain later father. There is no threat, but I'm sure our Dwarvish friends would like to look upon and learn what has happened here," James stated. His father turned away without speaking, but they knew he was displeased. The army moved away and was soon out of sight. Melchizedek and Corvil who had been forced by Zebethar, to ride at the back of the procession, now came forward.

"Thank you, James," Melchizedek said. "I am a mixed bag of emotions at the present. I know Nargaroth had many faults, treacheries, and detestable practices, but I cannot help but feel sorrow at the destruction of a city I called home my entire life."

"I understand," James replied. "But I think if we go up to the main gate we will find things quite different from what we thought."

They carefully picked their way through the sea of fallen warriors, eventually leaving their horses and continuing on foot. The smell and destruction of the battle made them gag and would have made them turn back but for the sight of a campfire outside the main gate. Drake smiled to see two men sitting around the fire and a large white Taruk behind them.

The man facing them smiled and stood to his feet, his arms outstretched as he came towards them. Drake smiled as though someone had told him a great story and he wanted to hear it again.

"It is good to see you all!" Aiden exclaimed. The man next to him smiled, his eyes conveying his approval as he also stood to his feet. He carried a great wooden staff and commanded presence even as he stood. "I trust by now you've all met-"

"Yes, we have!" Melchizedek exclaimed. "I have known him for many years, but only now do I fully understand everything that he has done for me!"

"You've all done very well and we're very proud of you," Aiden said. "You've stood your ground; stood for the one who makes all things possible. You have done very well!"

"Sometimes we don't feel that we did," Corvil replied.

"Well from me to you, I would gladly say all of it again!" Aiden declared.

"What happened here?" James asked.

"Justice."

"Looks like death to me," Corvil countered. "Did you have to cause such destruction?"

"Yes we did," Aiden said. "For generations, upon generations, there has been death, prejudice, hatred, murder, immorality…things that should not be and were never meant to endure. The Sorcerer's reach is long, but he forgets his limitations. It was time that they paid a price for their actions." Corvil remained quiet. "I sense that you are wondering how this destruction could be good and just. Allow me to explain.

"Let's say someone you know comes and kills your family. He's not sorry for it. He keeps killing people. You take him to the courts and explain the crime that was committed, but then the judge turns the accused away; chooses not to see it, and lets the man go. Would that be just? Would that be right?"

Corvil shook his head.

"There is always a price to pay for that which separates us from Lathon. It may seem like the nation of Nargaroth has not had the chance to learn the error of their ways and right what was wrong, but they have had many signs, wonders, and people who have reached out to them. Only to be killed by the people of Nargaroth. In the years to come the ultimate price will be paid and all who call on the name of Lathon may be saved, but it is not the time for that just yet."

They all fell silent, lost in their thoughts, pondering the words that Aiden had said.

"It's good to see Elohim again," Drake stated. "Is it safe for Destan to return?"

"Not for a while Drake," Aiden answered. "But don't worry he is hard at work in other parts of the wide world." Drake and Rachal both smiled at the thought.

"Who's Elohim?" Corvil asked.

"The Taruk behind Aiden," Rachal answered.

"I don't see a Taruk," Corvil replied.

"Then let he who has eyes see!" Aiden said. In an instant everyone, save Rachal and Drake, gasped in amazement as they could now see the massive Taruk in all his glory.

"Is he safe?" Melchizedek asked.

"He is not a tame Taruk," the second man said. "But he often brings strength to those who need it, when they need it. When the three are together who can stand against them?"

The others all took turns cautiously approaching Elohim and running their hands over his skin. He rumbled in pleasure, which was enough to scare Corvil into retreating.

They laughed and sat down by the fire, passing the remaining daylight with fellowship. Finally, the last hint of sunlight had vanished from the sky, leaving the stars to stare down at them. Drake and Rachal gazed upwards, grateful that they could look up at the beauty the sky held.

At length, Aiden stood up.

"I'm afraid that I must be going, but I've most enjoyed the fellowship we've shared tonight. But now, though you are likely sad, I have some good news for you. Corvil and Melchizedek, I task you two with the job of rebuilding and leading this city out of the darkness. Though the armies may have come to waste, there are a great number of people hidden deep in their caves, whose hearts are ready to hear the truth. And along those lines, I know that this place will become a very prosperous kingdom if you rule it with justice and morality in accordance with the will of Lathon."

"The work of Lathon will be done!" Melchizedek affirmed. Corvil nodded his head.

"And to you Drake, Rachal, and James, I will see you again. Keep your heads up, your hearts loyal, and remember all that Lathon has done for you." They embraced and said their final goodbyes until finally he climbed upon Elohim's back and was lost to the night sky.

***

Much to Isabel's relief, the days passed slowly as the five of them talked about their different adventures in full detail, so much so that they did little else than sit and talk for nearly a week.

When it was time, a great feast and celebration was held in Nain as Darrison and Iyla were officially married. After the excitement settled down, a week or two later, they began the long and tedious process of sorting through all the crates to see just what they had.

Rade, Isabel, Iyla, and Borea all worked diligently alongside their spouses in their separate roles; but also worked together translating a large number of žodis boxes and experimenting with other strange treasures found in the crates.

Captain Borea and his men were paid handsomely for their services, vowed fealty to Rade and Temperance, and were immediately assigned to a ship in one of the shipping routes. Darrison and many of the other crew members also joined Borea on his new ship *The Belofte.*

The Prater, which was too large and recognizable to be used regularly, was put in a special dry dock in the cliffs of Deuln, a day's sailing from Nain. There they kept the ship secret until they would finally begin the process of retrieving the other stashes that Catterick and Durio had hidden throughout Cordell and other nations. *The Prater* was regularly guarded and maintained, but otherwise forgotten by the people of Nain.

Using Taruks, Isabel and Morgrin also took trips to see Drake and Rachal, and the name of Lathon was praised and exalted in all their homes.

Much to their sorrow, Lily died of her illness and was buried in the town where they lived. Several years passed before Afador sent word to meet Ellizar the dwarf. Ellizar happily returned to meet Afador and lived the rest of his days in Jermin where he lived as a guest of honor and found friendship with Afador.

When he died he was given a burial of honor and was laid to rest next to the the former kings of Tuthar.

Afador's men found Drake in Rinevah and a great friendship grew between them and they visited each other as often as they were able...

Chapter 32

KING OF THE ELVES

One year later...

Aramis shifted uncomfortably. What had started as a strange, hastily thrown-together trial had turned into a nightmare.

It had been seven years since the Emperor and his wife, Jezebel, had been removed from power within the Goshen Empire. In their place Saul and Alexandria had risen and had proved to be wise and fair rulers. Pilas and himself had been allowed to keep their jobs, though the rules that governed them were now less drastic and controlling.

Overall the people of Avdatt were experiencing the most freedom they had ever known, while still having the protection of the Goshen government. On days like today, both Pilas and himself wished they could dismiss their jobs.

Though many approved of what had happened in Goshen, many did not. And the political situation was hardly desirable.

Especially today.

The sun had barely begun to light the sky, but already a mob of people had gathered in the streets of Avdatt.

It had been around midnight when Pilas and Aramis had first received word of what was happening. Now they stood on the steps of the Governor's palace. The courtyard before the palace was filled to capacity with untold numbers of people screaming and yelling their various insults. Guards were posted at the bottom of a large set of grand stairs. At the top of the stairs facing the mob was Pilas, and standing next to him was a person in chains.

Aiden.

Aramis watched intently as the crowds roared in fury. Pilas held up a hand and waited for several minutes until everyone quieted enough that he stood a chance of being heard.

"What is your problem with this man!?" Pilas cried. The crowd began to raise their voices again but they were quickly silenced by a hand from the head Farsee—Karfur was his name.

"We wouldn't have handed him over to you unless he was a criminal!" Karfur returned.

"I'm asking *you* what crimes this man has committed. I find no fault in him!"

"He has blasphemed the name of Lathon!" Karfur yelled. The crowd roared in approval.

"Lathon?" Pilas asked. "The God of the Elves? I am not Elvish, and therefore I do not have any concern for the Elvish ways. If he blasphemed the name of your God, then this is a matter for your jurisdiction, not mine!" The crowd began to raise their voices but were quickly silenced.

"Our laws do not give us the right to put someone to death!"

"You want this man put to death?" Pilas asked. The crowd erupted in noise and chants. "I have told you already if he has not committed a crime worthy of the death sentence in the eyes of the *Goshen* government, then why should I care?"

Boos and jeers came from the crowds.

"He called himself Sherados! The son of Lathon! Ask him yourself and see the treachery that spills from his lips!" Karfur yelled. The crowd erupted.

"Bring him," Pilas said. The crowd grew louder as Aiden was led inside. Pilas motioned to another guard and told him something before he went inside. The crowd settled down as Aramis slipped inside.

Pilas approached Aramis. "Keep a careful eye on this elf. I am baffled by this, in a way I cannot express," Pilas said. "Bring him in!" Pilas ordered. Aiden was led like a dog on a chain, and only now could Aramis realize how badly Aiden had already been beaten.

"Your accusers say you have claimed to be the son of Lathon. Is this true?" Pilas asked. Aiden was silent for a moment. "Why do you not speak in your defense?"

"Everyone knows what I teach and have taught regularly. My message has not changed no matter what town, city, or temple I have ever been in. I have not spoken in secret. Why are you asking me these questions? Ask those who heard me. They know what I said."

Pilas paced, lost in his thoughts.

"Is that the way to answer the Governor?" one of the guards reprimanded.

"If I said anything wrong, they must prove it. But a quick look through the ancient scrolls will reveal that I speak the truth."

"The Elvish scrolls?" Pilas asked.

"They were given to the Elves, but are meant for all races. Lathon doesn't play favorites."

"I'm unfamiliar with Lathon, but if he is your God, and you have claimed to be the son of this God would that make you king? Your own people and Farsees have brought you to me for trial. Why?

"Let me put it this way," Pilas said, slipping into his thoughts for a moment. "As far as the government of Goshen is concerned, I do not find you guilty of anything. You hardly strike me as a revolutionary. I've been at odds with the Farsees for some time, but I don't understand what you have done. What is this all about?"

"Their hearts have been hardened. They cannot understand," Aiden replied. "My kingdom is not an earthly one. If it were, my followers would fight for me. They would seek to stop me from being handed over to you."

"So, instead they do nothing?" Pilas looked at Aramis, confused. Aiden looked at Aramis and then at Pilas, a smile on his lips.

"He understands...all too well," Aiden said. Pilas looked at Aramis with intrigue written on his face. "My kingdom is not of this world."

"So are you a king?"

"You have said it," Aiden said. "I was born and came into the world to testify to the truth. All who like the truth recognize that what I say is truth, and some don't agree with that."

Pilas stepped back as if finally understanding the situation. He seemed to shrink a little in size, not as confident as he had been at first.

"Where are you from?"

Aiden remained silent.

"Will you not answer? I have the authority to release you or have you killed. You know that right?"

"I know you would have no power over me unless it was given to you from Lathon himself!" Aiden answered. "The ones who have handed me over to you are guilty of far more than you'll ever be."

Pilas pondered and paced for another moment or two before finally motioning everyone outside, immediately the entire assembly fell quiet.

"I find this man guilty of nothing. I wish to release him!!"

The crowds erupted in anger, threatening to become violent. "Kill him!" the crowd roared.

"You wish me to kill the king of the Elves?" Pilas asked confusion tainting his voice. The crowd roared louder.

"He is no king of ours!" Karfur yelled. "Are you not scheduled to execute a prisoner of state today?!"

"So it is scheduled, but I find this many not guilty!" Pilas roared. The crowds became even more unsettled. Pilas thought deeply and didn't speak for some time. Finally, he silenced the crowds.

"Fine! I give you a choice! Today was to be the execution of an elf named Geramond." A prisoner in tattered clothes was brought out of the compound. "Geramond is a well-known revolutionary, who had killed many of your own! Shall I release him in place of this elf, Aiden?!"

"Release Geramond!" the crowd roared.

"Here is your king! The king of the Elves! I do not find any fault in him! For I believe he is who he says!" A great burst of anger came from the crowd, soon they quieted and he spoke.

"Since you will not relinquish your quest for this man's blood then what shall I do with him?"

"Kill him! Kill him!" the crowd chanted.

"Fine!" Pilas angrily agreed. "I have tried to set him free, but you will not have it. My hands are clean of this!" He turned to the guards. "Release Geramond. Take Aiden away, and do as they request!"

Pilas motioned and Aiden was led away, the angry throngs of people following. Minutes later, the only ones left were Aramis and Pilas.

Pilas sat silent, unmoving, unspeaking.

Aramis was speechless.

Neither of them noticed Merderick standing in the shadows smiling.

The Story Continues...

DRAKE THOMAS: PART FIVE
RINGS OF KORAZ

MAPS

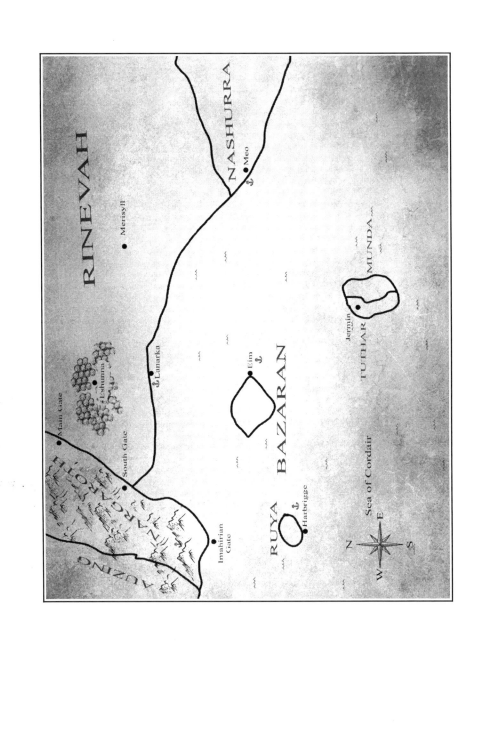

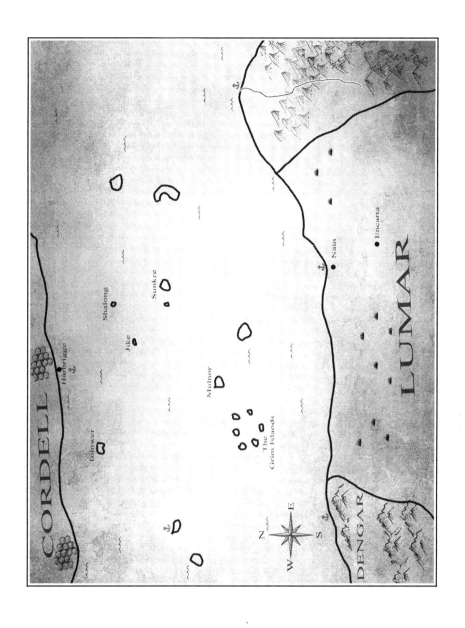

Stories & References

Pg: 41 – Wedding at Cannan - John 2:1-11

Pg: 55 – Genisis 4:7

Pg: 89 – History taken from book of Joshua

Pg: 98 – Ropes under ship – Acts 27:17

Pg: 129 – Matthew 12:25

Pg: 149-150 – Acts 17:22-32

Pg: 170-174 – Taken from 1 Samuel 5

Pg: 247 – David & Goliath – 1 Samuel 17

Pg: 256 – Parts taken from Daniel 3

Pg: 265 – Parts taken from Lions Den/Feiry Furnace – Daniel 3 & Daniel 6

Pg: 266, 289-294 – 1 Kings 18:19-38

Pg: 299-302 – Luke 8:26-37

Pg: 331 – Ezekiel 37:1-14

Pg: 349-351 – Story of Sampson – Judges 13 – Judges 17

Pg: 369 – 1 Samuel 10:17-23